PRAISE FOR JESSICA STRAWSER

CATCH YOU LATER

"Strawser increases tension by telling both [sides of the story] propulsively, leading readers hanging from one chapter to the next . . . Readers will flock to this fresh take on the missing-girl trope."

—*Booklist* (Starred Review)

"Exactly the kind of smart, twisty, heartbreaking, and ultimately satisfying novel that I love; a book with totally relatable characters which raises so many questions I knew within the first pages that I was going to devour every word until I reached the end. Don't think you can guess where the story is going; just put yourself in Strawser's capable hands and enjoy the ride!"

—Karen Dionne, author of the #1 international bestseller *The Marsh King's Daughter* and *The Wicked Sister*

"Where did Mikki go? That's the central question of this tightly plotted psychological suspense. Jessica Strawser deftly explores female friendships, the ties that bind you to the place you're from, and the things that can pull you away from everything—and everyone—you know. Along with trying to solve the mystery at the heart of this fantastic read, I found myself wondering whether I'd make the same choices, which is what all the best novels do. Pick this one up. You won't regret it."

—Catherine Mack, *USA Today* bestselling author of *Every Time I Go on Vacation, Someone Dies*

THE LAST CARETAKER

"Strawser's latest fast-paced page-turner (following *The Next Thing You Know*) grabs readers at the start and doesn't let go. For fans of Sally Hepworth and Liane Moriarty."

—*Library Journal*

"Ms. Strawser, author of Book of the Month bestseller *Not That I Could Tell*, gives readers a master class in distrust through the eyes of Katie . . . Readers might finish the book with a new sense of right from wrong—or, at the least, question their own beliefs, which is the power of a good book."

—*Pittsburgh Post-Gazette*

"You're never sure who to trust or where everyone's loyalties lie in this latest from the very talented Jessica Strawser. Deftly written with an undercurrent of unease, *The Last Caretaker* is a relevant, harrowing mystery with page-turning suspense, a powerful storyline, and relatable characters that readers will think about for a long time to come. Strawser's fans will love this!"

—Mary Kubica, *New York Times* bestselling author of *Just the Nicest Couple*

"A powerful and atmospheric tale that is equal parts emotion and suspense as a woman takes over as caretaker of a remote nature reserve, only to discover the barn is part of a dangerous underground network for victims of domestic violence. In *The Last Caretaker*, Strawser perfectly captures the perils of living in an isolated part of the world and the desperate measures some women must take in order to survive. A richly emotional page-turner with an important message."

—Kimberly Belle, internationally bestselling author of *Dear Wife*

THE NEXT THING YOU KNOW

"Grab the tissues."

—*People*

"[A] deft exploration of connection, death, and grief."

—*E! News*

"A magical tale of love and loss . . . bittersweet yet ultimately comforting."

—*Publishers Weekly*

"Jessica Strawser does it again—first-rate storytelling, a fresh, unique premise, and a didn't-see-that-coming twist, resulting in a book that's unputdownable! Strawser spins a wise, thought-provoking story that crackles with tension and intrigue. Perfect for book clubs, *The Next Thing You Know* will have you pondering end-of-life issues and guessing the final, shocking twist."

—Lori Nelson Spielman, internationally bestselling author of *The Life List*

A MILLION REASONS WHY

"A standout novel . . . seamless writing style, complex characters, and a layered plot. The high concept will attract book groups and fans of Jodi Picoult."

—*Booklist* (Starred Review)

"This emotional family and medical drama from Strawser will appeal to fans of Jodi Picoult and Liane Moriarty."

—*Library Journal*

"Riveting . . . a provocative family tale."

—*Publishers Weekly*

"A thrilling story of what happens when a long-held family secret comes to light . . . [Strawser] shows that no one is ever truly a villain or a hero, but instead, we are all a beautiful and messy mix of both."

—Associated Press

"A fascinating foray into the questions we are most afraid to ask: What constitutes family, what are our obligations to those we love, where does American health care fail the most, what secrets are unforgivable? And in case you need another reason to read this book: there are two massive twists you'll never see coming."

—Jodi Picoult, #1 *New York Times* bestselling author of *Small Great Things* and *A Spark of Light*

"Don't miss this searching, fraught family drama by a master of her craft. Jessica Strawser gives us a twisty plot, combined with deeply emotional content, in a novel that examines the most profound questions of our hearts. This is a story that will stay in your heart long after the last page is turned."

—Susan Wiggs, #1 *New York Times* bestselling author

"*A Million Reasons Why* is a heartbreaking, absorbing story with an irresistible premise: A random DNA test reveals you have a sister you've always wanted, a potential lifesaver. Strawser skillfully explores what it means to be family, to rethink the pivotal hinge points in a person's life."

—Angie Kim, bestselling author of *Miracle Creek*

FORGET YOU KNOW ME

"Masterful."

—*Publishers Weekly* (Starred Review)

"Strawser is a clear master of the craft."

—*Booklist*

"It's been a long time since I've been so lost in a book that when I looked up, I had to remind myself what day it was. From the very first page of *Forget You Know Me*, I was putty in Strawser's hands . . . [it's] that book you can't put down and can't stop thinking about when you are finished."

—Sally Hepworth, *New York Times* bestselling author of *Darling Girls*

NOT THAT I COULD TELL

A Book of the Month Club Selection

"Full of slow-burning intrigue, Strawser's second novel will appeal to fans of Liane Moriarty's *Big Little Lies* and Jennifer Kitses's *Small Hours*."

—*Booklist*

"*Not That I Could Tell* is a psychological thriller of the highest order, as well written as it is structured."

—*Providence Journal*

"[An] engrossing, taut tale."

—*Publishers Weekly*

ALMOST MISSED YOU

"A taut psychological thriller . . . leaves the reader breathless."

—*Richmond Times-Dispatch*

"Fans of smart women's fiction mixed with a fast-paced plot should not miss this startling first novel."

—*Library Journal*

"*Almost Missed You* is a skillful, insightful debut: a deft exploration of the mysteries of marriage, the price we pay for our secrets, and just how easy it is to make the worst choices imaginable."

—Chris Bohjalian, *New York Times* bestselling author of *The Flight Attendant*

"Once in a great while, along comes a novel that defies the odds, a true mystery that bars no holds and plays no tricks, leaving the reader both deeply moved and thoroughly astonished. *Almost Missed You* is just such a book, a debut that asks if we can ever really know another human being, by a writer's writer with talent to spare. You may not have heard of Jessica Strawser today, but by tomorrow, everyone's going to be talking about her and about this story."

—Jacquelyn Mitchard, *New York Times* bestselling author of *The Deep End of the Ocean*

The Quitters Club

ALSO BY JESSICA STRAWSER

Catch You Later

The Last Caretaker

The Next Thing You Know

A Million Reasons Why

Forget You Know Me

Not That I Could Tell

Almost Missed You

The Quitters Club

a novel

JESSICA STRAWSER

This is a work of fiction. Names, characters, organizations, places, events, and incidents are either products of the author's imagination or are used fictitiously.

Published by Lake Union Publishing, Seattle

www.apub.com

EU product safety contact:
Amazon Media EU S. à r.l.
38, avenue John F. Kennedy, L-1855 Luxembourg
amazonpublishing-gpsr@amazon.com

ISBN-13: 9781662534959 (paperback)
ISBN-13: 9781662534966 (digital)

Cover illustration by Jarrod Taylor

Printed in the United States of America

For my children, who I hope will never quit—except for when they should.

1

Marie

Marie approached travel the way she approached life: with a laser focus on what she could control and a tendency to forget how little that included.

The plan was to meet at baggage claim. Miraculously, all four of them had managed to time their flight arrivals within a fifty-two-minute window, with a rental car pickup booked eight minutes later. Just because they were celebrating their fortieth birthdays a couple of months late—on nobody's birthday in particular—didn't mean they were incapable of efficiency. Or optimism.

Marie arrived at Savannah/Hilton Head International right on schedule, beelined for the luggage carousel, and powered up her phone, only to discover Brooke's flight from Denver had been waylaid by a mechanical issue, while Lucy had gotten so engrossed in her laptop at a charging station in Chicago, she'd missed her boarding call and ended up on a standby list.

I'm so annoyed, Brooke wrote. It figures.

I'm so embarrassed, Lucy demurred. I have out-Lucy-ed myself.

There was, of course, no flight update from Collins, because she'd had the seat beside Marie—up until she'd flaked last night. Marie should've known better than to book the nonrefundable fare when

Collins got so worked up over leaving her house these days, let alone leaving Ohio. I'm so sorry, she'd texted, but I'm frazzled by all these packing restrictions since last time I flew. Do they seriously measure your bags? Before Marie could reply, the damage was done. I'm just gonna take the flight credit and drive. It's only nine hours! Send me your wish lists! I'll bring all the things!

At the time, the exclamation points had seemed convincing enough for Marie not to eat her ticket and ride along. This was her midterm break, after all. As a college professor, she was beholden to the university's schedule when class was in session, and she hadn't planned on spending half of this rare long weekend in the car. But she hadn't foreseen being the only one whose itinerary stuck.

Now, she stared at the group text of her old college roommates, the realest friends she had, mitigating her disappointment. Once, it had seemed impossible they'd ever grow so far out of sync. But she'd still do anything for them. Or, more accurately, overlook anything.

Well played, witches, she typed. I'm alone at baggage claim and didn't even check a bag.

Brooke's reply came instantly. You have to admit, this is all hilariously on brand.

Collins: It does explain why we haven't managed to be in one place for what, five years?

Marie's smile faltered. It had been two years since they'd gathered for Collins's late husband's funeral. But they'd all rather not count that.

Lucy's next text chimed in: Not to alarm you, Marie, but don't act suspicious. The air marshals might wonder why you're only pretending to look for luggage.

Marie laughed aloud, pocketed her phone, and followed the signs for ground transportation.

At the rental car kiosk, a bearded man whose company polo shirt looked much too tight informed Marie that her selected car was unavailable, but they were pleased to offer her a nice minivan instead.

"No offense," she said, "but this is my weekend off from being a soccer mom. Got anything else?" She wasn't playing to stereotype. Wade was the goalkeeper on his team, Connor a striker on his, and she felt a twinge at her own words, a pull of guilt about missing the boys' games this weekend—missing the boys, period. She'd made Kyle promise to send updates from the sidelines where he'd be watching from their usual spot: the tailgate of Marie's own minivan.

She didn't feel any twinges when it came to Kyle, though.

She wasn't sure when those had stopped.

The rental car clerk pulled at his collar. "It's a free upgrade," he told her, holding out the keys like that resolved it.

She climbed in feeling like anyone could tell by looking at her that she'd anticipated things would turn out differently. And not just today. This disconnection had plagued her lately, turning everything into a metaphor: the looping baggage carousel, the empty seats in her rearview now, the vacant beach house awaiting her. Though that part didn't sound bad. Most days Marie couldn't hear herself think over the running list of who needed to be where when with what for how long. She could do worse than a few solitary hours on the wide oceanfront deck pictured in the rental listing, getting a head start on the long weekend. The sea breeze, a book, first crack at the promised welcome champagne on ice. Who could be mad about that?

Her friends were right: This whole trip was starting on-brand. But what mattered was that the trip was starting at all. Finally, they'd have real time away, just the four of them.

They all needed this. *She* needed this.

Marie wasn't about to spoil it by admitting how much.

On the rare occasions Collins made an appearance these days, her arrival struck Marie as breathless and bustling—always bearing gifts or toting a little something extra. Marie suspected this was a clever redirection technique honed since Sullivan's accident, so people would greet her without looking too closely. Who would notice the gaunt shadows under her eyes when her arms were so full? *Oh, Collins, you didn't have to bring anything! Let me help with that.* This time, Collins had piled the drinkable contents of her trunk into a foldable wagon and wheeled it around back to find Marie stretched in a hammock, watching the waves and trying to recall why she lived in the Midwest.

"You made it!" Marie scrambled to her feet and took Collins in as she ran for a hug. She would not be distracted by the full-service bar Collins was rolling behind her. Even if Marie *had* been wanting to try that new brand of seltzer she spotted. And the celebrity-label tequila. And the "sip and support" selections from NPR Wine Club.

Collins looked . . . okay. More relieved than excited to be here. A little wan but smiling. Marie felt frumpy with her messy ponytail, in the joggers and tank top she'd traveled in, next to Collins's gauzy navy-blue jumpsuit and smooth blowout.

"Better late than never," Collins said, squeezing her tight. She pulled back to look around, nodding approvingly. Brooke had found this place—she was always the planner, sending emails that were so detail oriented, so fraught with over-explanation, no one dared respond with anything other than *Sounds great!* If she was trying to deter them from complicating things with questions, it worked. But more likely, she was just that eager. Brooke and her husband hadn't taken a vacation in years; they'd devoted their budget and paid time off to infertility treatments, and the rest of them knew to tread lightly around the subject. It really did figure that poor Brooke's flight had been rerouted. Luckily, she was already on another one.

"Brooke chose well," Marie said. A wooden ramp led to the deck, complete with four cruiser bikes and a golf cart for complimentary use. The dunes sloped gently, affording them a clear view over the seagrass where their private beach-access boardwalk stretched onto the sand. The whole back of the house was an oasis of shade and sunlight in desirable proportions, with an in-ground spa and outdoor shower, ceiling fans whirring above plush covered seating, high-top chairs arranged around a long dining table, cushioned hammocks swaying in the breeze, and chaise longues sprawled beneath clusters of Hilton Head's signature palmettos.

"I would have been happy anywhere with all of you," Collins said. "All this is whipped cream on the piña colada."

Marie helped pull the wagon through the sliding glass doors into the kitchen and gave her a tour. Now that half of them had arrived, it seemed fair to call dibs on rooms. Marie and Collins took the smaller bedrooms facing oceanside, with en suite doors to the shared bathroom between them. Across the hall, Lucy and Brooke would forgo the view but each have private bathrooms.

After unloading Collins's car, they returned outside to breathe the salty air, legs stretched in front of them, champagne flutes at their sides. Marie often felt awkwardly empty-handed on rare occasions when she wasn't doing *something*, busy with the kids or at class or running errands, unable to shake the feeling that she'd dropped some ball she was supposed to be holding. She used to know how to laze around, free her mind. Relaxing wasn't something you should have to concentrate on doing. If you were concentrating, you weren't doing it.

"I'm glad we're the first two here," Collins said, raising her glass. "Cheers."

Marie raised hers, too, and they both took a sip. "I'm glad too," Marie said, meaning it. "But Coll, I feel bad that—"

Collins held up a hand. "Let's not do the thing where we talk about how ridiculous it is that we live forty miles apart and have to come all this way to hang out."

Marie winced. "It is ridiculous, though."

"Of course it is. But it's my fault as much as yours. I know how busy you are with kid stuff and university demands—your priorities are in order. Plus, I'm well aware of how hard I've made it for anyone to be 'there for me.'"

Collins smiled reassuringly, looking like her old self, and Marie swallowed the lump forming in her throat.

"I could have tried harder," Marie said lamely. "Things with Kyle lately . . ." She didn't finish. She would not, could not, say a word of complaint about her husband to her friend who was still mourning her own. Collins and Sullivan had been married only a few years before his accident, barely time for anything to be less than perfect. It made Sullivan's death a dangerous thing to survive: easy to romanticize, hard to move past.

"I could've tried harder too," Collins said. "Let's pick up where we left off like usual, okay?"

"Deal," Marie said.

"Good. So. Things with Kyle lately have been what?"

Marie bit her lip. "Let's not do that thing either. Where we spend the trip rehashing every little thing so we feel up to speed. We're on vacation. Let's just be here, like you said."

"That would be a huge relief. I dread giving status updates on the estate."

Marie frowned. Sullivan Hartley had been the most high-profile visiting art professor at Ohio University, where Marie taught in the Women's, Gender & Sexuality Studies program, but his renown had grown since his death. The tragedy of the fire at his studio off campus made headlines nationwide. Collins, who'd been his manager throughout their marriage, suddenly found herself fielding exhibit inquiries with names like Guggenheim attached. There weren't many stained-glass sculptors of note, and Sullivan had been a prolific one. His outdoor installations were large and challenging to transport, while his smaller works were surprisingly delicate—and equally difficult to transport. "Aren't updates on the estate your full-time job?" Marie asked.

"Exactly." Once, the mention of Sullivan's artistry had lit Collins from within like a human version of one of his creations, a prism of refracted joy. Marie had faith the light would return, but she saw no sign of it now. And she had an idea of who was blocking the sun.

She tried to sound neutral. "Have Sull's daughters gotten used to that yet?"

"They have not."

Marie groaned sympathetically. Sullivan had designated one indisputable beneficiary for the house, its much-photographed sculpture garden, and oversight of his artistic assets: Collins. It didn't help that Sullivan's adult children had never warmed to the idea of her in the first place. Collins *was* technically closer to their age than his, but anyone could see she was an old soul. Sullivan always joked he'd had to wait a couple of "bonus decades" to be grown up enough for her.

Marie could never figure out how to navigate this subject without throwing more shade at his kids than was sensitive, given the circumstances.

Collins gazed longingly at the ocean. "Let's pretend we live here for the next three days. Like the Golden Girls, only much younger. We'll catch up on the rest when we're back in Ohio, vowing to do better at coffee dates thanks to our amazing weekend of beachfront bonding."

Marie raised her glass. "To the here and now," she offered. "And to us."

"To the here and now," Collins agreed. "And to us."

2

Lucy

Lucy looked around the table at her friends—these women who'd known her when, who loved her still—and was overcome with a whole-body happiness she hadn't experienced in far too long. Thank goodness, *thank goodness* she'd come. Now that she was here, the fact that she could barely afford it was beside the point. This was nourishment for her poor, bruised soul, worth every penny. Every second of airport anxiety, even.

Though Lucy had brought that last part on herself. It was almost refreshing, for once, knowing exactly how she'd gone wrong, making such an easily identifiable mistake. So much of her disappointment lately boiled down to *You did your best* and *No one can predict these things.*

Literary careers were like that, apparently. Even for "up-and-coming" authors.

Lucy was still waiting for the "up" part.

She'd been last to arrive, but Brooke had waited for her at the airport to split a rideshare. By the time they made it through traffic to join Marie and Collins at the rental, it was dinnertime, and they decided the house was far too nice (and, thanks to Collins, well stocked) to leave. Not surprisingly, Brooke had planned ahead for carryout, and in no time procured a feast of steamed shrimp and crab legs with salads, biscuits, baked potatoes, and all the fixings. They'd polished it off down to the last hush puppy, then carried blankets and wine onto the sand to watch the sunset, giddy to be together again.

Now they were back around the table, a decadent dessert of lava cakes warming in the oven, strands of white lights shining above them, citronella candles burning in glass lanterns.

"So, how are our old stomping grounds?" Brooke asked Marie. "I'm still so jealous you get to teach at OU. I miss it most this time of year—so pretty in the fall." Lucy sneaked a glance at Collins, who lived even closer to their alma mater than Marie, but if she minded being left off the question, it didn't show. Last Lucy had heard, Collins had been going out of her way to avoid the entire fine arts school, the Bicentennial Park and library where Sullivan's sculptures remained in memoriam, and other spots she'd frequented with her late husband. In a small college town, that didn't leave much else.

"The leaves are starting to change," Marie said. "To be honest, though, I haven't had a chance to enjoy it. My time in Athens is never my own. If I'm not in class or office hours, I'm running to get the boys. How can two kids have four places to be at once? It defies math."

"How many sports are they in?" Brooke asked. She was fidgeting, the way she always did when the subject of someone's kids came up. Not because she was disinterested; because she desperately wanted children and didn't want to be asked how that was going. They could assume: not well.

"Only one sport at a time. It's everything else that adds up—class projects or fundraisers or whatever else. When we bought the house between Columbus and Athens to split the difference on our commutes, I didn't realize what that would morph into. When we were talking preschool, enrolling the kids closer to the university seemed like a no-brainer. I have the flexible hours, and they could ride with me to forgo extended day care. Fast forward nine years, and Kyle is twice as far from everything they're involved in, all their friends and activities. We're not splitting any of that—it's all me."

"Aren't you the one teaching a class called How to Say No?" Brooke teased.

"A wait-listed class," Collins confirmed. "One of the most popular on campus. In fact, I've heard students refer to our dear Professor Welling as Professor No."

Again, Marie winced. "That has not escaped me. Although it's not like I didn't have the guts to say no . . . more like I never said yes to this specifically. But here I am."

Lucy knew that feeling—of a life you used to want morphing into something unrecognizable. She was starting to realize how easily it could happen if you didn't stop and ask yourself if it was still what you wanted.

Even so. She hadn't expected this from Marie of all people. Privately, Marie liked to insist her class was "*not* about harnessing big dick energy and perfecting resting bitch faces." Publicly, she cautioned students against enrolling just because it sounded easy and fun. Her curriculum required analytical thinking. Still, if you followed #howtosayno on social media, the class was a vibe. The week devoted to movies where women reclaimed self-respect by saying no was especially popular. It helped that *Pretty Woman* and *Legally Blonde* were both so quotable. ("What?" her students would joke in their reels. "Like it's hard?")

"I love working in Athens, though," Marie added quickly. "Even if I could see myself in Columbus at Ohio State, I can't give up tenure. And Kyle's company is top ranked. There's no equivalent wealth-management firm in a middle-of-nowhere college town."

"Maybe it's time for him to be the only one with a commute," Lucy suggested. "He drives twice as far, you parent twice as much. *That's* an even split."

Marie nodded without conviction. "If he didn't already complain about his hours so much . . ." Her voice trailed off. She looked tired, but more than that—sad. Then again, maybe Lucy was projecting. Marie met her eye, and something passed between them. A knowing without knowing.

"Anyway," Marie said, turning back to Brooke. "Athens misses you too. It's changed a lot on the surface, but the heart remains the same. Like us."

"Lucy and I should come to you and Collins next time," Brooke suggested. "Let's try to plan our next reunion in months, not years."

"That's drivable for me," Lucy agreed quickly. A free stay in Collins's spare room was the only way she'd be taking another trip anytime soon.

Marie tossed her a smile. "Driving does sound preferable. Is it too soon to tease you about missing your flight when you were *sitting at your gate*?"

Lucy groaned. "It will never not be too soon."

"You must have been really into the new book you're writing, at least," Collins said, refilling her wineglass and topping off the others.

Lucy felt her cheeks reddening. "I wasn't in some flow state. I just spaced out."

"Right. You spaced out enough to not notice everyone around you boarding," Brooke teased. "Was it a sex scene? A fight scene? Give us a preview."

Lucy would not be baited. "Don't take this the wrong way, Brooke, but you've barely even cracked open my book that came out last year. I'm not sure you qualify for a preview."

Brooke's face fell, and Lucy instantly regretted the dig. The truth was, she never expected friends to read her novels. It was too awkward when they launched into excuses about how they totally, super wanted to, they just hadn't found time to read *anything* in ages. Like that wasn't the last thing any writer wanted to hear. Whenever someone did mention liking one of her stories, she'd usually joke, *So you're the one who bought that!*

She had never mastered the art of self-promotion. It showed in many ways.

"Lucy, I swear," Brooke said. "It's not disinterest in your work. It's me, barely holding it together."

"Don't apologize. I shouldn't have said that. Lame attempt to deflect attention from my own stupidity. The gate agent looked at me like I was the reason she hates her job."

"Well, your books are immersive," Marie said. "If she read one, she'd understand how you could miss a flight writing one. Can you tell us the title, at least?"

"Maybe Lucy feels superstitious about discussing her art in progress," Collins said, coming to Lucy's defense. "Sullivan could be that way too. Let's leave her alone."

"I'm not superstitious." With her frustration mounting, this came out with indignance, the way you might insist *I am not racist.* Lucy threw up her hands. "Look, if you must know, I wasn't writing, okay? I said I was on my laptop—*you* all assumed I was writing."

Collins lifted a mischievous eyebrow. "Were you . . . online dating?"

"Worse. I was looking at job openings. For day jobs. And it was jarring to see how unqualified I am. For all the writing I've done, I don't even understand the language. I was sitting there panicking about 'corporate cultures' and 'performance metrics.' Whatever those are."

Brooke looked stricken. "Day jobs?"

"I read your last book the day it came out, Lucy," Collins said quietly. "I loved it so much, I reread all your others. Then I got angry they didn't have more customer ratings, and I posted reviews with every online retailer. Incognito," she clarified. "I'm Collin S."

Tears sprang to Lucy's eyes. "You never told me that," she said, blinking them away.

"Well, I worried you might rightly question how much free time I have. But you belong on the bestseller lists, not in a day job. One of your books will hit, and then the rest will too."

"I don't think so," Lucy said. "But I appreciate the vote of confidence. I think I'm ready for a change, so, we'll see where I land. Can we change the subject?"

"No," Marie said. She smiled. "See? I say it plenty."

Even Lucy had to laugh at that.

"Sorry, not sorry—but what's going on?" Marie persisted. "The logistics of my overscheduled life were one thing. You of all people switching careers seems like something else."

It was something else. They were saying all the right things, but . . . Lucy didn't want to hear them anymore. She couldn't work out how to circumnavigate these reactions. Nobody she told seemed to believe she was ready to move on. Least of all the people who knew Lucy best.

She'd set her heart on becoming a writer long before their days at OU. She used to want it so bad, she could feel it vibrating within her. She'd bask in the glow of her open laptop at all hours of the night, *aligning* herself with the inspiration, dreaming of the day these words were out in the world, and she'd look back fondly on how long she'd worked, how hard she'd fought, how much she'd sacrificed, because, deep down, she'd always known it would come to *this* validation that it had all been worth it. She didn't doubt she was capable, and she didn't worry the odds were against her. When it came to her writing, she'd embodied the kind of stubbornness that would be rewarded by the universe if she was patient.

The universe had not kept its end of the bargain.

In fact, it had toyed with her, strapping all her hopes and goals to a fat carrot dangling out of reach. Once in a lucky while, she'd manage to just graze it—an offer from a new small press, a starred review, a rave from an A-lister—and that was incentive enough to keep her stretching forward like a hungry little bunny.

She didn't know what, exactly, had changed. It was as if one day, she'd caught a glimpse of her sweaty, strained reflection hopping across the mirror and wondered, *What in the world am I doing?* She had so many writing-adjacent side hustles, her definition of "me time" involved her word count. She worked longer, odder hours than anyone she knew for far less return. Wasn't it kind of amazing that she'd lasted this long?

Wasn't it kind of stupid that she'd never seriously thought about just . . . stopping?

"You don't mean that," her mom had said with a dismissiveness that irked her. If human instinct was to automatically contradict each other's doubts, was every reassurance that empty?

"I think I do mean it," Lucy had said.

"But you love writing. Or, what's that quote on your office wall? You love having written."

Lucy could only shake her head while her brain supplied a truth she wasn't ready to voice yet. *I used to love it. Now, the best I can manage is to wish it had loved me back.*

"I'm not saying this lightly, Mom. I'm not some starry-eyed kid. I'm an adult still paying off my carpal tunnel surgery."

"Well, what else would you do?"

"Does it matter? My last editor left publishing for a career in Bitcoin. I'd make more as a barista at this point. My fallback freelance gigs are being outsourced to AI. Especially copywriting, and that paid best."

"Surely not. How do robots have time to copywrite while planning human extinction?"

Science fiction and horror were the only two genres Lucy did not read. It tracked that they'd team up in real life and make her pay.

"I'm sure this is just a phase," her mom went on. "We all feel discouraged sometimes."

At the time, Lucy had granted that maybe it was. But that was months ago.

Now, she sat up straight and looked around the table at her friends.

"I'm not giving up because I can't hack it—but if you knew what hacking it was like, you'd understand why I don't want to anymore."

With that, she drained her wineglass, and her friends exchanged glances, looking like they were waiting for some kind of catch.

"That's quite the firm explanation," Collins said finally.

"Well," Lucy said. "Everyone's eager to tell me I'm wrong. Even friends at my monthly writers' brunch, who should get where I'm coming from, were all, *You can't quit. You've come this far. Give yourself some time.* But I don't need coddling. That's not what this is."

In truth, her writer friends had recoiled from her, as if her attitude might be contagious. The stakes weren't as high for them. One had a CEO husband who funded her book tours. One was in such heated competition with her rival from her MFA program, she'd write out of spite until he quit first. Another was close to retiring, coasting out her final years on sheer nostalgia. Lucy had more skin in the game—and suffered more for it. But it wasn't her job to manage everyone else's insecurities. Her own were more than enough.

On her best day, she believed her friends and family: She *was* good, *had* come far, and it was bad form to shrug off the compliments. But none of it had been enough. Lucy had poured her heart into everything she wrote, her actual heart, and she was tired of pretending it didn't hurt when no one cared. It had been one thing when the heart was energetic and gritty, but it had turned forty this year. It had made some mistakes. And so had the people she'd trusted with it.

"I admit," Collins said, "my first thought was, you're too good *not* to keep doing this."

"I appreciate that," Lucy said. "But maybe it's the opposite. Maybe I'm too good to let it get ruined for me. Maybe if it's a hobby, not a job, I can learn to love it again."

Her secret worry was that it was already too late for this. She'd taken the source of her purest joy and worked it over and over until it was nothing more than a ball of anxiety bearing little resemblance to anything she'd loved in the first place.

"I was more comfortable when you were all making fun of me for missing my flight," Lucy said. Everyone laughed, and the good feelings flooded back in.

They might not be the best at staying in touch, but they were great at reminding her it was okay to laugh at herself.

Lucy leaned forward. "Here's what I don't get," she said. "Maybe this is a question for Professor Marie. In my mind, I am reading the writing on the wall and trying to be practical and smart. And it would be helpful to have a sounding board. But no one will let me talk through this honestly. They only want to talk me down like I'm up on some ledge threatening to jump. It's pathological. Publishing has given me a *concussion* and all anyone does is encourage me to keep hammering my head against the wall."

Marie considered this. "Maybe it's because we all fantasize about quitting things from time to time," she offered. "And if someone else goes through with it, that reminds us it doesn't have to be fantasy. Quitting big stuff can be scary even when we want to, like leaping without a net. Maybe those reactions are more about other people's fears and not about you at all."

"It's drilled into us from a young age," Brooke agreed. "Quitters never win. Like there's shame in giving up on something, even when that thing isn't serving us anymore."

"Of course there's no shame," Marie said quickly. Shame was definitely on her syllabus.

"She's right, though," Collins said. "Sticking with something isn't always good advice. That's the kind of thinking that makes people stay in toxic relationships. But you can't talk about quitting anything without people treating you like a . . . well, a quitter."

"We talk in my class about reframing things like this, to shift the power or agency," Marie said. "Like, there's this stat going around parenting groups claiming by the time your kids are twelve, you've already spent seventy-five percent of the time you'll ever spend with them. It's meant to perspective-check us into slowing down and being present, but it's depressing. I don't get why anyone would want to think like that."

Lucy raised a skeptical eyebrow. "Because they want you to shut up and be happy for the chance to be at your family's beck and call, even if it's grinding you down?"

"Ouch," Marie said. "I can only handle so much self-reflection in one night."

"But what if it isn't bullshit?" Brooke asked. "I mean, when we graduated, none of us realized we'd already spent ninety-six percent of the time we'd ever spend together."

That landed. Everyone seemed to take a collective breath. Everyone but Collins. "There's more to life than time," she said firmly. "Sometimes the thirty seconds we spend in our group chat are the best thirty seconds of my day. Plus, I've spent a hundred percent of the time I'll ever spend with Sullivan, but he's still an important part of my life."

Brooke paled. "That's not what I meant, Collins, I'm sorry."

"It's okay," Collins assured her. "This is the most interesting conversation I've had in a while." Her face colored. "It might be one of the only conversations I've had in a while."

Lucy squeezed Collins's hand under the table. She admired how her friends never turned their complaints into a contest to see who had it worst. But if they did, Collins would win.

"I know it's cliché that turning forty is a wake-up call," Lucy said. "But it's true. We're not waiting for our lives to start anymore, you know? We are well underway. And when you feel that, and then you look around and don't like what you see, it's jarring."

"Life comes in phases," Marie said. "Sometimes we have to stick the tough ones out."

"Sometimes," Lucy agreed. "But when we're doing more of the same and expecting different results, we have choices. We're just too busy keeping up with our obligations to realize it."

Collins seemed to be steeling herself. "I know about being stuck in phases." Her eyes were wet, but she looked determined. "When Sullivan died, it was hard not to think my life was ruined. I didn't know how to be a gracious widow at thirty-eight. Then I read that grief is really love without anywhere to go, and that resonated. So I leaned into the grief, like it proved how much I loved Sullivan. I chose to give myself over to it—like being caught in a riptide, you know? You'll drown if you fight it. You have to let the current take you and remain calm. But now, it's been years. The current is weaker now, but it's carried me so far, I can't see shore anymore. I know I need to start swimming again, but I've forgotten how. Or maybe I'm just too scared I'll go the wrong way, and it feels safer to float indefinitely."

They were all deep in the conversation now, the way they used to take for granted during their late-night heart-to-hearts. They might have had too many drinks for such a serious conversation, but then again, without their inhibitions lowered, they might all still be pretending everything was fine.

This was what they'd really come for. Not just the chance to reconnect. The chance to be *real.* Lucy had finally done it. It was only her first night here, and she'd unloaded this weight on her mind—and these women she loved had tried to help unpack it for her. She was one step closer to being free, moving on. They all could be.

Lucy breathed it in, every aching bit of it. Then she leaned over and put both arms around Collins, hugging her friend tight.

"We're your shore," Lucy said. "Swim toward us."

3

Brooke

As far as Brooke could tell, she was the first one up. The house was quiet as she padded downstairs barefoot and slipped outside. The sun must have only just risen, but the sky was too overcast to tell. Brooke headed toward the water, inhaling the humid, salty Atlantic air, so different from the dry altitude back home in Colorado. A long walk through the wet sand would be the perfect start to the day.

She expected her friends to be sleeping off their hangovers for a while. Becoming a lightweight had its upsides—she'd floated high on a couple of drinks last night and awoken clearheaded. Peering down the beach, it struck her what a novelty it was to walk in a flat, straight line, the path stretching as far as she could see. Not that she didn't appreciate the winding ups and downs of her usual walks, but she hadn't had a change of scenery in too long.

When her feet hit the foam, she headed north toward the high-rise hotels in the distance. A jogger zipped past her in running shoes, and, self-consciously, her hand went to the bloating beneath the drawstring of her terry shorts. No amount of the recommended low-impact exercise could counter the effects of so many hormone injections. There was no medical reason for the skin here to remain tender, but it prickled beneath her fingertips.

Everything about her was oversensitive these days.

"Brooke! Wait up!" She turned to see Lucy jogging toward her, sending up sprays of dry sand. "Mind if I join?"

"I'd love it. I didn't know anyone was up."

"This is nerdy, but I set my alarm. I don't want to sleep this trip away."

"I know what you mean."

They walked on in companionable silence, watching the pelicans diving for breakfast. Brooke could have walked miles without speaking. But it didn't feel right.

"Lucy," she ventured, "what you said last night . . . I take it you saw your book in my bag." The bookmark was obviously still just a couple of chapters in—where it had been for months. "I want to apologize again."

"Oh, stop. That was low of me to call you of all people out. I was out of sorts and feeling defensive. You preorder my books before my own parents do." Lucy caught her eye and winked. "As long as you buy them, I don't care if you read them."

Brooke laughed. "I didn't need to be called out to feel bad. I genuinely enjoy your books. It got me thinking how little room I make in my life for things I want to do versus have to do."

"That's no good, Brookie." A cluster of broken shells had washed up in front of them, and they stepped carefully around it. "I'm the one who should apologize," Lucy said. "I was a downer last night. Clearly, I'm working through some things."

"You weren't a downer." Brooke didn't say that it had been a relief to think about someone's problems besides her own. "I can't talk to anyone else the way I talk to you three, and I love that. We're *all* working through things. I woke up thinking about it. Some of the stuff you said, and Collins too . . . I think it applies to all of us."

Lucy hesitated. "Do you get the feeling something might be off with Marie and Kyle?"

Brooke nodded. "I love hearing her talk about Connor and Wade—she's obviously a great mom. But Kyle's name comes up, and she deflates." Brooke crossed her fingers, protecting her karma from her little white lie. She did *want* to love hearing Marie talk about her kids. She constantly reminded herself that envy was natural in her position and not the same as jealousy. The fact that infertility had turned her into a resentful shrew was one of the worst things about it.

"How are you and Mitch holding up?" Lucy asked.

"As good as people in our situation can be, I think. We don't take it out on each other. We're kind of . . . sad together."

"Yay?"

Brooke swallowed hard. She hadn't come all this way to spoil it by breaking down. "We found out a few days ago that our last transfer didn't take. That was the last of our frozen embryos. So, we'd have to start over with another egg retrieval to continue."

"Oh no." Lucy looked like she might cry. In every foursome, inevitably tighter pairs formed, unspoken yet understood. Theirs were Marie and Collins, Lucy and Brooke.

"Well," Brooke said, trying to keep it light, "there are worse times to find out you're not pregnant than right before three days of acting like you're still in college. Right?"

It was true. Brooke wanted nothing more than to be pregnant—she'd gladly sacrifice anything. But that was the thing: She already had. She'd spent thousands of dollars on treatments insurance didn't cover, she'd withdrawn from her trail-running club and wine-tasting club and nearly every other social circle, she'd tested her boss's compassion with all the days she had to come late or leave early, and she had nothing to show for it but jeans that wouldn't zip closed, bruised veins from blood draws that made her look like a junkie, and a possible increased risk of ovarian cancer. Was it so wrong to feel a bit of relief at a brief reprieve?

It felt wrong. It felt like a betrayal of her deepest desires to accept the consolation prize that for one long weekend, she could eat what she wanted, drink what she wanted, and pretend her life was not ruled by *behaving as if* she was pregnant, *in case* she was pregnant, only to remain nowhere near pregnant. Not so much as a false alarm.

"I admire your attitude," Lucy said. "But for what it's worth, I would've been more than happy to switch to mocktails in solidarity."

"I know." A rogue wave crashed high onto the sand, and Lucy leaped out of the way, but Brooke stayed where she was, letting the tide swirl and pull around her shins.

The truth was, she wasn't ready to go back—not to mocktails, not to sweating under long-sleeved shirts on hot days, not to any of it. When her flight had been rerouted, she'd caught herself wishing it was happening on the way home, so she could miss Monday's appointment. She always took the doctor's first available openings, even if she longed for a break . . . because what if this was it—the magical day, the next chance, the only chance, to get it right? But if an act of God delayed her, well, it was out of her hands.

What Lucy had said about realizing the thing you thought you wanted was making you miserable . . . Brooke related. Strongly.

But she was always so hormonal, she didn't trust her reactions anymore. With any rush of happiness, she'd check herself: *Would Normal Brooke be glad about this?* With a spark of rage, she'd question: *Am I overreacting?* This time, when they got the news, Mitch had held her until she'd cried herself out. As usual, he didn't ask if they'd make another appointment, only when. And then he'd sprung for tickets to the Broadway tour that was in town, letting the music fill the silence of waiting. But from her red-velvet balcony seat, she'd wondered: *If I never say half of the things I'm thinking, is Mitch doing the same? Do we even still know ourselves, let alone each other? For all the sacrifices we agreed to make, what else are our relentless efforts costing us?*

"Starting over sounds like a lot," Lucy said gently. "Is that what you and Mitch want?"

"I don't think anyone ever *wants* to do the treatments. It's about the end goal."

"I guess what I mean is, is it still worth it?"

Brooke had asked herself the same question more times than she could count. If it worked, it would be worth it. If it didn't, it wouldn't *feel* worth it. But she needed to know she'd done all she could.

The real question was whether she was at that point yet.

She didn't trust that she'd know it when she saw it.

"When I was a kid," Brooke said finally, "and people asked what I wanted to be when I grew up, I always said, 'A mom.' It's the one thing that has never felt negotiable to me. But I'm not sure my body is negotiating its stance either."

"Huh. You didn't say 'database administrator'?" Lucy said. They laughed. It was a running joke that nobody understood what Brooke did. Lucy's voice softened. "How many years of trying is this now?" Brooke could tell she was withholding judgment, trying to be a good friend.

"Let's just say no one used the term 'geriatric pregnancy' when I started. Now it's all I hear. Sometimes I wonder if we should have started trying earlier, but we really wanted to get established first, you know? All that careful planning, wasted. So much for manifesting."

"No chance Mitch will have a change of heart about adoption?"

Brooke shook her head. "I don't hold it against him. His mom spent decades searching for her birth parents and ended up wishing she hadn't. Rationally, he knows there are lots of beautiful ways to handle the process, but he's seen too many downsides. Even surrogacy is a gray area for him."

She'd promised him at the outset to respect those options as off-limits, and she'd never begrudged him his boundaries. It was only now occurring to her that she might have set a few herself. Like how long she'd give her body over to these efforts. She was, after all, the one being poked and prodded beyond recognition.

Brooke found it easier to talk about this while they walked. Like she was giving her grief over to the motion of it, as Collins had described. "Until now," she said, "the specialists have been happy to take my money. It's always, *You'll get 'em next time, tiger.* But now that I'm forty, odds of success with IVF go way down. And as much as I hated hearing everyone act like it was no big deal to keep trying at all costs, I'm more afraid to hear them say time's up."

Lucy linked her arm through Brooke's, and Brooke leaned in, grateful. She'd forgotten how nice it was to have an old friend walk an unfamiliar path with her. Wonderful as Mitch was, she didn't like relying on him for all things.

"This is unfair," Lucy said. "No one should have to go through this. Especially you."

Brooke knew the waiting room at the clinic was full of equally worthy people. But she appreciated the sentiment. She decided to level with Lucy.

"Are you familiar with Diana Nyad," she asked, "who did those long-distance swims from Cuba to Key West?"

"A little."

"She had this support team that would follow her on a boat, monitoring her pace and how far she had left. The day she finally made it, she almost lost steam with just a few miles to go, and they had to tell her, 'You're almost there, dig deep!' Without them, she might have stopped in view of the shore. She just couldn't see it from down in the water."

"You're afraid of giving up without realizing how close you are?" Lucy guessed.

Brooke nodded. "All I can see is open water, whether I'm five miles from shore or five hundred. And yeah, there's a boat—I can stop anytime—but there's no coach on it with GPS."

"I've felt that way too," Lucy said. "But you know, I think Diana Nyad nearly drowned multiple times, even with the coach."

"Well, I don't think this is life threatening. It's just torture." Brooke's joke did not land.

Lucy looked at her with concern. "Maybe," she said, gently, "when you started swimming, you didn't need a boat—you were doing laps in the pool. Then it turned into a lake, and you thought, *Okay, I can handle a lake.* You did everything they told you to do and swam beautifully, but now you're out there getting tossed by waves, and you're cold and exhausted, and no wonder. I know how hard this must be, for you and Mitch both. But you don't have to swim across the ocean just because you got into a swimming pool years ago. If you'd known the finish line was going to keep moving, maybe you two would have had some different conversations that you owe it to yourselves to have now."

Brooke was too choked up to respond right away. "I've been scared to talk even hypothetically about stopping," she said finally, sniffing hard. "I haven't wanted to jinx it." These thoughts had been crossing her mind more and more, and Brooke had to fight through guilt and self-flagellation every time. But Lucy's compassion felt validating. Maybe she was right: Maybe if Brooke and Mitch had acknowledged the possibility that they never would conceive, they wouldn't have jinxed themselves at all. Maybe they'd have made a plan B by now that would quell this rising panic.

She wiped away her tears with her free hand.

"I don't know what changing my mind would look like," she admitted. "What my life would look like, I mean. Or how Mitch might react."

"Of course you don't. You've been in the water. Maybe you have to stop swimming and dry off before you can think about anything else." Lucy squeezed their linked arms closer until they were walking elbow to elbow, hip to hip. "We're here for you, Brookie. Whatever you need. We don't have to be in the same place to figure this out together. We can help each other from anywhere. Whatever you decide. And whatever *I* decide. I'm going to need the support too." A horrified look crossed her face. "Not that I'm comparing my situation to yours. I'm not."

"It is a little like mine. I think we all have things it would be healthy for us to reevaluate. It's not bad to compare notes." Brooke slowed her stride. "Speaking of quitting. Maybe we should head back."

By the time they'd returned, the sun was peeking through the clouds, and their moods had brightened considerably. Brooke had been holding all her fears in for so long, it was a relief to find that talking things through could make them seem less hopeless.

There *were* similarities between them all. None of them wanted to have to let go and move forward another way—to accept that Brooke would likely never be a parent, and Lucy deserved a less fraught career, and Marie could no longer carry the brunt of her family's weight, and Collins had to find peace without Sullivan. But proceeding this way indefinitely was not a good option either.

Brooke felt oddly empowered as they bounded up the boardwalk to the beach house. Marie and Collins were on the deck with a pot of coffee and four mugs.

"What did we miss?" Lucy asked cheerfully, plopping into a chair.

Collins looked at Marie, who said nothing, and then to Brooke, who raised an eyebrow, sensing something was up.

"Not much," Collins said. "Only that Marie and the kids might come stay with me for a while, when we get home."

"Seriously?" Brooke asked. "Why?"

"Because I'm tired of feeling like a hypocrite," Marie said.

Collins cleared her throat. "Translation: She's thinking about leaving Kyle."

Brooke's hands went to her hips, a power stance she'd adopted in prenatal yoga. It had never actually brought her power, but today, it hit different. This wasn't the moment she'd ever wanted to face, but maybe it was the one she'd been training for all along.

"Welcome to the quitters club," she said wryly. "Got anything stronger than coffee?"

4

Marie

Marie wouldn't have believed it if it weren't happening to her in real time.

Once everyone's confessions were out in the open—once they'd said their deepest fears aloud, making them undeniably real—she'd worried she'd given too much power to her long-building doubts about her marriage. Instead, the damnedest thing happened.

Marie remembered how to relax.

By rights, she should have broken into a panicked sweat, wondering if she'd gone mad to consider leaving the home she shared with Kyle, doing something that she'd vowed to never do and could never be taken back—healed, perhaps, but forgotten, never. She should have been looking into couples counseling, seeking alternatives that would not disrupt co-parenting their beautiful boys. It *was* unthinkable to envision splitting time with the kids; she didn't even like being away from them now, much as she wanted to be here. But that was the thing: They were the only part of home she missed. She wasn't in the headspace to get to the root of that with Kyle yet. She'd been fighting her way through a dry, lonely desert, and she wasn't ready to talk about better footwear for the next leg of her journey. Eventually, she would.

First, she needed a drink of water. She needed to lie down in the shade and catch her breath.

So she did. Through some unspoken shared relief or solidarity, they all did. Nobody asked the others if they were still thinking about quitting or if anyone was having second thoughts. It seemed mutually understood that no one would have mentioned it, even in jest, if they weren't hoping for a friend to hold out a hand and say, *I see you, I've got you, it's okay.*

On the day she'd arrived, Marie had struggled to shut off her brain even to read in the hammock. How miraculous to find she was still capable, after all, of blissfully doing nothing in particular. She checked the boys' soccer scores and then left her phone in her room, tuning out the world to tune in to her friends. They went to long, late lunches and ate ice cream for dinner. They wore pajamas to the beach in the afternoon, and swimsuits beneath sundresses to happy hour, splashing through the surf on the walk back to the house. They danced to cover bands and chanted "Shake the salt!" to "Margaritaville" and "Hey, get laid!" to "Mony Mony." They napped in chaise longues and stayed up late playing rummy and searching for shooting stars.

They were extra gentle with Brooke. Every day she woke up to walk the beach, and every day a different friend went along and tried to carry her sadness beside her, giving and receiving the most extravagant gift any of them could have hoped for.

Four days of not worrying what they'd broken.

Four days of not obsessing about what they'd do next.

Four days of crying like babies, giggling like kids, and commiserating like old women.

Four days of thinking aloud without fear of judgment, refueling for what lay ahead.

It was as if by setting down their burdens, they'd freed themselves to reconnect with who they used to be, who they'd always been. Marie felt almost silly for ever having worried she'd lost herself. She'd been right there all along.

Waking to watch the sunrise together their last morning, there was a new energy, a collective sense that it was time to bring the trip full circle. Brooke was again the first one up and procured them a grease-stained paper bag of warm doughnut holes from a bakery a short bike ride away. The morning was chilly, a gentle reminder that autumn was in full swing back home, and they carried their pastries and coffees down to the sand, where they huddled together on one oversize blanket and pulled another one around their shoulders.

Marie watched Brooke help herself to a sugar-powdered ball and pop the whole thing into her mouth. Brooke's eyes widened in appreciation as she passed the bag around, and Marie took one, but her eyes never left her friend. As the horizon over the ocean brightened, Brooke looked the way Marie felt: Healthier than when she'd arrived just days ago. More comfortable in her own skin, with more color, more fight.

But none of them had gotten this far alone.

The words came out of Marie's mouth before she even knew she was going to say them.

"Anyone want to make a pact?" she asked. "Officially? To really go through with it. To go home and quit the things making us unhappy. To think of turning forty as a new start."

Three faces turned in her direction. Lucy was already nodding.

"I kind of thought we already did," Lucy said with a little laugh. "Then again, I think I was already halfway there. With or without this trip."

"I think we were all halfway there," Brooke said softly. "It feels a lot better knowing I'm not the only one doing it, though."

Lucy looked sideways at Brooke, searching, perhaps, for any signs of uncertainty. For Brooke, quitting would be a matter of biology, leaving no room for revisiting options at a later date. Marie didn't like to picture Brooke out on her morning walks alone. She knew that Mitch would try to shoulder the weight of her sadness—but that his own might be equally heavy.

"It's okay if you're not ready," Marie said gently. "I didn't mean that everybody has to."

Brooke smiled at her, a little sadly. "I think maybe we do," she said.

Marie cleared her throat. If Brooke could be this brave, so could she.

"So," Marie said. "To be clear, I'm not saying I'm going to leave Kyle for good. But if the boys and I go stay with Collins for a bit, that could be eye-opening for Kyle and I both. I'm going to quit making everything so damn easy for him. And I'm going to quit accepting that it has to be so damn hard for me."

Everyone nodded respectfully, as if waiting for her to say more. But what else was there to say? Marie had come to believe marriage was like politics: People tended to discuss couples at the ends of the spectrum, the best and worst, but most fell somewhere in the middle. Hers had been on a gradual slide away from the good stuff. No wonder she'd never talked to her friends about things falling apart until now: There was no big thing to blame—no infidelity or jaw-dropping betrayal. Only a million little things that sounded like nothing at all. She remembered a neighbor once contemplating leaving her husband, listing run-of-the-mill complaints until another friend piped up and said, "Sorry, but what do you think is different in our houses? Should we all lawyer up?"

It had made Marie's own unhappiness feel petty too.

But it didn't feel petty now.

Lucy cleared her throat and sat up straighter. "I'm going to quit chasing another book deal," she said. "I'm going to pursue a less thankless career."

Brooke's eyes were teary, but steady. "I'm going to quit blindly continuing infertility treatments that don't make sense anymore."

They all turned to look at Collins, who was staring into the doughnut bag with great concentration. She looked up and blushed.

"These aren't doughnuts," she announced, licking the powdered sugar off her lips. "They're balls of funnel cake in a breakfast disguise. How did we only discover them on our last day?"

She was obviously trying to change the subject. But after a beat, Lucy played along.

"Thank God," Lucy said, helping herself to another handful. "My appetite for eating my feelings seems bottomless. It's like I'm going through a breakup."

"You do talk about your story ideas like they're crushes," Collins mused.

Lucy pulled a face. "Maybe my writing is the reason I'm single. I mean, it's the main reason I often prefer to be alone. Maybe I'll do the old-fashioned thing and trade my career for a man."

Marie grinned. "People usually have a specific man in mind before they do that."

"I can gold-dig," Lucy said defensively. "I know exactly where to do it in Chicago: The Gold Coast. It's right there in the name." She held up a hand. "Don't ask me why I haven't done it yet if it's that easy. But Coll, whenever you're ready to try getting back out there . . ."

Collins bit her lip. "That's just it. I'm worried I don't fit with this pact in the first place."

"Of course you fit," Brooke assured her. "That's the messy beauty of it—that we all have a phase of our lives we want to leave behind."

"Exactly," Lucy agreed. "Don't let anyone ever tell you that you're not a quitter."

Clearly it was supposed to be a joke, but none of them mustered a smile.

"It's different with me," Collins said. "You're all gearing up to make this big, brave change, but my situation feels so passive and pathetic. Everyone else wants to stop torturing themselves over something they've been trying really hard at. I just want to stop torturing myself, period. It's embarrassing. If this was one of those novels where characters alternate telling their sides of the story, I bet I wouldn't even have a point of view." Collins blinked back tears. "I probably don't deserve one."

Marie shook her head. "That's not true," she said firmly. "If you have anything to be embarrassed about, where does that leave the rest of us? You haven't done a thing wrong. All you did was love the guy."

"Marie's right," Brooke agreed. "Even I share responsibility for the way my infertility treatments snowballed. I should have been more open with Mitch and asked more questions instead of plugging my ears to shut out odds I didn't want to hear. Losing Sullivan was a freak tragedy that happened *to* you."

"If anyone's quitting is shallow by comparison, it's me," Lucy chimed in. "At the end of the day, it's only a job." Marie and Brooke exchanged a look. Writing had been a core piece of Lucy's identity long before it had ever earned her a dime. But Collins was picking at the blanket, her cheeks still red. "Hey," Lucy said, laying a hand on Collins's arm until she finally looked up. "Of *course* it's hard, losing the person you love most in the world. You're pioneering uncharted territory we're all going to find ourselves in sooner or later. It's an honor to walk that with you."

Lucy's words hit Marie hard. She was right. She was inexcusably, unapologetically right. Collins had asked her not to dwell on this, but to hell with it. "The truth is," she told Collins, "we *haven't* been walking it with you the way best friends should. I live the closest—it's on me to keep showing up whether you want me there or not. You've been holding your head high on your own, and there is nothing pathetic about it. In fact, I don't want to hear you say that word again."

"Why?" Collins smiled ruefully, snagging another doughnut. "Does it sound too . . . pathetic?"

Lucy and Brooke chuckled, but Marie watched Collins closely. Despite the pep talk, she looked unconvinced. It emboldened Marie for the next phase of her own plan. Collins might have only offered her guest room to be nice, but Marie being there would be good for them both.

"Is anyone worried we're just psyching each other up?" Brooke asked, sounding uncertain for the first time. "I mean, here, with you, I feel empowered. Free. But what happens when we all go home? If one of us loses our nerve, will we all go down like dominoes?"

"We won't let that happen," Lucy insisted. "That's the beauty of doing it together. By myself, honestly, despite all my tough talk . . . I might not stand a chance."

"Same," Marie agreed.

"Same," Brooke said.

"Already tested and tried," Collins admitted. "Okay. I resolve to quit sitting alone in my grief. To quit my holding pattern. To at least, you know . . . leave my house more."

Lucy reached over and squeezed Collins's hand. "You'll have Marie with you," she said, then looked around the circle at the rest of them. "And we'll be there in other ways. We'll keep the group chat active, do accountability checks, plan video calls, whatever it takes. Whenever someone stumbles, we'll all pick them up. And I for one will take you up on the invite to visit Athens before long too. Who knows if I'll even stay in Chicago. Wherever I end up, I'm going to need you guys."

At last, the sun broached the horizon, and they all huddled closer, watching it rise in silence. Every new day was a chance to get things right. Perhaps, especially, this one.

Impulsively, they all grasped hands in the center of the blanket.

"I wish we could stay here longer," Collins said.

"Nah," Lucy teased. "Better quit while we're ahead."

They all laughed, delighted to have found some positive connotation for quitting after all.

It would hit differently later, though. Because none of them had ever really been ahead—that was the whole point.

And they had no idea just how close they'd come to leaving one of their own behind.

5

Lucy

Lucy had never mastered the art of navigating the backend of her website, but as it turned out, deleting things was infinitely easier than posting them. The contact page that had taken her a whole Sunday afternoon to format was gone in the mere seconds it took to swig from a rocks glass of whiskey, with time left over to sputter and clutch her chest as she remembered why she never drank this stuff. Never mind. This was part of the quitting experience: It was *supposed* to burn going down. The pop-up window for newsletter sign-ups was just as deceptively simple to get rid of: Click the mouse, sip the drink, say goodbye.

She'd thought about taking the whole domain down, but the idea wasn't to negate the work she'd done—she was still proud of it, more so now that there would be no more. The idea was to avoid any invitation for future contact or any implication that this page would remain up to date. She disabled the comments and contact forms, then toggled open the lead post on her homepage—typically a "What's New from Lucy" teaser—and pasted in the essay she'd started writing on the flight home. Once she'd gotten going, the thing practically wrote itself, as if *this* had been her magnum opus all along. Oh, the irony.

She'd never promised to quit without having the last word.

"From now on, if you find it hard to turn down an offer, try saying *don't* instead of *no*," Marie had suggested. "It's a trick I give my students. Instead of 'No, I won't visit your book club,' you might say, 'What a lovely invitation, but I don't visit book clubs anymore.'"

Lucy shook the ice in her rocks glass, took a third sip, and tried it aloud now.

"I don't write anymore," she said. In the empty room, her voice sounded hollow with uncertainty. It would take practice, but Lucy had never shied away from putting in the work.

She boldly capitalized every clickbait-laden word of her headline, and with trembling fingers, hovered her cursor over the "Post" button.

Her eyes slid sideways to the whiskey bottle, gifted to her last Christmas. The brand was called Writers' Tears, the kind of inside joke that had never really been funny. Well, it was tailor-made for her now.

She clicked.

That was it, then. It was posted, done. She loaded her URL on her phone to be sure, and just like that, she was palming the grenade that would firebomb her career.

Disbelief gripped her for a terrifying moment, as if she'd called her own bluff. She logged out of the website, then onto social media to share the link to her "update." Then, she disabled her two-factor authentication methods and logged out of them too. She wasn't much for social media. She used it only to monitor her professional accounts. And to wrestle with envy over what more successful writers were doing. What a relief it would be to quit that too.

Uninstalling the mobile apps was just as easy. Drag and drop. The whiskey was going down smoother with every sip. It figured that *now* she'd develop a taste for the stuff.

"I don't write anymore," she said again, louder this time. With authority.

She splashed another finger of the Writers' Tears into her glass, flipped open the desktop notepad she'd prepped earlier, and called Collins, who seemed least likely to be caught at an inopportune moment. There was no telling what kind of conversation Brooke and Mitch might be in the thick of right now, let alone Marie and Kyle. Collins answered on the first ring.

"Hey, Coll. Can I bug you for a quick favor?"

"Always. What's up?"

"I need you to write down these usernames and passwords for me. Do you have a pen and paper?"

"Can't you just text them? Or email?"

"I'm worried that's not secure. I got hacked last year, and—can you just do it?" Admittedly, Lucy didn't want a written record for herself either. Even if she deleted it from her sent mail, there was nothing to stop Collins from replying and sending the info right back. She couldn't trust herself to resist any future moments of weakness.

"Okay," Collins said. "Found a pen."

Lucy recited all the info and Collins diligently read it back. "What's this for, anyway?"

"The web host one is for my website, lucymayerwrites.com. The others are my professional social media accounts, @lucymayerwrites."

"You want me to have these as backup?"

"No. I want you to log in and change the passwords. As soon as we hang up."

"Did you get locked out or something?"

"Not yet."

"What do you want me to change them to?"

"Anything. I don't want to know what they are. Keep the new login info in a safe place, in case of emergency, but I can't imagine what that would be. In fact, don't ever give me this info, even if I claim it's an emergency. So I guess just . . . put it in the vault."

Collins went quiet, and Lucy could hear the tap of her laptop keyboard in the background, followed by an audible gasp. "Your homepage . . . Is this . . . Did you . . ."

"Yes. Which is why I'm trusting you to ensure I can't undo it in a moment of weakness. Which could come on anytime."

"Hang on, I want to read this."

"No!" Lucy felt her face redden. "Not while we're on the phone. It's too weird."

"Okay, but Lucy, locking yourself out seems drastic," Collins said. "Can't you just disconnect your Wi-Fi or something, until the urge passes? I mean, you're going to want access to this stuff eventually. This is years of work."

"When you quit a job, you don't get to take the keys to the office with you. This isn't any different. I'm firing myself. I don't want the temptation when I'm disgruntled or drunk or desperate or . . . any other *D* words."

"If you're sure. I just know what it feels like to regret something. To blame yourself later." Her voice gave way to a weighty pause. "It's the worst feeling. And if it's avoidable . . ."

"Collins, you're not supposed to question me on this; I'm calling you in for backup. Quitters united, remember?"

Collins sighed. "Quitters united."

"And I don't want you *using* the passwords once you change them. Don't try to help me, okay? If people are leaving comments like *Oh, so sorry to hear that, Lucy, we love your writing*, no going rogue with some campaign to rally the support of my nonexistent fans. I know you'd mean well, but you have to trust me that it wouldn't be helpful."

"But if people do say that, wouldn't it make you feel better? I mean, wouldn't you want to know?"

"Honestly? It makes it worse. That's the thread I've been hanging by for years. It's nice hearing compliments, but they're not paying my bills. It's time for me and my ego to move on."

More silence. "Oh, Luce, this essay is so beautiful—it's going to make me cry."

"If you're going to keep reading, I'm hanging up."

"Sorry. Couldn't help it. You're just such a good . . . I mean, you *were* a good . . ."

Lucy's grip on her rocks glass tightened. "Thanks."

"Lucy?" Collins's voice was quieter now. "Are you okay?"

"I'm going to be. I appreciate this, Collins. You're the best."

She ended the call and downed the rest of her whiskey in a gulp so big she started sputtering again. When she thought back on this moment, that's what she wanted to remember: Not the sweet longing that things could've been different, but the inescapable pain that they hadn't been.

6

Brooke

Brooke took two steps inside her front door, dropped her duffel, and burst into tears. She hadn't intended a dramatic entrance—in fact, she hadn't planned on anything emotional today beyond gushing to Mitch about how good it had been to see her friends. She thought it wise to sleep on her decision one more night, in case her own bed made a difference.

But the instant she saw Mitch reclined on the couch in front of the Colorado Rockies game, looking so positively dad-like in his worn raglan tee and askew baseball cap, her composure went out the window.

Mitch jumped to his feet. "Babe? What's wrong?" She could only shake her head, crying harder, and he crossed the room in a few giant steps, placing his hands on her upper arms as if bracing to physically lift her out of her despair. That was Mitch—always there to catch her before she fell. Even when she was tripping up everything he'd ever wanted. She couldn't look at him. If she looked at him, it would be real. "Are you sick?" he asked. "Hurt?"

"No. Yes." She sniffed and forced herself to meet his eye. "I think we should cancel tomorrow's appointment."

"That is completely up to you," he said, visibly relaxing, and she cringed. He thought they were talking about scheduling. About time—her wanting more of it, instead of them being out of it. She tried to memorize the way he looked in this last moment before she let him down for good. He looked understanding. Compassionate. Concerned. His eyebrows twitched the way they did when he was flirting—like he was paying her so much undivided attention, he'd forgotten to keep control of his face.

The word "unconditional" came to mind, and a fresh wave of tears threatened to overtake her. She'd do anything for this man. But she couldn't get her body to give him the thing they most wanted to share. She'd always known that if she admitted defeat, her own disappointment would be difficult to bear, but the idea of shouldering his felt worse. Impossible.

She took a slow, unsteady breath. "What I mean is," she said, "I think we should quit trying."

Mitch stiffened, like maybe he thought he'd misheard. His hands tightened on her biceps, his eyes searching hers. This was her chance to take it back, to hastily add some qualifier, like *just for a month or two* or *if that's what you want.* But after seeing how distant Marie had grown from Kyle, Brooke didn't want to take even one step down that road. Certainly not now, when she and Mitch were already at their low point through no fault of their own.

"Quit trying, huh?" he repeated. His tone was not disbelieving, just clarifying. She swallowed hard and nodded, giving the room over to another beat of silence.

"Okay," he said. He sounded . . . well, sincere. Brooke's eyes narrowed.

"Okay?"

She must have looked as skeptical as she felt, because he softened. "Oh, Brooke. I've been wondering when . . . It felt wrong for me to be the first to suggest it, but . . . I'm on this journey *with* you. Wherever you go, I follow. So if you're sure, or when you're sure, you can count on my answer to be the same: Okay."

An ugly sob escaped her—a strange tangle of relief and despair. On a day-to-day basis, Mitch didn't always say the right thing. In fact, sometimes he was maddeningly dense, quick to reduce any problem to a cheesy baseball metaphor. But when it really mattered, he knocked it out of the park. And it had never mattered more than this. He engulfed her in his arms while she cried, waiting for her to be the first to let go.

When she did, she saw that he'd been crying too. But he smiled at her, bravely.

"I almost forgot." He held up a finger, backing out of the room. "I have just the thing."

She heard him fumbling with the cupboard under the stairs, rummaging around. He reappeared in the doorway holding a Barbie-pink sandcastle-shaped bucket with "F*ck It" written in permanent marker on the side.

"Oh, for the love—" She laughed out loud. "You saved it?"

"I more than saved it." He held it out like a peace offering. "I restocked it."

They'd made the F*ck-It Bucket as an inside joke, an homage to a David Sedaris audiobook they'd listened to on their move out west, where Sedaris recounted how his foul-mouthed but big-hearted younger brother, "the Rooster," sagely recommended such an aptly named bucketload of candy as a remedy for days "when shit brings you down."

Now, she peered inside and saw a veritable buffet of things she'd denied herself during this my-body-is-my-temple era of trying to conceive. There was indeed candy but also gourmet aged cheeses tagged with sticky notes that said "Redeemable for six glorious ounces of forbidden feta" and "Almost as good as goat cheese—trust me." There were airplane-size bottles of tequila, a split of champagne, and even some of Colorado's finest cannabis edibles—a legalized throwback to their long-gone days of passing joints at Red Rocks concerts.

Brooke fingered the offerings with a mixture of awe and confusion. "How long have you had this ready to go?"

"Since your first treatment," he said, matter-of-factly. "I had to keep checking the expiration dates and replenishing. I thought I'd bring the old F-It Bucket out for a little break whenever you complained that this was starting to be too much." He tapped his finger under her chin until she looked at him. "But you never did. Not once."

"You're really not mad?" she asked. "Not disappointed, I mean?"

"Not at you," he said simply. "I'm *with* you. Never forget it."

~

They were sprawled on their bed half dressed, surrounded by candy wrappers and empty bottles. Brooke had rinsed off the ick of the flight in a long, hot shower, then pulled on one of Mitch's worn T-shirts and settled in to binge-watch mindless TV, a rotation of familiar movies she could quote by heart and lifestyle shows with increasingly outlandish themes. Did people really roam the world in search of the tiniest hotel room or the spiciest hot pepper? And if they did, was that any less sane than what she'd been doing, subjecting her own body to years of hormone injections and invasive procedures for, apparently, no reason at all?

As soon as Mitch had heard her tearing into his bucket stash, he'd turned off the game and come to join her, mixing Irish coffees for them both and slanting the blinds against the afternoon sun. A few hours later, they'd come down off the emotional rush, sated into something like contentment.

They used to do this when they first married—lounging around, indulging in lazy afternoons—but Brooke couldn't remember the last time. Everything had turned get-up-and-go, with a near manic focus on controlling uncontrollable variables. Her daily workouts had become unskippable, her quick dinners replaced with time-consuming meals made from scratch, and her pile of catch-up work was ever present due to unavoidable appointments during weekday hours.

Some people waited until they had kids to let relaxation get pushed out of their schedules, but Brooke and Mitch had forfeited all their unoccupied hours just to try.

"I feel bad you didn't come along to the beach," she told him now. "I didn't realize how much I missed the ocean until I got there. It's been years. I couldn't get enough."

"We should go again," he said easily. "You deserve more than a few days away. If we're not doing any more treatments, our schedules are wide open."

Brooke rolled onto her back and stared at the ceiling. "If only our bank account wasn't wide empty."

Mitch shrugged. "Staying out of debt is overrated. Everyone else seems to be in it. We'll pay everything off eventually. Or maybe if we're lucky, global warming will destroy us first."

They both laughed. Gallows humor had kind of gotten to be their thing, as tended to happen when one was stuck awaiting an uncertain fate. It beat the alternative—she'd seen too many other couples at the clinic rendered humorless.

"If the future is a nonissue, might as well sell our house and quit our jobs," she said, feigning nonchalance. No one would believe she and Mitch had never speculated about a plan B—especially given all the planning and effort that had gone into plan A—but it was true. And it was, admittedly, weird. Enough so that bringing it up felt scary. Half joking was easier than total truth, so she doubled down. "We'll just travel until the money runs out and hope we don't need a real plan by then."

"Why not sell our cars too," he said, playing along. "We could pay off our medical bills and have plenty leftover to see the world." He reached across her for the bucket. "Any more dark chocolate in here?"

Brooke caught his arm and hugged it to her stomach. She wondered if he could feel it doing flips.

An idea was forming in her brain like a word she'd just unscrambled—though the letters had been there all along, shaking around like tiles in a bag, trying to find the right order.

"We could, you know," she said.

"Could what?"

She handed him the bucket and sat up, hugging her knees to her chest.

"If parenthood isn't going to happen for us . . ." She caught herself: No more ifs. She started again: "Now that we're accepting parenthood isn't going to happen for us, we should talk about what we want our life to look like. Which could be anything, right? I mean, when we bought this house . . ."

He met her eyes, and she didn't have to finish the thought aloud. Of course he knew; everyone knew. The house was a three-bedroom in a good school district, in a family-friendly suburb, with a flat, fenced yard that begged for a swing set and sandbox. For years they'd paid taxes for a community they longed to be a part of . . . but weren't yet. This house, this neighborhood, this lifestyle—it was all hard to look at without seeing the plans that would never come to fruition. The room she'd pictured as a nursery. The finished basement they'd intended as a playroom. The places she'd lain crying every time the clinic called with more bad news.

"It wouldn't be a bad idea to start over somewhere else," Mitch agreed. "More walkable? In a trendier neighborhood, closer to work?"

She nodded. The whole way home, she'd been dreading walking back through this door—and not because of Mitch. Because of all the rest, so many reasons she'd only been able to ignore when she'd been able to convince herself they were temporary.

"Moving is definitely on the table," she said carefully. "But there wouldn't be a rush to put down roots anywhere else."

Mitch unwrapped a square of chocolate and popped it in his mouth. "What are you saying?"

"I don't know." She was starting to think she did know, but again, her emotions were getting ahead of her. This was a lot to lay on him all at once. She'd pictured so many scenarios where things went sideways as soon as she got home: Mitch storming out, saying he needed to think; Mitch talking her into one more egg retrieval; Mitch deciding he was young enough to find another wife whose body performed basic womanly functions better than Brooke's did. She would have hardly blamed him for any of that, but he'd done none of it.

In that respect, she'd gotten very lucky. Almost lucky enough to make up for all the rest.

She'd be a world-class idiot to go too far out on a limb and lose him now.

But she thought of the pact she'd made with Collins and Lucy and Marie—of how they'd promised to hold each other to it. They weren't just going to quit the things making them unhappy and slink away into submission. They were going to quit boldly. They were going to stand strong. They were not going to wait around to see if things got better. They were going to damn well make things more fulfilling—or at least more interesting.

"We don't have to do anything rash," she said. "But we could *think* about doing something rash. No harm in trying it on for size."

Mitch dumped the contents of the bucket onto the bedspread and balanced it on his head like a hat. "How's this for a perfect fit?"

She raised an eyebrow. "You look like a deranged drum major."

"This is it, baby," he teased. "Just you and me and this F*ck-It Bucket, from now on." His smile faltered, like the joke might not be okay, so she nuzzled closer to let him know it was.

"I'd follow you anywhere," she said, echoing his words from earlier. "And I invite you to test that theory."

7

Marie

Kyle used to look at Marie a certain way and she'd think, *Holy gods, how soon can we be alone? Take me now.* It was something in his expression, like he didn't know what to make of her but admired the hell out of her anyway, that made her want to throw off her clothes and show him exactly what she was made of.

Now, when he fixed his eyes on her across the bedroom as she was repacking the suitcase she'd never fully unpacked, all she wanted was to slink away before he could ask too many questions.

And before she could lose her nerve.

"I appreciate that you want to be there for Collins," he said. "But surely there's a way to do it without literally moving into her house?"

Originally, she'd planned to wait until the following weekend to set her plan into motion. She'd known what she'd come home to after four days away—the boys happy but dirty and sated on fast food, the refrigerator empty, and Kyle feeling self-congratulatory and entitled to a break, climbing over the laundry heap on the mudroom floor to load up his golf clubs and head to the driving range. It would take a day or two just to get things back in order, and by then, they'd be in the thick of her Monday-through-Friday chaos management.

One more week, she'd told herself. *Then I'll rock the boat.*

But the instant she'd stepped through the door, she'd known: She had to go now.

On the surface, nothing had changed: She'd been pretending everything was fine for a long time. But now that she'd made her decision, she didn't know how to pretend anymore.

Besides, if she had to restock groceries anyway, why not do it at Collins's? If she needed to do laundry, why not fold it directly into their bags? And how much notice did two preteen boys need to grab some things? If it were up to them, they'd wear the same hoodie day in and day out—and often did, despite her protests.

"A friend stopping by at three in the afternoon isn't what Collins needs, Kyle," she said. She dumped a basket of clean clothes on the bed next to her suitcase. "She needs a friend at three a.m. She's lonely and depressed—she didn't reach out for help lightly. And she wouldn't have had to if I'd been there for her in the first place."

So, maybe she'd exaggerated how much of her leaving was about Collins needing a friend versus Marie needing a break. She told students it was rarely a good idea to make big life decisions when feeling overwhelmed or, worse, afraid—and she felt both.

"Fine, but if you're this worried about her," Kyle asked, "are you sure it's a good idea to have the boys there too? I mean, do you think she's in danger of doing something rash?"

"Don't be ridiculous," Marie snapped, sounding more defensive than she'd intended. Using Collins as an excuse to buy herself time was one thing, but she wasn't about to throw her under the bus. "Collins has never done anything rash in her life. That's part of the reason she needs help. If I wait for the convenient moment to get over there and clean out Sullivan's things and drag her out of her hiding place, it will never come."

He wrapped his arms around her from behind, and she had to force herself to lean against him instead of pulling away. His nearness had once felt comforting, and she longed to have that back. Of course she didn't *want* to find her own husband's body an intrusion on her personal space. The problem, she suspected, had more to do with every inch of her life being occupied by someone who wanted something from her. The kids were in their own category, priority number one—but pile on top of that her absentee spouse, her colleagues, the other parents in her rideshare rotation, the wait-listed students begging her to squeeze them in . . . Maybe if she could just get a few minutes in her day that weren't already claimed by so many outside forces.

Maybe if just one person would invite her to simply take up some space of her own, wanting nothing in return, she could breathe again.

Collins had. She also knew Marie's kids were part of the deal.

Marie eased out of Kyle's arms to turn and look at him. "This doesn't have to be a big thing. I am *always* back and forth to Athens with the boys. If we stay with her, we'll have way more downtime without the commute. They'll fill her house with so much energy, she'll forget how quiet and empty it felt. We'll be home every weekend—or at least the boys will—and take it a week at a time, see how she's doing. Maybe alternate weeks for a while."

Kyle sighed. "Look, you had all weekend to get used to this idea, but it feels sprung on me. You could have asked how I felt about it before you started packing."

Marie hesitated. She'd learned the hard way not to ask Kyle questions she didn't want answers to. Because, taking a page from Marie's teachings, Kyle had no trouble saying no.

Might you negotiate to work remotely two days a week, so we could transfer the boys to school closer to home? What about applying for this job in university financing—less pay, but less stress too? Could you adjust your hours to handle soccer on Thursdays? Are you open to hiring a lawn service so we don't lose you to the mower for a couple of hours every Sunday?

The answer was always no. And after she'd asked, where to go from there?

"Well, it might not be a bad test," she ventured, unable to resist, "to see what it's like for most of our family to sleep in the place we spend most of our waking hours. And I *have* asked you about that before, many times."

This time, Kyle didn't get a vote. If she told him the hard truth—that she suspected they'd failed each other, and she wasn't sure they could find their way back—it would put him on the defensive. She wasn't about to inflict that kind of pain without taking time to further investigate her own thoughts on the matter.

Maybe if she stepped away to get some perspective, she'd see all was not lost. Maybe he'd get some perspective too.

"This is not going to make our lives more stressful the way you think it is," she went on. "I predict the opposite."

For a terrifying instant, she could tell he was wondering if there was more to this than geography and friendship and guilt. But he said nothing as his eyes searched hers.

Maybe she wasn't the only one who'd learned not to ask questions she didn't want the answers to.

"The timing isn't great," he said, finally. "I have a huge new client portfolio under review."

Marie squinted at him. It was almost pathological, the way he'd stopped trying to see anything from her point of view. "Doesn't that make this a better time for us to go?" she pointed out. "If you'll be working longer hours anyway?"

The door to their room burst open, and the boys tore in, a frenzy of energy. Wade hugged a football to his chest, laughing uncontrollably, trying in vain to outrun the taller, faster Connor, who tackled him onto the bed. The boys writhed in a tangle of legs and arms.

"Boys! Enough." Kyle either didn't clock that it was in good fun or didn't care. Only when Wade flung out an arm that nearly overturned Marie's open suitcase did she chime in.

"Okay, off the bed. You're going to have to practice your tackling on the floor."

Miraculously, they listened. Their eyes had lit on their suitcases.

"I can't believe we seriously get to stay in Athens," Wade said. "Mom, will Aunt Collins let us have friends over? Her house is so much closer to *everyone*."

"Bro," Connor said. "Dylan only lives like two streets over too."

"No way. Bet."

"I'm sure we can work something out," Marie said carefully. "As long as we're respectful of her space and her home."

"Her house is legit cool," Connor added. "Everyone is going to be jealous."

This outward excitement was becoming rare for their twelve-year-old, and Marie could see it rubbing Kyle the wrong way.

"I wasn't aware your friends were so interested in an infamous sculpture garden," he said.

"What's infamous mean?" Wade asked, and Marie threw Kyle a warning look.

"Do you mean the statues in the backyard?" Connor asked. "I was just talking about the porches—stacked right on top of each other! They have the coolest chairs that hang from the ceiling. Like nests. And mom said we can hook up the Xbox *in our room* there."

"Did she." Kyle shot a look back at Marie.

"We don't want to invade *all* of Collins's space, but we'll still have screen time rules," Marie said quickly.

"Well, I can see you're all really going to miss me." Kyle's tone was good-natured, but his facsimile of a smile was too tight.

"Aw, Dad, we will," Wade said. "But we hardly see you on school days anyway."

It was Marie's turn to smile tightly. Kyle looked away.

If she believed he was sorely going to miss them, she might have thought twice. But he was mainly bothered that they weren't worried about how they'd manage without him.

All four of them already knew they could.

Driving to work had never felt so symbolic as Marie turned onto her usual route bound for Athens, while Kyle veered the opposite direction toward the Columbus rush hour. Marie's van was full: The kids in the back seat, backpacks and lunch boxes stacked between them, and their bags in the trunk, along with a box of classroom files from her home office and a mound of sporting and gaming equipment. In the rearview, her back windshield was partially obstructed by the bikes strapped to their trailer hitch, which wobbled precariously as she accelerated.

The boys chattered as if it were any other school day, and she vacillated between being glad they were well adjusted enough to embrace this change and thinking something must be terribly wrong in her family for this to be so.

They were really doing this. Tonight, they would not come home.

And not tomorrow either.

Marie had been so resolute, but now she felt unmoored. She hadn't considered how obvious this would look with her overpacked van parked in the faculty lot, how people might talk. She had no time to head to Collins's before class. Unlike most of her colleagues, who vied for later class times, her day on campus was front-loaded so she could pick up the boys from school. Afterward, they'd unload and settle in together. As a family of three.

With Collins as an honorary member.

She wondered how her other friends were faring. She wondered if she might have gotten swept up in the spirit of quitting, carried away. She wondered if she'd cheated by not coming cleaner with Kyle—if she was only prolonging the inevitable.

Then she ran out of time for wondering. The boys ran into school, and moments later Marie speed walked to her eight a.m. class, hoping she had this in her today.

If it was anything but How to Say No, she'd have felt surer.

"Welcome back," Marie began, addressing the students. "Hope you had a nice fall break." The lecture hall was double the size of the classrooms she usually taught in, with tiered seating on a semicircle slope.

Only a few seats remained empty as the students settled in, removing coats and opening laptops.

"I'm curious," Marie asked. "Did any of you use something you learned earlier this term during your time off?" An affirmative murmur went around the room, heads bobbing.

A sophomore near the front raised her hand. "It sparked an argument with my dad," the girl volunteered. "Not on purpose."

Marie leaned back on the edge of her desk. "Do tell."

The girl sat up straighter. She was wearing an oversize T-shirt and striped pajama pants, her hair falling out of its ponytail, but her eyes were wide awake. "He called this class a waste of tuition," the girl said. "He said, *No is a complete sentence. What do you need a whole class for?*"

"What did you tell him?"

"I told him no one ever taught me how to say no. Or how to set boundaries. And that since he hasn't done that job, I was happy to spend my tuition on someone who would."

A cheer went up, with a smattering of applause. Marie waited for it to fade.

"All right," she said. "I'm glad you shared that. Let's put it to the room: Raise your hand if you've ever heard the phrase, *No is a complete sentence.*" They all had. "Now, keep your hand up if you find that dismissive instead of empowering." Arms went limp, unsure.

"Look, if that wasn't a gross oversimplification, this class *wouldn't* exist. I certainly wouldn't be interested in teaching it. Yes, no *is* a complete sentence, but why is that unhelpful?"

Only a few hands stayed up. Marie pointed to a first-year sipping coffee in the front row.

"Because I feel mean saying no without explanation?"

"Hmm. Is *mean* the best word for how you worry you'll come across?"

The freshman bit her lip. "Bitchy," she said. "I feel like they'll think I'm bitchy."

Marie nodded. "Who thinks *bitchy* is the right word?" Every hand went back up. "Who else has a reason a one-word *no* feels insufficient when someone really wants to hear yes?"

One of her favorite students, a guy named Randall, called out from the back. It was easier learning the names of the men because there were so few of them. He was wearing a Pride T-shirt, and he twirled his pencil like a baton. "Because people want to know why. They look at you like they expect an apology or something."

"Sometimes I *want* to explain," the girl with the coffee volunteered. "Sometimes I feel torn. Like, I'm worried about missing out on an opportunity, even if I'm overextended."

"Now we're getting into it. We talked in the first half of this term about how women especially are conditioned to have a hard time saying no. But it isn't just about wanting to be liked, or to be generous, or to avoid hurt feelings. Saying no is a balancing act. Once we've established parameters for drawing boundaries, we can acknowledge that we don't want to be pressured into things . . . but we do want to be nice. Both can be true."

Marie often looked out at her students and saw variations of her younger self—and of Lucy, Brooke, and Collins too. How many nights had they spent huddled in their dorm, trying to separate what their parents wanted from what they wanted, what their boyfriends liked from what they liked, what their textbooks taught from what was true? But now, as her eyes passed from one eager face to the next, she saw glimmers of how she felt today, at forty. She seized the moment, improvising.

"Maybe we could all drop this class and read *Eat Pray Love* instead," she said. "We'd get the message that saying no to someone else can mean saying yes to ourselves. And it might be effective for a day or two. But we're after long-term solutions, not bursts of bravado."

Marie thought of her van outside, packed full of *no. Not anymore. Not right now.*

She instructed the students to take out a piece of paper and a pencil, old school.

"I started the semester by asking why you enrolled in this course, and you gave thoughtful answers about your families and roommates and employers and dating and feminism. But now that we know each other a little better, we can talk about why you're *really* here. Even if it's just to prove your dad wrong." A chuckle went around the room. "I'd like you to share three things with me, in brief. One: how the reason you're here has evolved since the start of the semester. Two: an example of a time you've tried a strategy from this class and what the result was. And three: what you hope to learn in the remainder of this semester. Leave them with me on your way out."

Without hesitation, the scribbling began. Only one face in the corner stayed upright, and it took Marie a second to realize it was Collins, who'd slipped in unnoticed. Marie smiled quizzically, blushing at the impromptu pep talk she'd inadvertently given in front of her friend.

A couple of students gathered their things and made their way down to Marie's desk to hand in their responses. Collins got to her feet, hanging back until the early finishers were through. Then she handed Marie a thin stack of pages—not the exercise, but a printout.

Marie recognized the header from Lucy's website. She started to skim, her heart beating faster. It was internet official: Lucy was not going gently into that good night.

"Thought you might need a burst of solidarity today," Collins whispered.

The girl who'd argued with her dad over the break shyly approached. When Marie motioned her forward, she handed over her paper, then hesitated.

"Did you use lessons from this class too, Professor Welling?" she asked. "Or is it all so second nature you don't think about it anymore?"

Marie could feel Collins's eyes on hers. "You know what?" Marie said. "I did."

"I did too," Collins chimed in. "I'm not even in this class, and it's changing my life." The student held out her fist, and the three of them bumped knuckles. Marie smiled at Collins as the girl walked away. She hadn't realized how alone she'd been feeling until this moment.

"I'm proud of Lucy," she whispered. "This took guts. Thanks for bringing it."

"I think I needed to hear you say that," Collins whispered back. "I was a little scared for her."

Marie felt overcome with gratitude that Collins had come. They could do this. They could be proud of themselves and terrified at the same time. Relieved and anxious. Ready and yet hesitant. Like she'd told her students: *Both can be true.*

"See you at home?" Collins asked Marie, smiling bravely.

Marie smiled back. "See you at home."

8

Lucy

Lucy fidgeted in her chair, wishing she'd worn something more businesslike. She'd figured college campuses were low key—all she had to do was look like a grown-up, right? But this enrollment counselor seated across the desk from her wore a button-down and blazer that made her dip-dyed pullover and leggings look the wrong kind of whimsical.

She'd expected to feel a little out of place at this meeting. She hadn't expected the enrollment counselor himself to be this hot. Hollywood hot. Like if a casting director spotted him on the street, they'd start writing another *Ocean's Eleven* just to put him in it. Also, he looked roughly her age—far from the gray-haired counselors she remembered from her time in academia.

Did people really open up to this guy to talk through a career crisis?

"So," he said, "tell me why you're interested in an MBA."

He folded his hands on the desk, and that's when Lucy's mistake hit her. Intimidated by the volume of colleges in the greater Chicago area, she'd chosen the business program that claimed the highest success rate: better job titles, better salaries, better everything. Talk about wishful thinking.

This wasn't a place people came for career salvage.

Only to make successful careers *more* successful.

"Well," she began, clearing her throat. She was here now, so she might as well try to get something out of it. She tried to picture him with a beer at a baseball game, someplace more human, doing something less . . . businesslike. But the strategy backfired.

Because she could imagine that maybe he *was* more comfortable in street clothes. Maybe he was just toeing the line to impress the would-be execs who came in here. And that prospect only made him hotter.

"My career in publishing has involved a lot of project management," she explained. "Production deadlines, collaboration on marketing and design and PR strategies, input from both in-house staff and freelancers—a lot of moving pieces, a lot of . . . balls in the air."

She grappled for the kind of office speak she'd never had to use. The kind she made fun of when people said things like *Let's pull that idea into the parking lot until we designate a Slack channel for broader-reaching initiatives.*

"I see," he said, straight-faced. "So, end goal, you'd like to advance to a higher level of project management in publishing?"

"God, no." She shuddered. "But I thought those skills might translate to another field. In business administration. Hence the MBA."

"Business administration," he repeated, his mouth twitching toward a smile. Almost like he suspected her of reciting the words of the degree without understanding what they entailed. Which was 100 percent true, but a bit rude.

"You know," he said, "it's true our MBA program will accept students with any kind of bachelor's degree, but it's not one-size-fits-all. There are plenty of other paths for professional advancement, and we have comprehensive resources to help you find a pathway you'd enjoy."

Lucy shook her head. "I'm not looking for enjoyment," she assured him. "I had that. I mean, sort of. Until I didn't. Career enjoyment is overrated. I'm looking for career stability."

"Meaning . . . a higher salary?"

She was getting irritated. Wasn't it obvious she of all people knew what words meant? *Business administration* notwithstanding?

"By stability, I mean *stability*," she said.

"Could be culture shock," he observed, "to move from a creative industry to one that's all about the bottom line."

"You'd be surprised," she said, and at last, he smiled . . . the way you do when you're trying not to laugh in church.

"Okay," he said, shrugging. "Well, we're one of the top-ranked MBA programs in the country. We do offer flexible part-time options and online learning, but what sets us apart is our robust full-time experience on campus, complete with co-op and study-abroad options that allow you to focus on professional development without juggling outside pressure. Do you currently have a full-time position you're looking to work around?"

"No position," she said, her face coloring. Usually, whenever she talked about her writing career to a nonwriter, she felt like a misfit. But this was new: feeling like an unemployed loser. "Am I too late to apply for spring semester?" she asked.

"Not if you hurry. The cutoff is December first, so you'd have about a month to get your application together—but there are components that can be challenging to rush, like recommendation letters from professional mentors."

"That shouldn't be a problem," she said.

It was very much going to be a problem, depending on how they qualified *mentor*. But Lucy was resourceful. Plus, she had Marie—would a gender studies professor have clout at a business school?

"I was comparing all these MBAs online," she explained, "and got overwhelmed. Which is why I made this appointment. But now I feel unprepared. Like I should already know how long this will take or how much it costs." She grinned sheepishly. "Sitting here talking about how all I want is stability . . . I realize I sound like a horrible dating prospect. Ain't got no money, no job." She held up a hand. "I'm not sleeping on anyone's couch, though. So I have that going for me."

Never mind that she'd sort of been *wishing* she was sleeping on someone's couch. For the past week, Marie and Collins had been flooding the group chat with pictures of them together: posing with Marie's boys around the backyard fire circle, roasting marshmallows in the rosy light of Sullivan's stained-glass sculptures, toasting another day of quitting with glasses of wine, propping their fuzzy slippers up on Collins's porch railing. Lucy knew they were going through big, scary changes, too, but at least they had each other. They seemed to have settled back in to being roommates like old times—like the days Lucy longed to do over.

The admissions counselor flashed that half-hidden smile again. "Good thing you're not here looking for a dating prospect," he said. "Only a degree program."

"Good thing," she agreed, eying him sideways. Was he steering her back on topic, or flirting? Hard to tell.

"I'll level with you," he said. "Most universities, you suck it up one year if you want to go full time, eighteen months or two years for a part-time hybrid or online program. Here, it's two intense years, even full time."

She blanched. "Two years of accruing student debt?"

"Two years of accruing student debt while paying living expenses in Chicago. If you're truly after stability, that might not be it."

Lucy's mind raced. "That's a long time to put my whole life on hold and then have to dig out of a hole before I can get ahead."

"Many prospective students agree. Our offerings aren't the right fit for everyone. You might rethink your next steps. Look at making a job change or reducing your living expenses before applying." He skimmed her resume. "Are you set on staying in town?"

She shook her head. "I'm not set on anything."

"Well, I see you went to Ohio University—they have a robust MBA program. Nine concentrations, plenty of flexibility, and I know for a fact their on-campus option is fast-tracked. Maybe you're not open to moving back, but . . . if you have any contacts on campus, that could help expedite things."

Lucy thought about their last check-in call, Collins and Marie together on the screen, side by side on the couch with their cocktails, debating where to begin tackling projects around Collins's house. Lucy wondered if she was the only one who hadn't realized Collins was still living with her dead husband's clothes hanging in his closet, his office untouched behind its closed door. Thank goodness Marie would help her work through all that. Marie, meanwhile, had looked like a woman who knew she was on borrowed time. If she decided to try to work things out with Kyle, she'd likely head home for the holidays.

Before the new year—and new semester. And Collins might miss having a roommate.

"Thank you," Lucy said, getting to her feet. "This has been helpful after all."

"I'm glad after all."

His smile turned more genuine, relaxed, and Lucy smiled back. "How do you know so much about OU?"

He slid open a file cabinet and pulled out a Bobcats cap, which he perched on his head with a grin.

She had imagined this correctly.

His off-duty persona was in fact hotter.

"No way," she said. "You too?"

"OU, oh yeah," he said. This was the unofficial greeting of alumni who were sick of having their spirit wear mistaken for the football-crazed Ohio State Buckeyes by out-of-staters, who would yell "O-H" at them on the street and expect an "I-O!" in response.

"Well, if I *was* here looking for a date," she said, "that would be major brownie points."

"Too bad you're not," he agreed. "If you were, I'd ask if I could buy you a drink at the pub on the corner at five."

Lucy blushed. Wasn't this always the way? The second you weren't looking for something, the second it became an actively bad idea . . .

But what was wrong with having a little fun while she figured things out?

She cocked her head at him. “Is this a pity drink because I ain’t got no money?”

He laughed. “More of a challenge,” he said. “Since you were so clear about not being interested in enjoyment.”

The temperature in the room jumped ten degrees.

“Well,” she said, as casually as she could, “maybe I’ll see you there at five anyway.”

“I hope so.” He hesitated. “As long as I’m reading this right that you’re no longer interested in applying here? Because if you are, then I shouldn’t . . .”

“I am no longer interested in applying here,” she confirmed, clocking another bonus point for professional boundaries as she turned to leave.

“If you could *look* interested on the way out, though,” he called after her, “or at least not mention that I sold you on a rival program . . .”

“Understood. I will sing the praises of—” She stopped. “Did you tell me your name?”

“Enzo. Short for Lorenzo.”

Of course it was. She waved and turned to go again.

“Actually,” he called again, “don’t sing my praises. Because then if someone sees us together later, they’ll think I’m crossing a line.”

Lucy laughed. “You had me going. I thought you were smooth. I thought I was the only one in this room who overthinks things.”

“I am smooth at my *job*,” he said, with mock defensiveness. Then, his expression turned honest. “I’ve only ever been employably good at one thing,” he admitted.

The heat in Lucy’s chest softened into a genuine warmth. She had not been wrong to come here. She had aimed high and found exactly what she needed, in a roundabout way. A referral. And a connection.

“I know the feeling,” she said.

9

Brooke

A lifetime ago, at Brooke's bridal shower, Lucy had staged a version of *The Newlywed Game* where Brooke had to sit up front in an armchair, veil on her head and mimosa in her hand, and guess the answers Mitch had given to a list of personal questions. One of them asked about his idea of a perfect Saturday night together: Out on the town or home on the couch?

Brooke loathed quizzes that forced blanket decisions. Wouldn't most people's answers depend on their mood any given day? But when she'd closed her eyes, she'd seen Mitch in their apartment's tiny kitchen, comfy in plaid flannel pants, shaking martinis at the bar counter.

"Home on the couch?" she'd guessed, and as soon as Lucy nodded that this was correct, a chorus of *aww* went around the room. In the end, Brooke had not missed a single answer, but the game's real winner was Mitch—what a catch he was, that all he needed in this world was Brooke herself. Brooke had blushed with pleasure as her friends buzzed about how blissfully content she and Mitch would be together, how they'd never be like those couples who referred to their marriage as "hard work," how lucky they were to already have everything they wanted.

"No games at my baby shower," Brooke had joked to Lucy later. "Too much pressure."

Of course, there never was a baby shower. Brooke wanted to reach back into the memory and wipe the smug expression off her own face. Could it remain true that she and Mitch were perfect for each other if they were a mismatch on the most primal, biological level?

She tried not to think about that. She reminded herself, instead, that for all they'd been through, Mitch hadn't changed. Funny how often she still thought about a silly party game—how much reassurance it had brought her over the years, even if it occasionally brought frustration too. Like on nights she wanted out of the house, and Mitch's homebody side had seemed sort of . . . well, uninspired. Maybe Mitch's answer to his idea of a perfect Saturday night did not, after all, depend on his mood. Maybe he felt no pull to connect with the people and places around them the way Brooke sometimes did.

Maybe that was why Mitch's about-face now seemed nothing short of amazing.

"Ready for this?" he asked, carrying two glasses of cabernet to join her at the desk where the virtual invite to their "Quitters Video Check In" waited on the laptop. He pulled up a chair next to hers and took a swig. He'd been drinking more lately, but she couldn't fault him for making up for lost time. Besides, she was the one who'd set up this meeting. She was the one, in fact, who'd instigated all of this: *What are we waiting for? Let's get this show on the road.*

His reaction had surpassed the best-case scenario she'd imagined. It was *good* news. Only . . . they had yet to tell anyone who didn't react with stunned silence that read a little like judgment. Brooke's doctors had been carefully neutral. But then came her parents. Mitch's family. Their respective bosses. None of it was a fair test, because the people they'd told first, by design, were directly impacted by their decision. Brooke's friends, on the other hand, only wanted her to be happy. Which she was. More excited than she'd been about anything in years.

"Is it weird that I'm nervous to tell them?" she asked Mitch now. "I mean, I shouldn't be, right? Without their encouragement, who knows if any of this would even be happening."

He shrugged. "Accountability partners can be nerve-racking," he said. "Because you know they're going to hold you accountable."

His eyes held Brooke's, and she could see him trying to form a question. Maybe *Are you having doubts?* or *Are our parents right that we're rushing this?* No, she thought. And no.

"Good," she told him, tapping the button to initiate the call. "Let's get accountable."

Brooke knew their decision might seem fast to other people. The voice in her head kept reminding her: *A month ago, my whole calendar was ruled by when, not if, my next appointment would be. Three weeks ago, my first reaction to my last failure was automatic refusal to give in. Two weeks ago, Mitch and I just cracked open the door to discuss child-free options for the first time ever.*

But to Brooke and Mitch, this was a long time coming.

Her friends popped onto the screen, waving their hellos. Lucy's video feed from her apartment looked dark—she stood to flick on a few lights and shrug off her coat, like she'd hurried home to log on. In the other square, Marie and Collins sat side by side on Collins's couch in their pajamas, each curled under a fuzzy throw.

"Hope you don't mind I invited an honorary quitter," she said, as they greeted Mitch.

"I don't want to intrude on the girl pact, but I *was* a key component of the baby-making initiative in question," he joked.

"We recall," Marie teased. "I'm scarred from the time I walked in on that in the dorm."

Lucy groaned. "You're lucky you only walked in on them once. Why was it always me?"

Mitch looked proud of himself, and Brooke laughed. It was nice to be reminded their sex life had once been ruled by lust, not ovulation. "Hey," she told Lucy, "it's not our fault you were always getting home from the lit journal at weird hours." Brooke winced at her mention of Lucy's writing days, but Lucy laughed good-naturedly. Her hair and makeup were done, and she had on a nice sweater instead of her usual loungewear, with a new lightness in her eyes. Brooke was relieved to see it. She'd been a little skeptical that Lucy should give up something she was ridiculously talented at. But maybe Lucy was right. Maybe talent had nothing to do with it. Was that affirming or depressing as hell?

"So," Marie asked, looking from Mitch to Brooke, "what's the big announcement?"

Mitch put his arm around Brooke's shoulders. Go time.

"We're quitting *everything*," Brooke announced. Mitch raised his glass to clink hers.

On-screen, Marie and Collins glanced at each other quizzically.

"What do you mean, everything?" Marie asked.

"Well, you all know we had no backup plan." Everyone nodded. Solid start. "So, once we stood back . . ." Why was she stalling? She coughed. "We don't have much tying us here. We practically traded in our social lives to see so many specialists, so all our local friends are more like acquaintances now. We haven't put work into the house or upgraded our cars—we've been on pause. And we've stayed put for so long, travel is at the top of our bucket list, but we've used all our vacation time for health care. Financially and logistically, this has been rough. We wouldn't be able to splurge on anything for a long while without making big changes."

"You mean downsizing?" Lucy asked.

"Majorly. Once we started weighing options, we realized liquidating our assets would eliminate a lot of stress. In fact, if we sold it all, we'd be flush for a while."

"You're selling your house?" Collins asked.

Brooke felt Mitch nodding along with her.

"Makes sense. Are you going to rent? An apartment in Denver or something?"

Brooke shook her head. "We're also selling the cars, furniture, and anything else that won't fit in a ten-by-twenty-five-foot storage unit. And—" She took a deep breath. "We're leaving our jobs. I've already given notice, and Mitch is fast-tracking a request to take a sabbatical."

Lucy looked suddenly hopeful. "Are you moving back to the Midwest?" Brooke shook her head, and Lucy shot her an *aw shucks* look. "Can't blame a girl for trying. Where, then?"

Brooke shrugged. "Nowhere. Everywhere. Europe? Asia? We're going to travel for as long as we can make it work, or as long as we want, and then . . . I guess we'll see."

"Whoa," Collins said. "Wait, you *already* gave notice? Have you listed the house yet?"

"It's a hot seller's market here. Our Realtor thinks we can bank on getting an offer. And we thought it was only fair to give a lot of notice. Friday before Christmas will be our last day."

Mitch finally chimed in. "Technically, I might have quitting-related options," he said. "Brooke's been burnt out at work for a while, so a clean break will be good for her. But my employer has job openings all over the globe. I've been quietly turning down opportunities for years. Which is why I think they'll approve my sabbatical while I reevaluate."

Marie raised an eyebrow. "Brooke never told us that."

"She didn't know," Mitch said, covering Brooke's hand with his. It was warm, weighty. "I didn't want to put that on her when our IVF cycles took priority. I worried she'd worry about me turning offers down when I was happy to put our treatments first. That's what's so wild—she suggested this leap of faith without knowing I might have leads that could make this realistic long term. There's no guarantee, but I've been working on systems integrations that have value to our overseas markets. Once I have an idea of where I'd like to be reassigned, it's not a long shot either."

Brooke smiled at her husband. She wasn't upset at Mitch for holding out on her. He was right—it *would* have wrecked her when she was trying so hard to keep her stress in check. And she also believed him that he hadn't been tempted by the offers. The bigger surprise, honestly, was that shifting their lifestyle on an international scale would appeal to a man so content staying home. Brooke was the one who'd spent countless hours on the Peloton watching Rick Steves travelogues. But this crossroads in their lives had uncaged something in Mitch. One minute, a night out had been a hard sell; the next, he was agreeing to relinquish their entire home base. She kept watching for signs that he was going along just to please her, but he seemed *almost* more excited than she was.

She clapped her hands. "So, we have until Christmas to plan the first leg of our trip."

"We're looking seriously at Italy," Mitch added. "Overtourism is such a problem in the hot spots there, we're thinking it would pay to go in winter when crowds are low. But where we're going isn't the point. The point is just to go. And keep going."

Brooke smiled. "Surprise!" she said, raising her glass again.

"Wow," Lucy said.

"Wow," Collins and Marie echoed.

"Wow," Mitch agreed, and they all laughed. Relief began to creep in.

"Let us grab drinks to toast with you," Collins said. She disappeared off-screen, and then Lucy did, too, leaving Marie looking alone and awkward.

"Is this something you've always wanted to do?" Marie asked. "I had no idea."

"Well . . ." Brooke hesitated as Collins returned to her seat holding a bottle of white wine, and Lucy a can of beer. How to explain? For years they'd been asking their doctors, the universe, and themselves: *What's next? What now?* And for years the only response was: *Wait and see.*

A couple could only spend so many nights with their backs turned, feigning sleep, each trying not to let the other see them cry, before their minds wandered to possibilities they'd rather not consider. But it would betray a confidence to discuss that with Mitch sitting right beside her.

She decided to draw on the universal language her friends would always speak: Movies they could quote by heart. "You remember in *While You Were Sleeping* when Peter wakes up from the coma, and they tell him he has amnesia?"

Lucy brightened. "When the nurse offers him JELL-O, and he says, 'Do I like JELL-O?'" She mimicked the bewildered look Peter Gallagher gave his family, and everyone but Mitch supplied his mom's one-word response in unison: *Yum!* Mitch shook his head like they were incorrigible.

"That's kind of it," Brooke said. "Like I'm waking up from a long, single-minded blackout. I mean, *do* I want to travel? Who doesn't?"

"I know it's a lot," Mitch told them. "I thought it was crazy at first too. When Brooke first suggested it, I even wondered if this might be a form of self-sabotage, like if we couldn't be parents, we didn't deserve the things we'd worked for with that goal in mind."

Brooke looked at him in surprise. He'd never told her that.

"Then I realized," he went on, "this is the opposite of self-sabotage. It's a lifeline. Neither of us wants to be that nice quiet couple that people talk about like, *Gosh, they would've been good parents, wonder what happened.* We've had our lives on hold and don't want to waste more time. We don't want to look at the choices we've made like they're second best. So, we're going all in on the kind of plan B people dream about, not the kind people settle for."

Lucy looked at Mitch like she couldn't have written him better if he was the love interest in a novel. "That doesn't sound crazy at all," she admitted. "It sounds brave. And bold."

Collins nodded. "I hope we didn't sound unsupportive with so many questions. We were just caught off guard. Lucy's right: Good for you two." She sounded sincere, though she looked like she was trying to channel some of that bravery and boldness Lucy had mentioned.

"You guys are absolutely sure?" Marie asked. "I understand everything you're saying, but if you wanted to test the waters, make sure things shake out the way you're hoping . . ." Collins must have elbowed her, because Marie clutched her arm and gave her a wounded look.

"I get why you'd ask," Brooke said. She wasn't oblivious to the risks. A nomadic lifestyle could suit one of them and not the other; they could reach a place where one wanted to stay and one wanted to go; they could deplete their savings too fast or have a medical emergency or any number of other unknowns. Starting over at forty would require a lot of trust in both fate and each other.

And faith that if things went south, Mitch wouldn't hold this against her. He was on board, sure, but they both knew whose idea it had been.

"Our parents looked at us like we were joining a cult or getting full-body tattoos," Brooke admitted. "Testing the waters isn't a bad compromise, but it would drag things out. We're going to embrace the spirit of adventure."

"Well, cheers to the spirit of adventure," Lucy said, raising her glass.

"Any chance we'll see you before you go?" Collins asked. "Let us throw you a goodbye party in Athens. A Christmas party, maybe?"

Brooke and Mitch exchanged a look. "Probably not," Brooke said. "Unless we have a layover in Chicago?"

Lucy took a long sip of her beer before she answered. "I'm not sure I'll be in Chicago."

"You're kidding." Brooke seized on the chance to change the subject. "Okay, your turn. Are we going to talk about your manifesto?"

Marie waved a paper in the air, and Brooke saw that she'd marked up Lucy's essay with enthusiastic circles and exclamation points. "Yes, please," she said. But Lucy shook her head.

"Can we talk about my going back to school instead?" Now it was Lucy who looked nervous. "If I could beg a few favors . . . in Athens? Starting next semester?"

Marie and Collins let out such a deafening squeal that Brooke and Mitch jumped.

"Back to school to do what?" Collins asked, clapping her hands excitedly.

"To get my MBA," Lucy said cheerfully.

Collins stopped mid-clap and they all stared at Lucy, disbelieving. *Lucy*, who once got so distracted by a fictional character that her dinner in the oven caught fire. Lucy, who took the long way around even if she was running late. Lucy, who had once written Brooke an acrostic poem for her birthday that read:

Beautiful
Resistance
Of
Outrage,
Kismet
Exemplified.

Lucy, who no one could picture doing something as buttoned up as business school.

Mitch was the first to recover. "Hey, that's great, Luce. What will you do with an MBA?"

She shrugged. "Get a real job, I hope."

"Have you met with an enrollment counselor about this?" Marie engaged faculty mode.

Lucy beamed. "Does it count if I just had my second date with one?"

Mitch raised his glass again. "My cue to exit the chat. Lucy, congrats. Quitters unite?"

They orchestrated one more toast across the miles, mismatched wineglasses and beer cans in the air, and Mitch gave Brooke's shoulder a knowing squeeze as he slipped out. Fading fertility hormones still coursed through her system, and she couldn't *not* get emotional thinking of her friends gathered without her back where they'd met, digging into their reserves of strength and solidarity while she ventured into the unknown with Mitch.

But I don't want to be looking back, she reminded herself. *Forward, from now on.*

Lucy launched into the play-by-play of her meet-cute with Enzo, and they all leaned closer to their screens, eager for the details.

It had to be a good sign that things were coming together so serendipitously, didn't it? After years of Collins looking like every overture took effort, like she couldn't wait to crawl back home and get back to hiding from the world, now she appeared visibly relieved not to be alone anymore. Brooke was amazed at how little it had taken for the rest of them to turn their lives upside down, yet here they all were, smiling bigger, dreaming deeper. Ready to take the next big step, hand in hand, knowing they'd all made mistakes.

Hoping none of them was about to make another one.

10

MARIE

As Thanksgiving approached, Marie was most grateful for the things she did not miss.

A month into her stay at Collins's, she did not miss her own bed. She did not miss the nights she'd spent staring at the ceiling while Kyle started snoring the second his head hit the pillow. Nor did she miss stiffening at his touch, wondering how her body had become the one thing about her that wasn't content to go along to get along. She used to hate being without Kyle for even a night—she'd slept worse without him. Now, she breathed easier without the tension.

She also didn't miss devoting all her energy to regulating the emotions of everyone around her. The boys seemed more self-sufficient here. When they wanted a snack, they made it themselves; when screen time was up, they found something else to do without complaint. They followed the rules to keep their soccer net alongside the garage, where Collins assured her that Connor could safely take shots on Wade in goal without fear of damaging anything in the sculpture garden—even if the ball did bounce over the wall. Running out the door for school or soccer practice wasn't the hectic affair it used to be, because the gift of time wasn't the only perk of the shorter commute: They no longer needed provisions, because they were close enough to backtrack if anything came up: rain, hunger, a headache, blisters from a new pair of shoes. Fall really was the best time of year in Athens, the tree-lined pathways bursting with color among so many stately red brick buildings, and for once, they were free to linger and take it in.

Marie didn't miss the tension either. She could tell she wasn't the only one. All this time, the kids had been the main reason she couldn't fathom separating from Kyle. Her marital discontent stemmed from her growing aversion to living such a split-screen life, after all. Or, more specifically, from the fact that Kyle didn't seem to care that she didn't like it, behaving as if it was something she had to get over. Either way, her thought process, before coming to Collins's house, had gone like this: *Divorce would only widen the gap she already detested. She didn't want to see her kids less than 100 percent of the time. She wasn't unhappy enough to put everyone through all that. She was just burnt out, tired of not feeling heard or especially loved. Maybe it would pass. Maybe they'd rediscover each other after the kids went off to college. And if they didn't, well, they could get divorced then.*

Yet now, on this subtle pseudo–test run, she couldn't deny *everyone* was happier. Even Kyle was taking it in stride, though that probably had to do with him not realizing the depth of their separation. The boys had spent the weekends with him while she helped Collins pack up Sullivan's closet, home office, and garage. She did miss the boys then—of course she did—but the trade-off came in seeing for herself that Collins couldn't have done this alone. She could barely get through it with Marie. The house seemed full of emotional land mines. Like the one that blew up their Sunday afternoon when Marie found a letter from Sullivan's landlord, Evie, who'd owned the barn outside of town that had housed his studio. Marie had met her once, at Sullivan's open house unveiling his studio renovation, showing off all those north-facing picture windows that allowed his work to cast beautiful hues across the old, reclaimed space. Evie lived on the property, where she operated boarding stables, and had struck Marie as a woman more comfortable around horses than people. She didn't sound any warmer in her letter to Collins.

> Mrs. Hartley: I have left you countless unanswered voice and text messages regarding the items recovered from the site of the fire. I don't feel right about discarding them, but I don't have the space to store these things forever. Please contact me to arrange a pickup time. I have been as understanding as possible, but a two-year delay is inexcusable bordering on negligent.

When Marie offered to go get the boxes together, suggesting they use her van, Collins became inconsolable, tearing up the letter, crying that nothing that mattered could be "recovered"—nothing. It transported Marie back to the story whispered on campus, how Collins had run wailing onto the scene that awful day, among firefighters and medics, all too late to do anything but extinguish the out-of-control blaze where Sullivan and his studio had been moments before. The old wood and flammable welding and staining materials had proved a fatal combination. Only now did Marie understand, through her friend's gasping words, that Collins had never been back, not even to see the flower-strewn memorial his students erected there.

"And I never will," Collins said, eyes steely. "Much less bring one speck of ash from that day into this house."

Marie was too chagrined to do anything but drop it. What a terrible friend she was, to fail to realize Collins was avoiding this looming thing. Nobody had ever cast blame for the fire. The consensus seemed to be that if anyone had been careless, it was Sullivan himself, but that was no consolation to Collins. She'd mentioned it to Marie only once, after the funeral: "I should've stayed on him about safety."

Marie had hugged her tight. "I heard the fire chief tell you everything was up to code."

"He also called it 'an accident waiting to happen,'" Collins had pointed out.

Marie still didn't know what she should have said to that. She wondered if the saddest kind of tragedy was one that felt preventable. Like somebody should have known better. Even if that somebody wasn't anyone in particular.

"Why don't we take a break?" Marie suggested. "Go for a walk. Or to the movies?"

"I just want to get this done," Collins said miserably, adding, "please." So, they finished boxing donations and sent a "last call" to Sullivan's daughters to make sure they didn't want anything set aside. But Collins did it all with silent tears streaming down her face. When Kyle brought the boys back that evening, he clocked her swollen eyes and asked no further questions.

Marie had to talk to him. She couldn't avoid it anymore.

But not about Collins.

Marie had thought maybe he'd notice how well she and the kids had settled here, even in the shadow of Collins's grief. Maybe he'd draw his own conclusions about why. Maybe he'd come to her first, say they clearly should reevaluate how they'd been living, what was best for their family. Because even though Marie was grateful they were doing so well, she was sad too.

Because of what it might mean.

Kyle was coming to Collins's house for Thanksgiving. Collins didn't have much family—she was an only child whose parents hadn't made it to sixty-five—and they'd agreed having the meal here might make her feel like less of a fifth wheel. Marie planned to get through dinner and then pull Kyle aside and tell him they needed to make time to talk. At home. Alone.

Surely by then he'd have realized. Joining his family for a holiday in someone else's house, he'd glimpse what they were on their way to becoming if somebody did not *do something*.

School was out on the Wednesday before the holiday, and Marie had just pulled into Collins's driveway toting an obnoxiously American quantity of groceries when Collins's neighbor stepped outside and waved.

She'd noticed him before, looking like Athens' own Clark Kent. From the neck up, he was all coifed hair and bookish glasses, but his button-down shirts did little to hide his muscular frame. She'd seen no evidence of a wife, but two teenagers occasionally appeared.

"You have a hot neighbor," she'd observed to Collins once, after seeing them exchange a wave through the window. But Collins had turned it around on Marie, asking if she was already checking out other men, if she and Kyle were that far gone. Marie had changed the subject quick.

"Hi there," he called now, heading over. "I've been meaning to introduce myself. I'm Travis. Are you Collins's sister?"

"No," she said. "An old friend. Marie." She held out a hand, and he shook it.

"Ah, okay. I thought I heard your boys calling her Aunt Collins."

"Honorary title," she clarified.

"Sweet. It's been nice seeing so much life over here. I worry about her sometimes. I'm always telling her to let me know if she needs anything, but she never does anymore."

Marie clocked the *anymore*, looking at him more closely: sheepish smile, flushed cheeks, casual questions. Did Collins's boy next door have a crush on her? Maybe *that* was why Collins had shut her down when she'd asked about him. "How long have you lived here?" Marie asked.

His eyes softened, and he seemed to understand that she was really asking whether he'd known Sullivan. "Bought the place six years ago after my divorce, when my kids still cared about having a yard to run in. Sull was a good neighbor—sometimes he'd join me for a beer on my porch, argue about all the so-called improvements to campus. You know how he loved a good debate." His eyes flicked past Marie, to Collins's house. "He loved her most of all, though."

"He did," Marie agreed, watching his face turn wistful.

Oh boy. Collins *had* been holding out on her. All along, this eligible bachelor had been patiently waiting for her to work through her heartbreak? The made-for-TV movie wrote itself.

"How old are your kids?" Marie asked. "I hope mine haven't been too loud."

"I like the energy. Mine are a freshman and a sophomore at Athens High. They're supposed to be here more, but their mom teaches in their building, so we keep the arrangement fluid. I'd rather lose a little time than cause her or them any undue stress. Did enough of that while we were married." He smiled sadly.

Marie's brain lit like a motion-activated light. *Divorce is hard. On everyone.* But also: *How self-aware he sounds. How considerate of his wife's load.*

She hoped that kind of enlightenment didn't always come too late.

"Do you teach too?" she asked. "I haven't seen you on campus."

"I own a custom printing company uptown. Do most of it on-site, myself."

He ran a hand through his hair, and she eyed his biceps again. Maybe printing involved heavier lifting than she'd realized. "Near the courthouse?" she asked.

"That's the one." He nodded at her lanyard. "What department do you teach in?"

"Gender Studies."

"Right. Um. When I said I worried about Collins here alone, did that sound . . ."

Marie laughed. "Hazard of the job: Everyone's always explaining they're not sexist, when I never thought you were. I've worried about her too. That's partly why I'm here."

He nodded. "Well, I'm glad. And I'm still available to help—not that I think you need a man. But good to have a friendly hand next door."

She had an impulse to ask if he had anywhere to go for Thanksgiving but stopped herself. Not her place. "Maybe all three of us can have one of those porch beers together soon," she said instead.

"I'd like that."

Inside, she found Collins rolling out pie crust, an open bottle of champagne on the table. "Help yourself to a mimosa," Collins said, by way of greeting.

"Twist my arm." Marie set the last of the groceries on the table. "Met your neighbor."

"Which one?"

"The eligible one who seems sweet on you."

Collins's face flushed, but she didn't look up.

"Uh-oh," Marie said. "No chemistry?"

Collins worked the dough for a long minute before finding the words. "Travis is great. It's just . . . I can't see myself with anyone who was a part of my memories with Sull. It's too hard not to wonder what he'd think."

Marie got herself a champagne glass and topped Collins's off, not bothering with the juice. "I get that," she said. "It just inconveniently rules out most of the Athens population."

"I know," Collins said with a small smile. "That's why I signed up for a singles' retreat."

Marie's eyes went wide. "That's great. Where? When?"

"Last night. In bed. I couldn't sleep, and I saw the ad, and . . . impulse buy."

"I mean where and when are the *retreat*, Coll?"

Collins giggled and smacked her forehead, leaving a very un-Collins-like flour smear on her temple. "A ski resort in West Virginia. After Christmas. Before New Year's." She pulled a face as she pressed the dough into the pie plate. "Tell me I haven't made a mistake."

"Of course you haven't." Marie began stacking cans in the pantry. "I mean, you don't ski. And you hate winter. But otherwise, great idea.

Why find someone to love here when you could find someone out of town?" They both laughed.

"I know, I know. But you and Brooke and Lucy have been so inspiring, busting out of your comfort zones. This is my first try, and this way, if I mess up, it won't follow me home. Besides, I do hate the cold, but I like hot tubs. And cocoa. And if I'm not feeling the men, there's a spa. That time around the holidays can be lonely. It'll be good for me to get out of here."

Collins was right, of course. Marie had been trying not to think about Christmas. Christmas was family. Christmas was tradition. Christmas was the kids padding down to the tree in their festive pajamas and songs about being home for the holidays. Which there would be no excuse not to be. There was no school in session for her or the boys, no sports schedules to juggle, and now, no Collins to look after.

"I think it's a brilliant idea," she told Collins. "Even with the skiing. Good for you."

She tipped back her champagne, trying to flush the unease rising in her gut. If all went well with Lucy's application, which Marie had called in favors to expedite, by New Year's, Lucy would be on her way here to start school. Logically, she'd take over for Marie in Collins's house—perfect timing, where Lucy and Collins were concerned: Neither would have to face their next chapters alone. Marie already felt a little envious thinking of it.

But Marie wasn't some roommate being ousted from the sorority house. She was a grown woman, for goodness' sake, with a life that was tied inextricably to Kyle and the boys.

She couldn't put off her talk with Kyle anymore. Because she couldn't imagine spending Christmas anywhere but at home with the kids. But when she thought about going back to the aura of resignation surrounding her marriage, and another new year of the same old routine . . .

Well. Sometimes no *was* a complete sentence.

Marie had to stop using Collins as a crutch.

This year, Christmas might be a turning point—a sign that this break was something more. Marie couldn't keep pretending it wasn't.

No matter how much part of her wanted to.

~

Marie was on her first bite of buttery turkey and mashed potatoes when Kyle told the boys he had a surprise for their mom.

"Auntie Collins has agreed to keep you two here tomorrow night while we go on a special date, just the two of us, since your mom and I haven't seen enough of each other lately."

Special date? Just the two of them?

"What kind of special date?" Connor asked.

Kyle had that casual look of someone trying not to make a big deal about something that he hoped was, in fact, a very big deal. "We're staying downtown, in Columbus. My company owns a suite that no client is using over the holiday, so I got permission. We have dinner reservations and tickets for a stand-up comedy show. But *you* get to have a movie night here."

Wade turned to Collins. "With ice-cream sundaes?" he asked.

"Brownie ice-cream sundaes," she promised.

Marie couldn't help feeling suspicious. This had come out of nowhere. Whenever Kyle called, he barely asked about her. Only the boys. "You knew about this?" she asked Collins.

Collins met her eye with a look that said *Don't blame me*. But also, maybe, *Give this a chance*. "All his idea," Collins deflected. "I only agreed to watch the kids. Which I'm always happy to do, by the way. When's the last time you two went on any kind of real date?"

Marie honestly couldn't remember. Did her faculty awards banquet last spring count? Or his corporate Christmas party? "Real" dates were a thing of the past. She might float the idea of trying a new restaurant, and he'd point out how much less expensive it was to eat at home or how long his day had already been, and that was that. If they took the kids to try a new mini golf place, it was at Marie's suggestion; if they went on vacation, she did the planning.

From the time the boys were born, she'd read the articles warning against not making time for their marriage. But the alternative meant nagging him to do things he was disinclined to do.

"What do you say?" Kyle asked her now. "We don't have to hurry back in the morning. We could do brunch. See the Christmas displays, whatever you want."

He looked pleased with himself, but tired. Like it wasn't lost on him, after all, that he'd had to book a suite out of town to spend more than a few harried minutes with his wife. But was going along even a good idea, when she'd been gearing up for a very different kind of talk?

She waited to start feeling defensive. But her usual knee-jerk response didn't come. In fact, she was almost . . . Was she flattered? Was she on her way to being . . . excited?

There was only one way to find out.

11

Lucy

Lucy's agent, Delia, was on the phone. The first she'd heard from her since Lucy had called to explain her "career shift away from writing." Delia hadn't taken the news with the relief Lucy had imagined—*I'm off the hook!* But she'd taken it gracefully. *I understand. Take some time away.*

Until now.

"I'd love for you to take this essay down." She wasn't one to dance around the point.

"What essay?" Lucy asked, feigning innocence.

"Let's see. The one titled 'Why I Love Books Too Much to Keep Writing Them.' The one you failed to mention to me?"

"Oh, right. Why?"

"Have you ever heard that advice that if you have to think hard about whether you should say something, that means you shouldn't?"

Lucy laughed. "Not bad advice, but I'm not sure it applies to writers. Can you imagine if Gloria Steinem followed that advice?"

"With all due respect, we're not talking about Gloria Steinem. We're talking about a rare talent on my midlist."

"*Formerly* on your midlist."

"Well, you never know if you might decide to publish again. Unless you leave this essay up. In which case the choice might never be yours."

"Delia, I appreciate the sentiment. But with due respect to *you*, that essay has been up for over a month, and you're just now calling about it. Even my own agent doesn't read my website. And that's no dig on you. You're the best."

"Then do me the professional courtesy of taking this down. Do you know I had two other clients call me, vowing to quit writing after reading this?"

Lucy had not known. She sat up straighter.

"Look," she said, "I couldn't remove it if I wanted to. I don't have access."

"To your own website? Explain how that's possible."

Lucy did. Delia insisted she call Collins and get the passwords. Lucy refused.

"Lucy, do you know what image comes up on my phone when you call me?"

"That diorama I built to illustrate publishing? With the sharks circling the leaking boat?"

"A memorable craft, but no. A screenshot of that *Tribune* review I told you to put on your tombstone."

Gutsy, beautiful, and smart as hell, the review had said. But Lucy was done hanging on to sparse compliments for dear life. "Goes to show," Lucy said, "we've been discussing the death of my career longer than we want to admit."

One good-natured call from her agent wasn't going to change her mind about quitting. Just like a couple of excellent dates with a guy she'd just met weren't going to change her mind about moving.

But they both did make her feel a little better.

If also a little worse at the same time.

~

"What was your last serious relationship?" Enzo wanted to know. He'd taken her to a historic lounge called the Game Room, full of polished billiards tables and antique chessboards that made her feel like she'd stepped inside a Clue gameboard, minus the murder. She'd already beat him handily at table shuffleboard, and now they'd settled into some leather high-back chairs to sample the cocktail menu.

"I'm unsure any of them have been all that serious, to tell the truth," Lucy admitted. "You're meeting the version of me who is between jobs. Normally, I'm . . ."

She grappled for the right word.

"A workaholic?" he guessed. But he sounded skeptical, like he couldn't picture it.

"People don't see you that way when an office isn't involved," she said. "But writing was my focus in a way that half my brain was always thinking about it. It's been nice letting that part of it go—to be honest, I found it kind of annoying too." She gave a little laugh. "Nothing like having a deadline a year away and knowing it will nag at you *every day* of that year."

Enzo considered her. "I don't know," he said. "I think it's kind of amazing. I mean, that's the reason so many people say they're going to write a book and then never do, right? Not everyone can manage that kind of long-term discipline."

Lucy was oddly touched. And surprised. Most people glossed over that stuff. "Well, thanks," she said. "The flip side is, I've never minded being alone the way some people do. Not that I haven't been open to meeting someone, but that person will always need to be okay with the fact that I like having headspace. Most of my relationships have petered out around a year, on good terms. They just didn't stick." She shrugged. "How about you?"

"Similar cutoff," he said. "It's like my girlfriends are set to a timer that expires at eighteen months. No more, no less. But I'm not self-aware enough to have figured out why yet."

"So that's why you're still hanging out with me," she teased. "To break the trend."

"Absolutely. As soon as I found out you didn't have eighteen months left in this town, I knew this would be the way to kick the curse."

Lucy laughed. "What does it say about me that I'm good with that?"

He lifted an eyebrow seductively and flashed his most dashing smile. "I think the real question," he said, "is what does it say about *me* that you're good with that?"

"It says you're bad at shuffleboard," she deadpanned. "And I like to win."

He was right, though—the fact that they were still spending time together said a lot about him. Enzo was so much fun that it kept Lucy from overthinking the choices she'd made. Why sit around and obsess when somebody you really liked could keep you gloriously busy?

She wasn't going to read too much into it. And thanks in no small part to him, the weeks that might have otherwise crawled by in agony flew.

Collins was the first person Lucy called when she got her acceptance letter. She was trying not to always call Brooke. Brooke had her hands full with her plans to become drastically unreachable.

"I am officially enrolled in Ohio University's intensive MBA program," Lucy said.

Collins squealed. "I am officially impressed. And relieved. I'd feel lonely having this whole house to myself again. Even if it is a little crowded now."

Lucy was relieved at how genuine her friend sounded. It was hard not to feel like a freeloader when you invited yourself to move in with someone who knew you couldn't afford rent. Lucy planned to make herself useful by housesitting while Collins went on her singles' retreat, but after that . . . she didn't have much to contribute. Except her humbly indebted presence. "How's it going?" she ventured. "With Marie and the kids staying there?"

"There's been an interesting development. Marie is dating Kyle."

"She's dating her husband?"

"Yep."

"Wow. How's that going?"

"I think it's confused her. She says it's the best sex they've had in years."

"Sounds like a good problem to have."

"Tell me about it." Collins paused. "I don't want to make light of it. Kyle has been sleeping through what's going on in his own house for a long time. I'm not sure if this has been the wake-up call he needed or if he's just lonely. For the past couple of weeks, every time she's ready to confront him, he preempts her with some romantic gesture. Yesterday it was flowers. I can't decide if he's incredibly clever or incredibly dense."

Lucy thought about it. "Marie is always saying two opposing things can be true at once."

"True." Another pause. "Did you ever think Sullivan wasn't right for me?"

"Never."

"Outside of our relationship, I mean. Did you ever think that him taking me on as his manager and his assistant and his . . . everything on top of being his wife was too much?"

"No." Lucy paused. "I do remember thinking it would have been too much for other people. But for you two, it made sense."

"I always thought so too."

It was the past tense that made Lucy take notice. Collins usually made a point not to speak of Sullivan that way.

"What's this about, Coll? Why do you ask?"

"No reason." Collins sounded tired. "Everyone else has gotten so introspective about all this quitting stuff. I guess it's inevitable to rub off on me."

"Did somebody say something that got under your skin? Don't tell me his kids are still being awful to you."

"Mostly just Sara. She seems to be the spokeswoman."

"Spokeswoman for *what*?" In a backward way, Lucy had admired Sullivan's candor in taking responsibility for the state of things with his daughters, half sisters from two ex-girlfriends who Sullivan admitted "deserved better than I was at the time." He'd been absent for much of the girls' childhoods, evolving into someone they came to only for money. *The price I rightly pay,* he'd admitted, *for being obsessively single-minded about my art for too long.*

It was Collins who'd changed that, though some of it was probably timing. Sullivan had finally discovered the sweet spot between his starving-artist years and the level of fame that would come only after his death. He'd begrudgingly agreed to start teaching and discovered it genuinely fulfilled him while keeping his ego in check. For a brief window of time, he'd found balance, peace, and love. After the lifelong bachelor had settled down with Collins, she'd encouraged him to make more effort with his adult children, but Sara and Lea hadn't been receptive. They both had full lives in Michigan, Sara in Saugatuck and Lea in Ann Arbor. Sara hadn't even invited him and Collins to her wedding. But now that he was gone, she wasn't above staking her claim to her late father's legacy.

Sullivan had not been cruel; he hadn't snubbed them in his will. He'd left them the only thing they'd ever asked him for: money, in lump sum. But in assuming they'd take it and let Collins be, he'd miscalculated. Everyone wanted a piece of his estate now; even unfinished work sold for top dollar. It was hard enough for Collins to weigh what he would have wanted. The last thing she needed was his ungrateful daughters fighting her every step of the way.

"I hear from Sara less since Marie moved in," Collins said, dodging the question. "She's a wonderful shield. Her reputation precedes her."

"With everyone but Kyle," Lucy observed.

"True." Collins sighed. "You know, if Sara wanted more art to remember Sull by, I'd gladly hand it over. I wish that was it. Her tactic of threatening to contest the will is a stressful nuisance. And it's not like my own lawyer has been much help. After Sull died, he basically just told me to keep doing what I was doing and forward him copies of anything relevant, for posterity. Which I do. But you'd be surprised how busy the estate still keeps me. Most exhibits are temporary, sales lead to resales, and donation requests are endless. Maybe that's some comfort, when it comes to your books? Legacies really do live on."

"Especially when you take over one at thirty-eight," Lucy sympathized. She wasn't about to let Collins change the subject back to her so easily. "Has it eased enough that you might take a side job? Just to have something new to channel energy into?"

"I don't know . . ." Collins sniffed. "You and Brooke and Marie were always so sure what you were going to be," she said. "I was the one changing majors, bouncing around jobs and boyfriends. Until I met Sull. Becoming every kind of partner to him—personally, professionally, artistically—it gave me purpose. I didn't care that I'd put all my eggs in one basket because that basket was forever. Losing him is the ultimate identity crisis. If I'm not his wife and assistant and manager, what even am I? Besides his widow?"

Lucy considered the question. In truth, Collins was still most of those things, but obviously it wasn't the same now. She had to admit, maybe the reason going back to Athens felt so right had more to do with their friendship than with the MBA. But what was wrong with that?

"What about going back to school?" she suggested. "We could go together."

"Campus would be too—I can't. I wish I still viewed it the way you all do."

Lucy recalled a similar tone from Collins on the last day of their trip, when she'd clammed up about not belonging in the pact.

"Hey," she said. "We'll figure it out. Together. I'll be there soon, right? Can't wait."

"Yeah. Me too."

But Lucy hung up with a nagging worry that maybe Collins was right. Maybe she wasn't going to be able to tap the same momentum fueling the rest of them.

Maybe they could only do so much for her until she was ready to help herself.

12

Brooke

Brooke spread the picnic blanket on the carpet of their newly empty living room, among the indentations where their sectional and dining set had been up until this morning, while Mitch carried in the takeaway from their favorite burrito stand.

A prerequisite for leaving the Southwest: gorging on local favorites while you still could. And a casualty of posting your furniture for sale the day after your open house drew multiple offers above asking price: Everything might sell immediately. They were regressing to floor level in stages. Sitting on the floor, eating on the floor. After the next scheduled pickup, they'd be sleeping on the floor, but who could complain? Things were going better than they'd dared hope.

"So, we're set on Venice," Mitch said, as he sat cross-legged across from her and popped the tops off two Coronas. "Let's not second-guess it anymore. It makes total sense to start with the places that are too impractical for us to stay longer term if we go full expat."

"Agreed," she said, arranging the chips and salsa between their foil-wrapped mounds of smothered burritos as the homey smell of green chili warmed her sinuses. She was trying not to do that thing where she missed something before it was gone. Coloradans incorporated green chili into everything from burgers to pizza, for a habit-forming flavor she had yet to find replicated elsewhere. But the Roma tomatoes and garlic on deck in Italy weren't a bad trade. "Want me to book a week in that flat we were looking at, near the San Silvestro vaporetto stop?" she asked, squeezing limes into the long necks of their beer bottles.

They'd been fantasizing about making their way down the Italian coast once they had their fill of Venice, hitting tucked-away towns with narrow stone streets unchanged for centuries. She looked forward to this initial phase of sightseeing with no strings attached, even with Mitch already thinking ahead to exploring places with longer-term potential.

He popped a tortilla chip into his mouth, grinning broadly. "Took care of it on my lunch break. My reward for finishing the first tier on Duolingo."

Brooke hid her surprise behind a long, cold drink of her beer. The novelty had yet to wear off of enjoying whatever she wanted whenever she wanted—one of many ways she now moved through the day without guilt. Like no longer worrying she'd talked Mitch into something he didn't genuinely want. His enthusiasm really had surpassed hers.

"Keep this up and I won't know what to do with myself," she teased. "Obsessing over details has always been my thing."

"It's still your thing. If you hadn't planned the girls' trip, there wouldn't have been one, the quitters club would not exist, and who knows where any of us would be. Some journeys are too much to plan alone, though."

Brooke knew this was true—truer even than he probably realized. A wave of nostalgia washed over her. "Remember how romantic it seemed to eat on the floor when we bought this place?" she asked. Looking around the room, she couldn't help but think as much as this scene looked the same as it had ten years ago, it couldn't feel more different. Less full circle and more like coming out on the other side of something, permanently changed by everything that had happened in between.

"I remember how romantic it was to do other things on the floor." He waggled his eyebrows, and she laughed. But Brooke felt a pang. She hadn't anticipated how hard it would be to say goodbye to their things.

She knew they were just material possessions, and they didn't suit her purposes anymore. But she'd bought them all with such specific hopes in mind that getting rid of them felt like cutting a remnant of her dream loose all over again. Mitch seemed to have made peace with the whole decision at once, whereas Brooke had to keep reminding herself this was the right choice.

This morning, when she got an email confirming their dining set sold, she'd felt a pain in her side so intense that she'd actually looked up the symptoms of appendicitis. Of course, it had passed just as all the other pains had. It took a minute, that was all. She told herself Mitch's evidently pain-free state balanced them out. For all she knew, it would all hit him when they boarded their first international flight, whereas she'd have dealt with her feelings by then and be breathing a big sigh of relief.

"Speaking of," Mitch said, tearing into his dinner, "hope I didn't keep you up last night. I got sucked into the forum about our Frankfurt office expanding. Maybe we put Germany on the list, after Italy? And it turns out one of my favorite former colleagues has been transferred to London. I should drop her a line, too, reconnect. It's unbelievable how well everything is falling into place. Christmas with our families, New Year's in Piazza San Marco. It's like you saw the whole path forward before I even realized I'd been ignoring road signs all along."

He beamed at Brooke so brightly she could do nothing but beam back. So why did she feel this glimmer of unease? She didn't doubt that he'd rather be prepping their house for a baby. She didn't want to admit that maybe their parents had been right about them moving too fast either. Brooke's fundamentals hadn't changed; all she'd done was adjust them. Two people could be a family. A home could be portable.

Maybe the unease had nothing to do with Mitch.

"Should we rethink swinging by Ohio to see the girls?" Brooke asked. "I mean, I thought we might only be gone six months or so, but if there's a chance of months turning into years . . ." She felt especially guilty about Lucy, who kept wistfully asking, *You're really not worried about getting a job, huh?* It wasn't that Brooke was overconfident; simply that she didn't much care where her paycheck came from. She'd spent the last ten years managing such a specific inventory database that she couldn't muster concern that the skills wouldn't translate. Of course they wouldn't. And good riddance.

Mitch was looking at her thoughtfully. "Everyone's holidays sound pretty busy," he said gently. "Lucy has the move, Collins has the retreat . . . Are you asking for them, or for you?"

Brooke shook her head. "Forget it. You're right. It's just a last-minute nagging feeling, you know? Like we're going to forget something important. Like letting our passports expire."

She ducked her head, feeling silly, but Mitch caught her chin in his hand. Then, he kissed her with the kind of tenderness that said dinner could wait. The whole world could wait.

It was waiting, in fact—and had been all along.

"After years of everything going sideways," he said softly, "maybe all this good stuff is going to take some getting used to. But I'm not going to let us forget anything. Or anyone. I promise," he said, sliding his fingers under her waistline, "to be very thorough."

"I might need a little help," she said, tugging him closer. "Getting used to this."

He pulled her onto his lap. "I think repetition is key," he said, his mouth inches from hers. "One good thing after another. As often as it takes."

13

Marie

Marie flopped onto the bed next to Kyle, trying to catch her breath. Beside her, his chest rose and fell in quick rhythm with hers, and she couldn't help but think how good it felt to be in sync. Even if it was only physically.

It was a start. And a damn good one. Marie's whole body tingled with pleasure.

Kyle propped his head on his elbow and trailed a finger down her arm.

"Do you really have to go back to Collins's tonight?"

"I do. Early meeting tomorrow."

He gave her his sad puppy dog look, the one he always used to convince her to stay over when they were dating. Which, improbably, they were.

She was even starting to miss him when they weren't together. To look forward to telling him things about her day when he called. To slip out onto Collins's porch for a moment of privacy, to hang up smiling when he said he loved her. It didn't sound automated anymore.

Every weekend since he'd first surprised her with an overnight, Kyle had arranged to take her out. Now he'd upped his game on a weeknight:

She'd arrived at the house thinking he wanted to go over some health insurance paperwork, only to find it had been a ruse. He'd prepared a candlelit meal in their immaculately cleaned kitchen: perfectly seared steaks, wedge salads, roasted rosemary potatoes, cabernet from a vineyard they'd visited on their honeymoon, opera cream cake from her favorite bakery.

If she hadn't known better, she'd have suspected he'd read a book about marriage or seen a therapist or solicited advice from one of her friends. But the few times she tried to ask, he acted wounded, as if he'd been this version of Kyle all along.

"These nights we've spent just us," he said now, "they're good. We should do this more after you move home."

She looked into his eyes and simultaneously realized two things.

The first was that she had not, in fact, lost any semblance of love for her husband. It had just gone dormant while no one was paying any attention to it. This should have been a huge relief, except for the second thing.

Which was that the idea of moving back home still filled her with a low-level dread.

"Kyle," she said, "I really do love you."

He backed up a few inches, eyes narrowing. "Why did you say that like it's some kind of revelation?" He tried to laugh. "And why did you say it like there's a caveat coming?"

It is a revelation, she wanted to say. *And there is a caveat.* But now that her emotions were righting themselves, she was reluctant to confess how close they'd come to tipping.

She couldn't avoid this anymore, though. They had passed the point of rebooting their marriage with candlelit dinners, long term. They needed a reset to factory settings.

She turned to face Kyle, resting her fingertips on his arm until they mirrored each other, hoping he could feel how badly she wanted to see eye to eye again.

"I think we need to make some big changes," she said slowly. "When I picture coming home and everything going back the way it was, all I can think is . . . no."

His fingers stopped their trail on her arm. "No?" he repeated. "What is that supposed to mean?" She could tell that the irony of asking the literal professor of no this particular question was not lost on him. But he didn't take it back.

Marie sat up, gathering the sheets under her arms. "It means," she said gently, "I don't remember ever saying yes to the way our lives have evolved. To be fair, I don't think you did either. Neither of us grasped what the long-term picture would look like when we chose this suburb or when you got the promotion or when we enrolled the kids in Athens Elementary. But there are real downsides we did not foresee, and we're behaving as if we're stuck making the best of it. But we're not. We need to reevaluate what isn't working. We need another solution."

He ran a hand through his hair, his signature exasperated move, and pulled the comforter up to his hip. "A solution? I'm still catching up to the fact that I didn't know we had a problem."

This seemed willfully obtuse. Without thinking, she snapped back. "I moved out, and you didn't know we had a problem?"

A deafening silence fell over the room. "I knew *Collins* had a problem," he said, low and slow. "And I knew *I* had a problem until *her* problem was resolved. But no, I was not aware *you* had a problem. Why don't you enlighten me."

I don't want to have this fight, Marie thought, impatient tears springing to her eyes. *I want to be past it. I am past it. I want to work this out.* But she could tell from his expression that she had worked through too much of this alone.

"I have tried to tell you," she pleaded, "one little thing at a time. But all these little things add up to our entire lives. None of us like our commute—especially not me and the boys. We don't like you working too far away to have meaningful involvement in their school or sports or friends either. It puts way more responsibility on me, and it's not fair to expect me to keep carrying it when I keep telling you how hard it is to do alone. I don't like packing extras of everything like I'm going on some overnight rain-or-shine trek every day of my life because we're too far away to stop home. I don't like every interaction in our marriage feeling transactional. And contrary to popular belief, I don't like telling the boys no."

He waved his arms around the bed. "This?" he asked. "This feels transactional?"

She started to say that of course it didn't. But if she wanted to be cynical—which she didn't—she could point out Kyle hadn't taken any interest in wining and dining her until she'd distanced herself. If he was planning these lovely nights ostensibly for the good of their relationship, just to show himself he was entitled to sex when he wanted it . . . well, it was successful.

"I'm not saying that," she said carefully. "I'm glad you want me here. It's good to hear you say it. But haven't you noticed how the boys and I are happy staying in Athens? I'm not saying this to hurt you, only to point out that things are more stressful for us than they need to be when we're home. More stressful for us than they should be. I mean, the boys love their time with you, but not once have they asked me when we're coming back."

"What do you propose?" he asked, sarcastically. "Staying married but living separately?"

A lump lodged in Marie's throat. She forced herself to shrug. "People do it," she said. "Some couples swear by it. There's even a name for it: Living Apart Together."

"You're not serious. You've been reading up on this?"

"Casually." She cleared her throat. "I don't think it's as taboo as it sounds. Supposedly four million married Americans are doing it, and those are almost certainly underreported numbers. I'm not saying it's right for us, I'm only saying . . ."

Before she could finish, Kyle sprung from the bed and began pulling on his clothes. "Jesus, Marie. I'm glad this arrangement has been so fulfilling for you that you'd consider making it permanent. But what about me? I was happy enough before. You want to talk about noticing? Fine. Haven't *you* noticed how miserable I've been since you all left?"

Marie blinked at him. She had not.

"You were 'happy enough' before," she repeated, "even though you knew I wasn't? Because it was working better for you. But if you know it's not working for me, *that* should not work for you."

He shook his head with disgust. "Living Apart Together," he said, "sounds like the last step before a divorce."

"I don't want a divorce," she said quickly. Now that they'd reconnected, hearing him say the word was terrifying. "Let's leave divorce out of this. If you don't want to live apart anymore, and I don't want to go back to how things were, we need to find a third way. One or both of us investigates a job change. My tenure complicates things, but I'd never say never. Or we all move to Athens and resign ourselves to you having a longer commute. I don't know what the answer is, but I'm sure we can find one together."

"None of those sound any better," he said. "I know things weren't ideal before, Marie, but what about some smaller changes? Hire a housecleaning service or get a regular babysitter. We could invest in reducing your stress—the overall arrangement was fine."

This time last year, she would have been overjoyed at these suggestions. But now they seemed too little too late.

"It wasn't fine for me," she insisted. "And now that the kids and I are at Collins's, I can see that it wasn't fine for them either. If it was, I wouldn't be forcing this conversation."

"So you want to stick with Collins and raise them in a feminist commune?"

Marie would not dignify that with a response. "What if we put our house on the market and see what we can find in Athens," she suggested. "You could keep a second apartment, maybe just a studio in Columbus, for your busiest weeks when you can't stomach the drive?"

"That is not financially tenable, and you know it."

"Well, Collins's house is. And *you* know it's not a feminist commune."

"It'll be pretty close once Lucy gets there. You think she has room for both of you?"

Marie knew that Collins did. They'd already discussed it, in carefully hypothetical terms. *Good to know, just in case,* Marie had said, not defining in case of what.

In case of this, apparently. Marie had had the high ground until she'd botched this conversation. Kyle was justified in feeling like the wronged party.

But so was she.

"Let's not get off track," Marie said. "We should be able to talk through the logistics of our marriage at least once a decade. We can't do it if either of us is going to get this defensive."

"You want to talk through the *logistics* of our marriage," he said, "but I'm the transactional one."

Kyle wasn't just angry. He was hurt. "Please don't blow this out of proportion," she said.

"It's in proportion. My wife just informed me my family is immeasurably, shockingly happier living without me as if it's great news. The clarity I've been looking for."

"The only clarity in anything I said was that I love you," she said. "I want this to work."

"This isn't some theoretical problem you go off and research on your own. Testing your hypotheses at Collins's house, looking up statistics, for fuck's sake. What happened to communication? I assume you've talked to Collins about this? Her but not *me*?"

Marie felt as if she was chasing something on wheels downhill. Something she regretted she'd started rolling. Still, she seethed. "If you find that idea so offensive, maybe try asking yourself why your wife would need to talk to someone who actually listens to her."

"You never once came to me and said, *Our marriage is in trouble, we need to work on it.*"

Because I knew you'd react like this, she wanted to say. But that wasn't fair.

"You're right," she admitted, "I didn't. But I did not withhold any of the evidence for you to draw your own conclusions. You heard me say how impossible our situation felt every time I had a conflict with the boys' schedules and you were too far away to help. You saw me up late, grading papers while you watched Monday night football, which was as close to 'me time' as I ever got, because I literally didn't have enough hours in the day. You saw me gain ten pounds because I barely had time to cook, until I started waking up before dawn to get a run in. You saw me struggle to juggle it all, and every time I asked for help, you told me it wasn't that bad and everything was fine. But it was and it isn't. I'm sorry it's so inconvenient for you to acknowledge that what's working for you isn't working for the rest of the family. But it's your turn to shoulder the inconvenience for a while. Maybe it's you who needs to do some research into other options. It's exhausting feeling like the only one who cares enough to do it."

A mixture of regret and terror seized Marie as soon as the words left her mouth. But she'd meant them for a long time.

She watched Kyle's eyes cloud over with a storm of denial, shock, and realization.

"Have it your way," he said. "Go back to Collins's after Christmas. We'll give the boys a nice holiday here, and then I guess we'll see."

I guess we'll see? Panic gripped her. "I don't want to go back to Collins's," she said. "Not like this. I know we can find a compromise if we both try."

"I need time to think about whether I want to try," Kyle said icily. "In the meantime, I'd be *happier* without you here. Much less stressful that way. How's that feel? Try that on for size."

With that, he left her alone in the rumpled bed, heading to the kitchen to clean up the mess he'd made preparing such a fussy dinner for his ungrateful wife. His indignation was palpable in the air as she reassembled herself and headed back to everything else that mattered. Everything but Kyle.

14

LUCY

The last Chicago Christmas was the best Chicago Christmas. Lucy was glad she'd decided to stay through the end of December. In lieu of throwing herself any kind of goodbye party, she made plans with friends one at a time for a festive backdrop to their goodbyes, doing all the touristy things she'd eschewed for so long—ice skating in Millennium Park, window-shopping the Magnificent Mile, splurging on drinks with a view at 360 CHICAGO's CloudBar. She was from a big, blended family, half Jewish and half Christian and less than half practicing in any meaningful way, so holiday celebrations happened often enough that her family never pressured her into coming home to Cleveland for any given one. She'd see them all more often, anyway, once she was back in Ohio.

On this final gray, cold morning, wreaths still hung in perfect arches all the way down her street as Enzo helped her secure the rear doors of the rented U-Haul trailer hitched to her Honda. There was nothing left to do but say goodbye. They'd kept things loose, never once discussing keeping in touch long distance or turning this relationship into anything more, but she'd also seen no reason to stop seeing him. Enzo made her laugh more and worry less. Sometimes when the twinkle lights illuminated his face a certain way, she'd caught herself wishing they'd met earlier.

"If you're ever back in Athens for Homecoming or anything," she said, "look me up."

"My old roommates and I get a house in Hocking Hills every summer," he said. "I'd love to see you. And if you find yourself back in Chicago . . ."

She nodded overeagerly. They'd done a wonderful job of avoiding this, but now that it was upon them, she clearly should have thought more about how she wanted it to go. In the absence of a plan, her impulse was to get it over with.

There is nothing to rethink here, she told herself. Getting cold feet wasn't an option. Her apartment had already been leased to another tenant. She had no fallback plan for a job here. She'd picked up freelance copyediting to hold her over, along with some shifts at the coffee shop where she'd been a regular for years, which had been only mildly humiliating. It had all been enough to get by, but not enough to keep from depleting her savings in the process.

"Thanks again for all your help," she told Enzo, gesturing at the packed U-Haul. "Not just with this. With . . . everything." He flashed her an intimidatingly handsome grin that took her back to that first day in his office, when she'd felt underdressed and underprepared. She'd never have guessed that he'd turn out to be one of the least intimidating people she'd ever met, as likable and approachable half asleep in the morning as he was when he patiently helped her fill out paperwork at night. The truth was, she'd have been lost without his good-natured advice these past eight weeks. She'd barely stopped to think about how in the world she was going to do this alone, because he'd walked her through it, without her even asking.

"You made me look good at our semester break meeting," he said, "being so intimately familiar with the procedures of our competitors. Even if you also made me envious that I'm not the one moving back to Athens. Have a Tom's Turkey at Bagel Street Deli for me."

He even made her favorite bagel sandwich sound sexy. She kissed him playfully. "I've enjoyed getting intimately familiar with the procedures of the competitors as well."

He pulled her closer, the kiss turning less playful, more intent. Finally, he pulled back.

"One last favor?" he asked. To Lucy's astonishment, he reached into his messenger bag and pulled out the hardcover of her latest novel. She was still gaping at it when he procured a second copy. Then a third. "Will you sign these? My family exchanges books on New Year's. One for my mom and one for my sister-in-law. This one's mine."

He tapped the top of the stack, looking shy about asking. His copy had the unmistakable look of a book that had been propped open in bed and on tables, carried around and concentrated on with pages that had been turned, corners that had been folded over. She couldn't hide her surprise.

"You read it?"

"I more than read it. I loved it." His face turned serious. "Although it did confuse me why someone capable of *this* would need, much less want, an MBA."

Lucy averted her gaze to the tips of her boots. It was one thing to walk away from the most promising boyfriend prospect she'd met in all her years in this city. And another thing to walk away from a job she'd been equally capable of loving unconditionally. But both of these heartbreaks together, making their last stand right here in front of her . . . that was harder to turn her back on. He'd never pressed her to talk about her writing when she'd made it clear she didn't want to. But of course he'd seen her résumé back on day one. She didn't know whether to thank him or demand to know why he'd waited until now to mention he was from the rare sort of family that started every new year with a new book, for crying out loud.

"It's complicated," she said, when she felt sure she could smile back at him without losing her composure.

"I know," he said quickly. "I meant it as a compliment."

She nodded. "It means a lot." She took the pen he offered and scrawled the inscriptions he requested—*to another year full of wonderful stories*—along with her name and the date. She had a long drive ahead of her to sort through her feelings on Enzo. Hours and hours of Indiana cornfields and miles and miles of Ohio construction. She had a feeling it wouldn't be enough, but ready or not, when she reached Athens, this would all be behind her. Literally.

This would be easier if you weren't so perfect, she thought.

"This would be easier if you weren't so perfect," he said.

It was later than she'd planned when she pulled to the curb in front of Collins's house and cut the engine. Traffic had been terrible around Indianapolis, and she'd underestimated her confidence in towing the trailer. She spent most of the drive in the slow lane, wishing she'd sold her desk and bookcases and everything else she'd gotten sentimental about dragging along. But as she turned off the interstate onto the old state highways, and the flat farmland rolled gently into the Appalachian foothills, she began to breathe a little easier. As the campus came into view across the Hocking River, an unexpected current of emotion washed over her. She'd always felt as if a part of her heart belonged to Athens. How surreal that now, for a while, it was home again.

A light was on in Collins's living room, and delicate strands of white icicle bulbs shone along both levels of the porch, a welcome reminder that it wasn't just Chicago lit up with magic this time of year. Of course it wasn't. Collins had explained all her lights were set to a timer, so Lucy's main job until she got back was to make sure the pipes didn't freeze. A cold front was coming, but it hadn't deterred Collins from the ski slopes, probably because she planned to spend the retreat in the lodge anyway. Lucy hoped some other good prospects had signed up for this thing—whatever it took for Collins to come home feeling glad she'd done it.

Someone like Enzo, she caught herself thinking.

She'd have three days here alone to forget him before Collins came home.

She grabbed her purse and the fast-food wrappers from the passenger seat and shouldered her overnight duffel. She'd deal with the trailer in the morning. She was halfway up the walk, panning the flower bed for the false rock where Collins had hidden the spare key, when she caught the shadow of a figure moving inside and the faintest hint of a woman's voice. She stopped, watching and listening, and again the light shifted, as if someone switched off a TV. Had Collins backed out of the trip after all and decided to surprise her? Her heart lifted at the thought of not being alone after all. She took the porch stairs two at a time and was about to knock when the door flew open.

It wasn't Collins. It took Lucy a few seconds to register that the gaunt, tear-streaked face staring back at her was Marie, swaying slightly, phone in hand. Before Lucy could ask what was wrong, Marie threw her arms around her. "Thank God you're here," Marie cried. "They just called me out of nowhere, and I didn't know what to . . . I didn't—"

"What's going on? Is it Kyle?"

Marie shook her head against Lucy's shoulder, and Lucy's dread grew in that nonspecific way where the meter in your emotional center starts recalibrating. *How bad is this? What gear of panic am I about to shift into? How hard do I need to bear down?* She held tighter, imagining the worst. Some crisis involving the kids. If only she'd driven faster . . .

"It's Collins," Marie sniffed and eased back, trying to pull herself together.

Lucy squinted at her in confusion. What had she missed? "Did you two have a fight?" she asked.

Marie's expression changed, and Lucy saw now that she wasn't just upset. She was terrified. "She's had a serious accident." Marie grabbed Lucy's hand. "We have to go now."

15

Brooke

The GPS showed only nine miles from Columbus's John Glenn International Airport to Ohio State's Wexner Medical Center, but after multiple flight delays, Brooke had lost patience. Mitch concentrated on the road as sleet pummeled the rental car. Everything through the wiper-streaked windshield, from the sky to the towering office buildings to the city pavement, was a sludge gray that reminded Brooke why they'd left Ohio for good.

They'd been wrapping up a Christmas visit to her in-laws when Marie called. But by the time they secured standby tickets for an overbooked flight to West Virginia, the decision had been made to transfer Collins from the remote Timberline Mountain area to the Level 1 trauma center closest to home. Nobody wanted to acknowledge the subtext—that this was unlikely a short-term stay. Nor had Mitch mentioned that their flights to Venice were days away. He'd simply rebooked their connection; there was no question they would come.

The bigger question was what they'd find once they arrived. Brooke had maintained a state she could only describe as *nauseated calm* for the past thirty-six hours. But now that she was finally close to joining the rest of their friends at Collins's bedside, she was bursting to bridge the distance, however miserable things might be—to breathe in the same antiseptic air and sip the same cafeteria coffee and brace herself to know everything.

Starting with whether Collins would be okay.

She *needed* Collins to be okay.

"I think this is it." Mitch nodded at a parking garage. Making the sharp entrance turn, he took a ticket from the machine. Brooke snapped into to-do mode.

"Did you let your mom know we landed? She's always so nervous . . ."

"Shoot. No, do you mind?"

Brooke fired off a quick text. Here safe. Thanks again for being so great about this. So sorry to cut the visit short. We'll keep you posted.

"Done," she said. "Though it's safe to say I'm not her favorite person right now."

"Please. You haven't done anything but be a good friend."

"Well, besides dashing her hopes of becoming a grandmother. And then talking her son into leaving the continent. And then ruining our goodbye visit."

He maneuvered into a space and cut the engine, turning toward her. "*You* haven't done those things. *We* have, and she knows it. Besides, this has nothing to do with that. You ready?"

Brooke blinked back tears. "Thank you," she whispered, reaching to squeeze his hand.

He squeezed back.

Inside, the hospital's fluorescent-lit corridors pulsed with nervous energy. Oddly enough, fertility treatments had made her dread hospitals less. The maternity ward, after all, was the end goal. She knew these walls held patients who were desperate to restore their health—but she preferred to think of the miracles happening in places like this every day.

If anyone deserved one, it was Collins. She'd been through so much already.

Outside the intensive care unit, Brooke spotted Marie first, standing with her phone to her ear. Then she saw Lucy behind her, sprawled across several seats as if she'd either been there awhile or planned to be. She broke into a jog, and the next moment she was wrapped in a cocoon of *You made it* and *So glad you're here*, of *Longest day ever* and *How is she?* The few other visitors averted their eyes respectfully, and then the friends were hugging Mitch too.

"They're getting her a room," Lucy said. "All we know is she's stable and has another surgery first thing tomorrow. We detoured to get her things from the lodge and try to get her refunded for the unused nights."

"How was that?" Brooke asked. Her friends exchanged a weary look, and her own exhaustion suddenly seemed inconsequential. Marie and Lucy must have been awake thirty-six hours and counting.

"Weird," Lucy said.

"Thank God she put me down as her emergency contact on the retreat waivers," Marie said. "Even then it was like pulling teeth to get access to her hotel room. I mean, I get it, but the accident happened *there*. They knew she wasn't strolling back in for her suitcase."

"Did you get a vibe there?" Mitch asked. "I mean, whether she'd been having a good time, before . . . you know."

Brooke caught another glance between her friends, but she couldn't read this one. "Her room didn't look very lived in," Lucy admitted. "Like, her toiletry bag was open in the bathroom, but . . . she hadn't hung up any clothes. Even the new dress she bought for the cocktail party was still rolled up in her luggage."

"We talked to the retreat facilitator," Marie said. "She said Collins picked up her welcome bag but didn't attend the opening mixer or speed dating or game night. Nobody was with her when she rented the equipment and signed for her lift ticket. She didn't ask about a ski lesson or say boo to anyone. The first time she scanned the ticket was that night. Nobody knows if she got on the wrong lift or misunderstood the difficulty of the slopes . . ."

Brooke frowned. "That's odd. I figured maybe she met people who were more advanced and got in over her head. Trying to impress someone, maybe?"

"Maybe she thought it would be easier to get up the nerve to try it after the daytime crowds were gone?" Lucy ventured. "Or maybe she wanted to ride up just to check it out. Maybe that was her plan, to enjoy the view and take the lift back down? Because she wasn't on the slope when she fell. She was—" She shook her head. "She must have gotten turned around in the dark. Thank goodness someone saw her slide over the ledge, or I don't know how long she might have been there before they found her."

Brooke tried not to picture Collins broken and half buried in the snow, turning blue, scared and alone. Her stomach churned. They hadn't managed a proper meal during their layover in Atlanta; the lines were too long.

"Have they assessed the extent of her injuries yet?" she asked.

"The head trauma seemed their primary concern. They set the fractures in her femur and her arm right away, but it's bad, Brookie. So much internal bruising and swelling. It's a small miracle she doesn't have a spinal injury, but it's a shorter list of what isn't injured." Marie began riffling in her purse. "They used a lot of big words. I wrote them down."

The double doors to the ICU opened, and a brisk woman in a lab coat strode toward them. "Is one of you Marie Welling?"

They all got to their feet, and Marie feebly raised a hand. The doctor eyed the rest of the group. "You were all skiing together when this happened?"

"No," Marie said quickly. "She was by herself. I mean, she was attending an organized retreat, but we don't think anyone was with her."

"I see. And what about her next of kin?"

"Collins's husband passed away a couple of years ago. Her parents before that. I've been staying at her house with her, trying to—"

"So you're her roommate?"

Marie cleared her throat, looking uncomfortable. Brooke had known Marie's living situation was a little . . . undefined. At the moment, she assumed the boys must be with Kyle.

Lucy jumped in. "We're both her roommates, temporarily," she told the doctor. "She lives near OU's campus and is putting me up while I go back for my master's."

The doctor sniffed. "ICU typically allows only family to visit. Does she have siblings?"

"She has an aunt," Marie offered. "And cousins. I've called them, but they're not local. They asked me to keep them posted but didn't offer to come. I guess it might depend . . ."

They all looked at the doctor expectantly, but her face revealed nothing. "I'm going to need you to give that information to a case worker, so he can verify you're authorized as emergency contact. That may mean making medical decisions for Collins, while she's unable. What about her late husband's family? Are they close?"

"No." Marie bit her lip. "I thought I'd wait to call them until we know what's what."

The doctor frowned. "Well, the next few days will be critical. I'll be honest—they did their best in triage, but it's challenging when a patient sustains injuries like these so far from a properly equipped trauma center. The right femur will require further surgery, and her left knee damage involves the whole terrible triad—ACL, MCL, and meniscus. She's also sustained deep lacerations, so we'll be monitoring for infection as well. Fortunately, her arm fracture was a simpler break. Initial scans showed no significant internal bleeding but a lot of bruising. Our first priority is monitoring her cerebral edema under deep sedation to allow her brain to rest and heal."

"They told us *medically induced coma*," Lucy said. "Is that the same thing?"

"Exactly. Given the other trauma her body has sustained, this is the safest state for her, short term. Her brain activity is steady, which is reason for cautious optimism. Still, it's wait and see."

"How long until she can wake up?" Marie asked.

"We will reassess that frequently."

"She's going to walk again, though?" Brooke winced at the crassness of her own question, but she'd heard enough *wait and see* advice from her own doctors to last a lifetime.

The doctor offered a small smile. "I've seen people achieve amazing things."

"My friends and I," Marie said firmly. "We're her family. She's not awake to tell you that, but . . . if we take shifts, can we be allowed in? Please? We hate the idea of her being alone."

"Why don't you come with me to see the case worker, and we'll see what we can do."

Brooke did her best to nod encouragingly at Marie. But she felt helpless standing with Mitch and Lucy as their friend disappeared through the ICU door.

"Oh boy," Lucy said, dropping into a chair. "Well, at least we're here for each other."

"Should we be worried?" Mitch asked, settling beside her. "That Collins's aunt or whoever won't cede responsibility?"

Lucy sighed. "I don't think so. She was kind of combative with Marie when we called her. Said the Collins she knew would rather, quote, 'poke her eyes out with a stick than participate in winter sports.'"

"That tracks," Mitch said, meeting Brooke's eyes. "Remember when she and Sullivan came to visit us on his spring break? With snow covering the Rockies, the only place we could get them was Mount Princeton Hot Springs."

"Well, don't repeat that to Marie," Lucy said. "Because her aunt didn't mince words. She said whoever put such a 'harebrained' idea into Collins's head should take *full* responsibility for whatever happens now." Her eyes filled with tears. "Guys, what if this is our fault? Maybe we pushed her into something she wasn't ready for. Or she was grasping at straws to appease us."

Lucy's eyes moved past Brooke, and she quickly stood. Brooke registered the scuffle of fast-approaching footsteps, turning in time to see Marie's sons run past her and into Lucy's arms. Brooke smiled self-consciously as Kyle appeared in the doorway. It was her own fault she didn't have that kind of rapport with Connor and Wade. She'd wanted her own kids so badly that she'd missed out on relationships with the ones she already had in her life.

Mitch stood and held out a hand to Kyle. "Good to see you, man. Tough circumstances."

"Likewise." Kyle lowered his voice. "This is no place for the kids, but I didn't know what else to do. They miss their mom and won't stop asking about Collins."

"Don't worry, Aunt Lucy, we helped unload your U-Haul," Connor said importantly, his tone switching from giddy kid to posturing man as only a preteen can. "The truck place tried to charge extra when we returned it, but Dad gave 'em hell."

"Language," Kyle said.

"What would I do without you guys?" Lucy ruffled their hair, and they both ducked away from this great public humiliation. "And hey, remember Brooke and Mitch? Our friends from Colorado? They came a long way to be part of Team Collins."

This piqued Wade's interest. "Have you ever seen a mountain lion?"

"No, but I heard one scream once," Mitch said. He scrunched up his face into a crazed roar, and the boys laughed. A familiar ache of longing started in Brooke's chest, but she stuffed it back down. *Yes, he would have been a great dad. But this can be enough. It has to be.*

"You know," Lucy told the kids conspiratorially, "I was about to raid the cafeteria for treats. Want to come?"

The boys looked to their dad, and at his nod, they took off running as fast as they'd come. Connor jumped up to slap the top of the doorway but wasn't tall enough, and Wade cackled.

Thank you, Kyle mouthed to Lucy as she hurried after them. As soon as they were out of sight, his face fell, and Mitch filled him in on the doctor's updates and where Marie had gone.

"Makes you think, doesn't it?" Kyle said. "Life is so short." He gave a little laugh. "I blamed the kids, but the truth is, I'm the one who needed to see Marie. We're spending all this time apart, and for what? Everything seems so trivial by comparison."

Brooke had a surge of certainty that he needed to say that to Marie, not to them. She hoped he would. She hoped it wasn't too late.

"Puts things in perspective," Mitch agreed.

"I'm worried about her," Kyle said. "Does she want all this responsibility? I mean, if she has to make tough judgment calls, it could weigh on her."

"Sounds like it's going to weigh on her no matter what," Mitch said. "Everyone's already beating themselves up that this happened at all. But Collins made her own decision to choose this retreat. It's not fair to blame the pact."

Brooke elbowed her husband hard, but there was no putting the words back.

"What pact?" Kyle asked.

"Nothing," Brooke said quickly, but Kyle's eyes narrowed.

Mitch backpedaled, catching on too late. "Yeah, like I said, nothing to do with that. They were all just supporting each other through some things they wanted to move on from."

"Move on from," Kyle repeated.

"Right. Brooke and I, you know, we needed to face facts that parenthood isn't in the cards. And Lucy, she's getting this MBA instead of chasing another book deal. Collins wanted to quit hiding at home, put herself back out there."

"So this *moving on* pact pushed her to book the first singles' retreat she saw advertised? Even though it was a terrible fit? And dangerous?" He wasn't looking at Mitch, but Brooke.

"Inspired her to book it," Mitch corrected. "Not pushed." He slid an arm around Brooke. "I mean, we'd have come around to the same choice eventually. The pact was just the nudge we needed."

Brooke tried to smile, but her face wasn't cooperating. Because Kyle didn't look away.

"And Marie," he said evenly. "What was it she wanted to move on from?"

Next to her, Mitch tensed, and Brooke averted her eyes. *Why* hadn't she gone with Lucy and the kids? She'd be eating dessert for dinner instead of bearing witness to this mess. Kyle read into their silence, and there was nothing they could do to stop him.

"I see," Kyle said quietly.

Then without another word, he got to his feet and was gone.

16

Marie

Marie had no right to any glimmer of comfort or relief. Not with Collins unconscious in the ICU, Kyle acting distant and strange, and the start of the semester approaching unthinkably fast. She had so many things to deal with before she could resume any semblance of "normal."

But she didn't have to do it alone. That's where the glimmers came in. Marie had forgotten what it felt like to confront a problem as a team, without carrying the full weight of the responsibility. Although the irony was that she *did* have more responsibility in this collective ongoing emergency, now that she'd been designated Collins's go-between, medically and otherwise. The first few days with Lucy, Brooke, and Mitch at her side had been consumed by exhaustion and worry, that surreal sense this was a nightmare they'd wake up from. They'd cried together, they'd consumed all the fast food they could handle, they'd played out worst-case scenarios, they'd cheered the news of every successful surgery, clinging to hope that one day their friend could fully put this tragedy behind her.

It was hard to believe the broken figure in the hospital bed was Collins at all, her face obscured by the ventilator and feeding tube, her body so braced and bandaged they were almost glad she wasn't awake to feel the pain. So many specialists were involved, it was hard to keep them straight, and though they framed their updates positively, one procedure invariably led to another. In between, there was a whole lot of nothing, beeping machines and a nursing staff rotation they came to know by name.

In the fog of it all, though, the sun had occasionally shone through. They'd held Collins's hand and huddled around her to whisper in her ear about hot doctors and the hilariously cranky patient in the adjacent room. On touch-and-go nights, they'd taken turns staying, curled up with a blanket and a book, while the others made the long drive back to Athens. Staying overnight was a violation of visiting hours, but the care team looked the other way, taking pity on the patient with no family and the friends who didn't know what to do with themselves. They'd debated booking a hotel near the hospital, but Collins's house was cozier. Every night, they'd claim they were going to fall straight into bed, then come back downstairs in their pajamas to pile onto the couches with snacks and wine and a remote control tuned to junk TV. They'd taken the boys to Columbus's Yuletide Festival on Gay Street, where thousands of Christmas lights draped overhead like streamers from a party nobody wanted to admit was over. They'd ridden the carousel and ice skated until their noses turned red, then lined up at the cocoa truck and joked about how much Collins would have hated the whole thing.

On New Year's Eve, the doctors declared Collins's primary surgical interventions complete and made the announcement the friends had been waiting for: Her sedation would be lifted on New Year's Day. When Collins opened her eyes—and they had to believe she would—they'd be able to tell her that her accident on the mountain was, thankfully, last year's crisis. She'd wake up to a fresh canvas of three hundred and sixty-five days, a chance to paint a new picture—whatever she wanted to see ahead of her.

They smuggled in a bottle of champagne for a toast next to Collins's hospital bed.

"I hereby resolve to make no more resolutions," Lucy said.

"Here's to seeing through the ones we've already made," Brooke added, shooting a quick smile at Mitch. They'd delayed their departure until Lucy and Marie would start school, in mid-January, so they could help get Collins sorted with whatever rehabilitation program awaited her. *Venice isn't going anywhere,* Mitch had said, unfazed. He gave Marie faith that she and Kyle could still find a way to be stronger together. Even if Kyle had kept his distance, relegating himself to a cooperative role. *Sure, I'll keep the boys another night. No problem, I'll reschedule their dentist appointment. Your hands are full.* She'd been waiting so long for him to acknowledge that—but she'd never wanted it like this.

Nobody felt like drinking more than a sip of champagne with ninety miles between them and the couch they all longed for. Mitch stayed behind for the last overnight shift to give Marie, Lucy, and Brooke one girls' night before they had to spring back into action. They hit the Jolly Pirate Donuts drive-thru on the way back and ate straight from the box as they watched the ball drop, pouring what was left of the warm, half-flat champagne over ice.

"What were you doing this time last year?" Marie asked them.

"Canceling plans because I hadn't met my revision deadline," Lucy said.

"Crying over another year of *not* being pregnant," Brooke said. She tossed the uneaten half of her glazed doughnut onto the coffee table and rubbed her stomach in displeasure.

When they both looked to Marie, she sighed. "Waking Kyle up every five minutes," she admitted. "It was supposed to be a family movie night, but he couldn't stay awake."

They sat for a minute in knowing silence, Ryan Seacrest keeping up chipper commentary from the TV. Then Lucy topped off their glasses.

"Next year will be better," she offered weakly. But nobody chimed in to agree.

And Marie missed Connor and Wade with a sudden ferocity that felt almost like fear.

~

If they'd expected Collins to blink awake, prop up on pillows to eat some hospital JELL-O, and tell them the whole story, they were mistaken.

She was disoriented, drifting in and out, in and out. They spoke to her anyway, gently explaining that she'd had an accident, and she was safe, and they were here.

The first time she really registered them, eyes flitting from one face to the next, she didn't look alarmed, exactly, or even surprised. Marie wondered if she'd been able to hear them trying to make their presence felt these last few days. It should have been a comfort, knowing their round-the-clock efforts had not been for nothing. But as Collins began to take in her surroundings, she looked more confused than grateful to be waking up at all.

And more defeated than confused.

"Throat hurts," she rasped.

"I bet," Marie said. "That's from all those tubes. It'll go away."

Collins stared down at her legs, as if they might belong to someone else. The left one was bandaged so extensively, it looked almost as uncomfortable as the cast immobilizing her right. Her bare toes stuck out from the sheet, and Marie hid her relief when she saw them wiggle.

"That might hurt a little longer," Brooke said gently. "So much for your Olympic downhill training, huh?"

Collins moaned, but this time, it sounded almost good-natured. She winced and lifted her lone unbandaged arm to rub her throat.

"You don't have to talk," Marie told her. "We're just happy to see you."

"Oh, come on," Lucy protested. "Don't let her off the hook. I've been dying to ask her if she met anyone cute up there."

Collins managed a small smile. "Move in yet?" she whispered.

"Sure did," Lucy said. "Only thing missing is you."

"What day?" Collins rasped. "How long . . ."

"January first," Brooke told her. "Badass day to wake up from a coma, if you ask me."

Collins's eyes widened at the word "coma." Then, after a beat: "Is this . . . soap opera?"

Relief overtook Marie. Not only was Collins awake, but she was herself. That ruled out the worst scenario she'd been imagining. "If this were a soap opera," Marie told her, unable to hide her grin, "you'd have amnesia. Do you remember what happened?"

Collins closed her eyes, and her shoulders moved almost imperceptibly. Another wince, or a shrug? "Not really. Stupid. Cold." When she squinted up at her friends again, her eyes were teary. Her gaze landed on Brooke. "You're supposed to be—" She gestured to indicate someplace far away.

"I'm exactly where I'm supposed to be," Brooke said firmly.

Mitch nodded his agreement, and Collins's tears spilled over. Marie perched on the bed and took Collins's good hand in hers, emotion choking her.

"Sullivan," Collins whimpered. Marie's eyes met Lucy's, and a current passed between them. If Collins didn't remember Sullivan had died, Marie didn't know how she could possibly be the one to tell her that he was gone. But then, Collins sniffed hard, seemingly pulling herself together. "He loved New Year's Day," she said softly. Marie remembered then. It had been one of his few artist's rituals, to start each year by visiting someplace he'd never been before and bring back some token or idea or sliver of inspiration for the next phase of his work.

Her heart twisted, thinking how much he'd have hated seeing Collins here now, like this.

"I take him flowers," Collins said. She looked helplessly at her legs again. "Could someone go for me?"

"Of course." Marie was crying now too. "First chance we get. You can count on us, for anything you need. You don't need to worry about the house, or work, or anything besides getting better."

Marie had obviously meant this as a comfort, but at the mention of work, Collins tensed, and the despondent look returned. "Exhibit," she mumbled.

"I'll handle it," Marie said.

A nurse came in then, crossing to check the monitor at the other end of the mess of wires attached to Collins's casted arm.

"You are lucky to have such devoted friends," she told Collins. "But now that you're awake, we'll enforce visiting hours so you can rest. These three don't know when to quit."

Marie gave Collins a quick hug as Lucy and Brooke waited their turns, and headed for the door, where Mitch stood smiling, giving Collins an encouraging wave.

"That's where you're wrong," Mitch told the nurse. "They definitely do."

17

Lucy

Lucy's eyes fell on the welcome basket Collins had left on the desk in her room. As usual, Collins had thought of everything: a College of Business Bobcats hoodie, a refillable coffee mug from Court Street Coffee, congratulatory champagne, prewrapped study snacks, and a package of cute notecards from Cross Court.

It was painful to look at, this reminder of how quickly things could change. A week ago, Lucy's mind had been consumed by her big move—thoughts of what it would be like going back to college and how it would feel having a roommate again after so long living alone, and what it meant that she already missed Enzo more than she wanted to. Meanwhile, Collins had taken time out of packing for her own trip to prepare these sweet extras for Lucy's arrival, expecting to be back home by now uncorking the bubbly together, letting Lucy drag her to their favorite old haunts and finding their way to a companionable new normal.

Now, Collins had a lot of work to do before she could ever navigate the simple pleasures of Court Street again on her own two feet. Lucy had read up on femur fractures—nightmare stories about one leg ending up shorter than the other, about persistent limps and persistent pain and the sheer force required to break a femur in the first place—and wished she hadn't. They'd spent some of the best years of their lives together bounding down those sidewalks and across the uneven brick streets, taking the physicality of life for granted, invincible in their youth. Nothing about Ohio's oldest college town was very smoothly accessible, though—not the street parking, the hills, or pedestrian-only campus greens, not even Collins's own front porch.

She snapped a picture of the basket and sent it to Enzo, in hopes that his response might lift her spirits. But she wasn't sure she deserved such an easy out.

The other day at the hospital, when Lucy had finally voiced her fears—*What if this is our fault? Maybe we pushed her into something she wasn't ready for?*—nobody had wanted to entertain the idea. Maybe none of this was anyone's fault. Back on their girls' trip, Collins had said herself she wanted to quit hiding at home. Collins had chosen the particular retreat and the particular moment to stretch her comfort zone. Collins had put on the ski gear and ridden the lift up the mountain and done something perhaps a bit . . . ill-advised.

But that didn't mean there weren't millions of tiny things any one of them might have done or said differently in the interim. Things that might have steered Collins toward a different choice. After all, when you did something ill-advised, shouldn't you revisit who was advising you? Or, perhaps more accurately, who was leaving you unchecked as you advised yourself?

Lucy knew her imagination could run wild. She told herself it was her novelist's brain, unable to shut down, left with nothing to do but script fiction into the reality around her. But there was one conversation she couldn't stop replaying.

The night Lucy had posted the essay that would end her career, Collins had told her: *I know what it feels like to regret something. To blame yourself later. It's the worst feeling. And if it's avoidable . . .*

Lucy hadn't let Collins finish the thought. She'd been so wrapped up in her own problems, she hadn't stopped to consider what exactly Collins had been referring to. She hadn't asked what Collins regretted, what she blamed herself for. And as a result, she knew only one thing for sure.

Without their pact . . .

Without Collins facing another holiday left to her own devices, caught in the middle of everyone else's transitions . . .

Without Lucy and Marie assuming that simply being present for Collins was enough . . .

Maybe Collins would be perfectly fine right now.

And Lucy would not be sitting here stewing on her biggest fear of all. The one she was loath to voice to her friends.

The fear that maybe Collins's accident hadn't really been an accident at all.

Don't try to help me, she'd told Collins that night.

When what she should have said was: *How can I help you?*

Fortunately, Lucy was *almost* too busy to ruminate. Only twelve days remained before Marie and Lucy would start the semester and Brooke and Mitch would depart on the first leg of their adventure. They wasted no time mobilizing with a shared calendar app, courtesy of Brooke, who'd long used its intricate system to track her injections and cycles and payments.

"At least my skills are still good for something," she'd said, too brightly, as she explained her color-coded method and how to sign up for hospital shifts.

They gave Marie first dibs, as the busiest of them all. Not only was she the only one with some sense of what Collins had been doing to manage Sullivan's estate, but her kids were headed back to school, and she had to show her face at a few faculty meetings and a lunch-and-learn series for professional development. Lucy still didn't know what was going on with Marie and Kyle and was trying not to ask, though it would've been nice to know if the living arrangements were changing anytime soon.

Not that Lucy was in a hurry for Marie to go. She liked the house full. Brooke and Mitch had taken Collins's bedroom, with Lucy, Marie, and the boys already in the three guest rooms. The kids helped lighten the mood, and Lucy was getting a little addicted to the race car video game they'd gotten for Christmas. Not that she was good at it, but they found it uproariously funny every time she crashed.

Collins had moved out of intensive care to the ortho floor, where she underwent a rotation of daily evaluations and preliminary physical therapy to preserve her "passive range of motion" until she was ready for more active movement. There were occupational therapists, case workers, and a support team currently focused on getting insurance to approve an eventual move to rehab, where Collins would start the tricky business of learning to walk again with plates and screws in one leg and that "terrible triad" of tears in the other. Since Collins wasn't an athlete who'd be putting real strain on her ligaments, the doctors had decided to take a conservative approach in hopes that her knee could adequately heal without further surgery. For now, Collins was in immense pain, heavily medicated, and usually asleep. Sometimes she'd stay alert long enough to answer a few yes-or-no questions, but she hadn't said much. The doctors hadn't, either, declining to give much prognosis beyond "wait and see." But that felt easier to do now that Collins could make decisions about her own care.

Mitch and Brooke took the bulk of the shifts, arguing that they might as well make themselves useful during their limited time here. "Besides," Brooke had pointed out, "unlike you two, we have nothing else to do. You'll have plenty of slack to pick up after we leave."

Although it made sense that Brooke and Mitch operated as a unit, Lucy itched to get Brooke alone. Brooke kept saying her body hadn't adjusted to the jet lag, but she looked so worn out that Lucy couldn't help but wonder if she was having some of the same second thoughts Lucy was having . . . about Collins and maybe about her own choices too. But Lucy wasn't about to ask in front of Mitch, who exuded enough energy for them both.

She could hear him downstairs now, coordinating dinner plans with Marie, asking what toppings the kids would like for a Taco Tuesday bar. She waited until she heard Mitch and Brooke leave for Columbus before venturing downstairs. She poured coffee into an oversize mug and found Marie in Collins's office.

"Good morning." Marie smiled at her from the desk as Lucy slumped into an armchair and took a long, grateful sip. "You know, for someone who left the house so seldom, Collins had quite the backlog of invitations in her mailbox." She started reading off the stack of letters in her hand. "A 'Fine Arts College Alumni Achievements' event. A benefit dinner for the Cleveland Museum of Art. A guest lecture for the Ohio Arts Council. A Valentine's Day sculpture series at Riverfront Park in Marietta." She dropped them onto the desk. "They all want her to say a few words on Sullivan's behalf or accept some kind of honor or represent the estate with a show of support. It's meant as a compliment, of course, but they act like it's easy—like a few minutes is all it costs her. Can you imagine how draining?"

Lucy shifted in her seat. "Has she talked about it much?"

"A little, but I didn't realize the extent of it. Every single one of these letters begins with condolences. You'd never know he'd been gone for years, not weeks."

Lucy met Marie's eyes, and she could tell they were thinking the same thing.

They'd made Collins a promise a couple of days ago. They'd put it off long enough.

En route to the cemetery, Marie detoured to show Lucy the memorial plaque for Sullivan affixed to his most accessible sculpture on campus, a treelike abstract in the school colors of green and white near the Convo Center. It was impressively front and center to basketball games, graduation ceremonies, and everything else hosted beneath the white dome. But for his resting place, Collins had chosen an unassuming cemetery outside of town that got little foot traffic.

Lucy arranged the flowers they'd brought on the simple headstone, while Marie stood reverently beside her. "Our girl sure does miss you, Sull," Marie said aloud. Out of the corner of Lucy's eye, she caught a flash of red, a cardinal swooping into a stand of barren trees.

"She'd be here herself if she could," Lucy told the headstone, linking her arm through Marie's. Thick cloud cover obscured the sun, and the mid-morning air felt damp. Beside her, Marie shivered beneath her coat, holding her arm tighter.

The last time Lucy had stood in this spot—the only other time she'd stood in this spot—had been the funeral. Then, Collins's raw grief had had plenty of company, a crowd of mourners shrouded in black and gathered in solidarity to say goodbye. It felt so much emptier to be here alone, while the rest of the world got on with things.

"We'll get her through this, Sull," Lucy said. "This year is starting out hard, but we'll help her turn things around. We promise."

Marie cleared her throat. "She came so close—" Her voice broke. "Thanks for watching over her. She's doing her best to do right by you too. But I guess you already know that."

Lucy had to bite her tongue not to say more. Because what she was thinking was that maybe Collins was doing too much. Maybe if Sullivan had known what this would be like for Collins, he wouldn't have asked so much of her. But it wasn't her place to say. And it certainly wasn't what Collins had had in mind in asking them to come.

They kept their arms linked as they headed back to the car. Marie had suggested they divide Sullivan's bouquet and take the other half to Collins, so she'd have something tying her to this ritual, and she could see the splash of color through the minivan's dirty windshield. From this distance, it didn't look like obligation. It looked like love.

"It's so unfair," Marie said. "She would've stayed happiest of all of us, you know."

"I know," Lucy agreed. They trudged on in companionable silence, and Lucy decided to take a chance. "Speaking of. What's the status of things with you and Kyle?"

Marie sighed. "I wish I knew. Before Christmas, things improved. Then we had a fight, and then Collins got hurt, and now . . ." She sighed. "I know we need to talk. And I know he knows we need to talk. But with all this chaos, I've only seen him with the kids around, and—well, we're both avoiding it. Or maybe he senses I lack the emotional bandwidth. You'd think this Sullivan stuff would be the ultimate perspective check. But he and Coll were on another level."

"I wish I'd seen more of them together," Lucy said. "I always wanted to come back for one of his open gallery nights, but I never did. I always figured, *next time*." The words landed hard, a cautionary tale. "Have you ever been back?" she asked. "To the site of the studio fire?"

Marie shook her head. "It's not far from here, actually. But Collins is adamant about staying away. The property owner has been hounding her to pick up some things, but even when I offered to go along, she refused." She wrapped her scarf tighter around her neck. "Those open gallery nights were something. People would wonder why he wanted a studio so far off campus, until they saw it for themselves. Then it was self-explanatory."

"What if we go now?" Lucy suggested. "I mean, if it's that nearby?"

Marie glanced over at her. "Really?" She seemed to be thinking it over. "I mean, we can't take anything back to the house. Not 'one speck of ash,' Collins said. I respect her wishes, but I did wonder if she'd come to regret letting that stuff get thrown away."

"Could we store whatever it is at your house?" Lucy suggested. "Maybe Kyle could meet you so you can talk. I can take the boys to soccer tonight. Indoor turf at the field house, right?"

Marie squinted at her in amazement. "You remember their training schedule?"

"Brooke color-coded that on the calendar too," Lucy said. Then, testing the waters: "Maybe she should add Kyle."

"Ha. We already have a shared calendar he never looks at."

Lucy clocked the resentment in Marie's voice. "Let the rest of us share responsibility, then," Lucy said. "Starting now."

Marie talked as she navigated the windy country roads, explaining Sullivan had chosen an old barn atop one of the most awe-inspiring perches in all of Athens County for his studio. It had been part of a family farm for generations, but they'd since built newer, bigger boarding stables and arenas for horseback riding lessons. In exchange for a break on rent, they agreed to let Sullivan handle the renovations, hanging industrial lighting and embracing an open concept where soldering, welding, and staining could share space with finished displays. The result was the perfect balance: When he invited the public, it felt like a destination, but the rest of the time, he could hole up and create away from overeager students and half-envious department heads.

"I get why this place holds too many memories for Collins," Marie said as she turned into the gravel entrance. "She was here almost every day. She wasn't just his manager, she was his assistant. His . . . everything."

The word lingered, definitive. But as Marie steered up the hill, pointing out the frost-covered field where the barn had stood, the energy around them felt more peaceful than sad.

"I hope it's okay to show up unannounced," Marie said. "The owner's not exactly warm and fuzzy."

At the top of the hill, the stables and a farmhouse came into view. If you didn't know the barn had stood here, you'd never guess; there was no longer any teddy bear–strewn memorial, no commemorative cross in the dirt. But the smell of fresh woodsmoke from a nearby chimney was sobering as it mingled with the animal scent of the paddocks. When they parked and stepped out of the car, a woman came out to watch from the porch, braid blowing back in the wind.

"Evie?" Marie called. "Not sure if you remember me from the Hartley Studio's open houses . . . I'm Marie Welling, one of Sullivan's colleagues on the faculty. We're friends of Collins." Evie moved toward them, but her face didn't soften. "I'm here to pick up the things you set aside for her. If you still have them?"

"About damn time," Evie said flatly, hugging her flannel against the cold. Then, with suspicion: "How do I know you're not like those students always out here snooping around for their true crime podcast?"

Lucy looked at Marie in surprise—but this seemed like news to her too. "*Crime?*"

Evie raised an eyebrow. "She hasn't mentioned it? Surely I'm not the only one they've been hounding." She put her hands on her hips, and Lucy could see they were not exactly selling themselves as Collins's closest confidantes. "Anyway, you can assure Sullivan's Collins I have no interest in granting interviews. And I told those kids none of this was her fault."

"Her fault?" Lucy asked. "Why would anyone think that?"

"Um. Because she micromanaged everything but the safety protocol he wasn't following? But Sullivan could take care of himself." She checked herself. "Well. So he insisted." Evie turned on her heels and headed for the stables, calling over her shoulder: "Don't suppose I care who takes the stuff anymore as long as someone does." A minute later, she emerged carrying a large green rubber bin. Marie popped the van's trunk, and Evie dropped it in unceremoniously.

"Happy New Year," Evie said, already retreating to the house.

Neither of them said it back.

As they pulled into the driveway at home, Lucy was surprised to see the rental car already parked there. Mitch and Brooke must have finished at the hospital early. Marie left the bin untouched in her trunk and headed for the side kitchen door. Lucy followed.

Inside, Brooke sat stiffly at the kitchen table, looking pale, a pack of saltine crackers and a bottle of ginger ale in front of her.

"Oh no," Lucy said. "You sick?"

Brooke shook her head. "I'm pregnant."

18

Brooke

The ultrasound tech had left the room to get the doctor, but Brooke was still lying on the table with her eyes squeezed shut, awash in disbelief. She was afraid to say anything before the official word came, and she guessed Mitch felt the same, because the room was so quiet he must be holding his breath. But there had been no mistaking the white flickering light on the ultrasound screen.

She'd been waiting for the moment this would turn out to be a false alarm. Home pregnancy tests could be unreliable—and her hormones must be permanently haywire after so many years of pills and injections and procedures. Without medical intervention, her periods ranged from inconsistent to nonexistent, so there had never been a sense that she'd skipped one. Every time she used the bathroom, she expected to see spotting. Even after she'd called the women's health clinic Marie recommended and made the appointment to have her levels confirmed in a lab, even after the nurse had called with the affirmative results of her blood test, she'd insisted on seeing an ob-gyn right away. She was certain once they reviewed her medical history, once they understood the reasons this outcome was impossible, they'd offer some alternative explanation.

Her eyes opened at the sound of the doctor entering the room. Brooke sat up and assessed her—sixty-something, stylish, with white hair in a chic pixie cut. "I'm Dr. Maren York," the woman said as she shut the door behind her, smiling first at Brooke, then Mitch. "Congratulations. We estimate you're six weeks and four days along."

Brooke turned to her husband at last and saw her own skepticism reflected there. Usually at their fertility appointments he sat beside her and held her hand, but now he remained standing, hands in his pockets, his focus on the doctor instead of her. She was glad he hadn't met her eyes yet; she was afraid of what he'd see if he did. They'd promised not to jump to conclusions, not to even think about reacting until this moment. It had made for an agonizing week while they'd waited for the clinic's first available appointment. Now the moment was here.

"I don't understand how this happened," Mitch said to the doctor.

"Well, there's only one way." Her expression said she heard this all the time, and that did it for Brooke. After years of *dreaming* to hear those words, here was a doctor speaking as if they were careless horny teenagers. She didn't know whether to burst out laughing or bite her head off.

"I'm not sure how to convey the extent . . ." Brooke began. She tried again. "It took a lot for us to give up. But we finally accepted this wouldn't happen for us."

"Isn't it funny," Dr. York said, more gently, "how sometimes that's when it does."

Brooke didn't want this doctor. She wanted her specialist in Colorado, who would understand that this was either a certifiable miracle or . . . what? A cruel joke? The universe dangling this carrot once more only to snatch it away again? Because despite Brooke's unshakable fatigue and nausea and tender breasts and volatile emotions, this didn't feel real.

It didn't feel like a miracle.

So how could it be?

"I bet you've already spent a lot of time in offices like this one. How lovely that this time it's with more joyful news," Dr. York said.

Mitch patted his pockets, as if he might have misplaced his joyfulness in one of them. "So what happens now?" he asked. "I mean, you'd think we'd know, but . . ."

The doctor's smile remained fixed as she nodded and addressed them both. "Cautious optimism," she said. "Given your advanced maternal age, there's a little extra monitoring involved for a number of heightened risk factors we'll want to keep an eye on, your history aside."

Brooke looked to Mitch, desperate for him to take over their end of this conversation. He cleared his throat. "I guess the main question we've both been afraid to ask . . . we, uh, read that as many as a third of pregnancies over age forty are not viable. Is that really true? I mean, that would put the odds of miscarriage way higher than our odds of getting pregnant in the first place."

"So you know people defy odds," Dr. York said evenly. "Which are in your favor, anyway. Two-thirds or more are viable, which is a healthier stat to focus on. But probabilities *are* elevated for other complications, and early detection is key."

Brooke managed to find her voice. "What kinds of complications can you monitor for?"

"Gestational diabetes is a big one. Also hypertension, preeclampsia, placenta previa, and there's a noninvasive panorama test, the NIPT, you can opt for after ten weeks to rule out certain genetic abnormalities. Perhaps you already discussed some of these with your specialist, but it's different when it's hypothetical."

Brooke waited to feel something, anything. Elation. Fear. Awe. Concern. The white walls around her looked glaringly bright.

"Your intake paperwork said you're here visiting friends," Dr. York continued. "How long are you staying? Do you have a provider back home?"

"We're not—" Mitch did meet Brooke's eyes then, with the look of a man choosing his words carefully. "We're mid-move," he said. "So we won't be returning to our old clinic. Brooke will need . . . What I mean is, this isn't our destination. We're going overseas next week."

Dr. York's brow wrinkled. "Where, exactly? For how long?"

Brooke had to force herself to answer. This appointment was starting to feel like a pop quiz they'd been doomed to fail. "Italy, to start. But it's kind of open ended. We planned on floating around."

"I see. Well, you may want to reconsider or postpone those plans. Wherever you are, you and your fetus will benefit most from consistent care from a clinician who you can develop a rapport and comfort level with. I'm not saying you need to walk on eggshells, but a higher-risk pregnancy is a journey a good doctor takes with you. Communication is key. If you think it's tedious bringing me up to speed now, imagine doing that over and over as you accumulate more and more data to convey. Especially internationally. Another doctor might advise you differently if your trip were just for a week or two, and it would be another matter if you were relocating to a new home overseas near good medical care. But this kind of travel . . . it's at your own risk."

"That makes sense," Mitch managed. "Thank you, Doctor. We'll—thanks."

"Of course. Pleasure meeting you both." She turned to Brooke. "If you decide to stay in town, I'd be happy to continue your care. Your blood pressure today was a smidge up—probably just all the excitement, but I'd want to see you back in two weeks to be sure. Then we'd go from there. I have a partner who's on call when I'm not, and we deliver at O'Bleness, here in Athens."

Whatever part of Brooke's brain was still processing new information managed to speak up. "I know that's a small hospital," she said. "I have a friend now who's being treated in Columbus because she requires more specialized care. So . . ."

Dr. York nodded. "Labor and delivery happens in small towns every day," she assured her. "If anything comes up that we can't handle, I'll get you to someone in my network who can. For now, the best thing you can do is try not to stress. Restart your prenatal vitamins and take care of yourself. Sleep, nutrition, exercise. I know infertility patients have some practice living like they're pregnant. The difference is this time, it's not a drill."

She pointed out where Brooke should leave her gown and closed the examining room door behind her. Brooke and Mitch stared at one another, wide eyed.

Then he closed the space between them, and she remained stiff in his arms, trying not to cry. "I'm sorry," he whispered. "I feel like I reacted all wrong. I think I'm in shock." He pulled back and looked at her. "Are you okay?"

She didn't think so. She didn't know. She needed air.

"Can we get out of here?" she asked.

~

The day Brooke had flown home to Colorado and told Mitch she wanted to stop their treatment was the day she vowed to quit other things too. Even before she'd dared imagine what might possibly come next, she'd promised herself:

To quit holding back.

To quit bottling up feelings out of fear they might hurt Mitch.

To quit putting her whole life on hold in pursuit of a dream that might not come true.

Now, she was breaking every promise at once.

Because there was only one thought running through her head, over and over.

It wasn't supposed to happen like this.

She couldn't bring herself to turn to Mitch and say the words out loud. Not because they felt cruel or insensitive or ungrateful—though they did—but because they felt wrong. She wasn't supposed to be thinking like this either. She already hated herself for it, and she couldn't bear for him to hate her too.

They'd found a table at Casa Nueva, craving the comfort of an old favorite. She forced herself to munch a dry corn chip while Mitch turned his water glass in circles, swirling condensation onto the wooden table.

"I guess this is like that John Lennon lyric," Mitch said. "Life happening when you're busy making other plans." He gave a little laugh. "I just wish we'd known it was happening."

Brooke was already doing the math, flipping her mental calendar backward six or seven weeks. The salty chip conjured a memory of grease-spotted paper bags, a picnic dinner on the floor.

"That day we sold the couch," she said. "I had some sharp pains, here." She patted the side of her abdomen. "I actually worried about appendicitis, but they went away and I figured I was just being, you know, my paranoid self."

"Really? You seemed fine that night."

"Yeah," she said pointedly. "I know." They both knew it hadn't been *just* dinner.

She saw that sink in. "Is it possible to feel yourself ovulate?" he asked.

"I mean, I don't usually ovulate without the trigger shot. Maybe?"

He pulled his phone out of his coat pocket and did a quick search. "That is a thing," he reported. "It's called mittelschmerz."

Brooke looked down at her lap again. "I thought I would know," she said. "I mean, I feel nauseous, but I don't feel pregnant. I know that sounds stupid."

"Of course not," he said. "Considering we couldn't do it on purpose, why would we think it'd happen by accident?"

There was more to it, but Brooke didn't know how to explain. Through all those years of hoping, she'd always held the possibility that biological magic could be unfolding inside. She'd rest a hand on the soft, warm flesh at her core and think encouraging, loving thoughts. Sometimes she'd even say them aloud. But she felt none of that tenderness now.

She'd kept her guard up, for years, and then she'd torn it down. But the instant she took that home test in Collins's bathroom—to rule out the slimmest chance—all that rubble had assembled into some impenetrable emotional shield. Protecting herself from . . . well, herself.

"Hey," Mitch said, reaching across the table for her hand. "I know this is a lot. But it's just us. We don't have to censor ourselves or steel ourselves for all the questions our parents and friends are about to have." He smiled weakly. "We're allowed to be happy."

Brooke waited a beat to see if this was what she was waiting on. Permission.

Joy did not rush in.

Nothing did.

"It feels too early to be happy," she confessed. "I don't know if I have it in me to get my hopes up before the second trimester at the very soonest. And that feels far away. I don't like the idea of telling anyone—normally we wouldn't, right? But I know we don't have much choice. Everyone will know we wouldn't do a one-eighty last minute without a big reason."

Mitch's parents would be thrilled, of course. Thrilled and judgmental that their son's life was in no state to welcome a baby, thanks to Brooke. They'd probably lobby for them to relocate to Florida. And Brooke's own parents would be right there with them.

"Even to get this far, though," Mitch said, "is supposed to be a good thing."

He didn't say it critically. More like he was trying to convince himself too. But there were those words again: "supposed to."

The very words Brooke had lived by.

She and Mitch had done everything they were supposed to, down to stereotype. They'd procured the suburban house and fenced yard. The stable jobs, the safe sedan, the top-rated school district and well-reviewed day care nearby. She'd embraced the textbook diet and exercise program, treated her body as her temple. And then she'd turned her back on it all in spectacular fashion. While cells in her uterus had been multiplying, she'd been adopting a junk-food meal plan under the stress of so many big life changes, pulling long travel days, sleeping in unfamiliar beds, embracing all the vices of the holiday season, fresh eggnog and soft cheeses and deli trays. She hadn't merely let herself indulge in things pregnant women weren't supposed to have; she'd been existing on them almost entirely. Like some kind of anti-prenatal-health pariah.

And look where it had gotten her. Nobody would believe such a backward approach could work.

"Everything will be fine," Mitch continued. "We'll figure it out. Obviously, we're not going anywhere. Not that we can go home . . ."

They *had* no home. The utter ridiculousness of the situation hit her in waves. It was too late to call their Realtor and undo their closing. Too late to fall at her boss's feet and beg for her job back. She felt idiotic.

The only thing dumber would be to rush to put back together the life they'd dismantled, only to find out it was all for nothing. To lose the baby. Or to have tests reveal a chromosomal defect incompatible with life. Or to have her own health compromised in a devastating way that would make carrying the baby to term the kind of moral dilemma no one wanted to face.

"Look," Mitch said. "The plane tickets are nonrefundable, but maybe we can get a credit. I'll call—maybe a doctor's note would help. At least for your ticket. We could go back to my parents' house, quietly wait this out? Or to your parents'. Or we could get a short-term rental somewhere, although the more money we can save, the better. Getting approved for a loan will be . . ." His mind was running a mile a minute, whereas hers seemed frozen. "At least we're still on my work's health insurance. I could call HR, see if it's too late to undo my sabbatical. Or if there's something stateside?"

It was too much.

"I don't think we should make any decisions yet," Brooke said. "We can't discount the possibility that this might not stick. We don't want to give ourselves whiplash, you know?"

Mitch gave a little laugh. "I think we already have whiplash."

"Well, I don't want to make it worse."

"What are you saying?"

What *was* she saying? She was clearly in denial. But denial seemed safer than the alternative.

Panic.

"The doctor said I should reconsider traveling," she said. "Not you. There's no reason you can't go. Like you said, it's nonrefundable. I'll fight with the airline over my credit, but you might as well get the other half of our money's worth. And if by some miracle this pregnancy does stick, this might be your only chance to do something like that for a long time."

Mitch looked at her like she'd lost her mind.

"Brooke, the flight is in two days. I've already rebooked twice. Even if I was willing to . . . I mean, as ludicrous as it sounds to take a *vacation* . . . that's too fast to process things and make a contingency plan."

"Maybe it's better that way," she said. "If we have more time, we'll end up making a new plan, and like I said, I don't think we should. Yet."

"No way," he said. "I can't leave you to deal with this on your own."

But maybe that was what she needed. Mitch had said not to self-censor, but she couldn't stop. She didn't want to. She was too afraid of what might happen.

She needed time to process her feelings first.

Brooke had to get on with this, before she lost her nerve.

"But I'm not on my own," she said, as convincingly as she could. "I have Lucy and Marie, and Collins won't be in the hospital forever. We can't go home, I have no job . . ." Saying this aloud, an edge of panic pressed on her rib cage. She hugged herself, pressing it back down. "There's not much I can do but wait, but there's plenty you can do. So you should do it."

She thought back to that conversation with Lucy as they'd walked along the beach—God, that felt like forever ago. They'd talked in metaphors, about swimming through infinite seas, about her fear of giving into exhaustion closer to shore than she'd realized, giving up on a distance she could have crossed.

And that was exactly what she'd done.

It hadn't been Mitch's idea. It had been hers.

He wasn't thinking about that now, of course. But one day, he would. He'd see that she was to blame.

"The doctor said there could be complications," he pointed out. "If something went wrong—I can't imagine being an ocean away."

"That is always going to be a risk," she admitted. "But I'm not sure it's a reason not to go. I have the girls—you've seen how they've been there for Collins. And you could hop the first flight back if it came to that. I'd be fine. Honestly, it would probably be harder on you than me."

Her husband stared at her, taking in her conviction. Trying to be sensitive to what she wanted, putting her first. She knew this look well. He used to wear it all the time. It must have been such a relief for him to take it off for the last couple of months. No wonder he'd embraced their new plans with so much enthusiasm. Enthusiasm that wasn't just going to fade away, no matter how much he wanted it to. Instead, he'd have to store it somewhere. Somewhere that it could fester into resentment while neither of them were looking. And then what?

The truth was, the last thing she wanted to do was put Mitch on a plane without her, to stay behind with a brave smile on her face and give him her full blessing to go ahead, live a little.

But that felt shortsighted next to the terror of losing him in a slow, irreversible way.

"Why don't we sleep on it," he said finally. "We don't have to decide today." He sighed and looked around at the familiar walls of the restaurant. This place was a brick-and-mortar memory. But they'd been so determined to stop looking back, to look forward from now on.

"Tomorrow, though," he said, looking as trapped as she felt. "Tomorrow we probably do."

19

Marie

"Wow," Kyle said. "So Brooke is staying for . . . how long?"

"As long as she needs to, I guess," Marie said. They'd met for lunch in the hospital cafeteria. She wanted to see Collins before the semester started tomorrow, so she'd taken today's shift. Lucy was busy with errands on campus, picking up course materials and her new student ID, and they'd figured Brooke and Mitch might appreciate having the house to themselves.

"Mitch never struck me as a guy who'd leave the country when his wife got pregnant."

Marie didn't like the way he said it. Like he'd finally gotten one up on everyone's favorite husband. And like Kyle of all people had any right to judge their friends' marriage.

The reality was that Brooke, not Mitch, was the one behaving strangely. It broke Marie's heart, the way Brooke had lectured that they weren't allowed to be happy for her—not until she said so. Brooke had always had a cautious energy, but the shock of this unexpected development seemed to have tipped Brooke past wariness into fear. Mitch, for his part, had gone respectfully quiet, perhaps understanding his wife was afraid. Afraid to let herself believe this was going to happen. And maybe more afraid of what would happen if he *didn't* go.

"Don't be so sure Mitch is leaving until his plane is in the sky with him on it," Marie told Kyle.

His smugness depleted. "Well, at least Collins has plenty of help at the house. Have they said how long it might be before she can head home?"

That was the question on everyone's minds. "They keep saying it depends. We'll have a better timeline once she's moved to rehab, but every time she's making progress, there's some setback. She's dealing with an infection in her left leg now, and there always seem to be more scans. The nurse said something about waiting on results, and I was embarrassed to admit I've lost track of what she was referring to. All I know is some surgeon is coming to speak with us this afternoon." Marie glanced at her watch. "I have an hour."

"Come home, Marie," Kyle said.

Marie took a deep breath and did the one thing she'd been keeping too busy to do.

She looked her husband in the eye.

Exhaustion shadowed his expression, but it wasn't the bone-tired, worried kind that she'd been feeling. His seemed more exasperated. Like the look he gave the boys when they wouldn't stop roughhousing. Or, more accurately, when *Marie* couldn't get them to stop roughhousing.

"Look," he said. "That blowup we had, before Christmas—I overreacted. I haven't had a chance to walk it back, because, well . . ." He gestured around them at the fluorescent misery of a hospital cafeteria on a January weekday. "But before that, we were doing better. Weren't we?"

"Kyle . . ." She shook her head. They *had* been doing better. But if he'd reconsidered his half of that argument, so had she. And she could see that this break from their everyday problems hadn't eased her resentment. It had only put it on hold.

"I understand the point you were making by leaving," he said. "But this has gone on long enough. We can't work through things on rushed phone calls and lunch breaks. Let Lucy and Brooke take over with Collins. You've done an admirable job of being there for her, but there's no reason to uproot our family any longer. Come home, and we'll find ways to compromise."

"Coming home *is* a compromise," she said. "But only for me."

"Why? Because it's going back on this pact you all made?"

Marie froze. *Shit. How on earth did he know?* She couldn't meet his eye.

"Were you ever going to tell me about it, Marie? Do you have any idea what it was like finding out secondhand from your friends? I wanted to forget it, honestly. How do you ask your own wife if it's true—that she wants to quit you? But don't you dare tell me I'm not compromising when I'm the one who's willing to overlook this humiliation, in the grand scheme of everything else going on right now, and ask you to come home."

Tears blurred Marie's vision as she stared at the linoleum of the cafeteria floor. He was right. She should have been more direct with him. She'd clung too hard to a hope that if she removed herself from the situation, she'd stop feeling this way at all.

But she hadn't, of course.

Not even now.

She forced herself to meet his eye.

"I'm sorry, Kyle. I don't know exactly what you heard, but you're right that you should have heard it from me. We did make a pact to quit some things that were making us unhappy. Just taking stock of things at midlife, like everyone does in their own way. But I never wanted to quit *you*. I only wanted to quit doing the same thing, day after day, expecting a different result."

He tilted his head at her. "Overall, though, you're . . . unhappy."

"That's not what I said."

He stared at her skeptically.

"Our kids make me happy, I'm proud of my job, I'm grateful for all our blessings. But our marriage, the way it's all divide and conquer—does it make *you* happy? I find it lonely."

He didn't answer the question. "So you thought leaving would shift things around and make me lonely instead of you? And then you saw you had leverage? Because I was bending over backward trying to win you over again?"

She sighed. "Give me a little credit. I'm not playing games. And I wouldn't call a handful of dates bending over backward. You seemed to be having a fine enough time yourself."

He threw up his hands. "So what now? This whole quitting idea has obviously backfired for Brooke and Collins. Jury's still out for Lucy. But you're going to be the one who stays with it, huh?" When she had no answer, he lowered his voice. "Look, no one could have anticipated everything you're dealing with right now. All the more reason neither of us is in a position to change jobs right this second or move house. Coming home doesn't mean we'll never figure out solutions. But it's important to me that our marriage is between us. No one else."

He spoke with such confidence that he was right. A wave of sadness washed over Marie. "I'm not sure that's true," she said. "The boys, for starters, are very involved in our marriage."

"You know what I meant."

"Maybe. But do *you* know that the boys have more of a support network than ever? We've all been shaken by what's happened, and Lucy and Brooke have been a huge help to them—and to me. Coming home removes them from that."

He rolled his eyes. "They'll hardly be without a support network. They'll have me."

"You're going to start rotating into sports carpools and help with dinner and their homework? You won't be too tired of being in the car to haul them to Athens in the opposite direction and somehow make the whole thing seem fun and not like a long slog?"

It was the same tired argument. All Kyle could do was sigh. "I miss them," he said. And she felt for him. But it hurt, the way he said *them* instead of *you*. At the end of the day, she didn't want to teach him some lesson, or to be right about any of this, or even to stay separated.

What she wanted was for him to care. To care about what she wanted, and how she felt each night when she closed her eyes to sleep, and how they'd lost what they once had. What she wanted was for him to do something to fix this. Not to beg *her* to fix it for him.

"Normal families don't operate like this," he said quietly.

Marie saw an opening then. There would never be a better time to walk through it. "I'd like us to try couples counseling. I think we could benefit from a mediator."

He didn't exactly groan. He didn't have to. She knew his attitude toward therapy from comments he'd made over the years—that it was fine for people who needed it, but he wasn't one of them.

"Fine," he said flatly. "I'll go to couples counseling if you come home." She waited for the sarcasm that would follow this, but none came.

"Seriously?" she said.

He crossed his arms. "Don't you think people are talking? This is embarrassing. I just want it to be over."

She had to hand it to him: It was the most honest thing he'd said.

Granted, it wasn't exactly the kind of approach that typically led to big breakthroughs. But maybe a therapist could help with that.

"Great," she said, careful to keep her voice as flat as his, lest any genuine enthusiasm make him rethink the concession. "I'll set it up. What days and times might work? And where should the office be? I could find one near here, if it worked around my class schedule . . ."

He shook his head. "I can't leave work to do it—you know Q1 is always nuts. Can we find someone with virtual appointments, maybe?"

Kyle loathed virtual meetings. In fact, after the pandemic, he'd led his company's initiative to get remote workers back in the office, though Marie had begged him not to.

"You said yourself we can't work through things on phone calls and lunch breaks," she pointed out. "If this is going to work, it has to be something we make time for."

"Isn't that what we're doing right now? Finding time for it."

Marie started to object—finding was not the same as making—then thought better of it. "Fine. If they're going to be virtual, I can do them from Athens."

She didn't really mean it. She only wanted him to see that he wasn't matching her efforts. He needed to meet her halfway. But his eyes blazed, incredulous.

"You're using my busy schedule as an excuse to keep rooming with your girlfriends?"

"No. *You're* using your busy schedule as an excuse to find the path of least resistance to appease me." She blazed right back. "I thought you'd done enough of that."

Kyle pushed back his chair, leaving his lunch unfinished. "That makes two of us."

Collins was sitting up in bed, alert and smiling for the first time. Her hair was brushed smooth, the circles under her eyes were gone, and she'd traded her hospital gown for a clean T-shirt and a cardigan with bell sleeves Lucy had ordered to fit over her casted arm. Marie had been prepared to force a smile, to shake off the tension from the cafeteria, but she found she didn't have to.

What a relief to see Collins looking like Collins.

"You look great," Marie said.

"The nurses brought this magic called a shampoo cap. I'm still dreaming about a real shower, though. Or a soak in my tub." Collins looked wistful. "It's a really good one. I hope you've been using it while I'm stuck in here, missing all the fun."

"We're saving up all the fun for when you get out." This was mostly true. "Any idea what this afternoon's meeting with the doctor is about?"

Collins shifted and winced. "All I know is if I hear the word 'irregularities' one more time, I'll scream. Like there's anything regular about laying here like a cartoon character in traction."

"Does it still hurt as bad as it looks?"

"Yeah. Does it still look as ridiculous as it feels?"

Marie sensed an opportunity and didn't want to say the wrong thing. She'd been afraid to ask Brooke or Lucy if they had any doubts that Collins's mishap on the mountain had truly been an accident. But she was pretty sure they were all wondering the same thing. Hearing Sullivan's landlord talk about how Collins had blamed herself for the fire, seeing the weight of the condolences still flooding Collins's inbox, recalling the untouched state of her room at the ski resort . . . it all made Marie uneasy.

Marie blamed herself for things beyond her control all the time. Everyone did. But if Collins had had any notion, even for an instant, that she didn't deserve to go on . . . If she'd taken her own interpretation of quitting too far, to the point of no return . . .

Then this was Marie's fault too. All four of them had made the pact, but Marie had been the one living under Collins's roof, going about life together as if it were undebatably worth living. She'd seen her friend's moments of hesitation and struggle and convinced herself they were perfectly regular, solvable, rather than consider the scary reality that maybe they weren't.

Collins had made it clear she didn't want to talk about the retreat, shrugging it off or changing the subject every time they'd tried to ask. But maybe now that it was just the two of them, Collins would open up. If Marie could find the right way to ask.

There was a knock on the door, and in whisked Lucy, waving a carryout bag.

"I know it's not my day," she said, breathless. "But when I saw they had Ho Ho Cake in the student union, it seemed like a sign to come here instead of back to the house."

Collins brightened. "Oh my God. I could not tell you the last time I had Ho Ho Cake."

Lucy grinned conspiratorially at Marie. Ho Ho Cake was a campus delicacy, brought out mainly for special catered events, after which students feasted on the leftovers. It looked like an unrolled Hostess treat but tasted homemade, superior to any packaged version. Even faculty got excited over Ho Ho Cake.

"This is out of the goodness of your heart?" Marie teased. "And nothing to do with not wanting to be a third wheel with Brooke and Mitch?"

"All of the above? I feel like I'm missing all the fun when I'm not in here with you two."

"I was just saying that about not being out there," Collins said.

Lucy laughed. "Well, it can't be that none of us are having *any* fun."

"Certainly not," Marie said, holding her heaping fork of cake in the air. "Look how fun we are. And with this, your return to Athens is complete."

Lucy was already devouring her first bite, eyes closed. "Mmm," she agreed. "I texted a picture to Enzo, and he offered me a handsome sum if I could get them to fork over the recipe."

"A handsome sum," Collins deadpanned, "or a handsome sumthin-sumthin?"

Lucy rolled her eyes, but the flush in her cheeks gave her away. "Oh boy," Marie said. "You *like* this guy. And you two are still talking?"

"We never planned to," Lucy admitted. "But he checked in to make sure I got here okay, and when I texted him back from an emergency detour to West Virginia . . . well, that's not the kind of thing you just let go, like 'Whoa, good luck with that.' So, we've been texting."

"At least one of us made a connection at my singles' retreat," Collins said.

Marie met Lucy's eyes, and she could tell they both recognized the opening. Lucy nodded at her, almost imperceptibly.

"Was it really that awful, Coll?" Marie ventured. "I mean, before . . ."

Collins sighed. "It wasn't the retreat's fault. It just . . . sounded better on paper. And once I was there feeling sorry for myself, I got mad about wasting all that time and money. Not only was I at a singles' retreat hiding from the singles, but I was at a ski resort hiding from the skiing. I had to go through with *something*. So I went with what felt like the least scary thing." She took another heaping bite of Ho Ho Cake. "Obviously, my instincts need work."

Marie wondered if this explanation sounded rehearsed. Then again, Collins had had nothing but time to lay here and think about how any of this had happened.

"What about the night of your fall?" Lucy pressed her. "I know you said your memories were foggy. But can you tell us what you do remember?"

Collins flattened cake crumbs onto her fork. "I just wanted to see what it was like at the top. It was prettier than I expected. The snow was bright, and everything below was lit up . . ." She shook her head. "I guess I got distracted. I can't explain what happened."

Marie wondered if Lucy had also noticed Collins's choice of wording. Not *I can't remember*, but *I can't explain*.

Marie's eyes fell on the flowers in the vase on Collins's bedside table. The ones she and Lucy had divided from the bouquet they'd taken Sullivan. You'd never know a week had passed since they'd brought them here. If anything, the blooms looked more brilliant.

"Can you believe they're not wilting yet?" Collins said, following her eyes. "How did you two know to bring me half, anyway? Did I ever tell you I always do that, when I visit him?"

"I don't think so," Lucy said. "We just thought that knowing Sull, he'd want to share."

Collins's eyes glistened, but she smiled a brave smile. "I swear, the flowers I bring home after leaving half with Sull always last twice as long as normal. I thought I was imagining it. But now you see I'm not crazy." She looked down at her fingers, fiddling with the cord of the bed she was practically strapped to, and dropped it with a laugh. "Despite evidence to the contrary."

"Nobody thinks you're crazy," Lucy said. "But if you ever think it might help to talk to someone who is trained to help navigate this kind of grief, nobody would think less of you."

Marie felt gratitude for Lucy, who always had the right words, even if she didn't put them on paper anymore. Lucy had come the closest to stepping with Marie into Collins's shoes. They still hadn't opened the bin from Sullivan's fire. But they'd felt the weight of what it carried.

"Do you remember being rescued?" Marie asked.

She shook her head. "Nothing until waking up here. Which is probably for the best."

Marie wouldn't put it past Collins to spare them the details, saying what they wanted to hear. But that didn't make it less of a relief to hear it. Besides, Collins was under round-the-clock monitoring. On the terrible off chance she'd ever been a danger to herself, she wasn't anymore.

"Travis asked about you," Marie said. She did not add that the rest of them had taken to referring to him as *Hot Neighbor* every time someone spotted Travis looking longingly toward the house. "He said he's left you messages."

Collins nodded. "I got them. I just . . . Like I said, I feel like a dolt."

"Nobody thinks that," Lucy said. "He seemed worried, in a sweet way. It's nice to see someone else looking out for you." She patted Collins's bed affectionately and gathered up the remnants of their contraband cake plates. "Even though we're not going anywhere."

Collins raised an eyebrow. "I heard. Tell me what's up with Brooke. You hear about this kind of thing happening, but . . . what do you think they're going to do now?"

"We have no idea," Lucy said. "It's weird, because on the one hand, I'm thrilled for her. And on the other hand, I feel terrible for her."

Marie nodded. "I can only imagine how she feels. Literally. Because she isn't talking."

A knock sounded on the door, and two doctors in lab coats filed in: Dr. Singh, the orthopedic surgeon who'd taken over Collins's care from the ICU, and a balding, bespectacled man who looked like he belonged behind the principal's desk in a strict boarding school.

Lucy dropped their plates in the trash and moved to the other side of the bed, sandwiching Collins with solidarity.

"Ms. Hartley," Dr. Singh said. "Sorry to interrupt your visit." Marie liked Dr. Singh. She found his soft-spoken voice and kind eyes a balm in the otherwise sterile environment. But he looked at Collins with hesitation, as if what he wanted to discuss might be a private matter.

"I asked them to be here," she said. "Less pressure for me to remember everything you say. This concussion has scrambled my brain."

Neither of the doctors smiled. Dr. Singh closed the door behind them.

With a definitive click, the noise of the hallway faded away, and Marie had an odd impulse to fling it back open, like the lack of privacy might shield them from any bad news.

"We're here to discuss your biopsy results. Let me introduce Dr. Madison," Dr. Singh said. "From oncology."

It took Marie a second to realize what he'd said. She looked to Collins, who was staring blankly at the doctors. "You had a biopsy?" Marie asked, puzzled. "Of what?"

Collins was turning pale. "I assumed it was a mistake," she said.

Dr. Singh looked from Lucy to Marie and back to Collins, patiently addressing them all. "There was a new attending on rotation in the ICU the day of her transfer," he explained. "He was reviewing her new CT scans, to be sure the most pressing acute injuries had resolved. And he noticed a mass in her lungs. Along with enlargement of several chest lymph nodes. We immediately ordered biopsies of both areas of concern."

"You think she has *lung cancer*?" Lucy shook her head. "Collins has never smoked."

"They said there are other things it could be," Collins said quickly. "I mean, I'm black and blue everywhere. Plus, lymph nodes swell when they're fighting infection."

"We didn't want to jump to conclusions," he agreed. "But the biopsy has confirmed it. I'm sorry. This is not the news we were hoping for."

Collins kept her eyes on the doctor, blinking in confusion. Marie's eyes met Lucy's in disbelief. When Lucy reached for Collins's good hand, Marie took the other, though with the cast in the way, all she could do was encase Collins's fingertips in her own.

Dr. Madison cleared his throat, and Dr. Singh inched back, ceding the floor. "We've seen an increase in cancer in young people in recent years. Many people with lung cancer have never smoked."

Under different circumstances, Marie would have been glad to hear forty called young. But not like this. Not spoken with such sadness.

"Because there is no routine screening for lung cancer," he went on, "and because it can be asymptomatic, we often discover it by accident, in the context of treating something else. As in your case."

Collins was shaking her head again. "I haven't had a cough or anything. It can't be very advanced—can it?"

"Well, we took another look at your fractures to make sure we hadn't missed a metastatic site there. Bones are a common secondary site, and it makes them brittle. Fortunately, we've found no evidence of metastasis. But your lymph node involvement is of concern. Next steps are a lymphadenectomy and molecular profiling, which looks at the genetics of the tumor itself to inform our treatment plan. We have better outcomes with more targeted therapy."

"What stage?" Lucy asked. "One? Two?"

The oncologist pursed his lips. "Three."

Marie's heart sank. She was no cancer expert, but everyone knew early detection was key. "How soon can she start treatment?" she asked. "Are we talking chemo? Radiation?"

"The molecular profiling takes three weeks to come back," he said gently. "If there's a genetic mutation, as there sometimes is with younger nonsmokers, there's a pill you can take. If not, standard of care would likely be a combination of chemotherapy and immunotherapy."

"Isn't time of the essence?" Lucy asked, incredulous. "To keep it from spreading?"

"It is. But she has to recover from her surgeries first. Chemotherapy impedes wound healing. To be a candidate for treatment, you need performance status—that means you're up and around. The head injury has delayed that, but now that your concussion symptoms are subsiding, we'll want to get you into the ARU as soon as possible." Seeing Marie's confusion, he clarified. "The acute rehab unit. You'll need to graduate as their star student before you can go impress the team over at the James Cancer Center. I'm not saying this to scare you, but to emphasize the importance of staying motivated and focused on your recovery. Insurance won't approve systemic therapy while you're in a rehab facility."

Lucy had gotten hold of a notepad and pen and was taking notes. "What benchmark does she need to hit to get into the ARU?" she asked.

"Participating in more than three hours a day of therapy. Occupational, physical."

Lucy and Marie exchanged a look. Marie had yet to see Collins last longer than thirty minutes with any therapist before collapsing in exhaustion and pain.

"Let me get this straight," Collins said. "I need to hurry up and heal from this trauma so you can put my body through more trauma?"

He smiled sympathetically.

"And I might die anyway?" she said. "What's the prognosis?"

"Patients beat this," Dr. Madison said. "I'd caution you not to get hung up on any statistics. They don't reflect the newer targeted therapies we're having better results with. And I hear you're a tough one. Look what you've already overcome."

Collins had a funny look on her face. Marie couldn't tell if she was wishing she'd broken her leg sooner or wishing she'd never broken it at all.

She looked more like a woman who'd stopped wishing altogether.

"So I'll just keep moving from one hospital wing to another? The whole time?" Collins's voice broke on the words, like this was the hardest part of the news. Maybe it was.

Dr. Singh stepped forward again. "No. The overall goal is to get you out of here as soon as possible. Part of what they'll do in the ARU is assess how you'll navigate things at home. You won't be driving anytime soon with that leg. And even once it's weight bearing, having the opposite arm broken presents some unique challenges for getting yourself around."

"Collins lives in Athens," Marie explained, trying to keep calm as she thought of the historic house's very many historic stairs. "Does the James have a location near there?"

"Most rural patients have a long commute, unless they have the means to make other arrangements. But let's not get ahead of ourselves. You'll be in good hands, at one of the best hospitals in the country for a diagnosis like yours. Care has gotten so specialized, we want to ensure all your teams are aware of what the others are doing and working together in your best interests. Waiting isn't easy, but you can use the time to consider logistics. We have a wonderful local organization for cancer support—I'd encourage all of you to take advantage of their expertise on everything from finances to housing to transport to mental health. We'll connect you."

Collins looked so pale, Marie marveled that she was sitting up at all. Marie stared at her vase of flowers, the link between Collins and Sullivan persisting still. She hated for the couple to have this in common too—freak bad luck. One gone up in smoke, the other with lung cancer. Like she'd breathed in the loss and it had settled there, refusing to leave her.

Which was almost exactly how Collins herself had described it, without even knowing.

"Collins has an amazing support system, Doctor," Marie said, finding her voice. "Whatever she needs, for as long as she needs, we've got her."

Maybe this was the real reason the four friends' paths had come back together. Because last year at this time, Collins would have faced this diagnosis alone in a big house some ninety miles from a hospital equipped to help, with no idea how she'd manage it all. And now the answer was clear.

They'd manage it together.

Lucy put an arm around Collins and echoed Marie's words.

"Whatever you need, for as long as you need, we've got you."

20

Lucy

Lucy chose a seat in the back row of Marie's classroom, grateful to have this one sure thing to look forward to today.

She'd inquired about auditing Marie's How to Say No class on a whim when she went to wrap up loose ends at the admissions office. It was full, of course, and she'd missed the deadline anyway. But the young staffer let it slip that there was no rule against sitting in on the lectures as long as the professor gave permission.

Marie turned out to be a surprisingly hard sell. "I don't know," she'd said, frowning. "I'm flattered you'd ask, but my colleagues might find it ethically murky. Students bring vulnerability to a class like mine, and I can't have it look like I'm letting random people wander in."

"Could I just come once?" Lucy had asked. "See how it goes? I won't create extra work for you—I don't need to participate. But when I look at my course schedule . . . well, I just really need something in there that still feels like me. Especially with everything going on with Coll."

The truth was, it felt strange going ahead with the term at all, after the bombshell of Collins's diagnosis. But when Lucy had wondered aloud if she should defer her acceptance into the MBA program,

Collins had said only three words: "Don't you dare." They'd come home loaded down with brochures, then gathered for a big family dinner—originally Mitch's goodbye dinner—to digest the news over the comfort of spaghetti, salad, and garlic bread. Brooke, distraught at having missed the whole thing, had done her own consult with Dr. Internet, and they were all unmoored by worst-case scenarios and trying not to show it. When Marie's boys cried at the news, Marie reassured them that Collins was in good hands, and it wasn't their job to worry about the specifics of treating her illness. Their job was to be there for her as much as they could and to keep living their own lives in ways that would do her proud.

Ultimately, this is what had swayed Marie. "I've been curious about your class for years," Lucy had pointed out. "It feels like a waste to be here and never get to see it."

So here Lucy was. Seeing her best intentions through.

Her first day had gone better than expected so far, intimidating as it was to have the word "analytics" in two of her course titles. "Descriptive analytics" turned out to be a fancy term for "trends," and after years of trying to understand which books became random TikTok sensations, she welcomed the idea of breaking down actual cause-and-effect data. And "prescriptive analytics" had to do with assessing how a business should pivot—which, again, yes, please.

In the MBA, her classmates didn't seem as different from her as she'd feared. Some were younger, yes, but many had left jobs or taken sabbaticals to be here. She'd forgotten how much she'd loved being in a room full of people who were there to learn. Her faculty adviser had not worn a tie, like Enzo's colleagues, but a cardigan that she was pretty sure had been knit by hand. In their introductory one-on-one, he'd reassured her that she'd chosen her concentration well in project management, even calling the communications management requirement a "no-brainer" for her. And she already had her eye on the advanced Change and Risk Management course, which seemed like something she should have sought out long ago.

Better late than never.

Only now as she watched the undergrads file into Marie's lecture hall did she feel out of place. She'd known these students would be two decades younger, but these kids looked indistinguishable from high schoolers. Some spotted friends and moved to sit together, laughing about drunken mishaps over the holiday break. Others scrolled through glowing screens. Social media hadn't even factored into Lucy's original college years—thank God. She felt ancient. Maybe Marie had been right that she didn't belong here. She was considering leaving when a line of chattering girls filed into her row, blocking the path to the exit.

Stop being such a coward, she told herself.

"Excuse me?" the girl beside her said. Lucy looked up to find the whole group of girls who'd taken over her row angling over one another's heads to look in Lucy's direction. To look, it seemed, at Lucy specifically. Her hand went to her messy bun, self-conscious. Did she look as old as she suddenly felt—like their surrogate grandma?

"Are you Lucy Mayer?" the girl persisted. The others nodded as if to confirm that they'd appointed her spokeswoman, and she leaned in, rephrasing her question. "@lucymayerwrites?"

This was a new one. Lucy never got recognized anywhere. She'd never even spotted one of her own books being read in the wild. She was lucky to find them in stock in a bookstore.

Then again, she'd gone to school here. Maybe alumni publications were displayed somewhere in the English college. There was definitely crossover between language arts and gender studies—after all, that's how she'd first discovered her love of Alice Walker's *In Search of Our Mothers' Gardens* essay collection, in a women's literature class.

"That's me," Lucy said, a bit shyly.

The girls exchanged a look, like they'd *known it.* One of them squealed. And that's when she realized they weren't turning up their noses at her, or even merely curious.

They were excited.

A second girl raised her hand, as if Lucy were the professor, but didn't wait to be called on. "The @lucymayerwrites who wrote the post called 'Why I Love Books Too Much to Keep Writing Them'?"

Lucy looked, mystified, from one face to another. They knew her from her *website*? Her monthly traffic was in double digits. Not that she'd looked at it since she'd locked herself out.

"The part about detaching your livelihood from an art form that brings you joy," the first girl said, "so you can stop worrying whether it brings enough other people joy? I felt that. Deep." Her eyes widened. "Do you think I should change my major?"

The second girl tilted her head and began to recite. *"Every day, I wake up, turn my face to the sun, and wonder if I'm obsolete yet. This is not the kind of life-on-the-brink anyone sets out for."* She grinned at Lucy in admiration. "Hey, what are you doing here, anyway?"

It took a beat to process that they didn't merely know her website—they were quoting it.

And now, they were looking at her expectantly. No: reverently. Like now that they'd found her here in the flesh, she must have more to say.

"You've read that?" Lucy had never felt more confused. Especially when they all burst out laughing, eyes wide at the realization that Lucy wasn't putting them on.

"Everybody's read it," a third girl said, eyes twinkling. "You're, like, famous."

21

Brooke

"Last chance," Mitch said, "to tell me what a terrible idea this is."

Brooke looked at the long stretch of airline ticket counters, the commuters bypassing the snaking lines on their beelines for security, the infrequent travelers looking lost. A few paces away, a woman had her suitcase open on the floor, yanking shoes from between layers of overstuffed packing cubes, snapping at her husband that the bag had *not* been overweight according to their scale at home. A security officer watched them with a bored expression.

"But it wasn't your idea," Brooke pointed out. "It was mine."

Mitch stepped closer, tipping his face down until their foreheads touched. "Which is why I'm not going to be the one to call it the wrong move." His eyes searched hers. "It's not too late. Say the word, and it's off, no questions asked, no rehashing or debating. I wheel my bag back to the car, and we figure out what's next. That would be perfectly okay."

Brooke loved him for it. But they'd been over this, and she wasn't about to reverse course now. Even if the last thing she wanted was to watch him leave without her. Asking him not to go felt selfish. For Mitch, the weeks ahead held an unforgettable first foray into Italy's most beautiful ports: roaming the streets of Venice, touring palaces, window-shopping Murano glass, sampling gelato, learning to make pasta, and soaking up a culture where food tasted better, accents sounded sexier, and wine flowed freer. For Brooke, the weeks ahead held an onslaught of doctors' appointments between her OB's monitoring and Collins's toggling between ortho and oncology, each calculating her odds, both bargaining with the universe for a better deal.

"Collins needs me here," she told him, "And I need to be here. So in that way, the timing lines up. The girls will take good care of me."

The truth was, her friends could manage without her. All they could do for Collins at the moment was keep her spirits up while she awaited a treatment plan and cheer on her recovery. But Brooke knew she'd feel more helpless being far away, reading between the lines of every text message, trying to figure out how her friends were really doing. She'd been wrapped up in her own treatments for so long, she hadn't been a great friend, and now their time with Collins might be severely limited. But she couldn't think like that. It was the very definition of unthinkable.

"I know they will," he said, smiling sadly. "Otherwise, no amount of prosecco could get me on this plane. Also, Collins might rather I *not* be part of her care team. That nurse last week who assumed I was her husband and launched into her sponge bath might've done her in."

Brooke laughed. "Have you thought more about inviting your brother or someone to meet you over there? I bet he'd love to take my place for a week or two if he can swing the time off work. I mean, besides the plane ticket, everything else is paid for."

"I've thought about it," he said. "But you know, I've never traveled alone. You talk about the timing lining up and—well, I wonder if it might be the kind of thing everyone should do once. And if so . . . this is it, you know?"

"This is it," she agreed.

Not one part of her was mad about this. But she couldn't help being sad, despite herself. And maybe a little confused.

She tried to tell herself that this would be good for her and Mitch, to have the time and space to think. Mitch would never admit he was also reluctant to get his hopes up about the baby. But ever since she'd insisted they hold off on any decisions, she could tell he was relieved. She didn't know how long Mitch would stay away—three weeks? Six? More? She tried not to worry that his wanderlust would stick. This was Mitch, after all. The man who'd barely left her side since they met. The man who wouldn't have given up his job or home, let alone be standing in this airport waiting to board a flight without her, had she not suggested it.

The man who'd told her, at the start of this journey, *Wherever you go, I follow.*

"It's not too late," Mitch said, "to get a second opinion from a different doctor who might see no issue with you joining me."

They'd been over this. "It is too late," she said. "This opinion has imprinted on me."

This was certainly not Brooke's first test of her comfort level with risk. She'd seen for years how a doctor's offhand comment that barely even registered with Mitch could keep her up nights. It all pointed back to what she'd tried not to acknowledge: that their journey through infertility had never really been the same. All the restrictions had been on her, while biology cast him in a supporting role. And that was truer than ever now. But she didn't begrudge Mitch his comparative freedom. There was no sense dwelling on it.

If she was still pregnant when he booked his return ticket, they'd have had plenty of time—separately—to figure out how they felt about it and what to do next—together.

And if she wasn't . . . well, there would be no return ticket. She'd meet him in Florence. Or Paris. Or wherever he was by then. The door that had cracked back open would close, and they'd venture off into the sunset as planned. Being more careful about precautions that hadn't seemed necessary, like birth control, to avoid the heartache of future false alarms.

"We'll talk all the time," Mitch said. They'd both already promised this, but she nodded.

"I want you to have fun. The best time. And we'll play it by ear."

It was his turn to nod. "Depending on what's going on."

Surreal, how *what's going on* could signify the existence of an entire human life.

Wild, how everything hinged on so much that wasn't up to them.

"I'll miss you like crazy," Mitch said. "I love you so much."

"I miss you already," Brooke said. "I love you too."

When he gave a final wave and walked into the fray toward the security lines, she didn't move, determined to watch his head bobbing in the crowd for as far as she could see it. His stride looked reluctant at first, and twice he glanced over his shoulder. She watched him stop in front of a departures chart before he passed the point of no return at the metal detectors.

She saw the moment he smiled at the screen, his face full of the excitement he hadn't dared let show in front of her.

And she didn't miss the bounce in his step as he started out toward his terminal.

Anyone could see that.

22

Marie

The first day back to teaching always drained Marie's energy. But she rallied, picking Wade and Connor up from school and heading out for burgers and milkshakes, just the three of them. Kyle had a dinner with clients, Brooke had gone from the airport to the hospital to sit with Collins, and Lucy had a late class, leaving Marie grateful for the family time. They stuffed themselves on shoestring fries and whipped cream and were almost sated when Connor showed her his broken jacket zipper. So with that, they launched an impromptu search for a new winter coat.

Marie wondered if this would mark the turning point that would have the boys whining that staying in Athens wasn't so great after all. Though a few chain stores and restaurants had crept in, the best shopping in Athens remained the boutiques—which did little for a boy who saw the Nike swoosh as a status symbol. But the errand turned fun as the boys improvised outlandish sales pitches for the most random items they could find in Marshalls—from sasquatch boxer shorts to ceramic cow-shaped table lamps. "Believe in yourself!" Connor beseeched them, holding the sasquatch boxers to his hip, and Wade giggled so hard she almost bought them. By a stroke of luck, the clearance rack delivered, and the silence in the car was content rather than sullen on the way home.

It was dark and snowing lazily by the time they pulled up to Collins's house, one of those winter nights that felt like one long bedtime, though it was barely seven o'clock. The boys thundered up the stairs ahead of her, with Connor calling dibs on the shower and Wade calling back, "Who cares—I don't need one!" He probably did, but Marie wouldn't disturb the peace by forcing it. Even the light glowing from under Lucy's door seemed cozy. Judging from the sound of her muffled laughter, she must be on the phone with Enzo.

Lucy had finally come clean and shared photos from the last couple of months in Chicago, and Marie could see he'd be hard to walk away from. Not because he was undeniably attractive—though he was—but because they looked so damn happy when they were together. Which apparently had been way more than Marie had realized.

She tidied the kitchen, sorted Collins's mail on the counter, then added to the running list she kept in her note-taking app under Collins's name:

Find out which bills are set to autopay.

Get bank login, bring laptop?

Where checkbook?

The list kept getting longer instead of shorter, mostly because she never crossed anything off. As soon as she set foot in the hospital, everything on it seemed too mundane to bother Collins about. So, she let it wait until tomorrow. Then the next tomorrow. Though Marie knew better than anyone that problems didn't solve themselves.

She'd hoped Kyle might say he'd reconsidered couples therapy, or at least suggest another date night, but he hadn't even tried since that failed candlelit dinner a month ago. She had a sinking feeling that their brief second honeymoon was over, that any future deviations from their status quo would be similarly short lived.

She reminded herself to take one day at a time. This one had been productive in other ways, she'd been fully present with the boys tonight, and now her pajamas were calling her name.

Upstairs, she was surprised to find Wade had beat her to her room. He was curled up on her bed, waiting for her with an uncharacteristic patience that signaled something was up.

He and Connor were tall for their ages and carried themselves with a teenage swagger—a function of Connor leveling up for middle school, and Wade perpetually leveling up with Connor. But snuggled in his Super Mario PJs, hugging her comforter like it might hug him back, Wade looked exactly like what he was: a vulnerable kid away from his real home.

This was it, surely. The night he'd ask what was wrong between her and Kyle. She'd been waiting for it. She'd just wished she had an answer.

"Hey, bud," she said. "Long day, huh?"

She perched on the opposite edge of the mattress, then thought better of it and lay down, taking the pillow opposite his and curling up to face him.

"Mom?" he asked, his voice small. "Will we have to move out? Since Aunt Coll is sick?"

This was not what she'd been expecting. Marie took a minute to right her thoughts.

"Well, we'll have to move out at some point, because this isn't our house. But as far as Collins being sick, I think she's happy to have us here, keeping an eye on things."

"I like it here," he said. "Sometimes I forget it isn't our house. It feels like it is."

She smiled. "Maybe that's because home is more about a feeling than about a house." She was about to say that, for her, home was wherever he and his brother were, but she caught herself. That would leave out one key member of their family who was supposed to signify home too.

But Wade was nodding. "I wasn't sure about having Aunt Lucy or Aunt Collins around so much. It's nice, though. Kind of like having extra moms." He grinned at her. "No offense. You're the best one."

She was about to ask if the extra moms came in handy because he'd been missing Kyle, but he turned serious again.

"Is Aunt Collins going to die, maybe?" His lip quivered.

It was the "maybe" that threw her. She didn't believe in lying to kids—but shielding them from worry was part of the gig. Plus, she was kind of getting by on lying to herself right now.

"The doctors are doing everything they can to make sure that doesn't happen," she said.

"Are you sure? Because when I asked Connor, he said 'maybe.' He said that's what Dad said, man to man. But that I was too young for man to man."

A rage flared within her, and reflexively, she tried to extinguish it. Kyle had probably been caught off guard by the question. She was struggling to handle this too.

But seriously. "Maybe" was the best he could come up with?

"Dad was probably being . . . existential," she ventured.

"Does ex-celestial mean sad? Because Dad seems sad lately. Even though Aunt Collins isn't even his friend."

The mispronunciation would have been adorable if not for the troubling observation that went with it. "Existential, in this case, sort of means nobody knows what tomorrow will bring. And we'll just have to say our prayers and hope for the best." She took a deep breath, steeling herself to say what needed to be said. "Also, Aunt Collins is too Dad's friend. But I'm sure he also misses having you and Connor around all the time—it must be hard sharing us with Collins so much. I mean, you probably miss Dad too. And other things about home."

There. She'd said it.

"I mean, I've wished Dad was here for stuff like that playoff game, when you guys didn't care that Joe Burrow threw five touchdowns and *still* lost. Even though he's the pride of Athens!" Wade picked at a thread on the comforter. "But Dad missed stuff like that at home too. Besides, you guys always say everyone is happier when you take turns. And it's not true about Xbox, but it is true about Collins's house."

Marie stifled a smile. "It's important to know you can be honest with me, okay? You don't miss seeing your neighbor friends more often or having your old bedroom all to yourself? Or knowing that you don't have to pick up the phone or wait for the weekend to talk to Dad?"

"I have better friends here. And I know Connor says I'm annoying, but sharing the same room is kind of fun. Besides, I don't miss spending so much time in the car."

She looked at him earnestly. "Have you talked about any of this with Dad?"

He shrugged. "We don't want to hurt his feelings. Like I said, he seems sad."

"Who's we?"

"Me and Connor. We were so bored back at home after Collins had her fall. We knew you had to go to West Virginia, but it sucked without you. Dad kept saying we were going to do fun stuff but then was on his phone the whole time."

"I think Dad was trying to help out extra even though he had work to do, buddy."

Wade snuggled closer. "But you always have work to do," he said sleepily. "And extra is normal for you."

Marie didn't trust her voice to say anything else.

Kids had a way of making you feel flattered and floored at the same time.

All she could do was silently agree.

Extra is normal for me.

~

Downstairs, she found Lucy in the kitchen, wrapped in a blanket and pouring water from the electric kettle over loose-leaf tea. "I know it's freezing, but I need some air," Lucy said. "Want to come out to the porch swing with me and watch for Brooke? She's late."

"I will if you have enough tea for two."

Lucy reached for a second mug, and Marie gathered the throw blankets from the living room. In class today, Marie had gotten weirdly nervous about doing her thing in front of such a close friend, but she needn't have. In fact, Lucy had already been chatting happily with some other students when Marie walked in, despite her conspicuous age difference. When Marie had mentioned that an MBA student may be observing the class now and then, and that anyone uncomfortable with it was welcome to shoot her a note, nobody batted an eye. So Marie had told Lucy she could come as often as she wanted.

She grabbed winter hats and mittens from the closet, and soon they were ensconced on the porch swing beneath a mound of mismatched fleece, breathing in the steam from their mugs and swinging companionably in the glow of the porchlight.

"What's the verdict on your first day?" Marie asked.

"My professors seem great, present company included. And I love being back on campus. It reminds me of how it felt the first time." She went quiet for a minute. "Remember how we all just assumed good things would happen for us if we did the right things? Got the grades, showed up, put in sincere effort. Remember what that felt like?"

"Plenty of good things did happen," she offered, though she knew exactly what Lucy meant. If she found a nice guy, bought the house, got the job, had healthy kids, how could she end up *lonely*? And how could Brooke end up infertile? And how could Collins end up a widow, facing cancer at forty? She had to keep believing it wasn't too late for any of them to change things, though. To lean into the things that worked, and reverse course on what didn't. To fight.

"You're right," Lucy agreed. Then: "Turns out I've gone viral."

Marie glanced at her. "Come again?"

"My essay. About quitting writing? It took off. A few influencers shared it, and I guess it's become a whole thing. There's this line people keep quoting in their own videos—'Every day, I wake up, turn my face to the sun, and wonder if I'm obsolete yet. This is not the kind of life-on-the-brink anyone sets out for.' Some of the videos are sincere, but the out-of-context ones are actually funny. Anyway. My Instagram account alone picked up two hundred *thousand* followers."

"Whoa. You weren't getting notifications or anything?"

"Well, they're waiting on me somewhere. I locked myself out of all my accounts months ago."

"So you seriously had no idea?"

Lucy shook her head. "I mean, my agent mentioned a while back that some of her other clients had seen it, but a few of us follow each other, so I thought nothing of it."

"How'd you find out?"

"Some of your students recognized me, believe it or not. They're creative writing majors, but still."

Marie's eyes went wide. "Does that mean your books . . . ?"

Lucy gave an odd laugh. Somewhere between bitter and giddy. "They're getting up there in the charts. I mean, in obscure categories, but my latest has a bestseller banner on Barnes & Noble. And my debut cracked the top ten in 'amateur sleuth mysteries' on Amazon."

Marie racked her brain. "Huh. I don't remember that book having an amateur sleuth."

"It does not," Lucy confirmed. "But who cares? Last time I looked, there were more than two million books ahead of me in *every* category where I ranked. No exaggeration."

"If you climbed that many spots . . . how many copies does that mean you sold?"

"Who knows." There was that laugh again. "More than ever."

Marie turned sideways on the swing to fully face her. "Lucy! This is great!"

"Is it?"

"Of course. Is this—I mean, you have to capitalize on this, right? Call your agent and update your profiles and, I don't know, maybe Little Professor bookstore would host you for an event or something?"

But Lucy just stared straight ahead into the darkness. "I can't capitalize on my viral post about quitting my writing career by un-quitting my writing career. That's like saying the most popular thing I ever wrote was a lie."

Marie opened her mouth to object, then closed it. "I see what you mean."

But this was decades of Lucy's work they were talking about, finally getting the attention it deserved. There had to be *something* Lucy could do.

"I've been thinking about something Collins said, the night I called her to change my passwords for me," Lucy said. "She said, 'I know what it feels like to regret something. To blame yourself later.' She called it *the worst feeling*. I assumed she was talking about wishing she'd had more time with Sullivan. Wishing they'd never wasted time on stupid arguments, stuff like that. But do you think there could have been more to it?"

"You mean like what his landlord said?" Marie asked. "About how she thought Collins blamed herself for the fire?"

"Yeah. Or . . . anything. I don't know. I feel like she might have been off that night—more than that night—and I missed it. Remember how the doctor explained how they missed the abnormalities amid all the other trauma? She has so much more to deal with now. I don't want us to get so fixated on Collins's physical health that we forget to make sure the rest of her is okay."

Marie nodded. She knew Lucy was right: They needed to stay on alert. But she also knew how skilled Lucy was at changing the subject.

"If it's any comfort to know, they do routine depression screens on her," Marie said. "I've seen the forms. But," she went on more gently, "I want to make sure the rest of *you* is okay too. I still can't believe you haven't heard about this. If not your agent, you'd think a writer friend would've reached out to say, hey, you're everywhere, have you seen?"

Lucy paused before answering. "I'm thinking they have," she said. "It's not obvious I'm not on social media, getting messages. And I do have emails I haven't opened. Things with Collins have been intense . . . I didn't have the headspace for obligatory New Year's catch-ups with colleagues I won't have reason to see again. When the subject lines said *congratulations*, I thought they meant on going back to school. I never imagined this."

Marie understood. They'd all let things slide. She had the to-do list for Collins to prove it.

"Okay," she said. "Well, there must be some in-between. Maybe you could post a thank-you for the overwhelming response. If, say, someone wanted to interview you—that wouldn't be taking anything back. There are other ways to put yourself out there or keep your options open."

Lucy sighed. "I know that's what my agent will say. Right after she eats her words for asking me to take the essay down." Marie laughed, but Lucy didn't look excited at the prospect. She looked exhausted by it. "You'd think it would be a dream to have my books sell themselves while I'm asleep at the wheel," she admitted. "But this is . . . confusing."

Marie took a long sip of her tea and shivered. These blankets were no match for the cold. She patted Lucy's knee. "Well, you've gone this long without knowing about it, let alone doing anything about it. No reason you can't go longer. You're allowed to be confused for a while. We're all confused. I'm confused. Hell, Brooke is *really* confused."

A pair of headlights turned onto the street, and Marie recognized Collins's car. Collins had insisted Brooke return the rental and use hers from now on. Her heart sank a little at the sight of the empty passenger seat, though she wasn't sure why. Brooke had insisted she'd wanted Mitch to go.

Marie just hadn't quite believed her.

Lucy and Marie watched in silence as Brooke pulled into the driveway, cut the engine, and took her time crossing to the porch steps. She climbed them slowly, looking down at her boots, and only when she reached the top did she meet their eyes.

"Hey," Lucy said softly. "Mitch got on the plane? No problems?"

"Mitch got on the plane," Brooke confirmed.

Then, her face twisted in anguish, and she burst into tears.

23

Lucy

Lucy was no stranger to a hurry-up-and-wait mentality. It was the essence of life as a writer. You'd work and work toward a self-imposed deadline, only to send the pitch off and not hear back for months. You'd hear that a publisher was considering your manuscript, hoping that meant a call was coming any day, and then spend the next month staring futilely at your phone. "They have the publisher and sales reps on board," one of her friends used to quip, "but they haven't consulted the mailroom intern's girlfriend yet."

But cancer diagnoses rocketed the anxiety of waiting to life-or-death stakes. That test results could take so long when you were already inside the hospital seemed unfair. All any of them wanted was reassurance that Collins was going to be okay, but that was a story that would take a long time to play out. In fact, this story could be playing out for the rest of Collins's life. Even if she had the best outcome from treatment, even if Collins woke up a year from now cancer-free, she'd live with the valid fear that it could return. She'd always be at risk, always need monitoring. This looming specter was something she'd have to get used to.

But of course, that was better than the alternative. Which was that she wouldn't have long left to worry at all.

It was hard to tell how Collins was taking all of this. She said all the right things about taking things a day at a time. But she couldn't seem to catch a break. She'd been switched to a new IV antibiotic for the infection in her leg and had a terrible allergic reaction—not just hives, but blisters so gruesome, they'd thought she had a secondary infection at first. Brooke had gone to sit with her through her antihistamine haze and come home with a slip of paper for Lucy.

"She said a little birdie told her you might need the passwords to your accounts back."

"I sure don't," Lucy had said, pocketing the paper without looking at it. She wouldn't let her friends know she'd fallen back into her old habit of incessantly checking her sales rankings. But later, in her room, her heart had lurched at the familiar sight of Collins's handwriting.

LucyIsntFinished1 and *MarkMyWords2*.

She'd gotten straight into the shower, where nobody could hear her cry.

Then she'd woken up with a new conviction: If all Collins could do was focus on today, Lucy would focus on making it better for her in some small way. For as many todays as it took.

Which is how she came to be baking pumpkin chocolate chip cookies first thing in the morning, relishing the quiet with Marie and the boys gone to school and Brooke still asleep, in time to spy Collins's hot neighbor staring at the house again.

Lucy kept catching glimpses of him through the window over the sink. First, he walked to his mailbox, though there was never delivery this early in the day. Then he'd circled his front yard, gathering fallen pine cones and twigs. Now he had the hood of his car propped open in the driveway while he topped off his fluids. Through it all, he kept glancing in Lucy's direction, though she knew he couldn't see her through the rare January sun reflecting on the window.

Finally, she loaded a few cookies onto a paper plate and shrugged on her coat.

"Hi, there," she called, slipping out the side door. "Seems rude to bake within smelling distance without sharing."

Travis didn't bother to look contrite that she'd caught him staring. He only looked relieved that she'd manifested in front of him.

"Are those for Collins?" he asked.

She jogged down the stairs toward him, holding out the plate. "Yep. Living with preteen boys, I've learned to double all recipes."

"Thanks," he said. "Lucy, right?" She nodded. Marie had introduced them in passing, but Lucy had to keep reminding herself he had a name besides Hot Neighbor. Surveying his greasy hands, he closed the hood and took the plate. "How's our girl holding up?"

Lucy wasn't sure how much he knew or how much Collins would want him to know. But she liked the way he called her *our girl.*

"She's putting on a good face, but she's restless." Her next thought came out of her mouth before she had time to consider whether it was a *good* thought. "Hey, I'm taking these to her shortly. I don't suppose you'd want to come along?"

He shifted his weight. "I'd like to, but I don't know if . . . I mean, she hasn't invited me."

Lucy flashed a smile. "I don't think people in hospital beds usually send out invitations. The engraving takes too long."

In truth, she had no idea whether Collins would be happy to see Travis. But it would be good for Collins to see that people were thinking of her. People besides Lucy and Brooke and Marie. They'd passed along lots of supportive calls and messages, but as far as Lucy knew, no one else had visited.

"I can get someone to cover me at work, if you're sure," Travis offered. "I'll even drive. I bet you're tired of going back and forth." He looked down at the bottles of blue fluid at his feet. "Come to think of it, has anyone checked your levels? The last thing you want is to run out of windshield cleaner in winter weather. Brooke and Marie too."

Lucy turned to survey her parked car, which was indeed coated with a film of dried slush and road salt. "I hadn't thought of that," she admitted, pulling the keys from her pocket. "You're sure you don't mind?"

Twenty minutes later, Lucy had packed up half the cookies for Collins and her nurses, piled her bags into Travis's back seat, and they headed off. Even after playing mechanic, he'd managed to shower and change into a quarter-zip sweater and dark jeans. His hair was damp, and his clean-shaven face carried a pleasant whiff of Old Spice.

"What all are you bringing her?" he asked, glancing over his shoulder at the bags.

"Clean laundry," she said. "Toiletry refills. And a book by one of my favorite authors."

"You like to read?" he asked.

Lucy glanced at him to see if the question was a joke, but he was totally serious.

And why wouldn't he be? He knew her only as Collins's friend who was here for her MBA. How strange to be disconnected from the thing that had always defined her.

"Yes," she told him. "I love to read. I know Collins doesn't usually, but desperate times."

"I've seen her read plenty," he offered. "She has a friend who's an author, and she's always talking about how great her books are and how more people should read them." Lucy's face burned, and she turned to look out the window, so he wouldn't see. "Hey," he went on. "Maybe you two could form a book club."

"I'm pretty bogged down with reading for my courses," she said.

"Good for you, though. So many people think about going back to school but never take the initiative to go after what they really want to do with their lives."

If he only knew.

"So you know Collins pretty well?" she asked.

His face twitched, as if in some internal debate about how much to share. "We're friendly," he said finally. "Neighbor stuff."

"Like topping off her fluids?" Lucy asked. As soon as she said it, all she could hear was the double entendre. *What was wrong with her?* But he did a convincing job of ignoring it.

"Sullivan stayed on top of that kind of stuff," he said. "After, though . . . I offered help, but she never took me up on it. Until she had a milk snake in the kitchen."

Now here was a story Lucy hadn't heard before. "In the *kitchen*?" She shuddered, looking back on her cozy morning in a slithery new light, and Travis laughed—warmly, not meanly.

"That's exactly what she kept saying. *The garage I could handle, but not the kitchen!*" It was a pretty good imitation of Collins's cadence, and they both laughed. "She'd brought some potted plants in out of the cold, and I think it was a stowaway," he clarified.

Lucy pulled a face. "So there isn't a kitchen milk snake infestation I should know about?"

"As far as I know. But we got to be better friends after that, so I assume she was keeping me around just in case." His mouth twitched toward a smile, and Lucy laughed again.

"I'm glad she had someone she could call," she said. "She's had a hard time. Now this . . . It doesn't seem fair."

"Tell me about it." They drove on in companionable silence for a few minutes. "There is something I've been wondering," he said. "Why did she go on a retreat all by herself? What was it for, anyway?"

"For singles," Lucy said. He looked over at her blankly. "You know, like, solo travelers who are open to meeting someone? I think they had speed dating, and . . ."

She stopped at the hurt on his face. He caught himself and flushed. "Sorry," he said. "I'm just surprised. She seemed like she wasn't ready to date. I mean, she made it pretty clear."

Lucy wasn't sure what to say to that. "Honestly, I don't think she was ready. I think she wanted to be and thought she could force it. Or at least, test the waters."

Travis kept his eyes on the road, but he was blinking fast. Almost as if he was trying not to cry. That's when she realized.

Travis didn't just possibly, maybe have a bit of a crush on Collins.

This was something more.

"Sorry," she said quietly. "I didn't know. Something happened between you two?"

He half smiled, but there was sadness to it. "Since she obviously never mentioned it, I'm sure she didn't want anyone to know. So now this is awkward."

"Hey," Lucy told him. "At this point, we're all Team Collins. Whatever happened before—that was before. What's important *now* is that Collins needs all the support she can get. There's nothing awkward about that. I'm sorry if I asked too many questions."

"It's my fault, anyway," he said. "Anyone can see she's still in love with Sullivan. But over the past year, I guess I thought maybe there might be room for someone new."

"Maybe there is," Lucy said. "Maybe she just hasn't realized it yet."

"I scared her off," he said miserably. "I wouldn't have risked our friendship. It meant too much to me. But one night last fall, we both had too much to drink, and when she initiated . . . well, I wasn't strong enough to say no to that. I mean, to her. I thought we were on the same, you know—but in the morning . . ."

"She freaked out?" Lucy guessed.

He tried to smile at her again, but it came out as more as a grimace. "It was the worst—seeing someone else regret one of the best nights of your life. The last thing I ever wanted was for her to get hurt again, and I told her that. I told her we could forget it had ever happened. I would have waited. But she said not to bother. She called herself a lost cause."

Lucy felt for him. He seemed so sincere. And patient. Sullivan had been gone for years, though she knew there was no time limit on grief. Truth be told, Lucy thought Travis and Collins would be adorable together. But this explained some things. She wished Collins had told them. They could have helped her feel better about it. They could have at least listened.

"You said last fall?" Lucy asked. "When was this, exactly?"

"Right before she left for a girls' trip," he said. "She was spiraling so hard, she canceled her flight and ended up driving all the way to Hilton Head. It was a mess. I was a mess."

Time seemed to slow as Lucy tried to absorb what he'd said, what this meant.

The last thing Collins had done before joining them at the beach was sleep with this earnest, gorgeous man, and then end up—what? Ashamed? Collins had taken the whole drive to South Carolina to pull herself together, and when they'd all made their pact to quit the things making them unhappy, she'd said she'd wanted to quit hiding from this world without Sullivan. She'd cried that she wanted to move on. Had she been talking about Travis? Had she wanted to go home and try again, try harder, find a way to bring herself to pursue something with him?

And if so, why hadn't she? Why had she gone to a singles' retreat at all? To prove something to herself? To practice for the real thing waiting for her next door? Or . . . what?

"If it makes you feel any better," Lucy told him, "the retreat was a bust even before her accident. She didn't participate."

He shook his head. "You know, for almost a year, I was her go-to person, any time she needed a friend or a hand—and I loved being that guy. It could have been enough for me. And I was so blinded by my own feelings, I ruined it. I should have tried harder to make things right between us. In some backward way, this all feels like my fault."

"Trust me," Lucy said, "there's plenty of fault to go around. But none of that matters anymore. What matters is what happens next."

Silence descended for a contemplative moment. "What does happen next?" he asked.

Lucy sighed. "The first goals of inpatient rehab seem to be preserving muscle mass—because atrophy makes recovery harder—and making sure she can take care of her own basic needs. They've been working with her on things like getting dressed and to the bathroom on her own, which involves getting in and out of a wheelchair and this platform walker thing that has a place to put her broken arm, but she isn't really tolerating that yet. They're already asking a lot of questions about her coming home, like accessibility—which you know she doesn't have at all—and who can drive her all the way to Columbus for appointments. Thank goodness Sullivan left her so financially secure. Not that anyone ever wants to rely on a life insurance payout, let alone use it for something like this."

Travis swallowed hard. "That's going to be a lot."

"I know. All from one freak accident."

He mumbled something, but she couldn't make it out. "What did you say?"

He took a long time to answer. "I said, are you sure it was an accident?"

Lucy's breath stilled. "You . . . think she did it on purpose?"

"I'm not saying that." He sighed. "But I think she might have been purposefully reckless. I thought as time went on, she'd put Sullivan's tragedy in perspective. Instead she seems intent on punishing herself. Like she's convinced that if something goes wrong, she deserves it."

This tracked with what Evie had said. But if people around Collins had seen her struggling with misplaced guilt, how had she managed to hide it from the friends who knew her best?

Unless they didn't know her best anymore.

"I'm not sure I understand," Lucy ventured. "I remember burn scars on Sullivan's hands. He knew his tools could be dangerous, and he knew the barn was flammable, and surely what precautions to take. I'm not saying it was his fault either. But I don't see how it was hers."

"Exactly. When it came to paperwork, he relied on her to micromanage everything. But as far as the actual craftsmanship, he insisted on being fully in charge. It's like the longer he's been gone, the more she's conflated the two."

"Maybe that's because now she *is* in charge of the artwork," Lucy pointed out. "He gave her responsibility over everything, and it's made it harder to for her to distinguish who did what before."

Travis considered this. "I bet you're right."

Lucy was starting to feel uncomfortable with the conversation. They weren't exactly talking about Collins behind her back . . . but she wasn't in front of them either. She wasn't sure she should have invited Travis along after all. But it was too late to undo it now.

It was too late to undo so many things.

"Listen," Lucy said. "I know we both care about Collins. We'll be neighbors for a while, so I'd like to be friends. No judgment, and we don't have to ever talk about any of this again."

"Thanks. If you ever have another milk snake in the kitchen, you can count on me."

She pulled a face. "I'm going to need you never to say the words 'milk snake' again."

"So if I see one, like, behind you, I shouldn't tell you?"

"I'd prefer you apprehend it quietly so I'm none the wiser."

He laughed, and any lingering tension faded. "Deal."

24

Brooke

Brooke was absolutely fine.

Sleeping in Collins's bedroom—because it was the only one left unoccupied, and Collins had insisted she make herself at home—didn't bother her. Why should it? Just because Collins might never return home the woman she'd been, just because Collins had spent countless nights curled up staring at the same ceiling, missing her own husband who used to share this same bed, that was no reason to ruminate on how short-lived wedding vows could be when forces beyond your control intervened. It was no reason to mind that Mitch was a literal ocean away right now.

This baby, if it came, would need Brooke to be strong. Not a worried mess, and not a codependent whiner. She might as well get back in practice now.

And just because she kept looking at real estate listings in their old neighborhood did not mean she was having second thoughts about having left. Just because the asking prices made her want to weep, just because she found herself drooling over that blue Southwest sky silhouetting the mountains, did not mean she resented Ohio's less picturesque winter. And as for her longtime employer taking down the posting for her old job? That didn't make her panicky at all.

She wasn't even looking.

Except just out of curiosity.

Very often.

Not even the six-hour time difference between Ohio and Italy was a problem. Even if she and Mitch had barely spoken since he'd left because their schedules were so out of sync, and even if he hadn't sent many photos . . . well, this was Mitch trying not to rub it in.

And as her mother's name flashed on her phone screen yet again, she wasn't rattled to be fielding what was sure to be another spectacularly unhelpful check-in. She was merely annoyed.

"Brooke." Her mom never bothered with "good morning" or "hello." "How is bed rest?"

"Mom. I keep telling you I'm not on bed rest. Bed rest is something else."

"Are you feeling nauseated? I've always thought morning sickness was a misnomer, you know. When I was pregnant with you, I felt sick all day. But nausea can be a sign the pregnancy is going to take. All those hormones doing their jobs."

She could practically hear her mom wringing her hands. The woman had turned fretting over nothing into a way of life—so when something worth fretting over materialized, look out. She had a silver mane to show for it, having skipped over gray and gone white in her forties as a self-induced point of pride.

"It comes and goes," Brooke said. She did not say that she felt so unsettled about Mitch's absence and Collins's illness that it was impossible to identify the source of her nausea.

"Have you thought about my offer to come do your bed rest here? Most people do prefer Florida to Ohio in winter."

"I'm not on bed rest," she repeated. Ever since Mitch had left she had, in fact, spent most of her time in bed, when she wasn't with Collins at the hospital. But that was beside the point. "Bed rest is when you are instructed not to leave bed for most, if not all, of the day. I've just been advised against traveling to a foreign country at this particular moment. Which is a reasonable directive that wouldn't be disruptive for most people."

"Oh, but it's so disruptive for you. If you come here, Dad could make some calls about jobs. Mitch's parents would be all for it. They're only a few hours' drive away, you know."

"Mom, we fully supported you all in choosing the retirement communities that were right for you. But we're not following you there to raise our kids. That's not usually how this works."

"Well, no, but people don't usually wait until so late in life to have children. If we'd known it would ever happen . . ."

Too late, her mother seemed to realize her insensitivity. But as was often the case with Brooke's mother, she sounded uncomfortably like Brooke's own nagging fears. How long could everyone tiptoe around the fact that Brooke was in a real mess of her own making? After years of making her life textbook-ready to welcome a child, she'd done the exact thing she'd been afraid of and given up on it all a heartbeat too soon. What kind of mother would that make her?

What if she'd used up all her patience and selflessness trying to get pregnant, and now that it had finally happened in the eleventh hour, she didn't have anything left? What if she'd stayed vigilant about her marriage all those years, knowing how infertility could tear a couple apart, only to come out the other side and end up resenting Mitch now, just for enjoying the trip she'd insisted he take without her? What if a salary and a place to live weren't the only things Brooke lacked in the expectant-mother department? What if the reason her treatments had never worked was because she wasn't cut out for this?

But Brooke's mother was the last person she'd turn to with these worries unless she was looking for help worrying harder.

"I apologize that you did not have a crystal ball so you could plan accordingly," Brooke snapped. "I can't imagine how that must feel. And may I remind you that we do not know if having this child will in fact happen. I've repeatedly asked you not to get ahead of yourself."

"Honey. You know I mean well. I'm just excited, and nervous, and—well, we want to be there for you while you figure things out."

The last thing she needed was a fight with her mom. They'd always been oil and water, and people had assured her that later in life, things would even out. But no such luck. Maybe if she *had* had kids earlier, they'd have had more common ground to bond over. But she hadn't. And they hadn't. She knew the way to de-escalate was to set her mom at ease, to say *of course I know you mean well.* But she was growing tired of managing other people's discomfort when nobody seemed concerned about her own.

"Collins needs me here," she said instead, the words sounding every bit like the rebuke they were.

"I don't mean to be insensitive to poor Collins. But Brooke, if she needs radiation, can a pregnant woman even be around that?"

The hair on Brooke's arms bristled. Leave it to her mother to pinpoint something Brooke hadn't thought to worry about yet. But she wasn't ready to think that far ahead.

"One thing at a time, okay? Nobody will let me be exposed to anything unsafe. Listen, I need to get going. Please try not to worry. When I have updates, you'll be first to know."

She hung up before her mom could answer. As was becoming her routine, she hid under the covers until she heard the last person leave the house for the day. The way Lucy had blended in with the kids and Marie, like one big chosen family . . . Brooke knew they were all going through challenges too. But when she heard the kids laughing and Lucy teasing and Marie conducting it all like an off-key orchestra, she had the feeling they'd all be okay, no matter what. That it was enough for all of them, at the end of the day, to have each other.

The same could not be said for her.

And maybe not for Collins either.

She felt a stab of guilt, having told her mom she was running out the door to see her friend. It was bad karma not to follow through.

So, she dragged herself out of bed, and she went.

Collins's room was dark, her still form on the bed turned away from the door. A nurse at the desk had warned Brooke that she was not having a good day. Side effects of a new antibiotic had kept her up all night with an upset stomach. But Brooke wasn't deterred.

Not until she went inside.

Brooke had added Collins to their shared calendar app so she'd know who to expect and when. Today, Marie was bringing her boys after school, then meeting Kyle for a family dinner. So Collins wasn't expecting anyone for hours. At first, Brooke thought she was sleeping. She entered as quietly as she could, hung up her coat and purse, and was settling into the visitor's chair when she caught the reflection in the heart monitor of Collins's face—and the tears sliding down her cheeks.

Brooke sank into her chair and touched Collins's shoulder. "Hey. Rough day?"

Collins stiffened but didn't respond. Brooke pushed aside a nagging suspicion that Collins defaulted to this state of agony when no one was around. Maybe Collins had been putting on a brave face for them, like they'd been doing for her.

Maybe the facade wasn't helping anyone.

"We're quite a pair, aren't we?" Brooke asked.

She expected no response to that either. But Collins mumbled something unintelligible.

Brooke leaned closer. "Sorry, Coll. What did you say?"

Slowly, Collins shifted onto her back but kept her head turned away. "I said sure, we're quite a pair," Collins slurred, groggy from sleep or medications or both. She sniffed hard, and when she spoke again, her voice was clearer. "Me, I have two unusable legs. A broken arm, head contusions, a concussion, surgical wounds, bruises I can barely stand to look at, and an allergic rash from hell—all of which needs to heal before they attempt to poison my cancer, like some sick race to see what kills me first. And the only person I want to hold my hand through any of it is already dead."

She turned then, the look in her eyes so cold, Brooke had to fight not to look away.

"And you," Collins said, "you're pregnant. After spending many years and thousands of dollars to get that way. So yeah. We're practically in the same boat."

Brooke burned with shame. She obviously hadn't meant to compare them. Only, in the vaguest sense, that they'd made a pact together and things hadn't gone to plan, leaving them both here, alone, today, unsure what would come next.

But Collins had a right to be offended. Brooke was supposed to be here as a comfort. Not to add insult to injury. And not to intrude on Collins's personal space with her inanely crass attempt at commiseration. They'd never even asked if Collins wanted them doing all these shifts; she hadn't thought to call ahead today before dropping in. As if being confined to a hospital made you give up any autonomy. And then Collins was supposed to, what, paste on a smile and grovel with gratitude every time they showed up? While they lived in her house and slept in her bed and drove her car and took over flirting with her Hot Neighbor?

Maybe Brooke wasn't so different from her own mother after all.

Maybe her maternal instincts needed even more work than she'd realized.

"I'm sorry." Brooke's voice broke. These hormones didn't leave her a moment's peace. She wanted to hold up her head and face this, face Collins, tell her she was right, but it had been hard enough to get out of bed, and now she could feel herself crumpling, collapsing inward, tears threatening to overflow. She forced herself to keep talking. "I shouldn't have . . . You're right. And I don't deserve to be . . . This is all my own doing."

Collins's one good arm shot out so quickly, Brooke didn't even see her move. She only saw the contents of her bedside tray sent airborne—water pitcher and ginger ale cans flying, plastic cups splashing across Brooke's lap before clattering to the floor.

"Do you think," Collins growled, "this is not my own doing?"

Brooke scrambled to her feet and backward. Collins's chest heaved, her wild eyes blazed. "This is all my own damned fault!" she yelled.

The lights flicked on, and a nurse appeared. Brooke sank to her knees and began picking up the mess, but Collins had started to sob again, and the nurse moved toward them, brusquely.

"I'll take it from here," she told Brooke. "Maybe tomorrow will be a better day to visit."

Brooke stood, chagrined, and gathered her things. She turned back toward Collins, wanting to apologize again, and to offer that they'd all call ahead from now on, if she'd rather. But when the nurse returned the tray to the bedside table, Collins swatted it again and let out a throaty scream that drowned out its clatter to the floor.

Brooke wheeled on her heels, hugged her womb protectively, and ran.

25

Marie

A woman was sitting on the porch steps when Marie got home from her office hours. The mild weather had put Marie in a good enough mood to walk the two miles to campus, but she'd been out of sorts ever since Brooke's phone call warning her to rethink going to the hospital later. She eyed the woman with reluctance. She seemed familiar, but too young to be a parent from the boys' school and too old to be an undergrad. Wavy dark hair hung down her back, and her coat looked skillfully hand-quilted, with oversize cream buttons fastened at her neck. It wasn't until she stood and waved that Marie placed her.

Sullivan's daughter, Sara.

The one Marie had left messages for about Collins's accident right after it happened. The one who'd never called back. The one who ran an art gallery in Michigan and sent Collins regular letters dripping with resentment and jealousy, taking issue with every decision she made.

I wish you'd consulted me before you'd said yes to that abhorrent curator.

I know you have no obligation to us, but we'd have appreciated an invitation to the opening . . .

My sister has decided to let this go, but it would have meant so much to me and you don't seem to care . . .

Marie stopped walking.

Sara stepped off the porch.

"I'm sorry to show up like this," she said. "My husband thought I shouldn't, but . . ."

Marie crossed her arms, waiting. Sara cleared her throat.

"I was hoping to speak with Collins directly."

"She isn't here," Marie said. "Which you'd know if you'd bothered to return my call."

"But I did," she insisted. "I mean, I called her, repeatedly. And she texted back and asked me to stop. So I knew she was, you know, conscious."

"Wow," Marie said. "How diligent of you."

"I think we might have gotten off on the wrong foot," Sara said. "Can we talk inside?"

Marie hesitated. They didn't owe this woman anything.

"I drove all the way from Saugatuck," Sara said. "Please?"

Nobody asked you to, Marie wanted to say. But she nodded.

Inside, Sara apprised the living room as if this were a house she used to live in, though she never had. Marie watched her gaze linger on her father's stained glass in the windows, and on the things that didn't typically belong here—the *Diary of a Wimpy Kid* books on the coffee table and the pile of women's slippers kicked off beside the ottoman.

"How is Collins?" Sara asked.

Notifying Sullivan's daughters when Collins had been in a coma was one thing. But now . . . it didn't seem Marie's place to share more personal medical updates.

"She's got a great care team," Marie said carefully. "But she needs to focus on her recovery. We're trying not to add to her stress with questions about the estate right now."

Sara nodded. "I figured. That's why I wanted to offer some help with that."

This was what Marie was afraid of.

"It's under control," Marie said. "We have two other friends staying here. Between the three of us, we've got everything covered." Never mind that Collins might not be able to resume her job for longer than they'd imagined.

"But do any of you know anything about exhibiting art? Or about licenses, or—"

"We don't need to. We are in constant contact with Collins."

"You said you didn't want to bug her with questions."

Marie had been about to offer the woman a cup of coffee but decided that was overly polite. "And we usually don't need to," she said. "I'm just saying, if anything comes up that we can't handle, it's not as if we have to guess at what to do."

"It feels strange not to step in when this is my area," Sara persisted. "I've been trying to tell her that for months, but we can't seem to get through a conversation without butting heads."

"So you're here because you want to make amends? And not because you saw an opening to worm your way in while she's down and vulnerable?"

Sara paled. "I wouldn't . . . No."

"Like I said, I've been covering for Collins. I've seen the bullshit you've sent her. Those letters were not attempts to make her life easier. They were written by someone who is bitter, who is going out of her way to make sure Collins never forgets how displeased you are. Who is determined to rip open her scars every time they start to heal. So regardless of your expertise, you're the last person we'd call for advice. I think you should go."

Sara's expression changed from defiance to acceptance to defeat. But she didn't go. She sank onto the couch with a sigh.

"You're right," she said quietly. "Those letters were from a bitter woman who will never stop being mad about this. But it's not Collins I'm upset with. I'm furious with myself. And now that she's so seriously hurt, I couldn't let . . . Well, that's what I came here to explain."

Sara looked so nervous, Marie wasn't sure whether to feel proud or chagrined about her rant. "I'm listening," she said warily.

"My dad came to see me," Sara began, "a few months before he died. He kept asking to visit the gallery, and I kept putting him off, so one day, he showed up unannounced."

Marie smiled tightly. "Runs in the family."

She blushed. "He was full of compliments on my eye for technique and how impressed he was with where I'd ended up. Stuff I'd always wanted to hear from him, back when I was getting art awards in school and he couldn't bother to show up for the ceremonies. But by then . . . I was not in a frame of mind to be receptive. I'm not proud of how I acted."

"Does Collins know about this?"

"No. One thing Dad and I had in common: We were both ashamed of how unsalvageable our relationship proved to be. He owned up to checking out when I was a kid, and he hoped things could be better between all of us in adulthood. My sister had so little in common with him, neither of them even knew how to try. But with me, it was different. Like I'd found a way to take after him even though he wasn't around. Which should have given us a starting point, but . . . I never could figure how to get over it."

Marie followed her gaze to a simple line drawing Sullivan had done of Collins, framed on the wall. It was the kind of thing never meant for public display, an intimate note between spouses. Which was what made it lovely.

"My dad tried, though," she went on, "and I know Collins had a lot to do with that. She encouraged him not to give up with me, but every time his efforts failed—well, I think he ended up feeling more ashamed. I asked him, that last time, if Collins knew he was there, and he said, 'I don't want her to know how bad I am at this.'"

"Maybe your dad was afraid," Marie offered, "that if you rejected him enough times, Collins would start to question why and end up rejecting him too."

"Honestly? That's what I was going for. Why should he get to have everything he wanted later in life, when he'd messed up my childhood in a way I could never get back? I was unforgivably petty."

"You thought you'd have more time to make things right," Marie said, as charitably as she could. "Why are you telling me this?"

"That day in my gallery, he asked me if I'd ever consider managing his estate when he was gone. He said he'd be honored to have me do it. But I said no."

Marie vacillated between surprise and skepticism. "You said *no*?"

"To be specific, I said Collins was the only one he could trust with his legacy. I said I'd trained my whole life so I could have my own career in art that had nothing to do with him."

"Wow," Marie said.

"Yeah," Sara said. "Wow. Obviously, he took me at my word. I was awful that day. I gave him every reason to believe I'd trash his legacy on purpose if I ever got the chance."

"Hence all that language in the will, making it sound like Collins was the only one he'd trust under any circumstances?"

"Yeah. He called my bluff. Joke's on me, right?"

"So, what? You've changed your mind about wanting the job?"

Sara's eyes filled with tears. "I've regretted it every day since he died. My therapist has helped me see how it could have been healing for me if I'd said yes. I only wish I hadn't waited until he was gone to talk it out with someone who could lend perspective."

"No offense, but . . . how would Collins verify this conversation with your dad happened? How do we know you're not spinning this to paint yourself in a better light?"

She gave a little laugh. "Yeah, because it paints me in such a great light." She tried to smile sheepishly at Marie, but Marie wasn't buying it. Sara turned somber. "Besides the fact that lying about this would be a supremely sick thing to do? I guess you have to take my word for it. But when Collins had this accident, I thought she might genuinely need help. And I feel guilty that it's my own fault that she doesn't have me at the very least as a partner. Because my dad wanted it that way, if I'd been receptive."

Marie stood up and started to pace, putting distance between them. "You know, if this happened the way you said, it's not just your dad that you let down. Do you know what handling all this alone has been like for her? If people aren't pouring their hearts out about how broken up they are over his death, they're spinning conspiracy theories about what happened. The only thing that's kept her going is the fact that Sullivan asked this of her, as basically his last request. And now you're telling me she's stuck in this mess because you turned it down?"

"Yes," Sara said weakly.

"Then what's with the nastygrams critiquing her every move? You can't harass her into defying what Sullivan put in writing. It's only making things worse."

Sara shook her head. "I'm not proud of the way I've acted. I knew I shouldn't take it out on her—she's been doing her best. But this has been hard on me too. Harder than I expected. I've been hating myself over this, and my anger didn't have anywhere else to go, I guess."

"Yeah, well, she didn't deserve it."

"I know. And then with her accident . . . The idea that she could have died thinking I'm just . . . Well, that's why I'm here. I can't accept there's no way to make this right, no shot at a second chance for either of us."

Marie couldn't help it: She was finding Sara persuasive. Sympathetic, even. But this was a big judgment call. She tried to summon her most objective self. The one she brought to the podium every day.

"I need you to answer something honestly."

Sara nodded.

"Is this more about the fact that if your dad asked you the same question today, you'd say yes? And you're trying to figure out how to change your answer even though he's gone? Or is your main goal to make things right with Collins, no matter what that looks like? No matter what it means for you and the estate?"

Sara didn't hesitate. "Both," she admitted. "But when I ask myself what my dad would want at this point, there's no question he'd care most about Collins being okay. At the very least, I owe her an apology. At most, I'd like to make it up to her. However I can."

That night, the friends gathered around the kitchen table, filling each other in in low voices so Wade and Connor wouldn't overhear. The boys were upstairs playing *Minecraft*, and now and then their joyful shouts floated down to the kitchen. *Bro! Bro, no way! Bro!* Marie would never understand that game, but she did know they were building worlds, working together to safeguard their creations from hostiles. Which seemed solid training for real life.

"I'm not sure any of this is up to us," Lucy said. "Sara doesn't need our permission to visit her stepmother. We couldn't stop her even if we wanted to."

"That may be true," Brooke said, frowning, "but after what I walked into this morning, I'm feeling protective of Collins."

"Maybe we tell her Sara is here and let her decide if it's too stressful to deal with?"

"Except that reminding people how unhealthy it is to stress out totally stresses them out," Brooke said. "Ask any pregnant woman."

Lucy perked up. "So we're allowed to acknowledge you're a pregnant woman now?"

Brooke shot her a look.

"My first reaction," Marie said, "was to tell Sara this isn't the time. But what if it is? What if the things she's come to say are things Collins should hear? We haven't even processed how much help Collins is going to need. Work is such a small piece of it, compared to the basics of everyday living—but what if it does require someone who knows what they're doing?"

"If Collins could trust that she's telling the truth," Brooke said. "And that's a big if."

Lucy was nodding slowly, the way she did when she was only half listening, deep in thought about whatever story she was dreaming up. "I could try asking Travis. See if Sullivan had mentioned anything to him about Sara—you know, before."

Brooke frowned. "Are we sure Travis's visit didn't contribute to Collins being so upset today?"

Lucy shrugged. "She didn't seem all that surprised to see him. More relieved to get it over with, if anything. I got the sense from both of them it would've been weirder if he didn't eventually go, you know? Then again, I was right there the whole time—I thought about giving them some privacy, but I worried she wouldn't want that. So, the three of us just hung out awhile, and it was fine. If he hadn't told me,

I might have picked up on a slightly awkward vibe at first, but it didn't last long."

"I still don't understand why she felt like she couldn't tell us what happened between them," Marie said. She knew she was taking this too personally, but couldn't help it.

Brooke bit her lip. "I can't stop thinking about the way she said this was her own doing."

"Travis said he wondered if she'd been *purposefully reckless*," Lucy said. "Do you think we need to directly ask her if she went up on that mountain with the intention of harming herself? And if she's had those intentions again? Because the stuff that she's facing now . . . if she doesn't want to get better from this . . . I hate to say it, but she probably won't."

Marie waited for someone to tell Lucy this was preposterous. Out of line. No one did.

"I started to ask her," Marie admitted. "She laughed it off so convincingly, I stopped."

"I know you two are closest," Lucy said, softening, "but maybe that's why someone else should do it. Collins wouldn't want you to feel like you could've done something to prevent it."

"I'll do it," Brooke offered. "I have the most time on my hands. Plus, she can't flip out on the pregnant lady twice in one week." At Brooke's second mentioning of her own condition, Marie and Lucy exchanged a little smile. "While I'm at it," Brooke added, "I'll get her permission to tell other people what's going on. You said Sara is staying at the OU Inn?"

Marie nodded. "She's in no hurry to leave, said business is slow in the offseason. I guess the art scene in Saugatuck relies on tourism, and her husband works in taxes and is buried in his busy season now. She hasn't been back here since the funeral and wants to see some of the memorial installations. I don't know if we can talk her out of whatever she's going to do, but I think she'll give us time. She seems to think it'll go better if she can get us on her side."

"Zero chance of us taking sides against Collins," Lucy said.

"That would be truer," Brooke pointed out, "if we knew Collins was on her own side."

Nobody knew what to say after that.

26

Lucy

Lucy and her agent had always been friendly but professional. They did not text; they called or emailed. So it felt both more casual and unusually urgent when she saw Delia's message as she left her Wednesday morning class in Copeland Hall.

Got an interesting call about you. Can we set a time to talk?

Her stomach fluttered. Part of her resisted responding—which Delia had probably anticipated, hence the text in the first place. But curiosity was going to eat at her—which Delia would also know. Lucy didn't like being so predictable. So she pocketed her phone, zipped her coat against the cold morning, and headed toward Alden Library.

As it happened, she already had some writing to do today.

Marie had never exactly suggested she complete the essay assignments for her class. She'd only made an offhand remark that Lucy wouldn't get as much out of the class by simply watching other people grapple with the concepts.

"Well, I have been grappling for forty years," Lucy had joked. "Twice as long as those 'other people.' They don't know the meaning of grappling yet."

But Lucy knew, in a way, that Marie was right. She did her best thinking on the page. And she'd never been one to do things halfway. In retrospect, that was probably a big part of why she'd never settled down with anyone seriously in Chicago. Half of her mind had always been otherwise occupied, bothered by its inability to reach the one goal she was set on trying for.

Lucy was pretty sure Marie's writing assignments didn't constitute cheating on the pact. Technically, when she'd quit writing, she'd been talking about fiction. She'd never been one of those writers who'd diversified into more practical areas. Still, she'd been avoiding *all* temptation toward old habits. It helped that so many of her favorite campus writing spots no longer existed: Perks Coffee House, the terrace of the old student union, even her dorm on the quad. She could rationalize that dabbling in nonfiction was harmless, especially if she didn't turn the assignments in. But the pull to do it was so strong that it felt a little too pact-adjacent for comfort.

She couldn't bring herself to stop going to Marie's class, though. She wasn't just impressed by it; she was awed. In front of her classroom, Marie was no-nonsense and elegant, resourceful and graceful, a diamond tumbled smooth. Lucy knew from their years of friendship that gender studies departments had always been under scrutiny—the strain had just gotten more public in recent years, alongside other so-called diversity initiatives on campuses. Marie had had to fight for their right to exist, and she'd emerged tougher, smarter, and better informed about policy and theory. While her colleagues in more "safe" departments kept their heads down, Marie had learned to anticipate threats, to be ready with a rebuttal for every argument, a patch for every hole someone might try to poke in her syllabus. At the same time, she was considerate to her students and open to new ideas. She'd even joked after Lucy's essay went viral that maybe Lucy should give a guest lecture about "saying no while everyone's watching."

That had been Lucy's easiest no yet. She was uncomfortable with the attention as it was.

Inside Alden, she found an out-of-the-way table on one of the higher floors, dubbed "the stacks." There were nicer, newer areas of the library, but she preferred the smell of old paper. Marie had assigned the class to write about a Shel Silverstein poem, "The Bagpipe Who Didn't Say No," from *Where the Sidewalk Ends*. On the surface, it told a silly story about a turtle who falls in love with an object he finds on the beach, simply because it never tells him not to. Lucy had giggled over it as a kid, especially the bagpipe's one line of dialogue: *Aaooga.* But as an adult, the poem made her uneasy. The assignment: to interpret why.

Starting a new document felt loaded with significance. But once she started typing, the words flowed. The turtle started out as lonely and sympathetic—but his behavior raised questions about consent and lack of boundaries. If you never said no, other people might take your silence as a yes and do whatever they wanted—but the poem also showed how failing to speak up could hurt not only yourself, but others. Sometimes, you needed to show someone who loved you what was in your heart, even if it wasn't what they wanted to hear. And sometimes important messages could hide in benign places. Like in a children's poem.

She'd always imbued her fiction with truth, but now she felt herself channeling real conviction, finding compassion for both the turtle and the bagpipe. Curious, she searched and found no other analysis of this particular poem. She marveled that Marie had come up with such an insightful exercise.

She was finishing up when someone knocked on the other end of her wooden table, as if it were a door. Lucy jumped, her hand flying to her heart.

She recognized the woman from a couple of her classes. "Sorry! Didn't mean to startle you. Lucy, right? I'm Paige, project management track. Same as you, I think?"

"Yes," Lucy said, gesturing at the empty chair across from her. "Want to sit?" Paige plopped down, grinning. She looked a few years younger than Lucy, but with a no-nonsense vibe Lucy usually associated with older women who were tired of putting up with most everything.

"You did undergrad here, right?" Paige asked. "Isn't it a trip being back? Where are you living?"

"I'm staying with a friend who lives in town," Lucy said. "More like housesitting, while she's—away." Lucy caught herself. She would not overshare with the first person in her program who showed any interest in friendship whatsoever. "How about you?"

"Apartments at the end of Union. I'd have preferred a house—I miss my garden—but I'm too old to rent from a slumlord."

Lucy laughed. "I couldn't afford to outgrow slumlords in Chicago," she admitted. "My friend is a godsend."

Paige brightened. "You lived in Chicago? It's meant to be. Chicago is the reason I sat down." She pulled a flier from her sling bag with "MBA Symposium Chicago" printed across the top. Lucy glanced at the date, over a month away. "My adviser suggested I approach a few classmates who were self-employed before entering the program. He said if we assemble a panel on our unique paths to pursuing a graduate degree, he could get our costs covered to attend. And there are excellent networking opportunities there. So, I'm motivated."

Lucy was impressed by Paige's memory. Early in their core classes, they'd been asked to go around the room and say where they'd worked, but all the responses had blurred together for Lucy. Probably because she'd been more worried about how she'd come across next to the corporate ladder climbers. "I'm not sure I represent self-employment success," she said. "I'm here because that didn't work out."

"Good," Paige said. "I'm not interested in people who are here because they want to bill more by the hour. I ran a coworking hub, and I'm not going back to that either. We were all the rage before the pandemic. After that, we went from a waiting list to barely being able to *give* the space away. Plus, a lot of those gig workers are struggling now that AI is threatening their jobs."

"That I can relate to," Lucy said.

"So I read," Paige said.

Lucy pulled a face. The English majors finding her essay in their feeds was one thing. But her MBA classmates?

"Why so sheepish?" Paige asked. "Unlike most crap that goes viral, you deserved it. Anyway, I figured we could all focus on the MBA as the hinge on which we plan to pivot. They're not asking us to be disingenuous or salesy, just to share how it's been so far."

"But we just got here."

"By the end of this semester, our cohort will be half done," Paige pointed out.

Lucy took the flier and read it more closely. But she wasn't absorbing the words. Because the symposium was being held *at Enzo's school.*

Which would give her a not-at-all-contrived reason to see him.

She had tried to stop texting Enzo so much. To decline his calls, keep him at a distance. But he was so often the brightest spot in her day. He was, perhaps, one of multiple passions she had failed to leave behind. But she was finding it harder to remember why she'd ever tried to.

"I'm in," she said. "Thanks for thinking of me."

"Great." Paige handed over her cell phone. "Mind putting your number in? I'll set up a meeting to get everyone's input into our proposal. I think the application is just a formality, but I still want to do a good job."

"Me too," Lucy said, warming up to Paige more by the minute. "It's pathological." Oddly, this had been one of her biggest learnings in her analytics class so far: That she'd always been more concerned with being easy to work with than about setting parameters of her own. Of course she'd burnt out: Like the bagpipe in the poem, Lucy had never actually said no. So there was no way to know what might have happened if she had.

"How did it feel to go viral," Paige asked, "if you don't mind my asking?"

"I didn't even know it was happening. By the time I realized, it was dying down."

Paige cocked her head. "Is that a good thing? To skip over the anxiety of watching? Or do you feel like you missed out on your fifteen minutes of fame?"

That was a great question. But Lucy had always balked at the fifteen minutes cliché.

Something within her still heard *fifteen minutes* and thought it wasn't enough.

Delia's unanswered message taunted her.

"I'll let you know," she said, "when I figure it out."

27

Brooke

Brooke was still in Dr. York's parking lot when Mitch's video call came up on her phone. With it came a flash of relief that her husband was still the guy who'd always stayed by her side at the fertility clinic. She hadn't reminded him of the appointment today, but he'd kept track on his own, time zones be damned. She cranked the heat and propped the screen on the dash.

"Hey!" Mitch said, beaming at her. "Wow, is it good to see your face." It was good to see his too. He was wearing a fleece and a knit hat, sitting outside on his hotel balcony. He looked well rested in that way that people get on vacation, when they have nowhere to be and nothing to answer to. And maybe that's what made Brooke feel as if they were further apart than she'd realized. In the inset frame on her screen, her own face was stretched taut, trying too hard to look like everything was fine.

Brooke missed her husband desperately. She'd kept this longing for him in check, feeling guilty and selfish every time she caught herself wishing he hadn't gone. Now, here, it was too much. She'd looked up the distance from Venice to Ohio—7,327 kilometers, or 4,553 miles. But she didn't need metric conversions to know the space between continents was too far. She didn't want her husband out of reach like they'd been these past weeks, missing each other's calls and guessing wrong who might be awake at what time or asleep for how long. She wanted him here, in Collins's car with her, taking her hand and reassuring her the bloodwork would come back fine.

The image on the screen pixelated, and Brooke's heart seized in protest, but then Mitch reappeared clear as day. If the connection had weakened on his end, he didn't let on.

"How did the appointment go?" he asked.

She found herself unsure how to answer. It felt crass to say *Still pregnant for now* and disingenuous to sugarcoat some pat response: *It was great!*

"So far, so good," she said. "Mostly."

A weighty pause. "Mostly except for . . ."

"My blood pressure was a little elevated again. She said that could have been from feeling anxious. Which I was. But since this is the second time, they're talking about maybe prescribing baby aspirin down the road. If my readings stay borderline."

"Should we be worried?"

The nurse had frowned when she'd compared the readings in Brooke's file on her laptop. But Dr. York had exuded a practiced calm.

"They say no," she told Mitch. "They're keeping an eye on it. Could be normal, especially for my age. I keep being reminded how ancient I am when I look around at the other patients."

She doubted anything about this pregnancy would ever *feel* normal, even if it was.

Mitch ran a hand through his hair. "So much for hoping they might say *never mind*, you can go ahead and meet me over here."

Had he been hoping for that? She'd done her own research, of course, into traveling internationally while pregnant, wondering if she might reconsider, say, just a quick week in Rome near a shiny modern hospital. But while plenty of people had done it, she'd found too many nightmare scenarios of women hospitalized abroad, emergencies on trans-Atlantic flights, and insurance plans refusing coverage after a doctor's recommendation had been ignored. She'd resigned herself to this fate, in part because, deep down, she shared the doctor's hypervigilance. "So much for that," she agreed.

"How do you feel?" Mitch said. "Still nauseated?"

I feel, she wanted to say, *like nausea is the least of my problems. I feel like I've always calmed my anxiety by following the steps, sticking to the plan, and now I don't know what to do with myself. Because not only did we not plan on this happening, but we planned on it definitely not happening. I'm lost.*

"It comes and goes," she said. "I've been walking around campus, though. The fresh air and movement seem to help. And Lucy found a yoga class she wants us to do together."

"Well, that's great!" he said with too much energy. Brooke held her smile. She didn't want to answer more questions.

"You're the one with the better stories right now," she said. "Tell me everything. Make me feel like I'm there."

"Well, I'll warn you: I've gone from Rick Steves superfan to evangelist. His books are my bibles now. So I'm going to need you to convert."

Brooke laughed. "Did you get a Keep On Travelin' tattoo yet?"

"Don't give me any ideas. The guy is a godsend, especially if you're by yourself. He has a way of making it all feel okay."

That gave Brooke an idea. "Hey, that means I could follow along, right? If I look up the episodes to match where you've been?"

"Love that idea." Mitch looked over his shoulder, as if something had caught his attention below on the street. "Although, honestly, the show barely scratches the surface, you know?"

Brooke didn't know. How could she? All she wanted was some detail she could sink her teeth into, something to make them feel connected. She tried again.

"What's the biggest surprise?" she asked. "The thing camera footage can't do justice?"

He thought about it. "This sounds obvious, but everything here is *so* old. The houses we're used to calling 'historic' would seem new here. It makes everything at home seem . . ."

He caught himself, the way you do when you realize the person you're saying something bad about is related to the person you're talking to.

"Seem what?" she asked, not wanting to be either of those people.

Mitch tried again. "I just can't believe I lived my whole life without experiencing . . ." He seemed to realize this angle wasn't an improvement, and Brooke felt for him, even as something like hurt squeezed her heart. An unfamiliar sensation where Mitch was concerned. "It reshapes your worldview," he said. "Like seeing the ocean for the first time or flying in an airplane. It's not a matter of what doesn't translate. It's more about understanding that you can't rely on a translator. Some things, you need to see for yourself. I wish you were here."

She wanted to tell him pregnancy felt the same way. That all the hoping in the world didn't prepare you for what it was like, and neither did seeing others go through it or reading about it or knowing biologically how it went down. That no matter how much she tried not to connect with what was happening yet—yet—she could feel it changing the chemistry of her body, recalibrating her priorities on a primal level. That today she'd received information on the Non-Invasive Prenatal Testing blood draw that would be done at her next visit—the first one that could detect genetic abnormalities—and she'd instantly felt anxious about the outcome, in an unavoidable, un-put-off-able way that came as instinctively as breathing. Because that was her job now, as an expectant mother. Even if she didn't know their plans anymore, even as she put off the practical suggestion that they'd better make some, she was clear that if she got to see this through to the end, she'd have one priority that took precedence over everything else.

In many ways, she already did.

No wonder she was so terrified. Her whole life, she'd longed so fiercely to be a mom that she hadn't questioned whether she'd be any good at it. Naively, she'd believed that wanting to do the job would be enough. But what if it wasn't? What if, by letting go of that longing for even a second, she'd proven herself unworthy of it? What if she was already doing it wrong, worrying too much, or too little, or about the wrong things?

Mitch was out there thinking she would have to catch up with him.

But she wasn't the only one with catching up to do.

Because she was miles ahead of him in understanding how the responsibility and the shifting weight of parenthood would feel. For Mitch, it was coming.

For her, ready or not, it was already here.

~

This time, at Collins's closed hospital room door, Brooke waited to hear her friend's faint "come in." Collins appeared to be shrinking a little bit every day. She was cradling the novel Lucy had brought her, though her despondent eyes looked either bored of reading or too tired to begin. But she didn't turn away from Brooke this time.

"What did the OB say?" she asked. "Everything okay?"

Brooke flashed a tentative smile. "You're stuck in one never-ending doctor's appointment, and you're keeping tabs on mine?"

Collins half smiled back. "I can't take credit. I have this overzealous friend who put everything into an app for me."

Brooke hadn't felt zealous about much lately. It was weirdly nice to be reminded that her friends still saw her as the capable, organized, proactive person she'd always been. Even if it wasn't always a good thing.

"The appointment was uneventful," she told Collins, pulling up a chair. "Thanks for asking. So far, all I know for sure is that I'm terrible at quitting."

Collins let out a little laugh. "We all are. It's like the universe thought we were trying for reverse psychology. You quit trying to get pregnant and got pregnant. Lucy quit trying to hit the bestseller list and hit it by accident. Marie left her husband and—well, I'm not actually sure what's going on with that."

Brooke shook her head. "I think Lucy and I really did talk ourselves out of the things we used to want and into something that seemed more gettable. But Marie . . . she never wanted to get divorced. She just wanted Kyle to wake the hell up."

"And that's not happening," Collins said.

"It is not," Brooke confirmed. She took a deep breath. "And you," she said. "You tried to tell us you didn't feel like you belonged in the pact. But we didn't listen, did we?"

Collins's eyes filled with tears. She didn't answer.

"I'm so sorry about the other day, Coll," Brooke said. "I'm sorry about all of it. And for what it's worth, whenever you're ready to talk again, I'm listening now."

Collins started crying in earnest. She wiped at her cheeks with the back of her hand, and Brooke grabbed a box of tissues from the sink behind her. She handed one to Collins and took one for herself when she realized that she was crying too.

"I'm the one who's sorry," Collins said. "I'm angry at the world, but I had no right to take it out on you. I wouldn't have blamed you if you didn't come back."

"Of course I came back." Brooke leaned closer. "The pressure must be so daunting, to graduate to the next level of rehab. But you're doing so well, Coll. Most people I know would be throwing tantrums every day, and you just had your first."

Collins wiped her eyes. "Now I'll be hell on wheels. They're finally taking the cast off my arm—which means I get my very own wheelchair tomorrow."

Brooke brightened. She'd witnessed Collins attempt the one-arm push technique on the wheelchair the physical therapist would sometimes bring. So much awkward, zigzagging effort just to move a short distance across the room. "Hey, that's great."

Collins tried to smile, but the tears persisted. "That's what we've come to," she sobbed. "Celebrating a wheelchair."

"Yes," Brooke said, as firmly as she could muster. "Yes, it is. And we're going to celebrate even more when you're puking from chemotherapy. Because it will mean you are closer to done with this horrible run of bad luck."

Collins took a shaky breath. "I don't know, Brookie. It's like the threat of the cancer spreading is supposed to be this great motivator, but it's scaring me shitless. My legs don't hurt less, my headaches aren't gone, and all these benchmarks are tough, yet I'm supposed to summon the superhuman strength to conquer it all like sheer willpower is all I need. But the truth is, I'm not feeling determined. More like all of this is prolonging the inevitable."

"It's natural to feel that way," Brooke said. It was now or never. She steeled herself. "In your shoes, it might cross my mind to wish I hadn't survived the fall in the first place."

She had more to say—a lot more. But she didn't want to fill the silence.

It was time for Collins to do that.

"There's a therapist here," Collins said, "who they sent in after my outburst. She said she hears a lot of that sort of thing. Old coots saying she might as well take them out back and shoot them." She rolled her eyes. "She said they were all going to love flirting with me over in rehab."

"And here you thought you missed out on the singles' retreat." Collins rewarded her with a genuine smile. "Do you think you'll talk to her again? Was it helpful?"

"Maybe. This one nurse keeps saying someone must have been looking out for me on the mountain that day, like a guardian angel swooped in. But I didn't feel Sullivan there, and I don't know why he'd save me only so I could die slower and harder, like this."

"He wouldn't," Brooke agreed. "Must mean you aren't going to die from this."

Collins scowled. "Well played."

"I'm serious, though," Brooke said. "If you think about it, without your fall, who knows how far your cancer would have spread before you developed symptoms. By the time they caught it, it could have been too late. The fall could have saved your life." Brooke hadn't fully thought this through, but now that she said it aloud, it felt powerful. Poetic.

"Maybe," Collins conceded. "Or it could mean I spend what's left of it miserable in hospitals instead of out there, happily oblivious to what was coming."

Brooke shook her head. "I'm not sure there's any such thing as being happily oblivious. Reality would get you on the other end, where you'd give anything to have known."

"Like with Sull," Collins said.

"Like with Sull," Brooke agreed, and they fell into contemplative silence.

"Is it hard without Mitch?" Collins asked. "Like . . . you don't know what to do with yourself?"

"Like I don't know who I am anymore without him here to lean on," Brooke said, without thinking. "Like I never thought I'd have to find out."

Collins nodded. Fresh tears came to her eyes, but she held them back this time. "I loved being called Sullivan's Collins. Even Marie let it slide, though she normally would've had a field day with that sort of thing, because she saw for herself that no one meant that I belonged to him. It was more like I had tamed the beast. He'd been in such a bad way before we met—I downplayed it, because you'd have wondered what I saw in the guy. I know Marie heard all the rumors on campus, though. He drank too much, his ex and his daughters despised him, his students feared him, and it was only a matter of time before his womanizing got him into trouble. But nobody ever called me Sullivan's Collins until after his reputation did a one-eighty. I never actually did anything to turn him around, you know. He just did it. I was so much younger than him, and he was not going to let me become some cliché. The first time I stayed over, I woke up to him boxing up all his liquor to give to a friend. And that was that. But I never asked him to."

"You can still be Sullivan's Collins," Brooke said. "For as long as you want to."

"That's the thing. On one hand, I have to stay Sullivan's Collins, who would never let his legacy down. But on the other, I'm just Collins Hartley now, and I have no idea who that is. To be honest, I haven't wanted to know."

"So making the pact with us was kind of like trying to have it both ways?"

Collins hesitated. "You know how you said Marie doesn't really want a divorce? She just wants things to be different, and that might end up being the only way to get there?" She shook her head, like Marie's example barely belonged in the same room. Except that they'd forced their problems into the same basket.

"I know midlife doesn't turn out for most people the way they plan," Collins said. "But I got a late start. And it was worth the wait. Because as I approached forty, there was nothing in my life I wanted to quit. Not a damn thing. But that fire quit it all for me. And where do you go from there?"

"Were you still feeling that way," Brooke asked quietly, "up on that mountain?"

"Going was a mistake. I knew I wasn't ready for that retreat," Collins said. "There was this thing with Travis—" She studied Brooke. "You already know, don't you?"

Brooke nodded, and Collins squeezed her eyes closed. "Most people in my shoes would love to have someone like Travis there for them. But I'd rather panic and run off to see if strangers are less scary. Spoiler, they're not." She gave a hollow laugh.

"Why didn't you tell us what happened between you two?" Brooke asked. "We hate to think that it was bothering you the whole time we were in Hilton Head, and we had no idea. It might've helped to talk through it."

Collins shook her head. "Maybe it would've. But I thought I knew what you'd all say."

"That forty is too young to be celibate for the rest of your life?"

She gave a weak laugh. "Exactly. I'd already told myself that . . . but it still felt wrong. Like I'd ruined everything. Both between me and Sullivan's memory *and* between me and Travis. The worst part was that after, I missed Travis a lot. I think I knew how he felt all along, but I could pretend not to know . . . until I couldn't."

Brooke smiled at her sadly. "None of that is anything to be ashamed of, though."

"Isn't it?" Collins sighed. "Do you know there's a true crime podcast about the fire? People have wild theories about who wanted Sullivan dead. Rivals, colleagues, students, me . . ."

"Absurd. Was there any real, fact-based question that it wasn't an accident? Ever?"

"Never," Collins affirmed. "It is absurd, and everyone knows it, but it still bothers me. Point being, shame doesn't always make sense, Brookie."

Brooke wasn't sure if they were getting further away from the point or closer to it. "Just because you think you know what we'd say is no reason not to talk to us when you need a friend," she said, as gently as she could. "For me, I never wanted to talk about my infertility, for a lot of the same reasons. But whenever I did, I usually felt better."

"Yeah," Collins said. "Maybe I was scared that I still wouldn't."

Brooke was afraid of the same thing. But she wasn't going to back down now. She took a deep breath and asked Collins again. "What really happened on the mountain, Coll?"

Collins looked her square in the eye. "I really can't explain it," she said. "My last clear memory is of how pretty it was, like the snow was glowing in the dark. So peaceful. And I was thinking I was glad I took a chance and went up. I felt grateful for the perspective." She shook her head. "Now that we've talked it out, I can only conclude that was the moment Sullivan's ghost pushed my ass off a cliff to make sure my cancer got cured." With that, she smiled. A real, genuine smile. "You're right," she said. "Saying it out loud *does* help."

And then, Collins started to giggle. A contagious, maniacal laugh that began to build. Brooke couldn't help it: She found herself laughing too. What else was there to do? It all sounded so beyond what any one person could possibly comprehend, let alone live through. They laughed until tears rolled down their cheeks. Finally, Collins pulled herself together.

"Sorry," she said. "Man, that felt good. I mean, it physically hurt. But I needed that."

"Me too," Brooke said. Impulsively, she pulled Collins into a hug and, for the first time since Mitch had left, felt lighter. Even with their pact falling apart, it had reunited her friends when they'd needed each other most. It was all so circuitous, and so messy, but finally Collins had opened up.

She just hoped it wasn't a mistake to believe her.

"I want you to remember how glad we all are that you're okay. Marie and her boys and Lucy and me and Travis. We love you. Promise you'll talk to that therapist again? When you're feeling low?"

Collins nodded.

"Good." Brooke leaned closer. "Because I don't want any confusion about what kind of quitting we've been talking about. Quitting on rehab or oncology isn't on the table."

Collins smiled wistfully. "Before my accident, you really were all so inspiring. You were killing it. Pivoting into your setbacks, being true to yourselves . . . I admit, I was a little jealous, bringing up the rear."

"If it's any consolation," Brooke deadpanned, "we've totally fallen apart since then." Collins laughed. "Speaking of," Brooke said. "Sara showed up yesterday, hoping to see you."

Collins's face registered surprise, then suspicion.

"I know. We almost sent her packing. But after talking with her, and now with you . . . I think it might be worth hearing her out. Are you open to that? We didn't tell her any details of your diagnosis without your permission."

Collins looked like she was going to object, but then she looked around the room as if to acknowledge that there would be no better time. "Why not," she said. "Go ahead. Maybe she'll go easier on me. She has been incredibly difficult."

Brooke nodded. "She admitted it, for what it's worth."

"Seriously? Maybe I should fall off a mountain more often."

"No need," Brooke said. "It's turning out one fall goes a long way."

28

Marie

Marie stood on tiptoe in her garage, cursing the too-high shelving, angling for a grip on the storage bin from Sullivan's landlord. Now that Sara had resurfaced, Marie figured she'd put off looking inside long enough.

"Need a hand?" Kyle's voice startled her, and she turned to see him standing in the open bay, a silhouette against the driveway. She hadn't heard his car pull up, but she squinted into the nightfall and saw the familiar sight of her van and his sedan side by side. Hers the functional workhorse, his sleek from the car wash, where his premium membership kept him client-ready.

"Yes, please," she said. "This was much easier to get up here than it is to get down."

Kyle hoisted the bin to the garage floor. If he was either bothered or delighted to get home from work and find her here, it didn't show.

"What's in here?" he asked.

She told him, and a somber silence fell over the garage as they both stared at the bin.

"It's always strange," he said finally, "seeing what survives a disaster. Like on the news, after floods and tornadoes, how the things you thought were sturdy are warped beyond recognition, but then there's a stuffed animal or a framed photo that's unscathed. It's the little things you don't expect that break your heart."

He raised his eyes to meet Marie's, and the glowing domes of the overhead lights seemed too bright, illuminating the relics of their family's rapid growth. The too-small bikes waiting for the next garage sale. The gear from sports the kids had lost interest in—the brief stint in tee ball, the askew Fisher-Price basketball hoop, the starter skateboard peppered with peeling stickers. And the tool bench where Kyle kept things he meant to fix. The broken desk lamp and the towel rack and the cracked plant stand that used to hold herbs in the sunny patch on the deck.

Things, she couldn't help but notice, that mostly belonged to her.

"You're home from work early," she said.

"I had a headache," he said. "I haven't been sleeping well."

"I'm sorry," she said automatically. He looked at her expectantly, like it was her turn to admit that she couldn't sleep, either, that nothing felt right away from home.

But while lying to him had once seemed kinder, she was trying to stop lying to herself.

He turned his attention back to the bin. "How long has this been out here?" he asked.

"A few weeks. A month? I didn't intend to keep it. Collins couldn't face it, and then it turned out I couldn't either. But his daughter is in town." She shivered. "Will you stay for this?"

Kyle dragged over two stools from his workbench, and they each perched on one. Marie unsnapped the bin's lid, and they winced at the smell of smoke damage. Half the bin was taken up by a small set of metal file drawers, the kind that might sit atop a desk or tuck underneath. They were locked. She gave them a shake but couldn't tell whether anything was left inside.

"Got anything that could pry these open?" she asked.

Kyle carried them to his workbench, where he rummaged through his tools. She peered into the bin again and extracted a blackened stainless-steel tumbler, her heart twisting at the art college's laser-cut logo on the side. She set it on the concrete at her feet, where she began arranging the other findings: a semicircular marble plaque commemorating his years on the Contemporary Arts Center board, a large geode that had been cut into two bookends, and an assortment of engraved metal placards that had once been affixed to frames. Finally, there were a few once-gorgeous pieces of clay-fired ceramic: an oversize bowl with an unfortunate chip in its ruffled edge, a vase with hairline cracks in the enamel, and a small mug that was the most intact of the three. Marie wasn't sure whether to feel comforted or disappointed that Collins really wouldn't want any of this. She'd been right to guess that the pain of the fire damage would outweigh any sentimental value.

But she stopped when she turned over the cup and saw the artist's stamp on the bottom. SAUGATUCK, MICHIGAN. Where Sara's gallery was.

Maybe there was one thing worth keeping after all.

"I'm going to order a lock picking kit," Kyle said. He held up his phone screen, with a video tutorial playing on mute. "Can this wait a couple days?"

"Of course," she said. "Thanks for your help."

She loaded everything but the mug, the plaque, and the geodes back in the bin and secured the lid. "I'm going to bag these up," she told him. "There's some bubble wrap in the basement."

"How about a glass of wine?" Kyle suggested.

"I thought you had a headache."

"I do. But you could probably use one after this."

"I could," Marie agreed. "Thanks."

A few minutes later, the salvaged items were safely sealed in her trunk, and Marie and Kyle perched at the kitchen island, nursing two glasses of wine.

"So you think Collins might want that mug?" Kyle asked.

"No. But his daughter might."

She filled him in on Sara's visit, and how Marie and Brooke had later searched Sullivan's home office but found no evidence to corroborate Sara's story. They found, however, that he'd kept tabs on her career as a curator. He'd printed out articles where she'd been featured or interviewed, some with handwritten notes in the margins, where he'd asterisked a quote or underlined an artist's name. The overall tone did seem to be approving.

"She's lucky you heard her out at all, after everything she's put Collins through," Kyle said. He set his glass down. "Why did you?"

Marie took another long sip before answering. "If she'd shown up before the accident, I wouldn't have. But filling in for Collins has made me see things in a different light."

"Different how?"

"I used to think she just needed time to get over the worst of her grief. But now that I've seen what it's like for her . . . I'm not sure she ever will. Not like this. I understand why she felt trapped, because I don't see a way out for her either. But I'm not sure managing the estate is healthy for her. And we all know Sara has been part of the problem. So if there's any chance she could also be part of the solution, I'm willing to listen."

"Are you worried that Collins isn't going to fight the cancer? That she'd rather just . . ."

Marie looked away. "She'll fight it," she said. "But it works better if your heart is in it."

A silence descended over the kitchen.

"Speaking of which," Kyle said. "I looked it up. This Living Apart Together thing."

Marie raised an eyebrow. "And?"

"And I can understand the appeal for couples who meet later in life. Their kids are in high school when they get together, and they don't want to rock the boat . . . I get it."

"But not for us?" she asked.

"But not for us," he echoed.

"I can't force you to try it."

He rolled his eyes. "I think you already have."

"No. I mean embrace the idea and see how it goes."

He shook his head. "Split houses can be hard on kids. It's not what I want for ours."

"Have you asked them if it's hard on them?" He shot her a look, and she raised her hands in surrender. "Honest question. Living in a house with tension isn't good either."

"Not for kids or adults," he agreed.

"Well, I've looked more into what it would mean to apply at OSU. I didn't want to make wrong assumptions about how difficult it would be to give up tenure." He waited, and she really did wish she had better news for him. "Unfortunately," she said, "higher ed will always be susceptible to politics, and everyone has been freshly reminded of that. The prevailing feeling is, if you have a job, hang on to seniority for dear life. And if you don't, good luck getting one."

"What about leaving academia?" he said. "Running a women's center or a nonprofit?"

She waited until she could see him answer his own question. Those sectors were faring no better. She'd never set out to do anything other than empower students trying to understand their role in the world. But she couldn't control how people saw her. And she wouldn't stop being who she was.

He did not offer that he had looked at jobs in Athens or that he would try. Nor did he point out that Brooke and Mitch were currently bridging an Atlantic-size divide, while Marie and Kyle acted as if a ninety-mile gap might as well be the distance between two planets.

He just rubbed his temples, like the headache was getting worse thinking about it.

Marie knew the feeling.

"Any ideas of things you might try?" she asked, trying not to sound as angry and defeated as she felt. "Or are all your suggestions for me?"

He opened his mouth, then shut it. Had she really expected him to have an answer?

"Look," she said. "I want to do whatever we can to work through this. But I need to feel like *you* feel that way. It takes two."

"You're the one who left," he said. Like that was all the response she needed.

Marie had learned a lot since she'd made the pact. She now knew how good it felt to have supportive adults under the same roof, confronting problems together and making each other feel seen and heard at the end of the day. And she'd learned how resilient her kids were. She'd learned that there were more important things than a job, but that if you were lucky enough to have a career that brought you purpose and fulfillment, it could become a part of your identity that could be hard to shake. And she'd learned that even the best-laid plans could be beyond anyone's control.

But Kyle didn't seem to have learned much at all.

29

Lucy

"Why, Lucy Mayer." The smile was audible in Delia's voice. That's how Lucy knew her agent wasn't as mad as her texts made her out to be. "You've become a hard woman to get ahold of."

She'd put Delia off with surprising ease for weeks. In Chicago, Lucy had only had her own to-do list to worry about, mostly built from guilt that she wasn't writing fast enough, cleverly enough, or lucratively enough—but even so, she'd tackled her deadlines on her own time, in her own space. Here, her coursework fluctuated at the mercy of her professors, her adviser, and Paige's prep strategy for MBA Symposium Chicago. Marie's boys had started their indoor soccer season, and Lucy and Brooke tagged along every Saturday as a cheering section. Collins had finally transferred to rehab, where her regimen was so painful, Lucy made it a point to always visit with some wellness-boosting treat: a protein smoothie or aromatherapy oils or a calming app with positive affirmations. If Lucy wasn't doing homework, she was combing cancer message boards or taking the boys sledding when they had a snow day off school and Marie did not. If she wasn't curled up by the fireplace with Marie and Brooke at the end of a long day, she was giggling on the phone with Enzo, thinking they ought to stop this soon.

All of which was to say: She did not have to distract herself from calling Delia back.

She lived in a perpetual state of distraction.

But this time, when Delia rang, Lucy was nursing a coffee stout at a table in the window of Jackie O's, reviewing notes for an exam in her evening class. Before this brewhouse had been built, a fire had destroyed much of this block, but a restaurant called Skippers had once held roughly this spot, where her creative writing workshop used to meet at long tables overlooking this stretch of sidewalk. The idea of finding herself here now and declining a call from the literary agent she'd dreamed of having then was too much.

"Sorry," Lucy told her. "In my defense, I did quit this job."

"You downgraded it from a job to a hobby," Delia corrected her. "Hypothetically, if you were going to write another novel, have you given any thought to what it might be?"

"I haven't had time for hypotheticals," Lucy said. "Or hobbies. I'm earning a fast-tracked graduate degree in an entirely new field."

"I wouldn't call it entirely new," Delia reasoned. "Publishing is a business. It's just taken longer than we hoped for someone to recognize you as a master."

Lucy rolled her eyes, but she was smiling. "Going viral does not constitute mastery of a writing career."

"True. But having your publisher beg you to come back does. Especially when you haven't even pitched them an idea, but they want to publish your next novel anyway. For triple your last advance."

"You're kidding." The last she'd heard from her publisher, they'd explained that their "directives had changed" in a way that no longer included her.

"I don't have to tell you this kind of thing does not happen," Delia said. *Not at your level,* she did not say. *Not with your track record.*

"What kind of novel do they want, exactly?" Lucy asked, unable to help her curiosity.

"The same as your others, but different," Delia said. "Same thing they always want."

"They didn't always want it from me, though," Lucy pointed out.

"Your backlist is selling like hotcakes, baby. It's a whole new ball game. So tell me: What would it take for you to go back out on that field?"

Lucy laughed. "Um. For them to reimburse my tuition? I'm pretty locked into my current path at the moment."

She could practically hear Delia's shrug. "So do both."

She said it like it was easy. Like Lucy could set her own deadline, make her own list of demands. Only then did it occur to Lucy that maybe that was exactly what was going on here.

Maybe she could.

But no, she couldn't.

"We did this unit in class," she told Delia, "about the promises every business makes to customers. How it's better to overdeliver than to overpromise. How the worst thing you can do is make them feel you've lied to them."

Delia laughed. "See?" she said. "I told you it's no different from writing. You already know how to do that, Lucy. Your plot twists are fair, your characters change in satisfying ways, and you keep the unwritten contract you made with the reader when she picked up your book."

"Exactly," Lucy said. "Then you understand."

"Understand what?"

"Why I cannot write another novel. It would mean my essay—the most popular thing I've ever written, by a long shot—was a lie."

She waited for this to hit Delia the way it had hit Marie. For Delia to see the depth of the problem through a lens that wasn't obscured by dollar signs and alluring phone calls from people she normally had to chase down for a response.

Instead, Delia said: "Bullshit."

Lucy blinked. "The essay," she reminded her, "was a proclamation that I'm done."

A silence fell over the line. But when Delia spoke again, her voice had lost its polish. This was the real Delia. The one you'd get over a beer at Yankee Stadium on a Saturday.

"No, it wasn't," she said. "That essay was a proclamation that a sometimes-brutal industry was breaking your spirit, that you were burnt out and exhausted and your heart wasn't in it anymore. It was a vulnerable confession about how much you longed for the day you could let yourself love writing again, and *that* is what resonated most. It didn't take off because people who love books the way you do wanted you to quit. It took off because people saw you for who you are—a kindred spirit. A creator and lifelong dreamer who found herself down on her luck, through no real fault of her own. You want to talk about broken promises? I'd say your essay showed how the world we're living in, and the business we're writing in, broke its promises to you. Until you couldn't find a reason to continue anymore."

Delia paused, letting that sit, and Lucy became aware of the ambient noise of the tavern before the dinner rush. Glasses clinking, waitstaff chatting, nobody hurrying quite yet.

"But now you have one, Lucy," Delia said. "If you think people who are buying up your backlist aren't going to cheer you on if you find the heart and strength to write something new *despite* the truth of that essay, well, you need to go back and reread your own words."

Classes must have let out. Students filled the sidewalks outside the window. Lucy took in their young, hopeful faces, their limber bodies that moved with their whole adulthoods ahead of them, all their biggest goals waiting to be realized, all their gravest mistakes waiting to be made. Then, she let herself do the thing she'd avoided ever since she'd dragged her U-Haul back here. She wondered if she might have gotten things right the first time after all.

If maybe the only thing she'd done wrong was to run out of patience.

"Actually," Delia said, "that's not a bad idea. I want you to go back and reread some bona fide Lucy Mayer storytelling. Not the essay, but the novels. The ones that lit you up, before you got into your own head. The ones that felt like the good stuff. The hell with how well they sold or what anyone thought of them." Delia laughed. "God, it feels good to say that to a client. You have an opportunity here, Lucy. I can buy you time, if you promise to at least consider it. In the fifteen years I've represented you, I've never asked you to do anything you didn't want to. But will you please keep an open mind? Then we'll talk and see where we are."

Lucy's mouth had gone dry, but she nodded absently. Maybe—maybe—running out of patience needed to happen to spur her into action.

Triple her old advance was still a modest sum. But this had never been about the money. It had been about faith and support and needing readers to know she existed at all.

Now, they did.

"Okay," Lucy said. "You've given me a lot to think about."

"Likewise," Delia said. "Here I thought I was almost as jaded as you were."

"Watch it," Lucy teased. "You're not allowed to quit on me now."

"I won't if you won't," Delia said.

Afterward, Lucy sat looking blankly at her analytics notes. She knew she had to get to class. But it no longer felt like the most important test she'd be taking today.

She was on her way out when she spotted Marie and Sara at a back-corner table. Still reeling from the conversation with Delia, she wasn't in the mood to see anyone. But Marie was already waving her over.

Only as Lucy neared the table did she see that Sara had been crying. But she was smiling through her tears as she dabbed at her eyes self-consciously with her soggy napkin.

"Lucy, you remember Sullivan's daughter, Sara?" Marie said. "From the—" She caught herself before the word "funeral," and Lucy and Sara both nodded quickly, eager to move past it. "Lucy is staying at the house while she gets her MBA."

"Of course. Did Marie show you this?" Sara asked. She held out a dirty kiln-fired mug with some lettering Lucy couldn't make out stamped into the glaze. "My dad bought this in my gallery the last time I saw him. For this to be one of the only things to be pulled from the fire . . . don't you think it means something? I mean, don't you think it has to be a sign?"

Lucy tried not to recoil as she realized what she was looking at: not dirt, but ash. Only now, at her own visceral reaction, did Lucy understand that Collins had been right not to want it in her house. And that Marie had been right to retrieve it anyway. Because Sara was taking comfort from this object that had been there with her dad at the end.

Grief was like that, Lucy had noticed. Different for everyone. You had to learn to know yourself, and you could only take your best guess at what might work for everyone else.

Lucy and Brooke had been home last night, Marie's boys asleep in bed, when Kyle had called to say he'd pried apart that file cabinet and found the contents incinerated. Whatever Sullivan had seen fit to lock away was gone now, without a trace. "It makes you think," Marie had said, "about what parts of your life you want to preserve. Doesn't it?"

Lucy had believed in signs once. Who was she to tell Sara that she didn't anymore?

Besides, maybe she did. Maybe she'd just stopped seeing them after she made up her mind not to.

"Lucy?" Marie's voice was gentle. "Are you okay? You look a little pale."

“I’m fine,” Lucy said. “Just late for class.” She turned back to Sara. “I’m glad it found its way back to you,” she said, inching toward the door. “I think your dad would like that.”

She figured it was what she’d want to hear in Sara’s shoes.

It barely mattered that there was no way to know if it was true.

30

Brooke

Brooke had traded the rhythm of her walks in the mountains for the uneven sidewalks and brick walkways of Athens. In Colorado, she'd had a series of trails mapped around elevation gain—nothing too strenuous, minimal fall risks. Here, nestled among the gentler Appalachian foothills, she varied her route daily, taking in a side of the town she'd never appreciated before. In Collins's neighborhood, the porches held none of the empty kegs and beer pong tables that earmarked off-campus housing closer to Greek life and the bar scene. Houses were more likely occupied by faculty, university staff, the usual middle-class families—nurses and real estate agents, managers and contractors—and creatives who'd fallen for the place and never left. Brooke liked trying to guess who was who. Their yards were a mash of the domestic and the eclectic, from kitschy gnome enthusiasts to scrap-metal sculpture junkies, from hippies with macramé planters to millennials favoring propane fire tables. She never ran out of new things to notice, from house cats curled in bay windows to old VW buses peppered with bumper stickers. She was grateful for every curious detail, the more unexpected, the better.

They were all welcome alternatives to the new set of worries weighing on her mind.

Not the baby. Not the future. The state of things with Mitch.

When he didn't call when he said he would and texted some excuse later, she walked.

When he said his brother was meeting him in Rome for a week after all, she walked.

When he said he was rearranging his itinerary to meet some old coworkers passing through, she walked.

She walked through missing him, through trying to be happy for him, through being more upset with him than she had any right to be. She walked through her own evolving complicated feelings about the pregnancy and the fact that Mitch wasn't here to share them. She walked through her envy when he said he'd met new friends at a vineyard tour and had been invited to off-season Capri, where they had a tip on a skipper willing to lead rare winter excursions to the Blue Grotto. She walked through her frustration that some of these friends appeared to be women, and she didn't want to sound jealous by asking if they were single.

She knew it was all probably lonelier for Mitch than it looked. In Collins's house, she always had someone to talk to, surrounded by friendship, love, laughter, and family. Mitch wasn't here, but he'd be back, and she tried not to wish away time with everyone else. Once, Travis met her out front and asked if he could join her on her walk, and they had a surprisingly nice chat. She could tell he was walking through some things, too, which made him easy company.

She was rounding the corner one afternoon when she heard a forceful *thunk thunk thunk* coming from the direction of Collins's house. As she quickened her strides, the thunks got louder, until she was picturing Paul Bunyan axing trees in the backyard. She tore down the driveway, ready to demand answers—and came face to face with Connor, kicking a soccer ball as hard as he could against the side of the garage, his fists clenched and his face red, as if daring anyone to stop him.

"Can I play?" she asked. He thrust his hands into the pocket of his hoodie.

"I'm not *playing*," he grumbled, as if insulted by the implication.

She nodded solemnly. "Can I have a go, is what I mean. Looks cathartic."

Skeptically, he tapped the ball in her direction. Brooke contemplated the angle and took a running start. She didn't let herself think about how lame it would be to whiff it—and she didn't have to. The inside of her gym shoe made contact, and the ball arched toward the wall and bounced back at Connor in a perfect ricochet.

"Bet," he said, and when he kicked the ball back, he let out a yell. He still wasn't smiling. But he no longer looked about to cry.

Brooke caught the bounce with her knee, then cried "Hi-yah!" as she smacked the ball into the bricks. This time, it flew so high Connor had to jump and catch it. "It's not karate, Aunt Brooke," he teased, sending it flying again with a growl.

Years of avoiding reminders of what she couldn't have had made her rusty on what it took to relate to kids this age. But she instinctively resisted the urge to coax him to talk about whatever had him worked up.

"Bazinga!" she yelled, kicking the ball even harder, and this time Connor laughed, positioning himself for a header back at the wall. The ball rolled at her feet and she kicked it again, ready with her next battle cry. "Hooyah!"

"Fire!" he grunted, shooting it back.

They went on that way, alternating their rallying words between silliness and fury. "Attack!" "Charge!" When she yelled "Skibidi," Connor had to pause and collect himself, he was laughing so hard.

"Do you even know what that means?" he asked.

"I think it literally means gibberish," she said.

"Gibberish!" he echoed. *Whack.*

"Ohio!" she cried with glee. *Whack.* That one shut them both down laughing, and when the ball rolled at Connor's feet, he picked it up.

"Want to go for a walk?" she asked.

"You already went for a walk."

"I could keep going."

"Can we walk to the gas station and get French vanilla cappuccino from the machine?"

Brooke peered at him suspiciously. "Aren't you young for cappuccino?"

"Mom says it's more like vanilla-flavored cocoa. She used to let me get it for the long drive home from practice on cold days."

This ritual seemed more significant than the drink, so Brooke decided not to question it.

"Okay, then. Should we invite your brother?"

"He's at a birthday party."

They set off. Brooke stole a look in his direction, but he kept his head down, hands jammed in the pouch of his hoodie, his cheeks pink from the exertion and cold. What kind of mother would she be if she didn't have the presence of mind to make the kid put on a coat?

"Rough day?" she asked casually.

A full minute went by before he answered with a shrug. "People were just saying stuff."

"What kind of stuff?"

"Asking if we live in Athens for real, and why Dad isn't here, and if Mom is a lesbian now."

The laugh escaped Brooke before she could stop it. "Do they think she's a couple with me or Lucy?"

"I told them you're my aunts, but then PJ said his dad said everyone who teaches women's studies is a lesbian. He said they're the only ones interested in studying women."

Brooke wasn't sure where to start with that. "Wow. PJ's dad sounds like a catch."

"PJ has never been taught respect," Connor said, with such adult seriousness that Brooke guessed this wasn't the first time he'd come home with stories about things PJ had said. At least the kid still listened to his mom enough to quote her earnestly. "Anyway," he said. "Nobody believed me that my parents weren't getting divorced. They said they just aren't *yet*."

"Does the living arrangement bother you? Or does it only bother you that people are asking about it?"

"I just want to be normal," he said.

"There's no such thing as normal," Brooke said. "But I get it. I remember thinking that was important when I was in school too."

"What if they're right?" he said. "What if my parents do get divorced?"

"Well, back to my question. Are you unhappy being in two houses right now?"

"No," Connor said. Even he looked surprised at how quickly he'd answered.

"What about your mom and Wade? Do you think they're struggling with it?"

He stopped to think about this. "I think things are less chaotic now for them too," he said. "Even if that sounds backward to say."

"Well, then I think that no matter what happens, you'll be okay."

He kicked a pebble out of the path, more gently than before.

"Isn't it weird that I don't think it's weird? Because, like, everything my friends are saying is technically true. No offense, but most people don't end up living with their mom's friends and thinking their dad is actually more fun when he doesn't live with them. But it doesn't feel wrong to me."

Brooke wasn't sure whether this conversation would make Marie proud or break her. Maybe it was both. Maybe everything was both, once kids were involved.

Little by little, she was remembering why she'd wanted them so badly.

Letting yourself see what you'd been missing could do that to a person.

It was daunting, too, knowing that this moment with Connor could really matter—not just for him, but for her. What he needed were the very maternal qualities she'd been doubting in herself. Instinct and insight.

"Maybe it doesn't feel wrong to you because it isn't wrong," she told him. "Families don't have to look the way other people expect them to. They don't even have to look the way you expected. And it's okay to feel sad about that. But I think it's great to have two parents willing to try different things to find out what works best for all of you. Whatever that ends up being, how it feels to you is a million times more important than how it looks to other people."

Connor shot her such a grateful smile she knew that, for once, she'd said the right thing.

And maybe she'd been talking to herself too.

Because a jobless pregnant woman with no permanent address and a husband abroad was no authority on what families should look like.

But for an instant, she'd done a convincing job of sounding like one.

All the doctor did was innocently ask where Mitch was. Normal exam room small talk. There was no reason for Brooke to start crying.

But once she'd started, she couldn't stop.

Maybe it was the NIPT blood draw making her emotional, even though Mitch had suggested he fly back to be with her for the test results two weeks from now and she'd refused. *That's like signaling to the universe that you expect the results to be bad,* she'd insisted. *Nobody crosses an ocean just to confirm things are business as usual.* Maybe she'd been more thrown when Dr. York flagged her blood pressure again, because trying to calm her own pulse only made Brooke feel caught in a helpless cycle of stressfully ordering herself to stop stressing.

Or maybe those excuses were like hormones—convenient scapegoats for harder truths. Because she felt so responsible for every little thing happening inside of her. And even at his most supportive, Mitch simply . . . wasn't. Before she knew it, she was blubbering their life story while the doctor calmly handed her tissue after tissue. The more she talked, the more she realized what she hadn't dared to say. She wasn't most worried that Mitch wasn't here now, exactly, or that he wouldn't come back when the time was right—rather, she was worried what would happen when he did. Because he was having the time of his life without her. She, on the other hand, was undergoing a serious reality check. And after he returned, nothing here would look the same. To either of them.

She was getting used to the idea of the baby. But what if Mitch came home feeling *more* torn about the whole thing? And what if she didn't stop resenting his time away once he returned? Parenting involved inevitable sacrifices—little daily concessions and big, life-altering compromises. She was finding this one hard to swallow, and the baby wasn't even here yet.

"What makes you think anyone finds it easy to swallow?" Dr. York asked. "Having kids doesn't mean you'll stop wanting other things. And wanting other things doesn't mean you won't be wonderful at raising kids."

"I just . . . I know that not following my husband on his European detour sounds small in the grand scheme." She sniffed miserably.

"Sure doesn't. Especially not knowing where you're going to live or when he might be back. You know," Dr. York said, "there is no reason you and Mitch can't spend time abroad after the baby gets here. People do. In fact, if you're interested in moving around with kids, it can be easier when they're not in school yet, with their own social lives and sports and whatever else. There can be wonderful benefits to early exposure to other cultures and languages. As long as you provide for their needs, you can do that anywhere. All they really need is you."

Brooke gave a nervous laugh. In a way, this seemed laughable, the kind of thing someone who knew nothing about infants might suggest. Except that it was coming from her ob-gyn, of all people.

"Appealing, yet intimidating," Brooke said. "I wouldn't know where to begin. I probably seem like a flake to you, but before I came here, I'd built my entire life around becoming a parent. The only thing missing was the baby. Now I might end up with nothing but the baby."

The doctor smiled. "That's why building your life around parenthood is a slippery slope," she said. "But building parenthood *into* your life, people find new ways to do that all the time."

It might have sounded like a platitude, but the doctor's expression was warm and earnest.

And the message sounded eerily similar to what Brooke had told Connor on their walk.

Families don't have to look the way other people expect them to. How it feels to you is a million times more important.

Dr. York scribbled on her prescription pad and handed it over. "This is a group I've heard good things about—they have a message board, a newsletter, everything. So you don't have to know where to begin: You can watch and learn and ask questions and see what you think."

Brooke looked at the paper: *Have Baby, Will Travel.*

"There are two branches that I know of," the doctor said. "Have Baby, Will Travel US and Have Baby, Will Travel Worldwide. No harm taking a look."

Brooke was pretty sure she'd used the exact same words when she'd floated the idea to Mitch, all those short, long months ago. When she'd found herself here alone, she'd assumed she'd been wrong. It certainly didn't feel like *no harm* was being done.

But maybe the jury was still out.

She thanked the doctor, like she did after every appointment. But this time, she meant it.

31

Marie

Marie had been looking forward to dinner with her friends all day. Their divide-and-conquer approach was efficient, but it didn't leave much time for them to all be in one place, especially not with Collins. It reminded her of an old proverb: *If you want to go fast, go alone. If you want to go far, go together.*

Collins was meeting with a nutritionist tomorrow about ways to nourish her body through recovery, so tonight she'd requested one last greasy pizza. Travis, who knew the owner of Goodfellas, had pulled strings to get them a giant sheet of bakery-style pizza, complete with an industrial insulated carrier on loan. They'd only ever ordered Goodfellas by the slice at the late-night counter, so this was adulting at its finest. They swung by Court Street for the pie, dropped the boys with Kyle, and sang along to an old playlist on their drive to the rehab hospital.

As they rode the elevator to Collins's floor, they were still dancing to the Backstreet Boys, miming their moves into the reflection of the door.

But when the doors opened, a woman burst in, sobbing, not even waiting for them to file out. The woman had her hands over her face, and Marie had to tilt the pizza carrier to slip past her into the lobby. That's when she recognized the quilted coat under the woman's arm.

"Sara?"

The hands lowered, and Sara's eyes—so much like Sullivan's—squinted at them through tears, looking mortified. Then, she lunged for the button to close the doors between them.

Marie stood in stunned silence, bookended by Brooke and Lucy, as the elevator descended without them.

"Uh-oh," Brooke said. "Did we know she was coming today?"

"We did not," Marie said.

Lucy had a funny look on her face. "You did tell her," she asked, "not to bring that thing you gave her anywhere near Collins?"

A bolt of panic shot through Marie. Of course she had. Hadn't she?

"I mean, it went without saying," she stammered. "Right? She knew the backstory. You don't think . . ." Marie felt lightheaded. Her grip on the pizza faltered, and Lucy took it from her.

"Let's not assume," Lucy said calmly. "Maybe that had nothing to do with us."

"Right," Brooke agreed. But Marie could tell her friends were worried. They moved as a unified front toward the door to Collins's room. It was open. Quiet. Nothing outwardly amiss. Maybe Brooke was right. Maybe Sara had gotten emotional seeing Collins in her condition for the first time. Or maybe the visit had brought up feelings she'd managed to hold in until she'd made for the elevator. Marie only hoped Collins was okay. They'd done what they could to facilitate peace talks, but if Collins wasn't open to reconciling, Marie could hardly blame her.

They stepped into the doorway. Collins sat in her wheelchair, looking out the window. It was hard to gauge her expression in profile.

"Pizza delivery," Lucy announced, crossing to set the box at the foot of the bed. Brooke followed with the bag of plates and utensils and brownies for dessert. So Lucy and Brooke weren't in Collins's line of sight when the wheelchair pivoted toward the doorway.

But Marie was.

Never had she seen such an icy expression in her friend's eyes. These were eyes that had made up their mind. Eyes that might never thaw in her presence again. Lucy and Brooke turned and registered the drop in temperature. They all hung suspended in the instant before irretrievable things were said. But Collins's gaze remained frozen on Marie.

"I've let you live in my house as long as you wanted," Collins said quietly, then swiveled toward Lucy. "All of you. I actually felt better knowing you were there—driving my car, eating my food, making nice with my neighbors." Lucy's face reddened, and Collins turned back to Marie. "I trusted you to answer my calls. To speak for me. To bring me the things that mattered. But at no point do I recall asking you to override me with decisions about *my* life."

Marie cleared her throat. "Nobody has overridden anything," she said uncertainly. "I'm not sure what this is about, but—"

"It's about you betraying my trust." Collins's tone maintained a frightening level of control. "You more than anyone know how I feel about Sullivan and his legacy and my role—as his manager, sure, but more important, as his wife. When I first found out you let Sara into my home, I understood why. I didn't expect you to throw her out or tell her off, because that would have crossed a boundary. And boundaries are important. Boundaries," she said, raising her voice an emphatic decibel, "are all I have left."

"What did Sara say?" Lucy asked. "What's happened?"

Collins didn't acknowledge her. "Now I find out that not only did you go behind my back to pay a visit to his landlord, when I was crystal clear that I *did not want* Evie's messages addressed, but you've handed over the results of that visit to his daughter to use against me."

Marie lifted her hands. "Hang on," she said. "Nobody is plotting against you. And I didn't go behind your back. We were just getting Evie off your case. We didn't bring anything she gave us into your house."

"You offered to get the things, and I said no."

Now Lucy and Brooke were looking wide-eyed at Marie. She floundered. "I offered to go *with* you, and you said no. I never took it to mean you wouldn't want it handled at all . . ."

"God forbid we let Evie throw them away on her own. Now Sara is convinced she has some bogus proof that he initiated a completely different conversation about her, not me, allegedly managing his art estate after he was gone. Because why not give the person who's been making my life hell more ammunition?"

"Come on, Coll," Marie protested. "You know me better than that."

"Do I? I know you're obsessed with this quitting pact, though you're the biggest coward in it. You've convinced yourself that if you focus on helping everyone else quit, then you won't have to face up to it yourself. You know what they say: *Those who can't do, teach.*"

Tears came to Marie's eyes. False accusations, she could take. But the truth hurt.

"Hold up," Lucy said. "I was with Marie that day. She really was trying to help. Neither of us thought being there was taking some loophole. Obviously, we wouldn't have done that."

Collins was unmoved. "Forgive me if nothing seems obvious to me anymore. Seriously, Lucy. Have you even told Marie and Brooke you have a book deal on the table?"

Marie couldn't hide her surprise. "You do?"

"She does," Collins confirmed. "I'm not sure if she's scared you'll talk her into it or scared you'll hold her to the pact. All I know is that somehow this supposedly empowering agreement we all made has twisted her around to think she has no choice but to throw out the baby with the bathwater if she wants to stay true to herself. Which cannot be right. Can it?"

Collins wheeled over to her bedside table and thrust a pile of papers at Marie. Her hands shook as she squinted down at them, but her eyes were too blurred by tears to see. "What's this?"

"The writing assignments Lucy has been doing for your class. I talked her into letting me see them, and it will come as no surprise that they're amazing."

Marie's mouth went dry. Lucy had been doing the assignments? Without showing her?

But Collins wheeled around again, this time on Brooke. "And you. You're lucky enough to have a husband who is an absolute dream, and you're behaving as if it doesn't matter that he's gone off without you, or how long he stays gone, because you have an infinite amount of time left in your future together. You all seem to have forgotten life can be unexpectedly short, even as I sit here with cancer that has an alarming fatality rate. And we're all pretending we haven't looked that up. We're all pretending every breath I take might not be *the* breath that spreads those lethal cells into my bloodstream while I'm waiting to start treatment already. You're all so proud that if it wasn't for the pact, I might not know about my cancer. But at least I'd still be standing on my own two legs, enjoying the life I have left."

"Sorry," Brooke said, and she did look sorry, "but you were not *enjoying* your life, Collins. If you were, you wouldn't have made the pact in the first place. And you're one to talk about taking good men for granted when you have Travis waiting in the wings. Every day, I watch that poor guy stare at your house like a lost puppy, and all I can think is how amazing it is that you could have another shot at being adored like that. If you ask me, that's what you're really afraid of. You're not worried that Sullivan wouldn't want you happy with someone else—we all know he would. You're afraid that if you let yourself love again, you might lose it again, one way or another. But you can't quit on love, Coll."

"Pretty transcendent for someone who won't let us acknowledge her pregnancy," Collins snapped. "At least Marie has the self-awareness to know when she's being a hypocrite."

"Thanks," Marie said drily.

Collins pointed a finger at her, a gesture that seemed to require a depressing amount of effort. It wasn't fair for one human to have to recover from so much at once. The strain of it gave the outburst urgency, like this was less about Collins getting things off her chest and more about things she thought they needed to hear, even though she didn't have the energy.

Because she might never get it back again.

"Way back when this was all just an idea, you're the one who said you were tired of feeling like a fraud in your class. But all you've done is add more hypocrisy. Because now our resident professor has lectured us about sticking to our guns and following through, all while keeping your own life in limbo. Remind us what you've quit, exactly? You all think I'm the one who botched this the worst—and yeah, I have the outward bruises to show for it. But at least I didn't hide behind any of you as an excuse for my behavior instead of owning my choices."

Marie couldn't deny evading Kyle. But she didn't like how Brooke and Lucy were looking at her with something like pity.

"That's what you all think of me?" Marie asked. "I mean, haven't we all backpedaled? Lucy, you would have told us about your book deal if you knew what you were going to do about it. And Brooke, you're already finding out that the second you have kids, no decision is just about you anymore. I can't let a deal I made with my friends dictate what's best for them."

"So you're the only ones making decisions that matter," Lucy said. "I mean, I chucked my entire career, but nobody cares except for me, right? Not my agent or my readers or the great guy I left behind in Chicago. And apparently not any of you."

Brooke was crying now. "I thought you and I had gotten closer through this," she told Collins. "But the whole time, you had all this resentment. Is this what you wanted, for us to turn on each other? Well, great. Now we can go from only having each other to having no one."

"What I wanted," Collins said, "was to rely on my friends during my medical crisis to step in and be there for me without stepping *over* me to run my life. This can of worms you've opened with Sara cannot be undone. We're not dumb college kids anymore. It's one thing for me to lay here in this bed and keep my opinions to myself while you all fuck up your own lives, but I'm not going to let you fuck up mine too."

"Collins is right," Lucy said. "I thought this was going to make us all braver. But I don't feel like I've done anything brave. Only impulsive and reckless." She turned to Marie. "You might feel like your stakes are higher with Kyle and the kids, and you might be right. But you haven't done anything irreversible yet. Whereas Brooke and I, we've given up a lot. And I'm not sure I made the right call." She shook her head. "No wonder we're still so afraid. All we did was give ourselves bigger things to fear. What happens next with my writing or my MBA or anything else is no one's decision but mine. You can count me out of the Quitters."

Brooke sniffed. "Me too."

"I'm not sure I was ever really in," Collins said. "But I'm definitely out now."

Marie's unease was solidifying into an uncomfortable suspicion that even in this cruel moment, these women could see her more clearly than she'd seen herself. How had she been so wrong about so much? How could she begin to make this right?

Marie wiped at her tears. "Guess it's every woman for herself now," she said.

She was tired of feeling so confused. But maybe that was because she had, indeed, spent too much time worrying about her friends' problems and not enough working through her own. It shouldn't matter to her if everyone else was done with the Quitters Club. Let them be.

She was just getting started.

32

Lucy

The MBA Symposium in Chicago came not a moment too soon. Lucy was eager for the escape from the awkward silence at Collins's house. They weren't fighting, exactly—they were exceedingly polite to each other, which was worse. Lucy was starting to understand how Marie and Kyle had stayed in limbo for so long; having Connor and Wade around kept the adults on their best behavior, but did little to ease the discomfort that had followed them home from Columbus. Lucy suspected nobody was mad at anyone in particular; they were mostly upset with themselves. What they needed was space to figure things out, and they tried to take it behind closed doors—but they were still too on top of one another, always in earshot, breathing the same tense air. March had arrived at last, but it still seemed as if winter would never end.

Paige had rented a van for their "Self-Employment Perspectives and the MBA" panel's seven-hour drive to Chicago, with Lucy riding shotgun to help avoid toll roads into the city. Their group got along, though they weren't really friends outside of class. Lucy's favorites were Paige and Gina, an outgoing woman who'd operated a smart array of side businesses from her country corner store until her property was earmarked for a new state route. Gina intended to use the payoff to start up an all-female trucking business called Broad Street with her wife, a long-haul driver. The panel was rounded out by Mick and Whit, two uncommonly earnest frat-guy types who had sold their organic microbrewery for an eye-popping sum. Everyone called them the "Brew Bros," which Lucy thought they were good sports about until she'd realized that had been their brewery's actual name. The symposium would kick off with tonight's Thought Exchange dinner, where they'd join their faculty adviser, who'd flown out the night before.

Enzo would be there too.

Excited to see you, he'd texted that morning. Any chance you're getting in early enough for a pre-dinner meetup?

If she'd known her room number, she'd have been tempted to text it to him right then—but it felt scandalous, not knowing where they stood. Besides, she was sharing a double occupancy with Paige. She couldn't justify the cost of the single, as much as she craved solitude now that things had gotten so tense at home. Enzo had his own apartment, anyway, and hadn't invited her there. Why should he? Their staying in touch had just sort of happened, but they'd never discussed what it meant. She looked forward to his messages and calls nearly every day, but she wasn't sure if he still viewed her as anything but a good friend.

"Lucy," Gina singsonged from the back seat. "I hear you have a boyfriend in Chicago."

Lucy turned to give Gina a side-eye and burst out laughing. Gina had one pink-legging-clad leg stretched lazily across the van's middle seats, while the Brew Bros were cramped into the third row, their heads nearly grazing the ceiling.

Gina grinned. "Womanspreading," she said. "It's the new manspreading."

Mick laughed good-naturedly. "We lost a bet," he explained. "Fair and square. And Lucy has been holding out on us?"

"He's not my boyfriend," Lucy corrected. "We dated briefly before I moved here, but not seriously."

Gina raised an eyebrow. "Has he dated anyone since you left?"

"I don't actually know."

"Hmm. And have you dated anyone in Athens?"

"No, but . . ."

Lucy's phone chimed. It was a picture of Enzo holding up a lanyard to display his symposium badge, flashing a big cheesy smile. A gorgeous cheesy smile.

"Oh my word, is that him?" Gina was half out of her seat, looking over Lucy's shoulder. "That is not the face of a man who isn't hoping to get laid."

"Gina!" Lucy covered her face.

"I can't see the picture, but she's right," Whit said helpfully. "No such thing as a man who isn't hoping to get laid." Mick nodded in solemn agreement, and the two high-fived.

"And his name is Enzo?" Gina whistled. "Sounds fast. Imported. Luxurious. What the hell are you rooming with Paige for?"

"Trust me," Lucy said, "I don't need to overcomplicate my life more than it already is."

"Well, take my room, in case. I was supposed to bring my wife, but she got called into work. I don't mind sharing if it's all the same to Paige."

"It's all the same to me," Paige agreed.

"I couldn't do that," Lucy said, feeling her face flush. "You paid more than me."

Gina waved a hand. "All I need is a bed. I'll do my womanspreading here. You do yours at the hotel."

Lucy couldn't stop herself from smiling, and everyone hooted. She decided right then to stop fighting good things offered to her. Everything had been so serious lately. How invigorating to feel excited about something again. Even something as impractical as Enzo.

He found her in the hotel lobby before she even had a chance to text him. He gathered her into a hug and swung her in a circle, then pulled back to look at her. She'd figured they'd both spend this weekend playing it cool, as if nothing had changed since they'd agreed to go their separate ways. Only something had. Because defying logic, they'd held on to one another. And now that she was here with him, it seemed like a terrible waste to spend the time at arm's length.

"I missed you," he said. "Even though I wasn't supposed to."

"Same," she said.

This was not the smooth operator she'd first met in his office. He didn't seem to know what to do with his hands as the goofy grin from this morning's photo expanded across his face. She was pretty sure she was wearing the same one. "I don't know whether it's okay to kiss you," he said more quietly. "But for what it's worth, I'd like to."

"Same," she repeated.

Lucy didn't stop to think. She threw her arms around his neck and pressed her lips to his. Then it was her turn to pull back.

"My life is a bigger mess than when you met me," she warned him.

"Same," he said.

They got takeaway coffees from the lobby counter, bundled up in hats and gloves, and set out for a walk, across the street and into Millennium Park. Enzo told her about how his mom and sister had loved their New Year's books and how they'd been on his case for letting her get away. He told her how work was less satisfying without any plucky writers bouncing into his office, pretending they knew what business administration was. How he didn't want to pressure her to commit, but he wasn't interested in meeting anyone else. How he'd wanted to say all of this for a while, but she'd had so much else going on, it hadn't seemed the place or time.

The next thing she knew, she was telling him all of it. Including the things she'd avoided admitting when she'd met him. About the pact, and how sure she'd felt when she'd begun the MBA—and how uncertain she felt now. How the temptation of Delia's offer had turned her head, and she hadn't managed to turn her focus back. How Collins had fed her worries that all of this had been a terrible mistake. How she liked the business program even more than expected but still didn't know what she'd do with the degree. How she was accumulating debt and missing her chance to capitalize on her new followers and in some ways felt more trapped than ever.

How she hadn't been prepared for so much that had happened, including meeting Enzo.

They walked and talked and really listened. There weren't many kids out on a weekday, and when they reached the playground, it was mostly empty. Lucy and Enzo climbed the highest play structure for a glimpse of Lake Michigan and stood looking out at it, shoulder to shoulder.

"Do you want my advice?" he asked.

Lucy appreciated that he asked before volunteering it. "Yes."

"You like the business program more than you expected. And you're only in one panel at this symposium?"

"That's right."

"Then I think you should take full advantage of being here. Go to every other session you can. Don't put pressure on yourself to know what you're going to do with your degree. But stop putting so much pressure on what you're *not* going to do with it."

Lucy frowned. "What do you mean?"

"I mean that you seem to have made up your mind to see your options as two very different paths. Either you go back to writing or see this MBA through. But I've been doing this job for a long time, and I'm not sure I've ever seen anyone, no matter what they did before, truly change careers starting from scratch. Instead, you build on the skills you have. You find ways to apply them as an asset to your new job, even if they aren't your main job anymore."

"Collins said I was throwing the baby out with the bathwater," Lucy admitted. "I think that's what she meant. But the thing is, I've always figured that being better at business might make me better at a writing career. That doesn't change why I wanted to leave publishing, though. Say I do have another shot at writing a book that will make a splash. That won't improve how anxious I feel about that splash or how short-lived it will probably be. It still amounts to chasing the next thing. And chasing was the thing I loathed in the first place."

"So don't use business to make you better at a writing career," he suggested. "Use writing to make you better at a business career."

He made it sound so simple, just as Delia had. *So do both,* she'd said. Lucy had assumed she'd meant stealing time to write on lunch breaks, moonlighting as a novelist the way so many people did at the beginning—the way Lucy didn't have the energy for anymore. Because Lucy wasn't at the beginning. She was supposed to be reaching the peak.

But maybe *supposed to* was overrated. Maybe she was overthinking it. Maybe it was okay to sit in the middle for a while and see what happened.

"Solid advice," Lucy said. "There are a lot of smart people here I could probably learn a lot from. Including you."

"I'll go with you, if you want, as much as I can escape our booth," he said. "I can translate the more insufferable business speak. But if you keep an open mind, I doubt you'll need me to point out where a creative communicator like you might be an asset."

She couldn't help but apply Enzo's perspective to their relationship too. She'd seen the possibilities as two different paths: yes or no, together or apart, everything or nothing. But maybe the best way forward was to stop putting pressure on what they *weren't* going to be. And not to fixate so much on where this might lead.

Ever since she'd met him, he'd been trying to help her, even if that help took her away from him. Lucy wasn't sure she'd ever had such a person in her life. That's when she realized: Just because Collins had been gutsy enough to voice some hard truths, that didn't make her right about everything. True, if Lucy hadn't quit when she did, she'd still be here in Chicago—but there was no reason to think she'd have met Enzo at all. If she hadn't quit, she wouldn't have walked into that admissions office. She wouldn't have found out what it was like to have strangers quoting her work and to have gotten a surreal book contract offered out of the blue. She wouldn't have been there for Collins when she was hospitalized. She wouldn't have gotten to hug Brooke the day she found out she was pregnant, and she wouldn't have challenged herself in Marie's class and learned how much she liked writing about what it meant to be both empowered and vulnerable without hiding behind a fictional character to do it.

She wouldn't be here now, with what she'd always claimed to want in front of her.

Options.

Yes, the decisions would be hard. But maybe this was a good problem to have after all.

How could she be mad about any of it?

33

Brooke

It was the first day of Brooke's second trimester. Any day now, her screening test results would be back, and she was eager to move beyond this interminable waiting. But as much as she'd built up this milestone in her head, she'd never pictured it like this.

Alone in Collins's room, she felt like a houseguest who couldn't take a hint—and with Lucy gone, like a fifth wheel on a family that could barely keep its chassis together. *I've let you live in my house,* Collins had raged. *I trusted you.* How could anyone feel good about staying after that? Collins needed them here, despite everything, but it wasn't the same as wanting them here, and they couldn't deny the difference now. Brooke knew no one would begrudge her if she left for her parents' house in Florida, but that would require switching obstetricians. And for what? For how long? She didn't want to be there either.

What she wanted was Mitch. She couldn't get Collins's words out of her head: *You're behaving as if it doesn't matter that he's gone off without you, or how long he stays gone.* Collins knew damn well it had always mattered—but why *had* Brooke tried so hard to act as if it didn't? She longed to run to the airport in one of those grand gestures from romantic movies, flying through the night to throw her arms around him and confess everything weighing on her heart. But she physically couldn't go. And with her friends barely speaking to her, she couldn't send one of them in her place either.

Besides. The more she laid low, the more she marveled at how much they all juggled.

When it came to Lucy and Marie and even Collins, admiration and frustration were not mutually exclusive. They might have made a mess of things, but every day they kept going, doing their best under tough circumstances. And even if Collins had been right that it wasn't good enough—well, didn't *all* women feel that way? They were habitually analyzing and trying to do better, to be mindful of how their actions impacted others, all the while holding themselves to impossible standards. What a tragedy that classes like Marie's were only for college kids. You never outgrew needing that kind of advice. You only grew into new ways to let yourself down.

She knew Marie was blaming herself for the things Collins had said too. She overheard her soldiering on with Connor and Wade and wanted to reach through all that false cheer to reassure her that Collins would come around, and that nobody but Marie could judge what it was like being married to Kyle.

But nobody knocked on Brooke's door to comfort her. Which left plenty of time to second-guess herself.

When the call came from London, Brooke declined it. Then, thinking twice, she logged in to the Have Kids, Will Travel forum to make sure her profile hadn't been hacked. The group had kept her company during these days holed up with no one to talk to, and maybe she'd accidentally clicked on an ad. Because she didn't know anyone in London.

She'd been pining over pictures of it, though.

The UK is a great place to start if you're nervous about traveling internationally with young children, one member had written, beneath snapshots of her family posed photogenically on cobblestone streets. *No language barrier eliminates one big, intimidating hurdle.*

This post had stayed at the top of the feed because it had spurred a debate about how one person's hurdle could be another's reason for traveling in the first place. But even in a heated discussion about the pros and cons of bilingual environments, the space was kinder than the average online hub. Maybe that was why Brooke had lost track of her hours spent here. It was only armchair traveling, but unlike Mitch's solo adventures, her fact-finding was focused on having a baby in tow. Which she still wasn't sure he would even be open to.

She kept asking herself: Will this still feel like a good idea when Mitch is stateside, and you're no longer lonely and paranoid about what he's off experiencing without you? Some days, the nomads in the group seemed extreme, packing only what they could carry or going rogue after their families disapproved of their plans. But most of them presented as typical, curious parents, open about the challenges of being a transient expat. Some moved from one long-term rental to another; others swapped houses or stayed with distant relatives; still others were following job opportunities or military deployments. Most spoke of living in the moment, planning to go home eventually, missing their families but deeming the homesickness worth it. As she pored over story after story, her impressions morphed from *People are doing this?* to *Can we do this?* to *We could totally do this.*

Because she found things in the thread that she'd never expected to see there.

Stability.

Intimacy.

Balance.

These parents weren't dragging their offspring around, trying to live as if they hadn't procreated. They were broadening their kids' worlds. These families, in fact, seemed closer than the ones she'd known in Colorado. They weren't manufacturing adventures to rediscover through their kids' eyes; they were having big firsts together. The community was amazingly resourceful. In moments of overwhelm, caring advice from someone who'd been there seemed mere clicks away.

Brooke had interacted with just enough of the posts that she assumed the London number was spam. But when a voicemail popped up, she listened.

And what she heard was Mitch.

"Hey, it's me." He laughed nervously. "Um. So, I'm at the Hilton Hyde Park hotel, in London. You probably are wondering *why* I'm in London. I wasn't going to—well, do you remember Briana Frenchman, who used to work with me in . . . You know what, it's too long of a story for a voicemail." He sighed in obvious frustration, and Brooke gripped the phone tighter.

"No, it's not," she said aloud. She didn't care how many voicemails it took, she needed to know why her husband had gone to London without telling her first. And who was Briana Frenchman? She sounded pretty—too pretty to be spontaneously, evidently, with Mitch right now at some fancy hotel across the ocean. "What the hell?" Brooke protested.

But of course, he couldn't hear her.

"Why I'm calling from an unfamiliar number is a shorter story," he went on. She could hear background noise, but it was too muffled to make out what *kind* of background. Voices, she was pretty sure, and music. Maybe traffic? Wind? "Apparently, there's a scheme here where you're walking down the street holding your phone, and a thief on an e-bike snatches it from your hand. Guess it's a real problem. Just wish someone had told me before." More nervous laughter.

Brooke seethed. What did he have to sound so nervous about? This couldn't be happening. Not with Mitch. She'd never even caught him in a tiny lie. He wasn't the kind of guy who'd withhold anything from his wife, let alone where he'd gone or who he was with or why.

Except, apparently, he was.

"Anyway," the voicemail went on, "turns out I'm screwed. You almost need a phone to retrieve a phone. Tracking function was useless. I filed a police report and had tech support wipe it remotely so my logins can't be hacked—but I can't get my two-factor codes to access anything else. No email or hotel or flight reservations. Kind of a nightmare. Mobile stores are closed for the day, so the soonest help desk appointment I could get is tomorrow afternoon. At least I have my wallet. Wanted you to know I'm okay. I haven't eaten all day and have a terrible headache, so we're going to grab a bite, and I know it's already late where you are. If there's an emergency, call the hotel and give my name—I don't have a room number yet. Otherwise, I'll call tomorrow once I'm sorted. So sorry. Don't worry. Love you."

She dialed the number back but got a busy signal. Impatient, she played the message again, then again, as if she might have missed some crucial info. Obviously, there was more to the story, but she'd have to wait to find out. Why hadn't she picked up? What was wrong with her? Why had it not crossed her mind that a European number, from *any* country, might have something to do with Mitch?

More important, why did his voice sound guilty? *So sorry. Don't worry. Love you.*

Taking a deep breath, she dialed again and got another busy signal. That couldn't be right—could it? A cursory internet search revealed it could be a network problem or an issue with her wireless plan calling internationally. Come to think of it, she'd only been calling Mitch's regular number since he'd left. But he'd said he'd call her tomorrow. Was it really worth the hassle to troubleshoot this?

When she ran a search for London phone thefts, his story checked out. The e-bikes were too fast to catch; the stolen mobiles were rarely recovered. She thought of all the times she'd walked around consulting a map on her phone, times she'd handed it to a stranger who'd offered to take a group picture. But she couldn't muster sympathy for Mitch. She was too annoyed with him.

Or maybe she was too annoyed with herself.

The next morning, Dr. York commended her on a healthy completed trimester and reported, at last, that her test results were normal. This time, Brooke's tears were pure relief. For one blissfully uncomplicated moment, she could feel nothing else.

"Do you want to know the sex of the baby?" Dr. York asked.

Brooke looked at her in surprise. "You can tell that already? From the NIPT?"

The doctor smiled. "Miracles of modern genetics."

But Brooke was shaking her head before she could even think it through.

"I'm not quite . . . maybe at my next appointment."

Dr. York nodded and gently asked if her husband might be back by then.

"He might be," Brooke said. Hearing the words aloud buoyed her. This fiasco with Mitch's phone might be the thing to take the shine off his travels. They'd never discussed an end date, but this second trimester milestone marked a shift in her thinking. Surely it would for him too.

Dr. York nodded her approval.

"What's the next benchmark," Brooke asked, "for confirming that everything looks okay?"

"We're going to start you on baby aspirin and continue to monitor that blood pressure—you meet the criteria for that as a standard preventative measure, and this is the ideal time to introduce that regimen. Then, around twenty weeks, you'll have a Level 2 ultrasound with a maternal fetal medicine specialist. Think of it this way: Until that point, you're still making the baby. Between eighteen and twenty-two weeks, you're ready for a full anatomy evaluation."

That was at least six weeks away. An eternity. So Mitch hadn't missed the whole baby-making phase of her pregnancy after all. He'd barely missed anything but a few routine checkpoints, if you thought about it. No alarm bells, no tough decisions, just steady progress. The thought comforted her in a way she hadn't fully understood she needed to be comforted. She couldn't wait to tell him. She could already hear him whooping in relief, sharing her joy the way no one else quite could.

"Have you had a chance to visit the Have Kids, Will Travel group?" Dr. York asked.

"I have," Brooke said. "It's great. Thank you for the referral."

The doctor's smile widened. "The way you lit up when you said that . . . it suits you."

Brooke blushed. "Well, it's fun to think about," she admitted. "But I don't know. Those parents make it sound so easy."

"Parenting is never easy," Dr. York agreed. "But sometimes as women, I think we do overcomplicate things. Often because we're used to taking on too much in the first place."

Brooke knew she was only beginning to grasp how true this was. Still, she left feeling hopeful. She and Mitch had so much to talk about.

But for the first time on an appointment day, Mitch didn't call.

34

MARIE

Marie stared at her dean in disbelief. "I must have misheard," she said. "Come again?"

The dean took off her reading glasses and sighed. "You didn't mishear. We'll be removing How to Say No from our offerings next year. Let me be clear, this was a top-down decision impacting a dozen courses across the university catalog. I played no part in this."

"Well," Marie said, sitting straighter, "I hope you can play a part in undoing it."

"I cannot. We all know the university has been navigating rocky terrain in terms of government funding and alumni donations. With regulations changing all the time, they've identified courses vulnerable to scrutiny, and it shouldn't come as a surprise yours was one."

It didn't. Last year she'd been called to this same office to field another "top-down" challenge about what saying no had to do with gender. Perhaps it belonged in sociology or psychology. Did women really struggle with boundaries more than men? And if they did, wasn't it amplifying differences to point them out? Wasn't she perpetuating cycles she wanted to break? To prove her point, she'd turned to her students, asking them to bring in examples of how *they* thought it related to gender. The results had not only successfully defended her course but become her favorite assignment every semester. In fact, they were doing it in class today.

"The students won't stand for this," she said now. "My course was the top rated in the entire department, last time I checked."

"Actually, we've gotten a few complaints this semester. That your attention seems to be elsewhere, and you've missed some meetings, dropped off a committee that was counting on your input. I was going to ask if everything is all right at home."

That threw Marie. Of course she'd been distracted. Her marriage was floundering, and her best friend was in a life-threatening medical crisis—even if they weren't exactly speaking at the moment. But Marie had tried hard not to let any of it show. Besides, that committee was a waste of time that met behind closed doors.

"Complaints from my students," she asked, "or my colleagues?"

"That's irrelevant."

"Not to me."

"But to the future of your class. I'm sorry, Professor Welling. You've been an asset to this college for my entire tenure, and this is not a reflection of anyone's faith in your abilities. In fact, I think you could be most impactful teaching more core competencies. If I have to advocate for gender studies to continue, no matter what they call it or how they package it, I need my best faculty covering the bases. And while I share your disappointment, I can't say I'm keen to offer electives that draw unwanted attention. We can revisit a year from now, if you'd like. But for the upcoming term, these changes are final. I wanted you to hear it from me."

Any other time, Marie might have had more to say. Much more. But not today.

This was too much to process on the fly, and the dean knew it. Marie had to get to class.

She walked across College Green slowly, forcing deep breaths to calm her fury. The idea of rolling over went against everything she'd ever stood for. But she had limits. She didn't have it in her to fight right now.

She couldn't argue that her attention hadn't been elsewhere, because her attention had been on her priorities. And with her personal life in flux, that wasn't about to change any time soon.

They had pinpointed Marie's vulnerability.

It seemed cruelly fitting that this was the day she'd cede her podium to her students to begin their presentations. On the one hand, she didn't know how she'd summon the poise to face them just now, and was relieved all she had to do was watch. But if Collins thought she was a hypocrite before . . . well, this was next level. They'd be sharing real-life reasons her course was crucial. And she'd be sitting there knowing it was all about to end.

She already knew what Kyle would say when she told him: that this was a sign for her to leave OU. He'd once accused her of looking for leverage, and no doubt he'd be all over this, looking for his. He'd act like this would make a change easier for her, for all of them. And it would make no difference to him that it came at a soul-crushing cost. That the contribution she was proudest of—the only one that had reached beyond the tightening boundary walls of her field—had been unceremoniously taken from her, through no fault of her own.

She'd been reevaluating, ever since Collins's outburst. Stepping back to view the past few months more objectively. After a lot of soul searching, she could honestly say Collins had been too hard on Brooke and on Lucy. Perhaps not unfair, but uncharitable. Although it was no wonder she'd been fired up about Lucy sitting on those essays. They were so fierce and heartfelt that Marie could only take it as a compliment that her class assignments had prompted them. But she wasn't going to pressure Lucy to share them widely. She'd learned where the lane ropes were.

Likewise, Marie would not backpedal from her own handling of things with Sara. Brooke had said it best: *You were not out enjoying your life, Collins.* Marie didn't regret trying to help, even if she'd botched it.

Sara had come by the house to apologize, on her way back to Michigan. "I had it coming," she'd told Marie. "Maybe not for this, but karma's a bitch, and I've been a bitch too."

Marie promised to stay in touch, but it was half-hearted. She was in no position to offer comfort to anyone else. Because when it came to Marie, Collins hadn't been all wrong.

Yes, they'd all entered the Quitters pact on their own. Marie's background, however, had made her the de facto leader, the one with relevant training, and the logical person to hold everyone accountable—except, apparently, herself.

She had spent months now living among the remnants of Collins and Sullivan's once-in-a-lifetime love yet feigned uncertainty that kind of marriage could exist. She'd watched Brooke and Mitch flex their biggest, most heartfelt goals for each other and dared to question whether it was possible to compromise without settling. She'd seen Lucy demonstrate stubborn resolve and never pointed out that choices didn't have to be all or nothing.

Because she'd been too scared to face her own choices alone.

Marie thought of all the other academics who'd walked these brick-lined paths of College Green—more than two hundred years' worth—and all those yet to follow. She'd never stopped pinching herself that she got to be a part of this worthy institution. As angry as she was with the bureaucracy at the higher levels, it wasn't the kind of anger that made her want to leave. The dean had said herself: She needed the best academics to stay. Choosing their battles was not the same thing as backing down.

In a numb daze, Marie pulled open the heavy door to her lecture hall. She felt outside of herself as she watched her students filing in. When the final bell rang, she forced a smile.

"This is a day I've come to look forward to," she began. "Our chance to officially reverse roles. You've all turned in three examples that illustrate why *you* think How to Say No belongs in gender studies. Now you'll speak about the one you feel is strongest. In the past, we've had equally wonderful discussions about pop culture and literature, celebrities and ordinary people, so no pressure to try to choose something that feels studious or highbrow. I'd much rather see you be authentic than pick something because you thought I'd like it." A chuckle went around the room. "Any volunteers to start us off?"

A girl who had something to say about everything raised her hand, and Marie nodded and took a seat in the front row.

She was not going to get emotional. She was going to try to enjoy this, one last time.

And she did. She sang along with the rest of the class to the cheeky chorus of Meghan Trainor's "Untouchable." She let herself be moved by photos from an exhibit titled "What Were You Wearing?" displaying clothes worn by sexual assault victims—a sobering mix of hoodies and pajama pants bucking the stereotype of short skirts and crop tops. And she welcomed the comic relief in a debate over a #hotguysreading hashtag—featuring photos of oblivious men lost in books on subways and park benches—and its double standard about exploitation and consent.

"If this feed collected snaps of women, it would be creepy," her student pointed out. "I mean, yes, they were in public, but they might not even know their pictures are here."

A guy in the back raised his hand. "To be fair, my species shares the blame. If it wasn't such a novelty to find men looking at books, this wouldn't be a thing. Also, I'll be reading behind the Scripps building after this if anyone wants to tag me."

When everyone laughed, sadness and pride washed over Marie. This. Whether her class was truly canceled or merely on hiatus, this was what they'd all be missing out on. These moments where people with different points of view related and sometimes even got down to the increasingly rare business of changing their minds. It encapsulated everything naysayers misunderstood about gender studies: that acknowledging their differences had a beautifully messy way of reminding them they were all only human.

"Nicely done," Marie called out. "Who's next?"

A girl approached the podium in head-to-toe spandex, as if she'd remembered mid-workout that she had class. Then again, if her flat abs were any indication, she was probably always mid-workout. An Instagram reel flashed onto the screen behind her.

"I don't know if this is my strongest example," the girl said, "but it made me maddest."

The video began to play. The person filming was among the spectators at the finish line of some kind of marathon or other footrace, cheering as exhausted runners came into view on the home stretch, numbers pinned to their shirts, waving at their family and friends.

"There's Mommy," a male voice off-screen said as a sweaty woman came into view, clearly spent but triumphant at her accomplishment, hands in the air. She was not someone you'd pick out on the street as a distance runner but rather someone who was running toward some healthier version of herself, doing the hard thing.

"Oh no," a child's voice said. "I dropped it." In the bottom of the frame, a small toy was visible on the pavement, on the other side of a loose barricade holding the crowd back.

"Mommy," another child called. The runner beamed at her family who'd been waiting to congratulate her. But the child only pointed at the toy. "Can you pick that up?"

In the exasperated moment that followed, nobody in the crowd reached over the railing to help. The father remained silent. No one congratulated the mom. The joy on her face dissipated.

"Why not," she said finally, stopping. "I wasn't doing anything important."

She handed the toy over and resumed running. The video ended.

A stunned silence fell over the classroom.

And a long-simmering rage tipped the boiling point in Marie's veins.

"Wild, right?" said the girl at the podium. "I mean, she must have trained for this race for weeks or months. And before that she was birthing kids. But she's out there having her moment, and they stole it from her."

A guy in the front row raised his hand. "I mean, she could have said no," he said. "She could have kept running. They'd have dealt with it."

The girl at the podium glared at him with an impressive amount of foresight for someone so young. "My point isn't that she could have or should have said no," she said slowly. "My point is that she shouldn't have been asked in the first place."

"It's just a kid," the guy said, but his protest was weakening. "They don't know better."

"It's *not* just the kid," she said. "This would never happen to a dad who was running, because the mom would step in. She would say, 'Oh my goodness, I'll get your toy in a second, but Daddy is doing something incredible right now. Let's cheer! Yay, Daddy!'"

"The mom would have been all over that before the toy hit the ground," someone else chimed in. "And not letting them climb the railings like this guy, totally oblivious."

The presenter nodded. "Women could say no more often, sure. But it would be better if people stopped asking ridiculous things of us."

She looked to Marie for affirmation. But Marie couldn't say anything.

She couldn't move.

All she could think was that she recognized her husband in that video. He was in the silence where support should have been. In the empty space where a partner could have helped. He was off camera, going through the motions of watching her without seeing her at all.

And though she'd never run anything beyond laps around the block, she recognized herself too. Pounding the pavement for longer than she'd thought she could, tired and looking for a high five or hug. Or better yet, someone to run beside her.

The girl who'd gone first raised her hand. "What she needs is a group of friends there," she said. "They'd be all *Yes, queen* and *Get it, girl!* They'd shame that dad right into shape."

Marie looked numbly around the room. She could see it all so clearly.

Her life, running the race. And Kyle, passive on the other side of the fence.

Deep down, she'd known for a while what she wanted, but she'd been waiting around as if her mind might magically change. Because she still didn't know if it was okay to want it, or if she was being selfish or unrealistic. Kyle wasn't a cheater or a liar or even a bad husband in any black-and-white way. What was she upset about, really—logistics? So what?

As a result, she'd stayed in the gray area, squandering time—not only Kyle's but her own. Perhaps that was the most unforgivable offense of all. Because as Collins pointed out, more time was never guaranteed. The morning after that terrible confrontation, Marie had researched couples counselors herself, texted Kyle three options, and asked him to please pick one. Three times since, she'd followed up. Three times since, he'd said he hadn't had a chance to look at them yet.

It wasn't mere logistics that the man she married didn't see her anymore. At the end of the day, it was pretty simple. She didn't feel fun around him because he didn't seek out opportunities to have fun together. She didn't feel supported around him because he didn't support her. And Kyle wasn't behaving like a man who'd gotten a wake-up call. He was behaving the way he always had, dragging his feet, expecting her to give up and come around.

Like the kids in the video, Wade and Connor were learning from example. Marie felt confident that even at her most scattered, her kids knew where they stood among her priorities—at the top. Living with Brooke and Collins and Lucy, they'd witnessed compassion and solidarity. But their dad was demonstrating that it was okay to watch somebody you loved try their hardest and offer very little in return.

Marie might not always know what was best for them, but she did know what wasn't.

No wonder her students were doing a better job teaching this class than she was.

As the room came back into focus, she became aware of how quiet the classroom had become. The girl in spandex was returning to her seat but stopped when she saw Marie's face. "Professor? Are you okay?"

Only then did Marie realize she was crying.

"No," she said.

This time, she was ready to do something about it.

35

Lucy

Lucy sat across from Delia in the hotel bar and got to the point.

"Did you see the new review at the top of my latest book's listing?" She pulled out her phone and recited aloud. "*I read this writer's announcement that she's going to quit writing novels, and I think that's the right call.* It's been marked 'helpful' 257 times."

Delia fixed her with a steady gaze. "One-star reviews from self-important wannabe critics aren't going to stop, whether you become a mainstay or not."

"I know that," Lucy said. She felt eerily at peace with it. "I also know readers still haven't responded to any of my novels the way they embraced that essay—the one thing I've ever published in my own voice."

"What are you saying?"

"I'm saying that voice meant what she said, and nothing that's happened has changed that. At least, not exactly. I've realized life is too short to try to become someone I'm not. Maybe what I need is to be more fully myself."

"Does this mean you are or are not done writing?"

"It means this experience has opened my eyes to ways I could do it more effectively."

Delia's face changed from disappointed to curious. Lucy thought she even detected a hint of pride as her agent flagged down a server to order them a round of drinks. "I have a feeling we're going to need them," she told him, but she was smiling as she turned back to Lucy.

"Okay," Delia said. "I'm listening."

~

Brooke picked Lucy up at the airport, looking like she needed a hug. Or maybe Lucy was projecting. Either way, when Brooke hopped out of the car to help Lucy put her things in the trunk, Lucy threw her arms around her right there on the curb.

"Are you okay?" Lucy asked her. Brooke pulled back and smiled weakly.

"That depends on if *we* are okay," Brooke said.

Lucy nodded. Now that she was back, she wanted nothing more than to clear the air with her friends and put the awkwardness behind them.

They were all on their own journeys, to be sure.

But she'd never again entertain the idea that they'd been wrong to start them together.

"Should we go see Collins?" Lucy suggested, as they buckled in and headed off. "I mean, we're here . . ."

"I think that's a good idea."

Nobody had given Collins the silent treatment, but they'd given her space, taking turns checking in. Thinking of you. Let me know if you need anything. And if you're up for a visit?

They'd mostly gotten one-word responses to their texts. But Marie was still listed as an authorized contact for Collins and called the facility daily for updates, sharing them with the group through notes in their scheduling app.

Her PT said she made good progress today.

They're monitoring for a potential blood clot but say there's no cause for alarm. Routine precautions; symptoms could be attributed to other causes.

Nurse advised minor complications might have an upside if they keep her there longer, given accessibility issues at home. Insurance continues to push for release. But ortho is more tapped into the realities of what she can handle. They keep asking financial questions I can't answer.

Lucy wasn't sure whether Marie had forgotten that Collins also had access to their posts in the app, but she liked the message it sent if Collins was paying attention: that they wouldn't give up on her over one disagreement that had gotten out of hand, and they hoped she wouldn't give up on them either. That sometimes the best friends were the ones willing to say the hard things. That they cared and remained on her side.

"What's the latest from Mitch?" Lucy asked, sneaking a look at the driver's seat. She thought she could spot the earliest hint of a baby bump, but maybe it was wishful thinking.

"I'd rather not talk about Mitch," Brooke said. Lucy didn't know what to do but nod. She simply could not believe he had not returned by now. Nobody faulted him for going, but hadn't he had his fill? Couldn't he sense his wife might need him more than she'd let on? Lucy had a mind to call him up and shake sense into him, but she refused to believe Mitch of all people needed to be told.

Many of her illusions had been shattered this year—big ones about life and purpose and love. She would not accept that Mitch could be one of them.

Brooke cleared her throat. "So. Was Chicago worth staying the extra day?"

"Definitely. As soon as I heard Delia was going to be in town, it was a no-brainer. She had so many meetings scheduled, I was lucky she could squeeze me in. The publishing scene there really picked up."

Brooke's eyes narrowed mischievously. "You know I wasn't asking about Delia. Though I want to hear about that too."

"Enzo was another no-brainer," she admitted, and Brooke squealed.

Lucy felt insensitive gushing about him, knowing how much Brooke missed Mitch. But she wouldn't wait too long.

After all, Enzo had promised to visit soon.

~

Collins was propped up in bed, icing her unbraced leg. She started crying when she saw them.

"How did you know I needed you?" She sobbed. "I'm so ashamed."

Lucy and Brooke perched on opposite sides of her bed.

"Hey," Lucy said. "It's okay. You have nothing to be ashamed of."

Collins dropped her face into her hands. Her voice came out muffled. "You don't understand. They're saying that I . . . that I . . ." She was crying too hard to get the words out.

Fear gripped Lucy as her eyes met Brooke's and saw her own worry reflected there. Not another setback. Please. This was all too much. Every time they tried to get a handle on it . . .

Collins lifted her tear-streaked face. "They're saying," she cried, "I can go home. Next week."

Brooke clapped her hands. "Oh, but that's wonderful!" She caught herself. "Isn't it?"

Lucy handed Collins a fistful of tissues. Collins pressed the whole wad to her eyes.

"I know it's supposed to be," Collins said, her face crumpling again. "They'll even send out a team to help make assessments and modifications. The thing is . . . I don't want to."

"Okay," Lucy said, taking a beat. "Yeah. It's natural to feel nervous about leaving. I mean, you have a safety net here. There will be physical challenges back out in the world."

Collins looked at them miserably. "I know," she said. "But that's not it. The thing is, though it's no picnic in here, I think it's been good for me to get away. Not from all of you, I mean, but from, you know . . ."

"The memories?" Brooke supplied.

Collins heaved some deep breaths, collecting herself before answering. "Not exactly. I love my memories of Sull. I could never get away from those, and I wouldn't want to. But the thought of going home . . ." She met their eyes with an unfamiliar clarity and candor, and only then did Lucy realize just how sorely that had been missing. "It's the *reminders*," she said. "Where I was standing when the phone rang about the fire. The corner of the kitchen I was facing, trying to absorb what they were saying. The spot on the floor where I was always tripping over his shoes, no matter how many times I asked him to put them *in* the closet, and how I should have been nicer about petty annoyances. I should be so eager to get out of here, but when I think of going home . . . What does it say about me that I'd rather live out my days in this cold clinic than in the house I shared with the love of my life?"

Finally, a question Lucy could answer. "It says you've been through a lot," she said firmly. "And there is no wrong answer."

Collins winced. "I guess. But I can't use that as an excuse for everything. Just look how awful I was to all of you."

"'Awful' is a strong word," Brooke said. "You said some things that needed to be said. Besides, the rest of us said stuff too." Lucy could see that this wasn't easy for Brooke, either, so she quickly nodded her agreement. But Collins looked unconvinced.

"I'm not sure Marie will let it roll off so easily."

"I can't speak for Marie," Lucy said, "but here's what I think: You are allowed to be mad at the pact. We're all a little mad at the pact. But I'm still not sorry we made it. I'm not going to sit here with the benefit of hindsight and act like I should've known exactly what would happen. Not everything is the way I'd have scripted it, but who knows, maybe some of it will turn out even better." Lucy didn't mean to sound annoyingly optimistic. But she kind of was.

"I'm not sorry I made the pact either," Brooke said. "It's easy to say that if I'd waited things out, I'd be pregnant in my Colorado suburb right now. But I don't know if another round of IVF would have worked—my body did this on its own. Without Mitch and I having quit, the alchemy wouldn't have been the same. I stopped stressing so much, and we got more intimate, and . . ." Brooke teared up. "Obviously, Mitch and I might not be in a great place right now. We're not even in the *same* place. But this has given me time to think about where we go from here, instead of jumping at my first instinct to settle back down. And I never would've had that otherwise. I'm just trying to keep faith we'll come back to each other."

"Might be easier to have faith if you didn't have bitter friends accusing you of squandering your time," Collins said. "Which is the last thing you need."

"Well, for what it's worth, I haven't been squandering it," Brooke said. "I've been using it to have a full existential crisis about whether I'm even motherhood material anymore."

Lucy and Collins gaped at her. "Oh my God," Lucy said. "Is that what you've been . . . Brooke, of course you're motherhood material."

"But I talked myself out of it. I fully committed to not being a parent after all. I got all caught up in what that life would look like. How could a good mom do that?"

"Very easily," Lucy said. "And as I recall, it was quite hard on you."

Brooke shook her head. "Some of the stuff that's run through my head since Mitch left . . . I want to be better than this. I want to have no problem putting the baby's needs or his needs before my own. I want to not mind that all my plans went to hell and now I have to start completely over, even though the thought of it exhausts me. Infertility made me dislike myself. I felt bitter and disingenuous. I thought getting pregnant would change that, but look at me."

"We are looking," Collins said. "Ever since my accident, you've been the most selfless of all of us. You're the only one who had no obligation to stay here—but you did stay. You've been here for me, for

Marie's boys. Not only that, but I threw a pitcher of water at you, and you came back the next day. If that doesn't prepare you for motherhood, I don't know what does."

They all laughed at that, but Lucy could tell Brooke wasn't convinced.

"Brooke," Lucy said, "of course it was hard to let Mitch go. But you insisted, because you believed it was best for him, and you believed it was best for the baby for you to stay. You're worrying whether you have it in you to do the selfless stuff, but you're already doing it."

"I'm not actually okay with any of it, though. I hate it."

"But you're doing it anyway. Hello? Selfless."

"Honestly," Collins said, "I wish I could be more like you. The way you've rolled with things. The therapist here has been kind of my only friend lately, and I've gotten my share of tough love too. She's helped me see where I need to let go."

Brooke met Lucy's eyes, like she was trying to decide something. Then she faced Collins and spoke more gently. "For what it's worth, Coll, I think Marie was trying to help with some of that. Maybe she did overstep, but . . . the rest of us talked with Sara too. And I honestly don't think there was anything underhanded about it. On either side."

"I know. It's just . . ." Collins sighed. "I *knew* I couldn't handle seeing anything from the fire, and then here Sara was waving that mug around like it was some kind of trophy, and I couldn't see straight. I think I actually lost my mind for a second—and then you all walked in. I can't even remember everything I said. Flashes keep coming back to me, kind of like with the accident. I know I owe Marie an apology. But Sara . . . I don't know what to say."

Lucy had been thinking about this. A lot. "Maybe we all wanted what Sara said to be true," she offered. "I mean, hypothetically, wouldn't it change things for you if Sullivan *had* wanted her involved? The way you're talking about the house being too much . . . If you feel that way about managing his artwork, too, that's a lot to keep asking of yourself."

Collins took the extra pillow from under her knee and hugged it to her chest. "Of course I want it to be true. That's why I got so mad. I hate myself for being tempted. Because how could I ever risk it when there's no way to know if I can trust her? I couldn't live with myself if I made the wrong call for Sull because of what's easier for me."

"What's easier for you is no small consideration right now," Brooke said. "Maybe going straight home isn't the best move for you regardless. Even if we did install a wheelchair ramp and chair lift and figure the rest out, won't you have appointments in Columbus all the time?"

Collins looked exhausted at the mere mention of it. "Sometimes more than one a day," she confirmed. "My molecular profiling came back—all that waiting, and it basically revealed nothing. No genetic markers for my cancer, no cause or targeted fix we can point to. So once I'm cleared to start treatment, it'll be what they call 'standard of care.' A port in my chest, IV chemotherapy in combination with immunotherapy for the first three months, followed by maintenance immunotherapy for as long as it takes. And physical therapy only gets harder once the brace comes off. I basically have to learn to walk again. But it's not like I can afford a rental in the city on top of everything else."

"Let us ask around," Lucy suggested. "Maybe there are opportunities we don't know about. Temporary housing for patients who qualify or—I don't know, something. We could try to crowdfund it, maybe. I bet all the people who care about Sullivan's art will line up to help. As much as we'd love having you back with us, let's take an objective look at what makes sense."

"Maybe," Collins said slowly. "I don't know. I don't want people to think I'm using his name for my own charity."

"Real question," Brooke said. "Do you think Sull loved his art more than he loved you?"

"No," Collins said. No hesitation this time. "Of course not."

"Of course not," Brooke echoed. "We all know how much Sullivan cared about his legacy, and how much you care about doing right by him. But we *don't* know that Sullivan would have asked all this of you if he knew how things would play out."

Lucy got up and began to pace. She'd spent too much of this day sitting down.

"I spent all weekend learning how clueless I am about running a business," she said. "But one takeaway was that there is always someone specializing in whatever you need. The most successful businesses are the ones with the smartest partnerships. Maybe it's time for you to consult with some legal experts. There might be a way to relinquish control with safeguards in place."

Collins bit her lip. "You mean a way to give Sara a chance without giving her enough power to screw it up?"

"Exactly. Maybe you could maintain approval over big changes but step out of the day-to-day. Only one way to find out," Lucy said. "As my agent says, conversations are free."

"I don't know," Collins said. "Even this conversation feels like a betrayal."

"A betrayal of who?" Lucy pressed her. "Nobody would begrudge you this when you have *cancer*, Coll. It's time to stop putting Sullivan's needs in front of your own. Even if he wouldn't have showed Sara grace—even if he didn't—that doesn't mean you can't. You and Sara are the ones with your lives ahead of you. You're the ones who need to figure out how to do this without him."

"Maybe she'll surprise you," Brooke offered.

Lucy smiled. "Or maybe," she said, "you'll surprise yourself."

36

Brooke

It was late when they got back to Collins's house. An unpredicted March snow had started to fall, blanketing the dark roads and their dreams of spring as if to say *not so fast*. All the bedrooms were dark, but Marie had left the floodlights on for them, illuminating the mess of swirling snowflakes with melancholy beauty.

"In case you were missing Chicago," Brooke said, gesturing to the weather.

"In case you were missing Colorado," Lucy said softly back.

Brooke nodded, but it wasn't Colorado she was missing.

The sense of peace she'd felt by the time they'd hugged Collins goodbye had dissipated on the slick, slow drive. Now, she cut the engine and sat in the sudden silence, reluctant to leave the car's warmth for the frosty dash inside.

"I know you don't want to talk about Mitch," Lucy said. "But I hope you're not putting too much stock into what Collins said before. Things will be okay with you two. I know it."

Brooke nodded. But she wasn't sure of anything anymore. Maybe looking death in the eye, the way Collins had, gave her insight into things the rest of them didn't want to acknowledge. Brooke already knew too well how an unexpected diagnosis could spur regret. What you should have done while you had the chance. What you could have held tighter to. What you would have seen coming, if not for your blind spots. Things that had once been unthinkable getting harder to deny.

Mitch had left her a frantic voicemail the day after he'd missed her appointment, falling all over himself to apologize. He said in the chaos following the phone theft, he'd lost track of what day it was, and fine—she could grant him that. But now he expected her to jump at the chance to make it right, returning his call at the first opportunity, for whose comfort, exactly? Hers, or his? He obviously wanted to get it all off his chest, explain why he hadn't told her how he'd ended up in a country that wasn't even geographically attached to the rest of Europe, with some woman she wasn't supposed to feel threatened by. But Brooke was still sour he'd put them in this position at all.

So she didn't return his call. Not when she missed a second voicemail from him either. Or a third. He'd texted: I'm sorry. Please call. And then, when she hadn't responded, he'd written: Just let me know you're okay? To that, she'd hit the thumbs-up emoji and left it at that. Much as he thought he wanted to hear from her right now, he didn't want this version. She'd reached a limit, fed up with questioning *everything* on her own, and didn't trust herself not to sound like an overprotective parent whose teen had missed curfew, or a jealous wife jumping to conclusions. Or a wet blanket forgetting what it felt like to be unencumbered and free.

She'd never imagined herself avoiding her own husband or feeling envious of Lucy's romantic weekend. It all felt like wearing an outfit that was uncomfortably tight and not her style. But she couldn't just take it off either. Like the zipper was stuck or something.

"Thanks for saying that," she told Lucy. "I'm glad you're back."

"Me too."

"Liar," Brooke teased.

Lucy laughed. "Nah, I mean it. Enzo can wait. I have things to do here first. I think we all do. Even if it doesn't feel that way."

Brooke nodded, but it required effort.

Inside, the friends tried to be quiet so as not to wake Marie and the boys. But the harder they tried, the harder they failed. First, Brooke's wet boot bounced into the umbrella stand, tipping it over. Then Lucy's coat caught in the door, sending her purse sailing across the hall. Lucy clamped a hand over her laugh, but a snort escaped, which made Brooke lose it. They clung to each other, dissolving into squeaks and muffled giggles, as they scuffled to the kitchen, away from the stairs and out of earshot.

Lucy stopped short in the doorway, and Brooke crashed into her, doubling over with laughter. She was wiping tears from her eyes when she realized Lucy had stopped laughing.

Marie sat pale faced and silent at the table, exactly the way Brooke had the day of her pregnancy test. Brooke could still feel the shock of that day, still see the questioning looks on her friends' faces, though that seemed like a lifetime ago. She snapped to attention as Lucy went still beside her. Marie looked at them through eyes swollen from crying.

"It's over with Kyle." Marie squared her shoulders, and beneath her sadness was a conviction Brooke hadn't seen there in a long time. "We're telling the boys this weekend."

Lucy pulled out a chair to join her at the table, and Brooke did the same.

"Is there anything he could say to change your mind?" Brooke asked.

Marie shook her head. "Too little, too late. Honestly, I think we both already knew that. I think we've known for a while."

"I'm so sorry," Brooke said. She wanted to assure Marie that the boys would be okay. That they were already halfway there. But she didn't want to sound glib.

"I'll find another place to stay," Lucy offered. "Give your family space."

"No, don't. *You're* family," Marie said. "Besides, I'm the one who'll need a new place anyway. I'll fish for leads at work. Maybe someone will take pity on me now that they've discontinued my class."

Brooke and Lucy exchanged a look. "They've *what*?"

By the time Marie finished relaying the details, Brooke was burning with rage. "They can't do that," she seethed. "This is outrageous."

"It is," Marie agreed. "But watching Collins has taught me sometimes we really can only tackle one thing at a time, no matter how pressing. And this time, I'd like to recognize my limits before I get to the point of no return. I'm not giving up, but for now, I'm going to be mad as hell and do my job anyway. Because on my worst day on campus, I still feel lucky to be there. I'm not better off without it. I can't say that about my marriage anymore."

They filled her in on their talk with Collins, her reluctance to come home, and the details of her treatment plan. By the time they were done, the clock on the wall had ticked past midnight.

"Well," Lucy said. "It's a new day. Literally."

"I'll do my part to make things right with Collins too," Marie promised. "For what it's worth, I really am sorry I spent so long fumbling my end of the pact."

Brooke smiled at her. "You know how you said even on your worst day on campus, you still want to be there? That's how we feel about our little Quitters Club."

They sandwiched her in a group hug, and Marie started to cry again.

"Cheesecake?" Brooke asked, crossing to the fridge. "Like the Golden Girls we are?"

They would all be exhausted tomorrow. But some things were worth staying up late for.

Only after Brooke closed her bedroom door did she let her tears fall. Marie was getting *divorced*. And though their situations had little in common, it felt too close for comfort. Her heart ached for her friends, and for Mitch—wherever he was by now—and for herself, in this situation that no one had asked for but everyone was trying to make the best of.

She was closing the blinds when movement caught her eye outside the window. And there, pacing the sidewalk below in the fresh snow, was Mitch.

She'd know him anywhere.

But even from this faraway angle, he looked different. As she watched him pivot away from her, reflexive joy and relief leaped in her heart and froze there.

The Mitch she knew did not pace. He was as steady as he was reliable, whereas this Mitch was nervous and jittery. Then again, she hadn't spoken to this Mitch in days, which was admittedly—partially—her own doing. But he'd flown home without so much as a text message letting her know he was on the way. And now he was wringing his hands outside instead of scooping his wife into his arms the first chance he got.

Something must be wrong. Wronger than she'd realized.

She grabbed a blanket off the bed, wrapping herself in it like a cocoon. Then she slipped downstairs, into her boots, and onto the porch.

Mitch turned at the sound of the storm door snapping closed behind her.

His eyes met hers.

For a horrible instant, he looked like he wanted to run to her, but some force was holding him back. Mere moments ago, she'd thought that feeling so far away from Mitch—physically and otherwise—was the worst she'd ever felt. But now that he was here, looking twisted up and terrified to tell her whatever he'd come to say, she was equally terrified to hear it.

Brooke swallowed hard, hugging herself as snow floated between them like static. Maybe it was static. Maybe she was imagining him.

"Brooke," he said, the word a plea. Her mouth went dry. Then, he scaled the porch steps in three big bounds and lifted her into his arms, and he was Mitch again, her Mitch, not some distant stranger in a snowstorm or a frozen frame on a laggy video call or a voice lost in London but the man she loved, back at last, and she didn't want anything else to matter. Tears streaked her cheeks, gratitude washing away her confusion. He was crying, too, clinging to her like she was his lifeline.

"I'm an idiot," he said.

He pulled back to look at her, and she searched his face. She'd almost managed to forget the name of the woman he'd mentioned in his message from London. She braced, suddenly frightened that she was about to hear it again.

"I know I have explaining to do," he began. "God, I missed you. I thought I could just do this, fix this, make it happen, but then I second-guessed myself, convinced I'd made a big mistake, and what started as a grand gesture turned into days of grand disasters. If it wasn't a lost phone, it was an airline that sold my seat, and if it wasn't a missed connection, it was a snowstorm . . . I don't blame you for not calling me back. I owed you more than a call. I was supposed to arrive yesterday."

Mitch's rambling was taking on a panicked tone.

"What are you talking about?" she asked. Vertigo seized her, but she forced herself to look him in the eye. "Just come out with it. What did you do?"

"I know I should've talked to you, but I went and . . ." He took a deep breath. "I got a job."

Brooke did a double take. "A job?"

He started talking even faster. "A few weeks in, I realized I didn't want to do it without you. Nothing is any good without you. But coming back didn't feel right either. So I called in every connection I'd ever said no to. I realize now I don't even know how you'd feel about raising a baby overseas. But it didn't feel right not to give them an answer after all the strings I'd pulled. I can finish out my sabbatical until after your due date. And then I've accepted a position for a year in London, with an option to transfer after that. I should have talked to you first, but it's a good opportunity. There's high demand for my skills there. They provide housing, and . . ."

Brooke started to sob. Mitch looked pained.

"I intended to tell you, but my phone got stolen in the thick of it. And then when I couldn't reach you, I thought I might as well come do it in person. It seemed simple, like I'd be here in a matter of hours, but my new device must not have been set up right. As soon as I left England, it stopped working, and then my flights kept getting delayed, and I was so worried you were trying to call and I was missing something important. But I swear, I've been making my way back to you this whole time."

Brooke couldn't take it anymore. She threw her arms around him. "You got a job!"

He'd gone very still. "You're not mad?"

She laugh-cried into his shoulder. This whole time, she'd worried about all the ways they were in such different places. She'd convinced herself they might take stock of their lives and come to wildly different conclusions about what came next—and then what? What if they'd become permanently too far apart? What if they'd lost something they could never retrieve?

But they'd gone on separate journeys and arrived in the same place.

She pressed her lips to his, and just like that, she knew exactly who he was again.

And she knew exactly who she was too.

She was Mitch's wife. She was carrying his child. And she didn't have to convince him to check out some Have Kids, Will Travel group online. He'd gone out and brought it to her, without her even asking. Everything she'd ever wanted, at her fingertips.

Mitch was home.

And so was she.

37

Marie

Clarity was a funny thing. Never had Marie felt such sadness and relief at the same time.

For too long, she hadn't known what to do.

Now, she'd done it.

The boys cried when they told them. The walls of their old living room closed in as Wade turned to her, hands balled into fists, and said, "I knew you were going to do this. I knew it." Tears sprung to her eyes, though she'd promised herself not to cry in front of them. She'd known this wouldn't be easy, and this was probably the first of many such outbursts as they all adjusted.

It was Kyle who surprised her.

"This isn't on your mom, Son," he said. He and Marie had been sitting, ironically, on the love seat, opposite the boys on the couch. Now, Kyle knelt on the rug at their feet, commanding their attention. "You don't need me to tell you how amazing she is. Even with four of us who sometimes all want or need very different things, she's the one who keeps our family on track. And she does that by understanding better than anyone what's best for you and your brother and putting you first. Which we're both going to keep doing, together, even if we aren't married anymore, because we'll always be a family. No one is to blame.

This is hard on her, too, and we won't make it harder by forgetting to show her respect, gratitude, and love. Okay?"

Wade came to put his arms around her, almost shyly. "Sorry, Mom," he said. Her heart ached.

"If we're not moving home," Connor asked, "are we staying at Aunt Collins's for good?"

Marie kissed Wade on the forehead and tried to smile. "Maybe just until school lets out," she said. "I think summer would be a better time to move, don't you?"

"Can we get a house *near* Collins?" he pressed.

"That would be wonderful," Marie agreed. "But I guess we'll have to see. Hey, nothing is very far apart in a cozy town like Athens, right?"

In truth, she worried she couldn't afford much on her salary alone. Especially not so close to campus, where demand was high. She'd assumed Kyle would eventually move to Columbus, but for now, he wanted to keep this place. Working out the details would take time. Even once he bought out her equity, it would be less than they'd have gotten on the market. She'd probably have to rent, and with most of those properties geared toward students, a condo or apartment might make more sense.

She was just going to have to be patient and look for things worth saying yes to.

Afterward, she thanked Kyle for stepping up the way he did. She didn't point out she could have used that recognition all along. It turned out she didn't need to.

"I haven't been the best listener," he said, "but I've heard you. My work benefits include an employee assistance program providing short-term counseling for situations like div—" He couldn't seem to say the word. "Like ours," he finished. "And I'm going to take advantage. Learn strategies for being a better coparent."

She nodded carefully. Once, this might have been enough for her to put the brakes on, to convince herself that maybe he still hoped to change her mind. All this time, she'd clung to her belief that their marriage was fixable—if only Kyle would take an interest in fixing it. Now, she could accept that this enlightened new side of him wasn't likely to last any longer than his efforts to rekindle their romance had. This might be the closest Kyle would come to admitting that she deserved better.

Now that he wasn't going to be her husband anymore, she could live with that.

As she let go of her unmet expectations, her resentment eased, too, and she could glimpse a more realistic future—maybe not too far away—where things were better between them. Where they might even become friends again.

Neither of them would ever know if he should have begged for one more chance or if she should have offered one. And maybe that was its own kindness. To leave something unknown. To stop the cycle of hurt before it became unbearable.

Even if it did come with a wistful sense of what might have been.

"That means a lot," Marie said. "Thank you."

~

She found Collins packing. The door to her room in the rehab center was open, and her wheelchair glided with a newly practiced ease between the built-in drawers and the pile of clothes she was stacking beside a duffel bag at the foot of her bed. "You'll never believe who found me an accessible apartment." She greeted Marie as if nothing had gone wrong between them. As if their last encounter hadn't found Collins as furious as Marie had ever seen her.

Marie played along. "Who?"

"Sara."

Collins tossed her a hoodie, and she perched on the bed and began folding. "You're right," she said. "I don't believe it."

"Turns out Lucy called her with some general questions about art estates. She has this final project due, and she wanted to use me as her guinea pig to show how a creative project manager could outsource my responsibilities during a prolonged medical leave."

This was the best thing Marie had heard all day. Why had Lucy not mentioned it?

"That's great," she said. "Win-win."

"Actually, Lucy's adviser says estate law is too complex for the project, and I'd tend to agree. But, she mentioned my housing dilemma to Sara, who put out a call. Wouldn't you know, one of her old art professors had transferred to Ohio State. He's doing a study-abroad exchange for the Studio Art MFA this semester and decided to stay overseas through the end of the year."

"And he needs someone to sublet?"

She shook her head. "He wasn't going to sublet. He said he can't trust anyone in his apartment with his collection—I guess it's quite something. But when Sara told him about me, he offered me the place for free. No strings attached."

"Wow. That's so generous. Did he know Sull?"

"Nope. He knew of him, but this was all Sara. She and her husband even came down to check it out before relaying the offer, to make sure it's not too good to be true. It's a roomy two-bedroom in a high-rise with an elevator and super close to the cancer center. There's a third-party shuttle offering transport to my treatments too."

Marie was still processing everything this meant. "Wait," she said. "Sara has been back?"

"Yep. Which was big of her, after the way I acted. And her husband seems nice."

"I think the way you acted was understandable."

"Understandable, maybe. But not acceptable. Not to me. And definitely not to you."

Tears pricked Marie's eyes. "Coll, I am so sorry. I shouldn't have put you or Sara in the position for things to go down the way they did. I get why you'd be suspicious of her motives. Even now."

But Collins was shaking her head. "Regardless, grief and pain don't give me license to be shitty. Sara proposed we take Sullivan's estate off the table—not up for discussion. She says she'd like us to have a relationship that has nothing to do with that. She even tried to get her sister on board, which didn't pan out, but . . . Honestly, she's been a lifesaver, and I have you to thank. If you hadn't given her grace, this wouldn't be happening, and I'd be screwed, financially and logistically. This buys me time to figure things out. Did you know the lawyer who handled this for Sull doesn't even specialize in this stuff? It was a friend-of-a-friend kind of thing, and he might have actually been out of his depth. So Lucy referred me to a lawyer who does. I hadn't even considered finding someone else, but he's looking at my options for the months ahead. I've relied on you to cover me long enough."

Marie was going to need a lawyer too. They were all in uncharted territory here. And for the millionth time, she thought how grateful she was not to have to go through it by herself.

"You can rely on me as long as you need to," Marie said. She took in the room, with its call buttons and railings and all the extras that made it easier for Collins to navigate. "You sure you're okay with not coming right home? It's just . . . you'll be alone. This is a lot."

Collins conjured a brave smile. "Well, I was hoping you wouldn't all delete that calendar app quite yet. I might need a hand, especially at first. But in some ways, this feels like the first time I've lived alone since Sull died. I've been living with his ghost. And it's time, you know?"

Marie nodded. In some ways, she felt like she was living without Kyle for the first time too—because before, she'd leaned on the fact that it was temporary, like a crutch. The mindset shift would take getting used to.

"I want you to know," Collins said, "you and the boys are welcome to my house for as long as I'm in Columbus. I heard you might be looking for your own place in Athens, eventually?" Her eyes were so sympathetic, Marie had to look away.

"You heard right. But listen, I hope we didn't factor into your decision here. We can take care of ourselves."

"I know you can," Collins said. "But you shouldn't have to. And I shouldn't have thrown that in your face. Forgive me?"

"Damn it, Coll, I came here to apologize. Stop interrupting me with your own apology."

"I can't," Collins said sorrowfully. "I was too big of a bitch, and there's an outside chance I might die soon. I can't have that on my conscience."

"Well, neither can I," Marie shot back. "Same reason."

They both laughed, the way they used to. The way only best friends could, and only after decades of friendship. With a healing combination of irreverence, sisterhood, and love.

38

Lucy

Enzo came to visit in April. By then, Collins's house was humming with new energy. Brooke's latest ultrasound had revealed nothing but a healthy, on-track pregnancy, and she and Mitch were finally exuding the joyful glow of expectant parents. They'd elected not to find out the baby's sex, in the spirit of their new appreciation for the unknown, and gone to spend time with their parents in Florida, making up for the holiday cut short with an extended spring break while they still could. Seeing Mitch and Brooke so happily reattached at the hip seemed to restore something in all of them—faith, balance, or a glimmer that some things really were forever. Not that any of them had seriously doubted Mitch. Mostly. But he'd out-Mitched himself, not just coming back, but bringing along the best reason for staying away so long. While his wife was torn between two worlds, he'd secured a plan for stability and adventure rolled into one. Lucy couldn't have scripted it better.

Her friends took instantly to Enzo. He brought Collins a care package of Chicago's finest, from Garrett Popcorn to Frango mint chocolates to fuzzy socks picturing the lions from the Art Institute, and he pushed her wheelchair around Lincoln Tower Park so naturally, no one would've guessed they'd just met. He charmed Marie with his enthusiasm for being back on campus, accepting her guest invite to a faculty mixer as if she'd offered backstage passes to a sold-out concert. He arranged for Connor and Wade to join him and Lucy at Bobcat hockey's Division 2 playoffs and taught them every lyric to the fight song. He even coordinated a reunion of Lucy's MBA Symposium panel at Jackie O's, laughing with Paige, Gina, and the Brew Bros as if they were long-lost friends rather than acquaintances from their fleeting Chicago weekend.

"Are we done pretending you aren't Lucy's boyfriend?" Gina teased.

"So done." He pulled Lucy close and kissed her right there in the window overlooking West Union Street. Outside, signs of spring were everywhere, car windows rolled down, leaves budding on trees, coats tied around waists. In some ways, not much had changed since she'd sat here taking Delia's call on a winter day. In others, everything had.

For her first few months back on campus, each day had felt like a long list of obligations to fulfill and challenges to overcome. Now, the muscle memory of student life had returned, and the momentum sped up time, carrying her purposefully bell to bell as her mind turned over all the learning in progress, projects and assignments and deadlines and ideas for how she could implement them in the real world. As a writer, she'd known that work came more easily when you weren't starting from a blank page. But now that she'd regained her rhythm, areas of her life that had once seemed disparate were coalescing in exciting ways, and she no longer worried if she'd been wrong to come here or where she might go next.

Because Lucy knew.

Her final project came to her the way her best fiction ideas used to. When she'd been doing figure eights around prospective characters and dramatic questions until, finally, she could see the invisible forces tying them all together. As usual, she'd had to work through the false starts—but this time, she hadn't done it alone. She'd had nudges from Enzo, guidance from professors, encouragement from Delia, and the kind of inspiration that came only when you stopped trying to assess the world around you and instead immersed yourself in it.

As far as she could tell, word hadn't yet gotten out about the quiet cancellation of Marie's How to Say No class—but it was about to. Fall enrollment was about to begin, and students who'd yet to secure a seat in the most popular gender studies elective would notice the omission. It was anyone's guess whether this would elicit mere half-hearted complaining or if all hell would break loose, but Lucy suspected this one wouldn't be shrugged off. A semester of How to Say No had shown her a new generation's low threshold for injustice.

The week before her final presentation was due, Lucy sought out Marie during her office hours. She didn't want to come across as blurring boundaries between business and personal.

Even if, ultimately, that was precisely what she hoped to do.

"Do I need an appointment?" she asked. Marie looked up from her desk and smiled. Ever since she'd called it quits with Kyle, she'd exuded a subtle heartbreak that made it clear how much she'd been holding in. Sometimes in class she looked downright vulnerable, though Lucy had noticed this seemed to inspire more confidence in her teachings, not less.

Marie waved her in, and Lucy closed the door behind her. "Did I ever tell you," Marie said, "how glad I am that you ended up coming to so much of my class? I always thought you'd eventually get too busy with your cohort. But now that I know this may be the last one . . ."

"It means a lot to me too," Lucy said. "In fact, that's what I came to talk about." She pulled up a chair and opened her laptop. "I've been working day and night on this slide deck to show my adviser. Would you be my professorial guinea pig?"

Flattery flickered across Marie's face. "I can't speak to what they're looking for over in Copeland Hall," she said. "But as your friend, I'm happy to."

Lucy couldn't contain her smile. "I think you can speak to a lot of it," she said, revealing her title screen.

Empowerment for Every Woman, it read. Beneath it, she'd mocked up multimedia iterations of her project: a self-help book, paired with a podcast, alongside a logo for the brand's social media presence. *How to Quit: A Movement by Lucy Mayer.*

Marie gasped with delight. "Tell me this isn't just a class project."

"It's not just a class project." Lucy advanced the slide to a graphic of clickbait headlines paired with numbers showing how widely they'd gone viral. Her own was in the center—Why I Love Books Too Much to Keep Writing Them—with the phrase Too Much highlighted as a focal point. All around it, other words popped in swipes of color. Emotional Labor. Endless Cycle. Breaking Point.

"You already know some of this," Lucy stage-whispered, "but I need to practice my pitch." Marie nodded, leaning back in her chair to listen, and Lucy cleared her throat.

"These headlines, individually, are about parenting, marriage, careers, dating, friendship, and finances. But the people who clicked on them were all looking for the same thing: examples of people who've walked away or made a big change without regretting it. Because we have never been taught how or when or why to quit. People want validation that it's okay to draw a line, and proof hard things can turn out to be a blessing in disguise. They're looking for justification, for permission. I'm going off script now, but: They're looking for everything you teach in How to Say No, amplified."

"And you're proposing to give it to them?"

"Well, someone should. Some of these people learned the hardest way: They wanted to quit but didn't, until they failed out of school or got fired or dumped, and ended up so afraid to tell people the truth that they kept up a ruse, sometimes for years. And they're the lucky ones, compared to women who stay in dangerous situations and pay with their lives. Yet most of the content on the market that has anything to do with quitting focuses on bad habits."

Lucy flipped to a daunting array of cover images promising to teach you, once and for all, how to quit smoking and drinking and overeating and porn and gambling and enabling and any other manner of self-sabotage imaginable. "What comes to mind," she read from her notes, "is how unpleasant this kind of quitting is. And how many people backslide and never succeed. Or endure a lifetime of struggle to escape poor choices made in the past." Again, she dropped her stage voice. And the pretext of practicing. Because before she pitched her professor, she needed to sell Marie. "Am I wrong?"

"There are important distinctions," Marie agreed. "Everybody knows these vices are bad. We do them anyway and roll the dice, hoping that it stays manageable and doesn't become a problem."

"Right. This isn't comparable to changing your mind about what you want to do for a living. Or falling out of love with a person or place or dream. Or hitting obstacles beyond your control, like infertility or infidelity or layoffs. Beyond our quitting pact, your class prompted me to consider the things that were never modeled for us. And I thought, what if we create a platform where we can all figure that out together?"

Marie was still nodding.

"I'm wary of self-professed gurus who claim to have answers," Lucy went on. "This isn't that. This is about inviting people to share their experiences and exploring ways to reframe our thinking—like you've challenged your classes to do."

Lucy flipped the slide. Sister Brands, the headline read. Sharing Sister Strategies. One Audience. One Mission. One Vision.

How to Say No: A Movement by Marie Welling.

Marie stared at her.

"Your syllabus deserves to be bigger than a class," Lucy said. "Let the university cancel it. You have the content to move to another level. I have the writing, editing, and publishing experience. For me, it's a matter of pivoting my skill set into a smart, new business model. For you, it's about scaling up. For both of us, it's about having more control over our outcomes."

Lucy held her breath, sure she'd sold it. But after a beat of silence, Marie frowned. "This is tempting. But I don't have the bandwidth. I have no desire to leave academia."

"I don't think you should. But the university likes to boast faculty who publish, correct? Being thought leaders and contributing to their field in relevant ways?"

Marie considered this. "I'm not sure they'd see this as a serious contribution. Or as serious, period. Plus, if it's seen as controversial . . ." She looked out the window, and a slow smile spread across her face. "Well," she said. "I guess that might be worth fighting for after all."

The more Lucy thought about this project, the more right it felt. "You'd ask forgiveness, not permission," she said. "Or you'd get ahead of the narrative and make it look like nobody here ever told you no—you had bigger plans all along. If we do have a guru, it's you, not me. With your expertise and my MBA and communications strategies, we'd make amazing partners."

"Partners," Marie repeated, like she was trying the idea on for size. Doubtless she'd thought a lot about partnerships lately. What a big commitment they were.

"My agent connected with a new multimedia company in Chicago focused on women's wellness," Lucy said. "They've been looking for empowering content to syndicate across platforms. She's only given them the basic pitch, but they're very interested."

Marie raised a knowing eyebrow. "Chicago, huh?"

"Only one of us would need to be there. I'd finish school first. And I'll be going back and forth to see Enzo anyway, so meetings should be easy enough to fit in. I have a hunch my professors will be flexible. Ideally, we'd get the green light this summer and have through the end of the year to strategize and prep content for the rollout. You'd get a decent advance for the book too. I could help with structure and editing if you want, but *How to Say No* is your baby."

"And *How to Quit* is yours," Marie said. Lucy wanted to remember this moment, no matter what happened next, the solidarity and respect between them stronger than ever. Even after everything. *Because* of everything.

Marie crossed her arms, evaluating. "So you're not moving back because of the guy?"

"As much as I hope it works out with him, no. If it doesn't, I wouldn't regret this."

Marie nodded, like she'd known but needed confirmation. Then she did a little victory dance in her seat. "I *knew* you'd find a way to be happy writing," she said. "I suppose you already have some case studies in mind?"

"Names will be changed to protect the innocent," Lucy promised. "Does this mean you're in?"

She flipped to her market analysis, with her subtitle square in the center. *An Everywoman's Guide to Quitting Your Way to Happiness.* Lucy wasn't sure about the wording—she wanted Marie's input, on all of it. But she was proud of how far the concept had already come. She wanted to get this right.

When Marie stood up and stuck out her hand, she looked taller than she had when she left the house that morning. And lighter than she had all year.

"All in," she said. "Partner."

39

Brooke

Brooke and Mitch stood hand in hand outside Collins's apartment door. She gave his hand a squeeze. "Ready?" she asked.

He squeezed back. "Let's do this."

Collins answered their knock right away. The art professor's loaner apartment was a perfect fit. His walls were painted rich chocolate and indigo, and original art in frames of all sizes adorned nearly every inch of them. But the furnishings themselves were minimalist, allowing plenty of room for the rolling walker and cane that Collins was transitioning to, plus a growing assortment of strength-training equipment for her home therapy regimen. Ever since she'd left the rehab center, she'd seemed more like a woman on a mission to heal and less like someone going through the motions to appease her doctors.

"Thanks for coming," Collins told them, waving them in. "I haven't been nervous about starting chemo, but now that it's here . . . well, I'm glad for the company."

"We figured," Mitch said.

Collins looked to Brooke. "Your OB is sure this is okay?"

"As long as I'm not cleaning up your bodily fluids, we're good."

"I'll hold your hair back if someone needs to," Mitch assured Collins. "You all held Brooke's for me during her morning sickness. My turn."

"I didn't, though," Collins reminded him. "I was recovering from a coma."

"Excuses, excuses," Mitch teased. "You know, I don't think that coma card ever expires. You can play that pretty much forever."

"Can't waste that," she deadpanned. "Guess I'll have to outlive this cancer thing."

Collins lifted herself onto the couch, and Brooke flopped onto the cushion beside her. She was starting to get twinges of lower back pain as her abdomen grew. It was the most blissful discomfort of her life.

"I really do appreciate you being here for the first round," Collins said. "Learning to navigate ortho alone has shown me I can handle a lot. But this is . . . something else."

Brooke met Mitch's eyes, and he nodded subtly, claiming the club chair opposite them. "We know," she said. "That's why we signed a short-term lease on an apartment down the hall."

Collins looked unsure whether she was kidding. "You what?"

"We all agreed someone should be here in Columbus with you, at least until you see how treatment is going," Brooke explained. "We'll give you space, but Athens is too far. We didn't want you having a hard day or night without one of us a quick call or text away."

"Who is we?" Collins asked suspiciously.

"All of us. As much as we've all loved being roommates again, it makes sense to leave Marie and the boys to reestablish their family, and to let Lucy focus on school and her new venture. Mitch and I just want a quiet place where we can get ready for the baby and look ahead to our London move. My OB is part of a Columbus-based network. And once Sara's professor friend put in a good word for us with the building manager, it was easy. Meant to be."

Collins hesitated. "Sara too, huh?"

"She's atoning admirably well," Mitch said. "For what it's worth."

"I . . . I don't know what to say." Collins's eyes filled with tears.

Brooke nudged her affectionately. "You don't have to say anything. Just know that this time, nobody is going to quit on you and go back to regularly scheduled programming. On days you feel like quitting on yourself, we'll be here to make sure you don't. We love you, Coll."

Collins seemed torn. "I don't want you to feel obligated or stuck. This is an exciting time for you. I don't want to drag you down."

Mitch rested his elbows on his knees and fixed her with a serious look. "That's funny," he said. "Because all we've talked about is how lucky it is we're *not* stuck. Being tied to jobs in Colorado and unable to conceive, that was stuck. Being across the ocean from my wife while she couldn't join me, that was stuck. Being obligated to be anywhere but here, when our closest friends are facing the biggest challenges of their lives—that would be stuck."

Brooke was tearing up now too. She adored that Mitch's love for her extended to people she loved. Including his knack for saying the perfect thing when they needed it most.

"Becoming a mom without any of my fellow quitters nearby to lean on," Brooke added. "That would be the most stuck of all. It's not entirely selfless, you know. And until the baby comes, we have a second bedroom for anyone who wants to come see you. Especially Lucy, racking up airline miles to Chicago out of Columbus. There's literally nowhere we'd rather be."

Watching Collins laughing through her tears, Brooke knew that Collins would really let them in this time—and they'd all be better for it. The months ahead wouldn't be pretty. Brooke had been cautioned that her blood pressure could in fact land her on bed rest, though she refused to believe her mother could have jinxed her. Collins would get sicker before she could begin to get well. Brooke hadn't let her guard down, and as a mom, she probably never would. No positive outcome was a given. But every day that a positive outcome felt possible—that would be enough. The mere act of hope, of imagining themselves on the other side of this, had felt out of reach when they'd begun these journeys together. Now, it was more than reachable.

It was reality.

"I guess we're all pretty lucky," Collins said. "What a powerful revelation on my first day of chemo."

Brooke agreed. "What a powerful revelation on any day."

40

Marie

The only good thing about meetings with the divorce mediator in Columbus was that Marie could reward herself with visits to Brooke and Collins afterward. Collins was planning a small baby shower for Brooke in the building's rooftop garden, so she'd invited Lucy and Marie over to sample cupcake flavors from the bakery she'd chosen.

"Everything tastes like metal to me," Collins had explained, matter-of-factly. Her skin looked closer to porcelain these days, and she shunned wigs in favor of a turban, which only made her look more at home in "the Guggenheim," as they'd dubbed her temporary apartment.

Marie was craving a space of her own too. She and the boys had been spoiled at Collins's house, where Lucy had insisted Marie take the primary suite after Brooke moved out, giving each boy his own room. Marie had always coveted the reading nook and the soaking tub, and now that summer had arrived, the boys were obsessed with the double-decker porches, where their neighborhood friends would appear daily to play intricate games involving walkie-talkies and makeshift forts. Still, as Marie got used to the idea of single parenthood, she felt pulled to nest someplace they could get comfortable for good.

Brooke and Mitch made it seem simple to establish home as a thing you carried with you—but then again, they hadn't had the baby yet.

Marie remembered her and Kyle's first year with Connor, how they'd joked about the household's smallest member accumulating the most gear. On their first vacation, they'd loaded a hotel cart just for him—portable crib, travel highchair, play mat, toys, and backups "just in case"—and the concierge had laughed at the sight of them. Marie and Kyle had been too in love with their son and each other to care.

Now, Kyle had planned his first vacation with the boys—without her. Lucy promised to keep Marie busy that week, collaborating with their enthusiastic new multimedia team in Chicago. Their travel expenses would even be paid . . . but missing out already stung.

Whenever memories sent her reeling, Marie used an old trick she'd learned for big decisions: She flipped a coin. It wasn't about doing what the coin said. It was about seeing if she felt disappointed at the result. *Tails, get a Realtor. Heads, rethink the divorce and try moving back in with Kyle.* Every time it landed on heads, her gut would twist in protest, confirming that just because this was hard did not mean it was wrong.

First rule of the Quitters Club: Sometimes, it really is easier to start from knowing what you didn't want.

Collins was standing in her open-concept kitchen when Marie arrived, looking so capable on her own two feet, Marie almost missed the cane leaning against the counter beside her.

"Hey," Collins greeted her. "How'd it go? You okay?"

Marie nodded. "I will be."

"Did you tell them the latest on the student petition to save your class?" Lucy asked. She was doling out sparkling water in champagne glasses, and Marie accepted hers gratefully.

"I heard the email campaign crashed the campus server," Brooke called from the couch.

Seeing her friends so proudly standing by her still caught Marie off guard sometimes. And with her students in the mix, what should have been the most difficult couple of months of Marie's career had instead been the most affirming.

"I can't tell which way it's going to go," Marie said. "But if nothing else, it's good PR for our new brand. Lucy was smart to start capturing email addresses. There's a box asking if they want to be notified when we go live, and almost no one opts out. It's brilliant."

Lucy bowed modestly and settled next to Brooke, while Marie chose a club chair and snatched a triple chocolate cupcake. Brooke was already licking frosting from her fingers. "We don't need this taste test," she said. "Not that I'm complaining, but they're all delicious."

"Well, it was a fun excuse to get us in one place," Collins admitted, making her careful, steady way to the chair beside Marie. "I wanted to run something else by you all too."

She took a deep breath and panned their faces. Lucy and Brooke exchanged glances, and Marie silently prayed this wasn't about a new diagnosis. She harbored real hope that Collins's tumors would respond to the initial chemo treatment well enough for her to move on to the good stuff. Immunotherapy had inspired an optimism that wouldn't have been warranted even five years ago. Cancer didn't play fair, but Collins had suffered enough. Hadn't they all?

"It's about me not moving back to Athens when this is over," Collins said.

Even in Marie's confusion, relief washed over her. Because Collin hadn't said *if I make it through this* or *depending on* or *we'll see* the way she usually did.

She'd said "when."

"When" was a word of confidence and manifestation and control. It was also a word Collins only ever used about the past. *When Sullivan was alive, when Sullivan died, when I had my accident, when we made the pact, when I lashed out, when I first got the news.* Every *when* carried more anguish and regret than the one before.

But this "when" reflected faith in the future. Marie detected no pain in it. Only peace.

Lucy reached out and squeezed Collins's hand. "Where would you go instead?" she asked.

"I'm not sure," Collins said. "Maybe Saugatuck." Their jaws collectively dropped, but she hurried on. "Sara says she personally knows of a half dozen artists who'd bend over backward for the chance to hire an experienced manager or assistant or whatever they want to call me. She's very tapped in and willing to make introductions. Maybe even offer it as a service through the gallery. She says the least she can do is help get me a new job if I'm giving her my old one."

It took a second for this to register. Marie wasn't sure she'd understood. "I thought the estate was off the table?" she asked.

"I put it back on. The lawyer Lucy found is a miracle worker."

Lucy sat up straighter. "Look at me, administering business after all."

Collins laughed. "You did! You were right. There are provisions to protect what I want for Sullivan's legacy. Sara respects that earning my trust will take time. But we also have things in common that no one else shares—things we've never had a chance to relate over before." She gestured, encompassing her bald head beneath her turban, her cane, her borrowed apartment, her friends, and everything that had brought them here. "This is not how I would have chosen to get clarity on what's healthy for me, believe me. But now that I have it . . ."

"Moving back into his house doesn't feel healthy," Brooke finished.

Collins looked to Marie. "Have you ever felt a physiological response, like your brain might be indecisive, but your whole body is saying no?"

"Quite recently," she affirmed. "And you don't feel the same way being near Sara?"

"I don't. Being near Sara isn't tied to old memories. It's doing something he never got to do. Something I think he would have come around to appreciating, even if it isn't how he'd have done it himself."

"So you're going to sell the house?" Lucy asked.

"We can totally help stage it," Marie chimed in, ignoring the twinge she felt at the prospect. "With Sullivan's name attached, you'll get way above market."

Collins's eyes never left Marie's. "I already have a buyer in mind."

Marie's heart slowed, and her breath caught. What a generous, loyal friend Collins had proved to be. But the offer was equal parts wonderful and impossible.

"I'm in no financial position," Marie said, putting her hands up. "Let me stop you there. You need the money, and I won't let you take less than you could get from a real buyer."

"Let me stop *you* there," Collins said. "The value I place on that house goes way beyond money. As custodians of Sullivan's estate, Sara and I both agree we can't let just anyone own such a showpiece of his art. I don't want to relocate the sculpture garden or remove the windows—he created them to stay there. We thought about approaching the university or founding a new residency program, but honestly, the only way I can feel good about giving up that house is to feel good about who's living in it. The only people I can picture there are you and the boys." She winked at Lucy. "Well, and a certain boarder who has a degree to finish."

"I'll pay Marie rent for my last semester," Lucy said quickly. "I can afford it now. I'm getting royalty checks for the first time ever."

Marie let herself picture it, just for an instant: Collins's big, beautiful house as the place she and the boys could start over in. The home office with all those gorgeous bookshelves, where she could write her book and record her part of the podcast. The side yard, where the soccer net could stay nestled beside the garage. The sculpture garden, which had never made her sad, always felt like a tribute to someone she'd admired, not only as a man who'd been good to her friend but as a colleague who'd shown them all how much people could change.

"You'd be doing me a favor," Collins said. "Unless staying isn't what you want?"

"It's not that," Marie said. "But . . . wouldn't it bother you when you visit?"

Collins smiled. "It'd bother me more not to be able to visit. If the house stops being right for your family, though, there's no catch. You can transfer the property like any other homeowner. The fine print will say Sullivan's estate can veto a buyer with questionable intentions, but I don't anticipate a problem. I trust your judgment."

Marie stared at her, overcome. "Coll," she said finally. "How can I ever thank you?"

Brooke burst into tears. "Sorry," she cried. "Hormones. This is just so perfect."

Lucy leaned her head affectionately on Brooke's shoulder. "Who'd have thought," she agreed, "that forming our own little Quitters Club could completely change our lives?"

"Marie did," Collins answered without hesitation.

She hadn't, of course. This kind of synergy didn't come from knowing things would turn out okay. It came from messing up, and losing yourself, and trying again, and rediscovering your worth in the process. It came from lifting each other up, and letting each other down despite your best intentions, and being brave enough to say sorry. It came from telling the truth, even when it hurt, and reserving the right to change your mind, and not settling for less than you deserved. Only then, it seemed, could such a beautiful ending become a new beginning too.

"The key was doing it together," Marie said, wiping away her own tears. "None of it would have turned out the same way alone."

She knew that despite what Brooke had said, nothing was perfect. Chances were, this might not all go to plan, for any of them.

Then again, there was always the possibility things could turn out even better.

EPILOGUE

Collins

Artists from all over the Great Lakes flocked to the natural beauty of Saugatuck's Oval Beach. Plein air painters propped easels in the dunes above throngs of summer tourists, photographers timed sunsets to the second, crafters scavenged driftwood, and jewelers sifted through rainbows of pebbles. No matter their talent, they could only ever capture a piece of it, one idyllic angle or symbolic treasure to conjure the vitality of that spectacular Lake Michigan coastline—the rustle of dune grass when clouds blew in from the horizon, the surface transformation from glassy calm to oceanlike waves, or the shifting sands of a landscape that was never as solid as it seemed. Even the most striking creation would fall short.

That was what kept them coming back.

If you wanted the purest inspiration all to yourself, there was nothing like an unseasonably gorgeous day in the offseason—the kind of day that reassured Collins she'd chosen her new home well. You could only luck into such perfection by living there, yet against all odds her friends had managed to pick just such a day for their visit. Eager as she was for them to see the cottage she was making her own, she'd asked them to find her here first, where the peak autumn foliage framed the beach in striking contrasts beneath a cloudless sky.

She stood with the lake at her feet, the rolling dunes at her back, and not another living soul between her and the distant breakwater, inhaling it all through her scarred lungs and wondering if they'd hold out as long as the doctors now said. Indefinitely. People claimed her limp wasn't noticeable anymore, but Collins still felt it, the subtle reminder of how close she'd come to another outcome, how easily everything could have been different. Maybe her stance was only one degree off, but that was all it took to know her scales had been rebalanced. She wouldn't have wanted to forget, anyway.

Her friends' lives were better because of the Quitters pact.

Collins was alive because of it.

It had been two years since their girls' trip to Hilton Head, twenty-one months since her helicopter ride to a trauma unit, one year since her last dose of chemo. She had yet to stop immunotherapy. They'd told her she might try weaning off, but she wasn't sure about risking it.

She had too much to live for.

People called the accident her saving grace, shaking their heads at how long her cancer might have spread undiscovered otherwise, and Collins always nodded along. It was a solid story. It renewed people's belief that there must be order to the universe after all.

She'd never told anyone the truth that there had been no accident, and she never would. Not because it would change the way they saw her—that she could endure—but because it would change the way they saw themselves. Especially her friends, who had so plainly feared they'd been complicit in her disaster. Nothing good would come of them retroactively searching for some missed distress sign, because there was nothing she wished they'd done differently. They'd behaved in a way that had helped steer her the long way around to the place she was meant to be.

And so had she.

She had never fantasized about ending things. She wasn't the planning kind. But seeing that moonlit mountaintop in a blanket of snow, it had struck her as profound that the world could be so peaceful and so treacherous at once. As she'd stood shivering, her grief came to life around her. How tired she was of finding herself alone in places she'd never really wanted to be. How thin the line could be between a moment of clarity and a moment of insanity. Grief *was* a snowy mountain that could kill you if you stayed out too long without protection from the elements. You could grow so cold that you couldn't remember what it felt like to be warm. In dark like this, you might give up hope of the sun ever rising again—for other people, of course it would, but maybe not for you. They might send a search party, they might try to rescue you, but they'd never truly reach this place you'd gone. Ultimately, you'd have to rescue yourself.

And from that height, Collins had seen the whole harsh landscape of what hard work that would be. What hard work it already was. She'd been in this place for two years and counting, and she was no closer to rescue than she had been the day Sull died.

She was not cut out for this. The harder she tried, the more miserably she failed.

In that moment, it seemed infinitely easier to just . . . let go.

She and Brooke had half joked about Sullivan being with her on that mountain. And maybe some divine intervention really had saved her. But not the way her friends thought.

They'd been right to question how her slide off the wrong side of the slope had happened. She'd managed to evade the hard questions while keeping the terrible truth to herself. How could she ever admit that she'd closed her eyes, bent her knees, and intentionally taken that terrible, shameful, ill-advised plunge when all seemed lost?

That night was the most wrong she'd ever been, about anything. The most miraculous thing of all was not only that she'd survived it but that she'd very likely survived *because* of it.

If she'd shaken off her melancholy and ridden the lift back down, she'd have developed a cough eventually, one she wouldn't have thought much of, because she'd have likely caught all the usual bronchial infections going around the college town. If she had gone to an urgent care, she'd have presented no differently from anyone else at the height of cold and flu season. She'd have continued to chalk up her weight loss as a normal part of widowhood. Her achy fatigue: the product of another bereaved winter. How long would it have taken until her symptoms had reached a stage she couldn't ignore? Until she'd coughed up blood or broken her leg some other way, because of a fatally latent metastasis weakening her bone?

Too long, she knew. Long enough that she wouldn't be standing here now. Or anywhere else, for that matter.

She still never missed an episode of the hit podcast, The Quitters Club, hosted by two of her favorite people. It had a religious following, and Collins was glad. Because you couldn't identify when it was best to quit if you didn't also understand when not to.

She'd done the wrong thing. She'd let despair win. And it had still turned out right. In part because she had never been as alone as she thought. Not with friends like them.

That was the real reason she was so lucky. Fitting, that she now carried the quiet knowledge with her, literally, in every breath and every step she took. There was a word for the swirl of emotions she felt every time she had a recheck: *scanxiety*. But Collins could handle it.

For the first time in her life, she trusted herself.

For the first time in her life, she had no regrets.

Not the pact, or anything that came after. Not selling the house, or turning over the estate, or coming to terms with being Collins, no apostrophe. Not taking the fixer-upper cottage with its distant lake view, or mounting one perfect stained-glass piece of Sullivan's on the covered porch, or trusting Sara, who'd become both colleague and friend. Not advocating for the work of messy, brilliant artists who reminded her of the other reasons she'd loved her job in the first place.

Not even Travis. They were friends again, real friends, but it didn't make sense to pursue anything more now that she wasn't going back. In fact, she suspected he might be developing a crush on the new woman next door.

She hoped so. She genuinely thought he'd be good for her. And vice versa.

"Collins!"

She turned at the sound of her name, and there they were, piling out of Marie's minivan into the parking lot. Even from here, she could spot the engagement ring glinting on Lucy's finger. Mitch stood with his hand on Brooke's shoulder, both looking happy but jet-lagged from the cross-Atlantic flight. Their toddler, sporting two tiny, curly pigtails atop her head, hit the sand running and promptly face-planted. Wade and Connor ran to help, laughing.

"Sorry we're late," Marie called out. "We got lost on the way. Took a wrong turn."

Collins took off running to meet them.

"There was never any rush," she called. "You're right on time."

ACKNOWLEDGMENTS / AUTHOR'S NOTE

In any ever-changing industry—particularly a creative one—it's important to have a constant, a partner or colleague with the faith and vision to help you grow while honoring where you've been. Mine is my agent, Barbara Poelle, who gives me new reasons to be grateful for her with every book—and who felt this one in particular, from the very start, almost as deeply as I did.

Marilyn Brigham, senior editor and Quitters Club honorary member, endless thanks for sharing our enthusiasm for this project and championing it to the rest of the Lake Union team. Jodi Warshaw, you're a dream of a developmental editor, and it's been a treat to team up for a second time. Working with the two of you in tandem has made revision fun, and this book is unquestionably better because of your wise perspectives and collaborative spirit. Appreciation also to production manager Angela Elson for her seamless oversight, art director Jarrod Taylor for the fantastic cover design, and everyone else at LU who had a hand in the bringing this project to fruition so well.

Heartfelt thanks to several professionals who generously lent their knowledge and insights to specialized aspects of this story: Lisa Ovesen's expertise as an oncology nurse proved invaluable (with thanks to Erica Kelley for making introductions) as she humored my many questions via phone, email, and text message with a superhuman patience that is the sure mark of a caring, compassionate, and wise health care professional. Dr. Deborah Kuzawa, on the faculty of The Ohio State University, devoted a humbling number of hours to reading an early version of this manuscript, in full, and advised on the nuances of Marie's character and career as only a college professor with a PhD and two master's degrees (including one in women's studies) can. Aaron Pertner of New Day Physical Therapy in Centerville, Ohio, helpfully weighed in on the rehabilitation of various leg injuries and walked me through (pun intended) hypotheticals that demonstrated the grace that he puts into his own practice. And Dr. John Sullivan generously lent his expertise in obstetrics yet again, cementing his title as the most consulted medical professional across several of my novels (and the most good-humored). With all of the above subject matter, I occasionally took creative license for the purposes of the story, and any perceived mistakes are entirely my own. On a side note, it's especially fitting to have met both Aaron and Deb in our sophomore-year dorm at Ohio University (oh, those late-1990s Perkins Hall memories); I couldn't be more delighted that a story set largely at our alma mater gave us reason to reconnect. I was touched by their kindness and willingness to help an old friend after so many years.

This speaks to the enduring quality of the student community at OU (oh yeah!) where I met some of my best friends to this day and spent four of my favorite years. I hope my unshakable love for the campus and town of Athens comes across in this story, though of course Marie and her How to Say No class (along with the specific challenges she encounters) are products of my imagination and, I want to be clear, *not* based on any real people or academic experiences. The ongoing difficulties faced by gender studies programs in general, however, are real—a fact I was blissfully oblivious to as an undergrad who majored in journalism but took several women's studies classes that left a memorable and positive impact on me. I had humble intentions in crafting the fictional one in this book and certainly no agenda (first I read everything I could find about saying *no*, and then I read widely about shouting *yes* from the rooftops, and as with most polarizing topics, perhaps the most honest answer, sometimes, is *maybe*)—but what began as a purely fun idea took a thoughtful turn that I hope, perhaps, might resonate with you too. Many of the examples used in Marie's class are loosely inspired by real life, from the Susan B. Anthony Project's powerful "What Were You Wearing?" exhibit to a widely shared Instagram reel of a very tired mom crossing the finish line of a race. All were fictionalized with utmost respect for the source material.

My heart goes out to anyone who can relate to Collins's grief after a sudden loss: In my experience, you are never as alone as you may feel—and thank goodness for that. If you need someone to talk to, please reach out to one of the many lifelines available; in the US, start with a simple call or text to 988.

The writing life would be lonely without friends and colleagues like my Career Authors team (Paula Munier, Hank Phillippi Ryan, Brian Andrews, and Dana Isaacson), *Writer's Digest* family (past and present), fellow Tall Poppy Writers, Fiction Writers Co-op (especially Catherine McKenzie, who is unfailingly generous with her time and experience, and who has more than once given me the right advice at the right time), and my local circle of writerly kindred spirits (Katrina Kittle, Sharon Short, and Kristina Purnhagen). Bonus thanks to Jane Friedman for decades of putting trust in my abilities as an editor and instructor.

My life has been immeasurably improved by my friendships with other strong women, and I never could have written a book like this if not for the longtime love of my college roomies (Marice, Cara, Amanda, Jen, and, in memoriam, Jackie, with a bonus nod to Megan), the sanity-saving sisterhood of my neighborhood walking buddies (counting down to our next game night at Abbey's), and (new this past year) the fun of Margarita Club and our mini Nacho Business Club sidekicks. I'm also grateful to *all* the other sideline parents who make such good company in cheering for our kids together, including on the non-sports sidelines (looking at you, Denise Weber).

My family is always at the top of my mind and the top of my list, with gratitude for the support of my parents, Michael and Holly Yerega; my brother, Evan, and his beautiful family; my in-laws on the Strawser side; and of course my husband, Scott. Most of all, to our two kids who make me unbelievably proud to be their mom every day: It's the absolute best watching you two grow up, even if you are doing it a little too fast for me sometimes. I know you are going at just the right speed for you—and I love you more than anything.

BOOK CLUB QUESTIONS

1. Growing up, were you told that quitters never win, and winners never quit? Was that helpful, or did it ever make it difficult to listen to your gut?
2. The four main characters in this book are struggling with some of the biggest areas that often come into question in midlife: career changes, marriage longevity, parenthood paths, and unexpected loss. Which woman's struggle did you relate to the most strongly? Were there aspects of every character that you could relate to in some way?
3. Lucy is intimidated by the idea of going back to school for her master's, but strangers are quick to praise her decision, as many of them have also thought about switching careers. If you were to do something different from your current livelihood, what field or job would you choose?
4. Marie likens marriage to politics: "People tended to discuss couples at the ends of the spectrum, the best and worst, but most fell somewhere in the middle." What marriages in your circle have you thought of in the rare "best" category, and what do you think makes them so?
5. Brooke and Mitch share the emotional burden of trying to conceive, but most of the physical responsibility falls to Brooke, which takes a toll over time. Do you think pregnancy inevitably impacts any given couple's dynamics? Does it change the balance irreversibly?

6. In an early chapter, Collins says, "If this was one of those novels where characters alternate telling their sides of the story, I bet I wouldn't even have a point of view. I probably don't deserve one." This is a wink to the novel's actual structure—until the epilogue, when Collins lets the reader see something that the other characters will never know. Did you find yourself wishing she had a POV earlier? Did you ever question, as she did, whether she truly belonged in the pact?
7. A student in Marie's class quotes her father's belief that "No is a complete sentence." Do you agree with him, or do you think that approach is easier said than done?
8. If "How to Say No" were a real course, would you be interested in taking it? What would you hope to learn, or what do you wish you'd known all along when it comes to saying no?
9. Perimenopause is having a cultural moment, with viral sensations like the "We do not care club." Why is it so important for women to relate to one another at a certain stage of midlife? Or is it *always* important for women to relate to one another?
10. Has this novel changed your attitude about quitting? Will it make you think twice the next time a friend asks for advice or when you confront your own doubts about a chosen path?

ABOUT THE AUTHOR

Photo © Corrie Schaffeld

Jessica Strawser is the *USA Today* bestselling author of *Catch You Later*, *The Last Caretaker*, *The Next Thing You Know*, *A Million Reasons Why*, *Forget You Know Me*, *Not That I Could Tell* (a Book of the Month selection), and *Almost Missed You*. She was editorial director at *Writer's Digest* for nearly a decade before becoming a novelist. Jessica is also a Career Authors contributing editor, a popular speaker at writing conferences across the US, and a freelance editor and writer with bylines in the *New York Times* Modern Love column, *Publishers Weekly*, and other venues. A Pittsburgh native and alum of the E.W. Scripps School of Journalism at Ohio University, she lives with her husband and two children in Cincinnati, Ohio, where she has been honored with Ohio Arts Council Individual Excellence Awards in 2024 and 2026 and served as 2019 Writer-in-Residence for the Cincinnati & Hamilton County Public Library. For more information, visit www.jessicastrawser.com.